# MOUSE IN THE BOX

## LEWIS ALLAN

STRETCHED STUDIO LLC

# DISCLAIMER

This book is a work of fiction. Although some descriptions are based on real locations and places, the specifics and details are fictionalized. Further, while some characters and case details may be reminiscent of real world examples, they too are fictionalized. Likewise, several events and other details are cut from whole cloth.

Any facts, details or specifics related to the same are not meant to represent reality. All the names, characters, businesses, places, events and incidents in this book are either the product of the author's imagination or used in a fictitious manner. Any resemblance to actual persons, living or dead, or actual events is purely coincidental.

ISBN 979-8-9882410-0-3

Printed in the United States of America

Cover Design by Marshall Hook

# PROLOGUE

"Yes, my client shot him in the face, but the guy lived! Be reasonable, Jean. Five years in, seven years out, and let's move on."

Mason Mitchell saw the man standing in front of the school doors watching him, and held up his index finger in a silent request for more time.

"Ok. You bet. I knew you'd see the light, Jean. Trust me, he's a kid who got in over his head. You're doing the right thing. Gotta run, I'll file the paperwork later today." Mason ended his call and bounded up the steps of James Madison High School. "So sorry to keep you waiting. Work never stops."

The man wearing an ill-fitting gray suit extended his hand to Mason. "Good morning, Mr. Mitchell! I'm vice-principal Jerry Adler. So happy to have you on campus today." With thin, sandy hair framing pleasantly dull features, Jerry Adler made such an unremarkable impression that it would be tough to pick him out of a lineup.

Mason felt mild disappointment that he didn't warrant a greeting from the principal, but reasoned that it was better than a run-of-the-mill teacher.

"Hi, Jerry. It's my pleasure. Looking forward to speaking with your kids."

Someone at the school knew someone at the Wisconsin Association of Criminal Defense Lawyers, and that someone had recommended Mason as the ideal candidate to speak to several hundred high schoolers about Justice In Society. In a moment of weakness, Mason agreed to do it. And that's how he found himself at the front doors of a suburban high school, his mind occupied by several pending cases and a pounding headache, shaking hands with the most vanilla man he'd ever met.

After a beat, Jerry realized it was time to move things along.

"Right, ok. We can head in now so you can get set up in the auditorium. The kids will assemble there in about fifteen minutes. Don't worry, I'll settle them down and make a quick introduction before you go on." Jerry opened the door to show him in.

As he led Mason through deserted hallways, Jerry broke the awkward silence, "So, working in the justice system...must be quite a stressful line of work."

"It has its moments," answered Mason, "but probably not as scary as teaching."

"Ha! I'm sure you'll do well today, Mr. Mitchell. They're good kids, just do us a favor and don't give them any ideas."

Mason forced a grin and held up his slim folder of notes. "Thanks, I'll just stick to what I know."

The vice-principal gave a nod of approval, his authoritarian impulse satisfied for the moment. "Well, the stage entrance is right here." He unlocked a set of doors, stuck his head in and flicked the lights on. "You can have a seat by the podium while I head to the office to make some announcements. I'll be back by the time the kids show up," said Jerry. With that, he ducked out into the corridor, the swish of cheap slacks fading as he made his way.

Blessedly alone, Mason stepped onto the stage and looked out over the room. It was larger than expected, and he hoped it would seem more intimate once the seats were filled. Mason didn't have a fear of public speaking, but the setting had unexpectedly put him on edge. High school memories were not a sweet spot.

Mason sat in one of the three folding chairs to the right of the lectern and opened his folder. His talk was all there, laid out in bullet points and broad strokes. He felt most at home when speaking off the cuff, so the loose structure was all he needed. Still, the sudden itch of mild anxiety would not leave him alone. He got up and stalked the stage, bent over his notes.

"They're just kids. Another half hour and you're out of here." he muttered. "Jesus. Keep your head together."

Mason scanned the auditorium to confirm it remained empty, then ducked into the wings, behind a thick black curtain hanging from the rafters. He fished a small flask out of his jacket and snuck a swig, then breathed deep as the vodka spread its soothing heat down his throat, into his chest. He downed one more shot for good measure, and his nerves began to settle. After this sacrament came three burning blasts of mint breath spray before Mason emerged back into the light, steady on his feet once again.

Right on time, the students began filing in and Jerry Adler joined him on stage, accompanied by Principal Gwen Lowry.

"So nice to meet you, Mason," said Lowry. "I know the kids are really looking forward to your remarks today." She lied smoothly and with a smile, a trait Mason reckoned to be more effective with school administrators than with students.

Lowry waved Adler away from the lectern and stepped up to deliver Mason's introduction. After a tepid round of applause, Mason opened his notes on the stand, adjusted the mic, and began.

"As Principal Lowry said, my name is Mason Mitchell and I'm a criminal defense attorney. I've been told you're all tackling a part of the Social Studies curriculum called Justice In Society. That's lucky for me, because I don't know much about chemistry or math." Mason paused for laughter that did not come. "So, I'm going to tell you what I know about justice, because I deal with it every day." He shifted from one leg to the other and focused on his notes.

"Over many years, our society has developed a system to dispense justice. Judges and attorneys, plaintiffs and defendants, all parties have an important role to play. By working together, they can produce outcomes that are fair to all parties and serve the interests of the community. Of course, that's the theory, and in practice it can get a little messier, but it's my job to never lose sight of what our system is trying to achieve."

Mason scanned the faces in the crowd – vacant, bored, some bordering on hostile. Many were clearly preoccupied, their faces lit by the glow of phone screens.

"A foundational principle of our system is that anyone accused of a crime has the right to a vigorous defense. No matter what a defendant is accused of, no matter how bad, it is my duty to defend them. By doing that, I'm really defending our society's concept of justice. Without our right to a defense, the powers that be could pick winners and losers, deciding that some of us don't deserve equal protections under the law. And if justice becomes arbitrary, it can no longer be called justice. Have you guys learned anything yet about trial procedure and the adversarial system?" asked Mason. There were scattered nods and murmurs from across the auditorium.

"Ok. Well, my job in court is important because the deck is stacked against the defendant. The state has a massive advantage because it has the most resources. And even though we operate under the principle of 'innocent until proven guilty', the harsh reality is most judges and juries are predisposed toward a defendant's guilt."

Mason paused to take a sip of water. His head throbbed. He regretted coming here even more than when he arrived, but pressed on.

"So, we see that, in our system, the state has the upper hand. That's why they have the burden of proof. In order to take away someone's freedom, the state must show that person is guilty beyond a reasonable doubt. That's the standard. Are you guys following me here?"

Apart from a group of honor roll kids up front, there was almost no audible response.

Mason took a slow, deep breath. Menthol seared his nostrils and gave way to the slow warmth of vodka settling in somewhere behind his silver tie clip. *I didn't haul my ass to the suburbs just to be ignored by a room full of teenagers.* He closed his folder and walked out from behind the podium, closer to his audience.

"I get it. Not that interesting. I know some of you might think the stuff I'm talking about will never apply to you. Well, maybe." Mason began to pace the edge of the stage as he spoke. "But have you ever had a bad day? A day when things just go wrong? Because sometimes, that's all it takes. Our jails are overflowing and the backlog in our courts is *years long*, because regular people get arrested every single day and end up sitting next to me in court. Sure, some of these people are there because they broke the law, sometimes on purpose. But some of them did not expect to be there, and don't deserve to be there."

Mason could see more eyes in the audience looking up, watching him prowl the stage.

"Believe me, there are all sorts of reasons you could end up in that courtroom. Sometimes it's just a big misunderstanding, or you were in the wrong place at the wrong time. Or maybe it'll happen because you're poor, or look different, or live in the wrong neighborhood. I see it all the time, and it could happen to anyone in here. You!" said Mason, pointing to a girl sitting on the aisle. "What's your name?"

She looked mortified to be singled out, and managed a meek, "Caitlin," as a flush colored her cheeks.

"You know, Caitlin, I had a client last week just a couple of years older than you. Wrongly accused of killing two teenagers in a hit and run, she was looking at thirty years in prison. I had to fight for her, to push back against the massive weight of state authority. I showed the jury that the eyewitness testimony was faulty, and my client walked free. In the end, justice was served."

In reality, last week's client was a nineteen-year-old gang member accused of shooting and killing two girls at a house party in Franklin Heights. Years of physical abuse in foster care had left him mentally impaired. He was in and out of school, and in trouble with the law from a young age. With that profile, there was almost no chance of a positive outcome in his life. His case was an automatic loss – dozens of witnesses and Mason's client still had the gun when police picked him up. He was sentenced to life in prison.

"But even with an innocent client like her, it wasn't easy. Because when the justice system gets its hands on you, it won't let go without a fight. The authorities have all the power and they use it. Did you know prosecutors are ethically bound to file criminal charges only if they believe a case can be proved beyond a reasonable doubt? By that standard, I should lose one hundred percent of my cases! But in the real world I have to defend clients against excessive charges all the time."

Mason was rolling downhill now, his notes long forgotten. The airy auditorium felt to him like a hushed courtroom.

"The justice system is a massive machine and when it comes for you, it's no joke. In a way, it's just like school; the authorities hold the cards and they make the rules. So, you have to fight to make sure they don't screw you over, and you'll need a good lawyer who gives a shit."

"Mr. Mitchell!" hissed Principal Lowry.

He turned and held his hands out in contrition. "My apologies, Gwen. I'll keep it clean," said Mason, before pivoting back to his audience.

He didn't care if it was the substance or the spectacle of his ad-libbed remarks, but he could feel the room coming over to his side.

"As I was saying, you want to make sure they don't...put you at a disadvantage. So, listen up. I get paid $300 an hour for legal advice, but I'll give you this one for free – if you are ever placed under arrest, never, and I mean *never*, talk to the police. Repeat after me," said Mason, raising his arms like a conductor, "I want a lawyer...I will not make a statement." As he repeated the mantra, more students joined the recitation, giggling and growing louder each time. "Very good. If you remember just one thing I've said today, let it be those words. You'll thank me later."

The call and response break had brought the audience fully to life. They were his now.

"Look, they didn't pick me to talk to you just because I had a free morning. They picked me because I'm very good at what I do. That means my innocent clients go free. Still, my job entails a lot of losing. Even the best defense attorneys, and I happen to be one of them, lose cases all the time. That's because many of the people I represent in court are guilty. And when they are sent to prison, that's one version of what our society calls justice. But if I do my job well, some of my not-so-innocent clients go free, too. That's how the system is supposed to work. A long time ago, a law professor drilled the idea into me – that it's far better for fifty guilty people to go free than for one innocent person to be robbed of their freedom. That's another version of justice, and just as important."

Mason walked slowly back to the center of the stage and leaned on the podium.

"So, what would I like you to take away from all this? In our society, justice can be elusive, but it's worth fighting for. And I fight hard with every client, every case, every day, because that's what it takes. I fight hard because justice is what I care about more than anything. And I will *do* anything for justice...in...society. Thank you."

During the Q&A that followed, Mason had trouble keeping up with the number of hands that shot into the air. After five minutes, Principal Lowry, clearly agitated by the morning's performance, cut the segment short. After a brief and insincere thank you from her and Vice Principal Adler, Mason was politely escorted off campus. When he made it back to his car he checked the time and smiled. "Fifteen minutes early."

**1**

R obin Key gripped the steering wheel tight to keep from shaking. She drove on autopilot, barely aware of her surroundings. Her pulse raced, breaths coming fast and shallow. No tears, she was still too frazzled for that. Now, finally alone on the drive home, she unraveled.

*Holy shit! What the hell was all that?*

She had seen that Michael wasn't himself from the minute he showed up at the barbeque. He was so touchy, spoiling for an argument. She knew she shouldn't have taken the bait, overreacted, but then everything got so out of control.

*Who called the cops? Some curtain-twitching neighbor across the street?*

Everyone at the park, her colleagues and neighbors, had watched the entire scene. Robin was still too worked up to feel embarrassed.

Her day had not gone as planned. Tiptoeing around at work, almost impossible to stay focused on the classes. Seemed like every bad decision was coming back to haunt her. Maybe once her heart stopped racing and she had a chance to shower and get into her sweats, she'd call Michael, try to talk to him, try to be civil. He was so insecure and suspicious these days. So insistent with his questions. She wasn't surprised. They had been trending in the wrong direction for so long.

She wasn't sure Michael was ready to hear what she had to tell him, but she could deal with that. At least, she thought she could. Hopefully the whole drama at the park had scared some sense into him. Both of them, really. Robin really wanted a big glass of wine but that wasn't in the cards tonight.

*Shit. What a mess. I just need him to hear me out and go from there. That's all.*

She almost missed her turn, hit the brakes and jerked the vehicle to the right. Too many thoughts swirling in her head. For Robin, the one saving grace of the whole incident was that it happened at the park rather than in front of their house. Everyone on the block already had notions about what kind of people Michael and Robin Key were.

Her body still hummed with anxiety as she rounded the last corner onto their street and pulled into the driveway. They had bought this house less than a year ago. Michael said this newer, bigger home would give them the stability and space they needed to get things back on track. She had reluctantly agreed.

Robin didn't care about the house anymore, or her job for that matter. She could find new ones. Maybe she would finally carry out her threat to move back to Philadelphia.

*Can't start fresh here. I'm so tired of this fucking city.*

First, Robin would answer Michael's questions and tell him exactly what was going on. She wouldn't be surprised if he had already figured it out himself. Then, even with all the fallout she would go on and handle the rest of life on her own. She was confident of that.

Robin switched off the ignition and closed her eyes. She took several long, deep breaths to slow her manic rhythm.

*Ok. It's ok. You've got this, Robo. You've got this.*

She realized her left hand still held the wheel in a vice grip and laughed at her false bravado.

Robin got out of the car and looked up and down her street. She saw tidy middle-class houses with well-manicured lawns. She heard a dog barking and the voices of children somewhere in the near distance but there was no one to be seen on such a pleasant night.

*Decent citizens in their nice little homes, with their nice little opinions about me and Michael. Fuck them. You've got this.*

She rummaged through her purse for the house keys as she approached the front door. The porch light was already on. A broad willow hedge that shielded their porch from the street and the property next door was home to a family of raccoons that were always setting off the light's motion sensor. When she reached the foot of the steps Robin heard twigs cracking.

*Yikes, those raccoons must be getting fat.*

A dark figure burst from the hedge and rushed in behind her. A gloved hand clamped over her mouth and she smelled old leather. Pain exploded in her right side, setting Robin's mind on fire. She felt the full weight of a man leaning into her back, then looked down and saw a blood-slicked knife blade before it swung again, disappearing into the flesh under her ribcage. She screamed behind the gloved hand as a fresh surge of adrenaline coursed through her. Robin set her foot against the middle step and pushed her attacker sideways into the railing. She turned her body away from him, ignoring the searing tendrils shooting through her abdomen, but his hand stayed in place, stifling her howls of agony. He was so strong.

*Keep fighting! Oh my god fuck fuck fuck keep fighting! Don't let him do this!*

She kicked and stomped behind her, searching for his feet, his knees, anything. She became conscious of warmth spreading over her blouse and jeans. Blood. Her blood. Lots of it. Robin twisted against his grip and reached back with both hands, her fingers curled like talons clawing at his face.

She raked the skin under his eye and down his neck and he grunted in pain but steadied himself and sent the knife into the middle of her back. With that her wind was gone and her legs failed. He fell on top of her, pinning her to the steps. Robin drove her thigh into his groin and he shifted briefly, but she remained trapped under him. He leaned onto her chest, driving the edge of the top step into her spine, sending fresh waves of agony to every corner of her body. Held in place, she could do nothing as he slid the blade into her throat. He paused there, his panting face just inches from hers, and looked into her dimming eyes.

"Now it's over, Robin," he said before withdrawing the knife from her neck. He wiped the dripping blade on her jacket and scrambled back into the shadowy wall of willows, his footsteps fading into the night.

Robin's head fell to one side, and she coughed. Blood spattered onto the boards next to her face. There was so much blood. On the steps. On her clothes. Running free in her abdomen. She couldn't feel her legs. Robin let out a low croaking moan that was cut short by the blood filling her throat.

She lay there, alone with the sounds of suburban dusk; barking dogs, kids laughing in someone's backyard, chirping crickets, the far off rumble of a freight truck. With a gurgling effort, she drew air into her lungs.

*You're not done. You've got this, Robo.*

Using her last reserve of ebbing strength she dragged herself up onto the porch landing. Through her tunnel vision the front door seemed so far away. The pain receded into a different section of her consciousness and now she felt heavy and so tired. Her keys and phone were all the way down at the bottom of the steps. She was cold now. Her voice would not come and there was no one on the street to hear her faint moans. Robin Key lay in a widening pool of her own blood, her left hand resting on the doormat that proclaimed YOU ARE WELCOME. Her heart slowed to a standstill as the porch light ticked away its sixty second countdown and then went dark.

**2**

"Michael Key?"

"Yeah," said Michael. He nodded slowly, wiping sleep from his blood-shot eyes. "Wha' time is it? Wait, whaddya guys want?"

"I'm Officer Hunt and this is Officer Koenig. Can you step outside, sir? We need to talk to you right now."

Michael opened the door wider and rested his unsteady weight against the frame. He held a hand in front of his face as a shield against the flashing blue lights. He could see Koenig, at the bottom of the porch steps, speaking into the walkie talkie on his shoulder, "Yeah, we have a black male, positive ID." Beyond him, Michael saw four more cops standing by the two squad cars that blocked the driveway. All eyes were on Michael.

"Hey, um, look I talked to you guys at the park and didn't go back to my house, just like you said. I haven't even spoken to her." Michael's voice was thick, slowed by the alcohol in his bloodstream.

"You can explain everything down at the station, Mr. Key," said Hunt.

"Whayoumean?" said Michael. His tongue felt fat in his mouth and his legs wobbled beneath him. He took a deep breath and started again in the deliberate, halting tone of the inebriated. "What'd Robin tell you? I texted her a couple times to say I was sorry, but I've been here all night."

Koenig drew his gun and held it by his side. Michael rubbed his eyes and surveyed the scene again – six white cops and him, no one else around. A ball of electricity bloomed in his chest and spread through him, piercing the cloud of booze in his mind. He slowly raised both hands to his chest, palms out.

"Relax, man. I'm all cool. I did what you guys asked. I came here," said Michael. Except for Hunt, the cops were tense, like dogs straining at the leash. "Just tell me what you want."

"Mr. Key, listen to me," said Hunt, "We need you to come with us and answer some questions about what happened to Robin."

"What are you talking about?" said Michael, his voice rising in alarm. "What happened to Robin?"

Koenig took a step up to the porch, both hands on his pistol grip. Hunt held eye contact with Michael and put one hand out to keep Koenig at bay.

"Mr. Key, I need you to come with us right now, ok? I am asking you nicely. When we get to the station, we can talk about Robin and get everything out in the open."

Michael kept his hands still and looked at Koenig, then to other cops, their postures full of latent menace. The air felt too thick to breathe.

"Wait, what the fuck is this?" whispered Michael. His vision returned to Officer Hunt and clung to him like a life preserver in a storm. "Ok, ok. I'll come with you. Just tell them to stay calm. My hands are right here. I just wanna know what's going on with Robin."

"Same here, Mr. Key. It's good that you're cooperating. Now, come with me and you can ride in my car, ok?"

Michael nodded numbly. He stumbled across the porch, a shuddering breath escaping his lungs.

"My buddy, this is his house. He's sleeping in the back. I should let him know I'm going."

"No need, Mr. Key. You come with us and the other officers will talk to him. Anything we should know about what's in that house?"

Michael squinted at Hunt, puzzled by the question, "What? Nah. Just ...just him. His name's Flip. I mean, it's William. I call him Flip."

Hunt ushered Michael down the walkway toward the car with a firm grip on his upper arm. Koenig opened the back door of the cruiser, his predatory stare locked on Michael.

The officers at the end of the driveway split up and approached the house in pairs with their flashlights out, two advancing around the back and two approaching the front door, still ajar.

"Just tell him I'll be back soon. I mean, he's just letting me stay on his couch. He's my friend." Michael realized he was babbling now. He stopped to search for the correct thing to say and came up with nothing. As the car door shut, his head spun with questions that had no answers, only dark possibilities.

"Don't worry, Mr. Key," said Hunt, "The officers can handle it. You sit tight and we'll be at the station in a couple minutes. Then we can have that talk."

**3**

C lyde followed Mason out of the bedroom and went straight to the glass door that opened onto the balcony. The dog liked to start each morning with a sniff of the fresh air and a survey of his kingdom four floors below, the intersection of Broadway and Chicago. Then he would waddle over to the low planter box Mason had made for him years ago and do his business. Clyde was happy to take his time with this routine because he knew that soon he would hear the staccato clinking of the food in his bowl. He knew Mason would place the food dish in his favorite spot on the polished concrete floor where, on days unlike today, the sun would hit. He knew Mason would take care of him.

Clyde wasn't wrong. To Mason, the dog was quite literally his best friend. He had drinking buddies, courthouse peers, and a dwindling number of old law school chums, but no real friends. Clyde was someone he truly cared about and tried to never let down. Maybe Clyde was the only one he never let down.

Mason's father was a hard man who spent thirty-five years in a foundry and never approved of his son defending 'those people'. His mother more than once expressed her disappointment that Mason worked so hard at law school only to become a 'mouthpiece for thugs'. Both had passed away years ago, and Mason's only sibling, an older brother who lived in Duluth, hadn't spoken to him in years. There had been no falling out. They were just different people who didn't care enough to stay in touch. He had been married to Hannah, his college sweetheart, for six years before she filed for divorce. And while it wasn't a lie when Mason told people that the split was amicable, it simply meant that he and his ex-wife were best when not in contact. Hannah lived ninety minutes away in Madison with their daughter, Kaylie. Between his eighty-hour work weeks and Kaylie's packed pre-teen social calendar, their visits had become less frequent, but Mason followed her life via social media, which allowed him to stay in touch while minimizing her embarrassment. He hoped that one day they would have a more normal relationship, but wasn't sure when that would be.

But Clyde was always there, encouraging Mason out of bed to face another day. The dog was someone Mason felt accountable to, someone who needed him. Mason's clients needed him, but that was different. Clyde never bashed his little sister's head in with a bat because she played her music too loud one night.

He was a sand-colored Pug Pomeranian mix, built like a cocktail sausage. Clyde had slowed down in recent years and bits of gray now crept into the black fur around his snout, but with his bulging eyes and breath that sounded like an outboard motor on its last legs, he remained comically endearing. On every walk, a smitten passerby would stop them, Clyde impassively accepting their scratches and belly rubs while Mason would force a grin and respond to questions about name, sex, breed, and age. Both were always more than happy to move on.

Mason's long hours and irregular comings and goings weren't ideal for pet care. He tried to make up for it with organic food, the finest dog bed money could buy, and an abundance of stuffed toys, one of which had become Clyde's long-term girlfriend. In any case, the little guy didn't seem to mind his alone time and they were too far into this relationship to split up now.

Clyde tapped at the glass door with his paw. Mason let him in and watched the dog trot to his food bowl. Mason was already halfway through his standard liquid breakfast; a strawberry, banana, and OJ smoothie. Frosty, a little tart, and ostensibly full of nutrients, it cut through the boozy fog in Mason's head. It took only five minutes to prepare and knock back twenty-four ounces of this fruit slush, and most mornings the thought of solid food was enough to roil his stomach.

Through some gift of genetics, Mason's alcoholic overconsumption did not curse him with severe hangovers, but the smoothie was like a protective talisman, fortifying him for the life and death nonsense of his workday.

Mason took another huge gulp while Clyde crunched away at his bowl. The brief but peaceful breakfast ritual they shared was a highlight of both their days.

Mason finished and rinsed his glass. He bent down to give Clyde a hearty back scratch.

"You complete me, you little goof."

Clyde paused his feast to lick Mason's hand, then returned his focus to the kibble.

**4**

Michael sat in a holding cell with a dozen other inmates. Bunks lined the walls, each comprising a slab of concrete and paper thin mattress. Not long after his arrival, an officer delivered bag meals to the cell, each one containing a bologna sandwich and fruit cup. Michael forced down several bites before losing his appetite. Exhaustion hung on his body like a lead blanket but anxiety set his mind racing. He had so many unanswered questions about Robin and what she must have told the police. He knew he should try to sleep but with the always-on fluorescent lights and the commotion of inmates coming and going, it wouldn't happen. Up to now there had been no questions, no information, nothing. He had been put in here and told to wait.

Michael had no watch or phone and there was no clock in sight, but he guessed it was around 8 a.m. when the guard unlocked the cell door and called his name. They led him to a square windowless room with cinderblock walls painted off white. It was not bigger than a broom closet, with just enough space for the two hard plastic chairs and a small table. The only decoration to be seen was a tin ashtray.

He was soon joined by a plainclothes detective who set a file folder and a pack of Newports on the table and took the other seat.

"Mr. Key, my name is Detective Bader. I'm going to go over some questions with you now." He pointed at the cigarettes. "You want one?"

"Don't smoke anymore," answered Michael.

Bader drew a laminated card from his folder, then read out the Miranda rights quickly and without emotion, like it was the disclaimer at the end of a commercial. "Do you understand these rights as I read them?'

Michael nodded.

"Out loud please, Mr. Key."

"Yes, I guess I understand."

"Having been read these rights, do you wish to answer questions?"

"Yeah ok, but can you tell me what's going on?"

"Great. It's also my duty to inform you that the audio and video of this interview is being recorded as standard practice."

Michael said nothing. His face showed a dawning sense of alarm.

"Mr. Key, do you know why you're here?"

"Must be because of what happened with Robin."

"That's right."

"I agreed to come down here, but now it feels like I can't leave."

"It's good that you're cooperating, Mr. Key. Can I call you Michael?"

Michael paused and reached for the Newports, "Sure. Got a light?"

Bader passed him a book of matches and continued, "Michael, we need you to fill in the details of the incident from last night, ok?"

"Yeah. Look, I want to know what Robin told you about what happened. Wait, last night? It was only like six o'clock."

Bader pulled a sheet from the folder. "That was the, um, incident at the park, yes. But our conversation is more concerned with what happened after that."

"What do you mean? The cops told me to go home, I mean, back to where I was staying. So I did. I told the other guys all this. Then I got a little drunk, tried contacting Robin a couple times on the phone but that's it."

Bader leaned back and folded his arms. "Is that really all you want to say, Michael? Because we can do this the difficult way if you want but it's not going to help you."

"What are you talking about? Can I talk to Robin? Really, there's been some kind of misunderstanding."

"Michael, Michael, stop. We know everything. We know what happened and we know it was you." Bader took a small stack of photos from the folder and laid them out on the table. Each shot showed a different angle of the Key's front porch. Michael stopped dead, transfixed by the images. Wide shots and closeups of Robin's lifeless body, her long blond hair matted in a pool of dark blood, garishly lit by the camera flash.

"What is this," whispered Michael. "Robin, no. What's going on?" He looked to Bader, uncomprehending, tears welling in his eyes.

"Michael. You need to talk to me about what you did to Robin."

---

Mason showered quickly, scrubbing himself down under nearly scalding water. His close-cropped hair needed little attention, but he cleared yesterday's stubble with an electric shaver. He gave his teeth a vigorous brushing and gargled with minty mouthwash to complete the ablutions and erase the traces of last night's bender. A dull but persistent complaint from the region of his liver was the only reminder.

He walked into his custom-built closet and turned on the wall-mounted TV. Local morning news hits played as Mason surveyed the well-organized collection of suits, shirts, ties, handkerchiefs, and shoes. He knew his wardrobe caused snickers among some colleagues. To them, the French cuffs, suspenders, vibrant colors, and hand-tailored pieces were ostentatious, obnoxious even. To him, this wardrobe was a public-facing business tool that communicated confidence and authority. This was a show for clients and juries, and they took notice. Sometimes it was as simple as 'he looks like a good lawyer, so he must be one.'

*"It's another rainy one today, with a high in the mid-fifties and a low pressure system that should stick around through the week...."*

Mason made mental notes for his upcoming case as he dressed. He started with a fresh shirt – always white, always crisp. This morning he selected a two-button, double-vented black pinstripe suit that was the most sober model in his closet. Crystal cufflinks, a hot pink tie, and a supple pair of black and white Allen Edmonds wingtips completed the look.

*"...found stabbed to death in front of her home last night. It's the 198th murder in Milwaukee this year, on pace to be the deadliest in city history..."*

Mason straightened his double Windsor knot and gave himself an approving once over in the full-length mirror. "Time to stick it to the man."

He grabbed his keys and briefcase from the hall table, which sat askew with one end now blocking the entrance. He used his hip to push it back into place and stopped at the dog bed to give the now slumbering Clyde one last head scratch.

"You be good. No parties or girls while I'm gone." Clyde gave a sleepy snort of acknowledgement and tucked his head deeper into the folds of his blanket. Mason made a note that both dog and blanket were overdue for a wash.

At the elevator, Mason ran into his next-door neighbor, Donna Hampton.

"Morning, Mason. Going down?"

"You bet. All good, Donna?"

"So-so. Dead tired. Couldn't sleep last night. You?"

"Slept like a baby."

"Ok, good. I thought maybe I heard something bumping around in your place late last night."

Mason had no memory of arriving home in the wee hours, but imagined he was less than steady as he stumbled in. That would explain the table, which was set against a wall he shared with Donna's unit.

"Oh yeah, sorry about that. Clyde got a little rambunctious. Unfortunately, I was at the office pretty late and I think he had some pent up energy. I've got to try and get him out for walks more often."

Donna nodded, satisfied with this explanation. The elevator doors opened, and Mason held out his arm. "After you, neighbor."

"You know, I'm around the house a lot during the day," said Donna. "Freelance life, you know?"

"Right," said Mason. He had no clue what she did for a living.

"I wouldn't mind taking Clyde out now and then if you need. Just saying."

Mason inwardly recoiled at the offer. He felt for Clyde sitting alone all day, but did not relish the idea of Donna Hampton having access to his home. Not that he didn't trust her, but in his estimation, a little distance made for better neighbors.

"Thanks, Donna. That's nice of you to offer. I'll keep it in mind."

After descending the final two floors in silence, Donna exited into the lobby with a polite wave that Mason returned with an impeccably civil smile.

One level down, Mason left the elevator and walked to his gleaming Mercedes sedan parked in a corner spot of the underground garage. He leased it new last summer and would flip it for a newer, shinier model in another year. Fine German engineering with all the bells and whistles meant the payments were steep, but then nobody wants a lawyer who drives a Kia.

**5**

The rain blew in off Lake Michigan as soon as Mason pulled out onto the street. The wet look wasn't doing Milwaukee any favors. Gray sky met gray lake water at an invisible horizon, the downtown skyline squatting more than soaring in the dull gray half-light. Mason navigated the rain-slicked streets, with the steady rhythm of the wipers making his drive look like a flip-book animation. He joined the traffic on Wells Street and could see the brooding bulk of the County Courthouse growing larger through the windshield. The blocklike mass of columns and pale stone loomed over its surroundings, promising stern but sober Midwestern justice.

Overlooking downtown to the west and the eight-lane trench of the I-43 to the east, the Milwaukee County Courthouse was actually a complex of three buildings – the Courthouse, the County Jail, and the Safety Building – connected by a labyrinth of corridors and skywalks.

The courthouse itself was a temple of the Roosevelt era's secular religion – public works. Completed in 1931, it boasted an imposing neo-classical facade and interiors of marble and mahogany. It stood as a symbol of muscular American goodness, grandeur for the greater good.

Now, it was a drafty relic clinging to its former glory, a collection of mysterious leaks and tricky wiring held together by a patchwork of repairs and sporadic good luck. Successive budget cuts had reduced maintenance to the bare minimum, keeping the building just safe enough to host the public. Most local politicians loved to complain about court backlogs but rarely loosened the purse-strings to solve the problem.

The building housed all manner of courtrooms and offices devoted to criminal, civil, and family law, along with a rabbit warren of offices for the County Executive.

Mason drove past the plaza in front of the courthouse and around the block to 9th Street. On his right stood the County Jail, a drab post-modernist take on incarceration standing directly north of the courthouse and linked to it by a glassed-in walkway one floor above ground. This austere concrete box, that let in almost no natural light, had been wreaking havoc with cell reception since the '90s. It housed the courts designated to address initial appearances and other preliminary court matters. This allowed in-custody defendants to appear in court without leaving secured areas. The courtrooms here smelled of musty furniture, mixed with the jail's pervasive scent of stale sweat and urine.

Out his driver side window, Mason could see the Safety Building, which had housed the original county jail. Half the building's square footage was made up of empty, decaying cells, taken over by vermin since the last inmates moved out thirty years ago. Now, the building accommodated all felony criminal cases, but the disjointed layout meant shackled defendants were often walked down the same hallways where jurors waited to serve on their trial. The Safety Building made the courthouse look ultramodern in comparison, and there were calls for it to be torn down and replaced. The building's two banks of elevators exemplified the overall state of disrepair – an older one originally operated by the county, the other installed decades later by the city. Different elevators, requiring different parts and different maintenance schedules, yet similarly unreliable. Mason gambled and became stranded enough times to know the stairs were the only safe option.

Mason turned left into the underground parking lot and found a spot two levels down. He turned off the car and closed his eyes. The courthouse could wait for a moment. Mason filled his lungs and exhaled slowly, then cracked open a mickey of vodka and took one equally deep swig before replacing it in the glove box. Mason's mood had taken a nosedive on the drive from home. Maybe it was Donna's prying, maybe it was the weather. Or maybe it was the prospect of spending his week representing a remorseless twenty-year-old who shot a man in cold blood. Another week, another losing battle. But first, Mason needed a breath mint.

He locked the car and walked down the dimly lit aisle, past a hum-drum collection of vehicles that stood in stark contrast to his freshly detailed Mercedes. The garage reeked of garbage and years-old rot, but he had long since ceased to notice. Arriving at the elevator, Mason recognized Derek Gill, a prosecutor he faced last month on an armed robbery case. "Hey."

Gill looked up from his phone and replied, "Hey yourself. You had to park all the way down here, too, huh?"

The hundreds of people that came to work at the Milwaukee County Courthouse formed a close-knit community. It could feel like walking the halls at high school – you knew most people by face if not name, there were well-defined tribes (lawyers, court staff, security) and smaller cliques with shifting memberships. Everyone played a role and knew where they fell in the hierarchy, professionally and socially. Still, proximity and basic courtesy dictated a level of civility, if not friendliness.

Derek Gill was one of the few black attorneys in the DA's office, and one of only a handful that worked felony trials in Milwaukee County. Lack of non-white representation was an issue at all levels of the court system, except among defendants.

Mason liked him as much as he liked any prosecutor. Gill was sharp, level-headed, and could be reasoned with. Unlike several of his colleagues, he didn't come off like a trumped up hall monitor. And Mason appreciated Gill's ability to pick suits that fit, a vanishingly rare trait among the State's prosecutors.

They stepped from the elevators and crossed the 9th Street tunnel to the courthouse's basement entrance. Prospective jurors, defendants, victims, family members, and random citizens thronged the security station line. Courthouse staff and lawyers were issued passes that allowed them to bypass the line.

"Damn it," hissed Gill, "I forgot my pass in the car."

"Shit. Um…want me to wait for you?" asked Mason and immediately regretted it. Too weird.

"What? No. But your chivalry is noted." Gill shook his head and turned back toward the garage, muttering, "Mondays. Always a fuckin' circus."

"You said it," said Mason, under his breath.

To members of the Milwaukee County criminal defense bar, the start of each work week was known as Manic Monday. With all due respect to The Bangles, this was a nod to the general mayhem that greeted attorneys as they arrived at the courthouse to find out if their case would go to trial. Each court in the building had a cluttered docket of cases stacked up on their calendar. Every Monday morning, this trial deck would be shuffled and one picked to go ahead, usually later that day. This was the system that dictated the weekly schedule of every criminal lawyer in Milwaukee County.

Citizens selected for jury duty were summoned to appear in court on a Monday, and these extra bodies milling around added to the atmosphere of disorder. The first line of jury the summons advised, "prepare to be in court for two days, starting on the Monday you were summoned," and if the prospective juror kept reading from there, they would find "or for the duration of the trial for which you get selected, which could be several days or even weeks." Most jurors never made it past that first line of the summons, and their dismay at being reminded of the potential length of their service to the County added to the charged atmosphere in the building.

This uncertainty of which trial was going and when caused all other appointments in Mason's work week to be subject to the 'MMD' qualifier, meaning 'Manic Monday Dependent'.

On this Monday morning, Mason had three potential trials prepped to start; two homicides and an armed robbery. Unlike what one might see on TV or read in books, Mason did not spend weeks preparing for every trial. The weekly lottery at the courthouse and the quick turnover of his practice did not allow that luxury. The window between the end of one trial and the start of another was never more than a few days, leaving little time to rehearse an opening statement, craft cross examinations, or write a soaring closing argument in advance.

And there were the incessant calls and texts from clients pestering Mason to pore over evidence and review documents long before their trial was scheduled. He told each one the same thing – 'When it's your week, I promise you'll get one hundred percent of my attention.' – but they only stayed patient for so long.

Mason normally reviewed evidence for each new case only as it was imminently pending. In most criminal cases, the defense did not call any witnesses, so preparation on that front was limited. He would file pre-trial motions, if appropriate, then make notes on the case's strengths and weaknesses. These notes formed the bulk of his trial prep. This allowed Mason to prepare multiple trials for the same week. But when one of his cases was selected for trial on a Monday, it held Mason's full attention for the duration, which usually was through Thursday afternoon. The rest of his workload would be compressed into Friday and the weekend. The result – all work and very little play.

He expected one of his homicide trials would proceed this week, in which the co-defendant had elected to testify against Mason's client, a common occurrence.

According to the rules of the prisoner's dilemma, if co-defendants trust each other and remain silent they will benefit, with a lighter sentence or maybe none at all. But if one of them talks to the cops, they will benefit and their counterpart will suffer. In Mason's world, the adage that 'snitches get stitches' was true but rarely a sufficient deterrent under intense police questioning. Cops routinely leveraged the fear of betrayal to convince one defendant to turn on the other, using that as the foundation for a criminal prosecution that would end up in court. Today's trial would be no different.

Mason stepped into the waiting elevator and was joined by a young lawyer he knew by face only. *Maybe Paul?* Mason nodded a greeting and went back to mentally plotting out his route through the court complex labyrinth – disembark on the first floor, get to the north side of the courthouse, take the skywalk from there that would deposit him on the third floor in the Safety Building, take the stairs to the fourth floor, down the hall to the left where he would find the courtroom in which one of his trial was scheduled.

"Sweet suit, Mitchell," said Maybe Paul. "Putting on a show today?"

"It is Monday. I've got three on the schedule," said Mason.

"Anything interesting?"

"Um, you like homicide? I've got one in Branch 38 that will probably go."

The doors began closing at a glacial pace but were stopped by the hand of a vaguely familiar victim witness advocate who scrambled into the elevator car. Her harried demeanor, jumble of dog-eared files, and floral perfume that did little to mask a recent cigarette made her the poster child for Manic Mondays.

Maybe Paul made room by moving closer to Mason and continued, "Safety Building?"

Mason nodded, keeping his eyes on the bank of buttons.

"Me, too!" said Maybe Paul. "You can tell me more while we head over."

The doors pressed shut and the elevator lurched into motion. Mason cursed his decision to skip the stairs.

"Not much to tell," he began. "My client got into it with the new boyfriend of his baby mama. They had a fight, my guy lost. So he went to his car, got his gun and started shooting. My guy is claiming the victim drew down on him but the eyewitnesses don't support his self-defense claim." Mason rolled his eyes and continued, "I told him to take the deal, but when the offer is thirty years it's hard to get the guy to swallow that pill. So, another trial for the books. What about you?" Mason gave Maybe Paul's attire a critical once over. "Are you putting on a show today?"

The doors opened, letting the two lawyers escape the cloud of smokey lilac and join the bustle in the corridor.

Maybe Paul fell into step at Mason's shoulder. "Not a show, but I have a shitty DV case before Branch 10." Domestic Violence was all too common on the dockets in Milwaukee County, and Mason some-times wondered if the acronyms, initials, and shorthand used around the courthouse desensitized them all to the daily horror of their jobs. Maybe that was the only way to keep doing the job. "Client broke into his girlfriend's house and started shooting. She barricaded herself in the bathroom, and took cover in the bathtub, until the cops arrived. The guy plead guilty to stalking and reckless endangering safety, only after they amended it from an attempted homicide. The State is asking for fifteen years in and ten out."

"Not a terrible deal," said Mason. He increased his pace as they entered the skywalk. It was less crowded and he needed to make up time. The dumbest way to start your week was to piss off a trial judge by being tardy.

"Yeah, but you try explaining to my client what a bifurcated sentence is," said Maybe Paul. "They never understand that time inside is the actual time they will spend in prison and 'good time' does not exist."

"My guys struggle with that too," said Mason. He really did empathize. To do this job well, you had to manage the clients. It made sense; these were people who were sinking fast and would frantically grab at anything to keep them afloat. A defense attorney often served as therapist or punching bag. Mason felt fiercely protective of clients who were screwed over by cops and overcharged by zealous prosecutors, but even the ones who were in court because of nothing but their own doing won his sympathy. It was one person against the system, and they only had him to rely on. On most days, that appealed to his mile-wide defiant streak and kept him coming back for more. Some days, it filled him with despair. He found a use for Tito's vodka on both kinds of days.

"Sorry, Paul. I really gotta run now." Mason tapped his watch as he opened the door to the stairwell.

"Yeah, no problem. And it's Scott, by the way."

"Got it," said Mason over his shoulder, and launched himself up the stairs, taking two at a time.

He walked into Branch 38, slightly winded, just in time to hear the first call of trials that morning. The courtroom was one of the largest in the safety building, with a gallery eight rows deep, separated from the front of the room by a glass partition which ran floor to ceiling. The deputy pushed a buzzer and a door in the partition popped open, allowing Mason to join the other lawyers seated in the unused jury box. He took the open chair next to Jean Lindeke. She would be the prosecutor in next week's trial; a family party that had gone decidedly wrong during a disagreement in the kitchen. What started with raised voices had ended with third-degree burns.

"Hey, Mason. Doing any good deeds today?" asked Jean.

"You know me, always thinking of others. Speaking of which, my client doesn't deserve seven years in. That's overkill and you know it. What can we do about that?"

"Her brother yelled at her so she threw boiling fat in his face. Not exactly a minor incident."

"Your so-called victim was brandishing a knife and for all my client knew he was about to use it on her."

"A bread knife, Mason."

"Oh, so if I had a ten-inch bread knife with a serrated edge in my hand right now you wouldn't feel the need to defend yourself with whatever was within arm's reach?"

She rolled her eyes. "I always feel the need to defend myself when you're around, Mason." Lindeke sighed. "Fine, I can go down to substantial battery, five in and two out."

"That's the spirit! But still a little harsh if you ask me. The two years of extended supervision is fine, but the upfront time? Five years, really?"

"She hit him on the head with the pan when he was down on the floor with a sizzling face!"

"That may be so, but if we go to trial. I'm going to pound you with self-defense and the brother's well-documented rage issues, the jury will lap it up, Jean. Let's go with three in and three out, joint recommendation and call it a day."

She looked at him with exasperation, "I'm going to agree to this, but only to get you to stop talking to me. Jesus, you're a pest."

"Thanks, Jean. I'll take that as the compliment you intended it to be. I promise not to bug you again until we meet up for a drink at the State Bar Christmas party."

Jean smiled and shook her head. "That might be too soon."

The court clerk for Branch 38 consulted her docket and announced, "State of Wisconsin versus Kevin Dixon, case number 21CF002382". This was Mason's trial case, appearing before the Honorable Michelle Borowski.

Mason rose from the jury box and hurried over to the defense table. His client was escorted into the courtroom clad in a plaid shirt and black pants, both of which Mason had purchased and dropped off at the jail the night before.

"Jacob Stevenson for the State," said the prosecutor.

"Mason Mitchell on behalf of the defendant, who appears in person, in-custody but dressed in jury clothes. Good morning."

"Good morning, does this case remain in trial posture?" asked the judge.

"It does from the defense perspective."

"Also for the State."

"Ok, we have some other cases to call this morning, but this is my number one trial," said the judge. "We will recall this case at 11 a.m. to start jury selection, so if you have other courts to go to, do it now because I intend to start promptly on the hour."

"Yes, your honor," said Stevenson.

Mason nodded. "Understood. I have a couple of courts I need to drop in on, but I'll be back in time."

He spent the next half hour navigating the courthouse complex, informing other interested courts that his week would be spent in Branch 38. While making his rounds, Mason called the office. "Linda, the Dixon case is going to trial. Can you clear off the week through Thursday or move anything that's urgent to early morning or after five? Thanks."

6

At 11:02, the thirty-person jury panel was brought into Branch 38. They walked single file, lined up according to their assigned number. In most cases, the judge, staff, and all parties would stand as the jury came in, but not when a defendant was in custody, like today. A bailiff led the panel to the cramped group of seats in and around the jury box, each one labeled with a number that matched a juror.

Mason sat behind the defense table, next to his client, who was allowed to wear street clothes in front of the jury. The floor length table skirt meant the jury couldn't see that the defendant's right leg was shackled to the floor.

This precaution was not always the protocol in Milwaukee County, but things changed after an in-custody defendant attempted to escape out of a courtroom window and was shot to death. This happened before Mason's time but every criminal lawyer in the county knew the story. It was a rite of passage to go see the square of replaced carpet in Courtroom 305 where the pool of blood had gathered. Since then, all in-custody defendants were shackled to the floor during any court appearance. As a result, the litigants remained seated while the jury came and went so the ankle chain wouldn't rattle and reveal a defendant's custodial status.

The selection process began with Judge Borowski and then the prosecution questioning the jury panelists.

*Is there any reason you could not perform your duties?*

*What is your highest level of education?*

*Have you or anyone you know been the victim of a violent crime?*

*Do you believe in the importance of community safety?*

*Do you have any life experience related to the facts of this case?*

By the time Mason rose to take his turn, he had a relatively clear image of each juror, their likes and dislikes, occupation, spouse's occupation, number of kids, what part of town they lived in. He knew if they were a hard-ass or bleeding heart. He also knew which jurors he would eliminate. With much of the work already done, Mason liked to use his time to mold the jurors and get them to think differently.

"Ladies and gentlemen," he began, "I'm sure when you got your jury summons in the mail you were thrilled." He paused for the smattering of polite laughter. "But in all seriousness, serving on a jury is one of your most important civic duties. This system only works when citizens of the community come together to hold the government accountable. So I thank you for serving and my client thanks you for serving." Mason walked out from behind the defense table and approached the jury box.

"Now, the questions that the judge and the prosecution just asked were meant to determine if your experiences and opinions are in any way biased against the State or Defendant. All of you have indicated you can be fair and impartial and that you don't have any bias. But let's be honest. No one likes to walk into a room full of strangers and admit to being unfair or prejudiced." Mason looked down at the floor, as if in contemplation, then continued. "Bias, unfair, prejudice. Those are loaded words in our society, ugly terms. But sometimes, it's acceptable to be openly biased, unfair, or even outright prejudiced. Like when you're watching sports." Mason paused, returned to the table and stood behind his client.

"For example, for most Wisconsinites, when Number 4 changed from the green and gold to that purple jersey, we all switched from loving him to openly and publicly hating him." The Brett Favre reference was a little dated but still worked even with the most casual Wisconsin sports fan.

"Clearly, that is not fair or rational, but that's being a good *Cheesehead*." A few more laughs this time. "Of course, we can't let that kind of thinking enter the courtroom. Because my client is a citizen just like you, but now he's here beside me. So, in a manner of speaking, my first question is," Mason laid a hand on the defendant's shoulder, "do you see my client in a purple jersey?"

"Now, I want you to be honest with yourself. It's ok if you see him that way, and please raise your hand to let us know your thoughts. It won't mean you are unfair, it may just mean you're not the right juror for *this* case. Is that fair?" Most members of the panel nodded in agreement.

"Good. I know we're all familiar with the idea of the presumption of innocence. Whether you learned it in civics class or from a TV show, you understand the general concept. But in *reality*, when sitting here in this courtroom, can you really apply that concept? To illustrate, I'll ask the question this way."

Anti-defendant bias was a well-documented phenomenon and to swing jurors the other way, Mason always put them through simple thought experiments.

"My client is sitting in a felony courtroom. There's a bullet-proof glass partition between him and the exit. You know the charge is homicide. Given all those factors, how many of you think my client must have done *something* wrong to be sitting here today? Raise your hand if you do."

After a long pause, a few hands were slowly raised. Mason surveyed the affirmative respondents and called on Juror Nine. "So, tell me why you think that, sir."

The man, who did not look happy from the start, was doubly unhappy to be called upon to speak in open court. "Well, I've never been charged with a crime, and I figure if he didn't do something he would not be charged with a crime." His gruff response was expected and Mason rolled on to his next point.

"What if I told you all that's happened is that a lawsuit has been filed against my client? And we all know about frivolous lawsuits. Like the lady who burned her legs with McDonald's coffee and sued because she hadn't been warned the coffee was hot." Mason offered with a distinct tone of sarcasm.

"That's all that has happened. The State of Wisconsin, the government, has filed a lawsuit against my client and my client is defending the lawsuit. My client has entered a not guilty plea, he has already said to this court and publicly that he is not guilty of this crime. He is saying the State must prove his guilt beyond a reasonable doubt." He went from speaking to all, back to one.

"So, does that make more sense to you, Juror Nine? Or do you still think my client must have done something wrong to be here?"

"When you put it that way, I guess not. I can see how the government needs to prove their claim."

Mason did not push it further. He had decided to strike Juror Nine before the man even spoke. The point about frivolous lawsuits was for the rest of the jury panel.

"What about this? Let's imagine that right now the judge said we are done, we are going to fill out the verdict for this case and go home. At this stage of the trial, given what you know about the case, who would vote not guilty? Give me a show of hands." None were raised.

"Ok, who would vote guilty?" One hand reluctantly went up, followed by two more.

"And who thinks we need to wait to hear the evidence before voting on a verdict?" Almost all of the hands shot up.

"Well, sorry to say it, you are all wrong." Another pause. Mason wanted the jurors to absorb this and wonder why before he gave the answer. "To be fair, all jury panels get this question wrong." He shrugged and smiled warmly to take the sting out of it.

"The correct answer is that you *must* vote not guilty! Think about it this way; a defendant always has the presumption of innocence, so that's our starting point. Since we are at the start of the trial, if you were to vote right now you would need to vote not guilty, right? And you can only change your vote if the State convinces you otherwise, beyond a reasonable doubt. Anything short of that and you must find the defendant not guilty."

Each deliberately delivered word hung in the stale air of the courtroom. All thirty jurors were focused on Mason as they grappled with this revelation.

---

As the trial of Kevin Dixon continued, it was clear that Mason was up against a substantial amount of damning evidence and a sharp, if uninspired, prosecutor. The jury listened to hastily composed opening statements delivered by both sides before the State presented its case. Mason did his best, probing for holes in the case against his client and making the prosecutor work for every point. But the evidence was clear, and the case was shaping up to be a cakewalk for the State. With no procedural mistakes by law enforcement, there was very little Mason could do but postpone the inevitable guilty verdict.

Judge Borowski, who prioritized her schedule above all else, interrupted the State's presentation of ballistics evidence to excuse the jury at five o'clock sharp. After a brief consult with his client, Mason escaped the dank confines of the Safety Building and by quarter past was driving back to the office. He checked in with Linda before she left for the day and promised to get back to her soon regarding the raise she had requested two weeks ago. Mason retrieved an unopened bottle of Tito's from his desk drawer before getting back behind the wheel and heading for home.

As Mason sat in a backed up traffic on Michigan Street, a news item on the radio caught his attention:

*"...the James Madison High School teacher and football coach has been arrested! Michael Key, a second-year coach, was placed under arrest and charged with the murder of his wife, Robin Key, who was found stabbed to death on her front porch. Key's initial appearance is scheduled for later this week. A police spokesman gave no further...*

Mason's eyes widened. *Jesus. I was just at that school.* Based on the media attention alone, every criminal defense lawyer in town would want a shot at a case like this. When his gang member clients killed each other in the street, it warranted a brief mention on the news in order to remind Milwaukeeans that some parts of town were just as unsafe as they assumed. But a local football coach accused of murdering his wife was sensational enough to lead the primetime broadcasts and provide a serious career boost. Mason handled so many violent defendants that he'd had brushes with the spotlight in recent years, and now he wondered who would be tabbed to defend the coach.

**7**

After arriving home, Mason changed out of his suit and took Clyde for a walk. They followed the Milwaukee River down to Erie Street Plaza, one of the little mutt's favorite places to relieve himself. Mason watched the black water slip past and thought about his never-ending supply of doomed clients served up for judgment. He knew his efforts would have almost no effect on what the future held for Kevin Dixon.

"What am I supposed to do for him, Clyde?"

The dog looked up at Mason and sniffed the air. The warm Autumn weather was waning, as the breeze now carried a hint of winter chill.

After returning home, Mason perched himself on a stool at the kitchen island. Clyde retreated to his bed, so Mason mixed a tall double vodka on the rocks to keep him company. He returned some emails and sketched out a rudimentary budget. He was spread thin and did not relish the idea of paying out more money to his disgruntled paralegal. She sometimes struggled with the heavy workload, yet Linda always got the job done, and while he trusted her, the relationship had become strained and it wasn't just about compensation. She never mentioned his drinking outright but he sensed her disapproval. Still, the hassle of finding someone new was too much to take on. Mason downed his vodka and drafted an email with a salary increase proposal he hoped would patch things up for the time being. He clapped his laptop shut, grabbed his coat, and tiptoed past a snoring Clyde, closing the front door behind him with a soft click.

41

—————

"So, like, how do you feel about what you do for a living?"

Here it was, the question she wanted to ask since they started talking. Mason had left Clyde at home an hour ago and headed to The Thirsty Oak, a whisky bar two blocks from his loft, where he promptly struck up a conversation with a lovely woman who sat alone at the bar. How many double-vodka-Sprites had Mason put away since he started chatting with…*is it Jada?* After opening with halting small talk, they bonded over snide remarks about the awkward Tinder date in progress by the window then fell into an animated back and forth that had finally come around to careers. He always enjoyed chatting up a woman as sharp and pretty as…*Jenny! That's right, her name is Jenny.*

When someone found out what Mason did for a living, he knew what they wanted to ask him. They might circle around it for a bit before popping the question, but they always asked. Mason decided to play coy and make her work for it.

"Do you mean how do I feel about being a trial lawyer?"

"No. What I mean is, and I'm genuinely curious – how can you represent people who do such awful things?"

"You work in marketing, so maybe I should ask you the same thing."

"Very funny," said Jenny, "but I'm serious. How do you rationalize it in your head?"

"Rationalize it? Well, first off–"

"And you can't just say 'because that's the way our system works.'" She smiled like she'd just scored a point at debate club, cornering the lawyer with her brilliant preemptive strike. Mason was so tempted to tell her how foolish she, and every person who subjected him to this line of questioning, sounded. He wouldn't tell her about the misery and broken lives he saw in his job, the people scooped up by a massive machine that crunched them like numbers and discarded them into one pile or another. Even the lucky ones had their entire existence upended and everything shaken loose. Instead, he swirled the ice in his drink, smiling graciously as he paused for effect. So easy to slip into courtroom mode. Maybe it was the only mode he had that worked.

"Fair enough, but it's true. Our system, even with all its flaws, is rightly based on everyone getting a defense. Everyone, no matter what. And the idea that some people shouldn't get that and be surrendered to... what? Your desire for revenge? Or to whatever the loudest voices say should happen? Before any facts have been heard or a credible accusation mounted and proven?"

He drained his drink in a gulp. "Doesn't sound too smart. That's no system I'd want to live under. And neither should you."

She took a second to reconsider her position, then plowed ahead.

"Yeah, but some of these guys rape and kill and when they get to court, you know they're guilty, everyone knows they're guilty. So who do you think you're helping by defending them?"

"Look, if you want me to say I'm terrible and my role is useless at best and at worst only helps depraved predators to go free, you're barking up the wrong tree."

"I wasn't saying that."

"Sure you were. I get it, to a point. But you'd change your tune in a heartbeat if you were in their position."

"I guess, but–"

"You'd be surprised at the number of people I meet and defend who are just like you." This was a bald-faced lie but now that he'd gotten her to back up a step, he felt like laying it on thick. Courtroom mode. "These people are scared, the deck is completely stacked against them, and the system is out for blood. I'm the only one on their side. The only one who can stop their life from being destroyed and make sure that justice is done." Mason let her sit with it for a beat. "But, I guess you could be right."

He saw the shift in her. He'd seen it before, that moment when the amateur realizes their righteous argument isn't quite so airtight and elects to steer things back to friendly ground.

"Ha-ha. Ok, Mason Mitchell, Attorney-at-Law. You made your point." She nodded at Mason's empty glass, then met his eyes. Her smile had gone from debate club to mischievous. "So, you want another drink, or should we get out of here?"

**8**

David looked down and saw crimson staining the front of his white shirt. His stomach was warm, and he didn't know why. He looked around, but couldn't find his bearings in the dim light. *I'm on the ground. Is that grass?* He ran one hand over his abdomen and it came back sticky with blood, now spreading from a wound on his right side. The mixture of adrenaline and party drugs coursing through his system dampened his pain. He tried to remember what happened before this but nothing clear swam to the surface. He squeezed his eyes shut but came up with nothing.

David could smell burning hickory and heard the crackle of a fire and music coming from somewhere nearby. What he did not hear was anyone calling for help or an ambulance. Did anyone know he was back here? *Right, I'm in the backyard.* He knew he was in trouble, losing blood. His heartbeat thumped in his ears, arms and legs getting heavy.

David wiped a bloody hand on his jeans and felt the familiar outline of his knife in the front pocket. And then it came back to him in a series of flashes. Leaving his wife talking with people at the party; scoring some pills from a dude upstairs; fooling around by the fire with his not-so-secret girlfriend, who was also there; his wife running at the two lovers in a rage. He had dumped the girlfriend off his lap as he scrambled to avoid his wife's blows. Then the two women were on the ground, fighting, while onlookers whooped and hollered. *She had to go start some shit. Stupid bitch!* He could remember intervening and pulling his wife away from the crowd that had gathered. He wrapped her in a bear hug and didn't let go until she stopped kicking and screaming. By then they had moved away from the fire towards a shed at the back of the property. To his left, David could see its outline against the night sky. *Wait, I know this place.* The home of his childhood neighbor, a one-acre residential property with the shed out back for the ATV. That's where it happened. That's where his wife stabbed him.

*How did I let that bitch do this to me? With the fuckin' knife I gave her for her birthday!*

The flash of anger gave David enough energy to haul himself up on two feet. He barely suppressed a wave of nausea and stumbled toward the house. The blood was soaking into his underwear. *Un-fucking believable! Should have done her in a long time ago.* He saw the rooms of the house lit up and people milling around inside. The music was getting louder and there was yelling that sounded like it came from the front of the house, but he couldn't make it out. *They don't know I'm back here! I'm going to bleed out in the dark. That bitch!* Blood loss and the mix of alcohol and narcotics in David's system made his legs unsteady and he labored to stay upright on the muddy, rutted pathway that led from the shed to the front yard.

David rounded the back corner of the house and saw blurry figures silhouetted against the bonfire. He tried to call to them but couldn't summon the air to push his words out. *One foot in front of the other, one foot in front of the other. They'll see me any second.* The glow of the fire showed that his front was covered in a pasty mix of mud and blood, a sight that drained the last of David's strength. He managed two more steps and collapsed, knocking over the garden hose caddy with a clank.

As consciousness faded, one thought filled David's head – *I'm going to make that bitch pay.*

**9**

"**H**ey, Lori. It's Lori, right? I'm Officer Logan. Look at me." The police officer snapped his fingers in her face. "Hey, I'm talking to you. Now let me see your hands."

Lori looked up from the pavement. She was crouched at the end of a driveway on a street she didn't recognize. A police cruiser was parked behind the officer, its front wheels resting on the front lawn of a house. The blue and red lights were so bright, throwing harsh shadows across the scene. She heard shouting from somewhere behind her.

"Where's David?" she asked. "Is he ok?"

"Don't worry about that right now. Just show me your hands!"

Lori slowly pulled them out from under her sweatshirt and the officer trained the beam of his flashlight on them. Her hands were empty but the left was mottled with dried blood and the right was nearly covered in it.

"Ooookay. Lori, listen to me. Put your hands behind your back and don't move, alright?"

Lori stared at her hands with widening eyes. "Oh my god. Where is David?"

She started to rise up from the curb, but the officer placed a hand on her shoulder to shove her back down, "I said don't move, goddamnit!"

An ambulance pulled up next to the cruiser. A second police officer emerged from the house and waved the paramedics in.

Lori's voice rose with alarm "He's hurt, isn't he? I need to see him!"

A young woman standing in the front yard took a step onto the driveway, "Not a chance, you fuckin' psycho!"

The officer rounded on her, "Ma'am, get back and let me handle this!"

"You need to lock her the fuck up!" said the woman and took a step closer.

The second police officer jogged over to move the young woman away. "You good, Rick?"

Logan now had Lori pinned face down in the grass at the edge of the lawn, "What does it look like?"

Lori's body went taut and she let out a scream of terror. "Gimme a hand here!" shouted Logan as he struggled to pull Lori's hands together behind her back.

"Stop it! I need to see David! He's hurt! He needs me!"

The second officer put a knee into Lori's back, "Stop making this hard, ma'am."

---

As the cruiser made its way through unfamiliar streets, Lori pleaded with the officers for information about David, for any details of what was going on, but was ignored. The car pulled into a bay at the rear of the Brookfield Police Department and deputies escorted Lori into a processing area where she was fingerprinted and photographed, her belongings taken and put into a plastic bag. An officer then sat her on a concrete bench and cuffed her to the steel armrest. She sat there numbly, unnoticed by the officers processing more incoming arrests.

An officer brought in another woman and cuffed her to the other end of the bench.

"I want my phone call!" said Lori. "You need to let me use the phone!"

The officer shook his head. "And you need to just stay quiet. You don't get a call 'til we say so." He walked to the intake desk and began chatting with another officer. They looked back her way and shared a laugh.

———

An hour later, Lori was taken to the communal holding cell. She paced the floor, tracing a six-foot circuit to and from the door. A half dozen other women were there with her, sitting quietly or lying on benches, some using a forearm to shield their eyes from the harsh overhead lights.

On the bench nearest Lori, a size 14 woman wearing a size 11 tracksuit fixed her with exhausted eyes. "Why don't you fuckin' sit down? It's annoying, all that back and forth."

"When are they letting us out of here?" asked Lori, her panic still close to the surface. "Isn't anyone coming back for us?"

The woman scowled and shook her head. From the opposite bench a young woman with hard eyes chimed in, "I hope they finna take you outta here if you can't sit quiet. People tryna sleep, you know."

Lori ignored her and kept pacing. "I'm not supposed to be here," she muttered.

The hard-eyed woman raised herself up on one elbow, "Don't make me come over there and make you get quiet."

Lori finally paused and stood still, but one foot tapped softly on the concrete floor. After a beat, she walked to the bars and strained to gain a better view down the empty hallway. "Look, I just want my phone call. People are worried about me."

"Good for you. Now shut the fuck up," said the hard-eyed woman.

"I need to call my mom."

"Fuckin' stupid. You need to call a lawyer," said the track suit woman.

"But I didn't even do anything," said Lori, prompting laughter from the others.

In the far corner, a wiry 50-something bottle blonde sat with her eyes closed, resting her head against the wall. She enjoyed plenty of empty bench space on either side, as if the others knew not to crowd her. With a sigh, she opened her eyes and turned to Lori, "Mason Mitchell."

Lori gave her a blank look.

Another sigh, "You need a lawyer, bitch. You call Mason Mitchell." A couple of the other women nodded their heads.

"She ain't lying. That's who I'm calling." said the track suit woman.

"Fuck you, you can't afford him," hissed the hard-eyed woman.

The wiry blonde laid her head against the cinder block and closed her eyes. "Now, all y'all shut the fuck up and let me sleep."

---

The booking officer had taken Lori's watch and cellphone but she could see by the clock on the wall that it was 3:49 a.m. when she was brought out of the holding cell to make her phone call.

With a disinterested officer sitting nearby, Lori picked up the receiver in shaking hands and began to dial the number. She had to stop and start over three times before punching the right buttons in the correct sequence.

"C'mon, pick up," she whispered. "C'mon, pleeeease pick up."

After eight rings, a sleepy voice answered, "Hello?"

"Mom? Can you hear me?"

"Lori? What's going on, angel? It's the middle of the night. Is everything ok?"

"No, not really, mom. I'm in jail."

"Oh my god!" Her mother's voice sharpened in an instant. "What happened? Are you hurt? Are you alright?"

"I don't really know. I'm so confused. I just...me and David were at a party, and he got hurt. Like, with a knife, I think. And I don't know if," Lori let a spasm of sobs wash over her, "if he's ok or what. They won't tell me anything."

"Oh no. Ok, let's calm down and figure this out."

"And I think maybe the police think," the sobs interrupted again, "maybe they think I'm the one who hurt David!"

"No. Lori, no. It's ok. Just breathe. Tell me where you are and I'll come get you."

"I'm at the police station in Brookfield. They put me in a cell, mom. They think I hurt David. Please help me. They won't tell me what happened, and they won't listen to me. I don't remember anything."

"Lori, listen to me. Stay calm. I'm going to call a lawyer then I'll be right down there to see you, ok?"

"Please hurry, mom. Everything is so weird. They're treating me like I'm a criminal or something."

"Don't worry, Lori. I'll find a lawyer and we'll straighten everything out."

"Mom?"

"Yes, angel?"

"Maybe I know a lawyer. I think it's, um, Mitchell. Mason Mitchell."

**10**

T he insistent vibration of his cellphone awakened Mason. He snatched it off the nightstand and squinted against the light of the screen, which read *Unknown Caller*. It was 3:58 a.m. Jenny slept soundly beside him, too drunk to be disturbed by the noise. He turned away from her and slid his thumb across the glass to answer, "Mason Mitchell." A woman's voice greeted him, she tripped over her words, urgency interrupted by sobs. Mason blinked away the fog of booze and gained his bearings as he listened.

"Mr. Mitchell, it's my little girl. I need your help *immediately*."

This was not the typical late night call from a pinched dealer or drunk driver. Mason kept her on the line as he slipped from under the covers and walked into the spare bedroom that acted as a home office. He popped in a pair of earbuds and kept talking, "Slow down. I can help you, but let's start from the top again."

He grabbed the sweatpants and well-worn Marquette Law School t-shirt laying across his chair and slipped them on, then woke the desktop computer. Mason methodically worked his way through a list of questions, typing the answers into a new file. Carrie Bedford's daughter, Lori, was in trouble. Late twenties, recently married with no children. A couple of months ago, Lori moved to Milwaukee with her husband and was trying to find her way in the city, working as a server at a trendy downtown steakhouse. Ten minutes ago, Lori called her mom from jail, confused and in trouble, saying her husband was hurt but she didn't know how badly.

"She said that maybe the police think she did it. But I know my baby girl would never hurt anyone, the police must have gotten it wrong." The mothers always defended their children, unable to accept their precious child did anything wrong, and Carrie was no exception. "I need you to find out what happened. You need to go there and fix this, go get my baby."

While processing the rush of new information, Mason wondered how she got a hold of his name. Almost all of his business came by word of mouth and Carrie Bedford didn't sound like she would know any of Mason's normal clientele, but the world was full of surprises. A few months earlier, he met a woman at one of his favorite after-work bars who sold him on the idea of spending money to 'increase his Google presence'. As that night wore on she could have sold him on any idea. Regardless, Mason had thrown some money at an 'SEO Guru' recommended by a personal injury lawyer he knew. Maybe it is bearing fruit now.

"Hold on, Mrs. Bedford. You need to hire me before I can start on this case. That involves signing a retainer and paying my initial fee."

Clyde waddled into the room, yawned, and curled up on top of his right foot.

"Whatever it takes. Just tell me how much," pleaded Carrie. "When can we meet? And when can you get her out?"

"First, she will not get out tonight. It'll be a few days before we can get bail set and posted. Second, I cannot meet or speak with Lori right away. Third, you must talk to no one else about this, and if Lori calls back tell her the same thing – no one! Don't speak to the jailers, cellmates, no one. Do not talk to her about the incident over the phone. All calls are recorded, so they can and will be used against her."

While reciting these stock warnings, Mason considered his fee. People like Carrie, who sounded like she was desperate and had means, would pay almost anything. He wasn't the type to gouge clients just because he had leverage but it sounded like Lori was in a real mess. He quoted an initial deposit of ten thousand dollars and Carrie agreed without hesitating.

"If you'd like, Ms. Bedford, we can meet at my office later this morning. Do you have a pen? Sure, I'll wait."

Jenny poked her head around the door, wiping sleep from her eyes. Now everyone was up. "You, ok?" she asked.

Mason covered the phone, "Yeah, all good. Sorry I woke you, but I have to take this."

She nodded. "Do you mind if I grab a glass of water?"

"Go right ahead. Anything you want. I'll be back in bed in a minute," he told her. Then, into the phone, he read out instructions, "Yes, Mrs. Bedford, it's 520 East Chicago, Suite 200, in the Third Ward. Let's say 7:30. We can arrange payment of the retainer then. Ok, I will. You, too."

He ended the call and leaned back in his chair, mulling the few details he had. Going back to bed wasn't an option. Mason was never truly off the clock, and had grown accustomed to the late night calls, usually from someone having the worst day of their life. Provided they could pay, he was on the case.

He entered the meeting appointment into the online office calendar, then began searching databases that held information for local courts and jails. Carrie hadn't given him much to go on. Most clients, and their family members, had limited and often inaccurate information at the outset of a case.

His search yielded little, but at this stage, he would take what he could get. He learned that Brookfield PD arrested Lori Wells (née Bedford) just after 1 a.m. and she was being held on suspicion of attempted first degree homicide. Mason noted the location as much as the charge. Brookfield was an affluent suburb of Milwaukee that saw little violent crime compared to the city proper. Most cases out there involved drunk driving or minor drug offenses, not attempted homicide. Given the limited number of violent incidents they handled, Mason guessed the Brookfield police would spend time and resources on Lori's case, making Mason's job more difficult.

By the time he looked back in the bedroom, Jenny had left without saying goodbye, so Mason grabbed Clyde's leash and took him down to street level for his morning walk. These daily tours of the neighborhood were the sole form of regular exercise for man and dog. They followed their usual route, west to the river and along the streets of Milwaukee's Historic Third Ward. This inner city district was once home to block after block of factories and warehouses that ran right up to the bank of the Milwaukee River. The structural remnants of this bygone age of Midwestern industry had become an enclave of trendy lofts, restaurants of the month, a multitude of bars, small art galleries, and the Milwaukee Public Market. Mason's condominium was a converted brewery from the turn of the 20th century that featured distinctive creamy yellow brick walls found in many buildings around the Third Ward. These bricks, made with magnesium-rich riverbank clay that lent a warm sandstone hue, were at one time so prevalent in the city's architecture that Milwaukee became known as Cream City. Mason learned that from the real estate agent who sold him the condo. He had always assumed the nickname was tied to Wisconsin's obsession with cheese. With an assumption like that, he was as bad as any juror.

**11**

The majority of Mason's clients were guilty, the kind of people you would call criminals, and he was one hundred percent okay with that. It came with the territory, and he suffered no pangs of conscience. They were citizens with the same rights as anyone else, standing accused of committing criminal acts and in need of representation in court. Mason didn't categorize them as bad people. They were simply people who broke the law, some of them with great regularity and shocking violence.

Almost all of his clients were men, most of them black. Many fit a certain profile – hard lives in rough circumstances, operating at the margins of society. Short-term thinkers who made lots of schemes but not many plans. Even when they had money they had few options. Their cases were Mason's bread and butter, and his practice existed mainly to serve them.

Gang members, armed robbers, drunk drivers, and drug dealers, sometimes all in one. That's how Mason made his money, and particularly with the drug dealers, that money came in cash. Several years ago, he had invested in two safes. One was installed in the wall of his office, hidden behind a print of one of his favorite paintings, Matisse's *Le Bateau*. This safe was for what he called 'accounts receivable' and he rarely let it hold more than fifteen thousand dollars. Mason didn't keep banker's hours, so once the stack of cash got too large, he transferred it to the second safe, behind a false panel at the back of his walk-in closet. And in each safe, Mason kept a loaded Ruger Max 9, one of which was given to him by a grateful client, Jalen Demps, who worried that Mason kept too much cash around.

Luckily, Mason never had cause to use either weapon. He hadn't hit the shooting range in a long time, but from the cases he tried, Mason knew that simply aiming a gun at someone was enough to win most arguments.

Unlike the majority of Mason's clients, Jalen was no short-term thinker. That's why he had arrived at the office unannounced, early on a weekday morning, and planted a brick of cash on Mason's desk.

"Retainer. As usual," said Jalen.

"Right on schedule, as usual," said Mason. He retrieved an electronic money-counter from a file drawer, placed it on his desk, and flicked it on. The LCD screen flashed '$00.00' three times on startup.

"You gonna count it? Really?" Jalen looked like he'd had even less sleep than Mason and his usual even keel was slightly off kilter this morning.

"No offense, but I always count the money. You know that. Then every-one's straight, right?"

Jalen nodded almost imperceptibly.

"Besides," said Mason, "one reason you're paying me this money is be-cause of my attention to detail." He removed the rubber bands from the bundle of cash then placed it into the cradle of the counter and pressed START. The two men waited as the machine riffled through the cash and beeped once.

"That's twelve thousand five hundred. I believe we had agreed on twelve thousand."

"The extra nickel is a tip. From the last time, with my cousin."

Jalen Demps had many 'cousins' and he sent them all to Mason when they had legal troubles, which was often.

"I'm touched, but the tip won't be necessary, Jalen. I'm your attorney, not a blackjack dealer."

"Give it to someone who needs it, then. We're straight."

Mason let it lie and set the five $100 bills aside. "Fair enough. You need me to draw up a receipt?"

"Bro, no need." Jalen tapped his temple. "You know me, I keep my records all up here."

Linda tapped at the glass door and peeked her head in. She was used to cash coming through the office, but human nature got the best of her and she gawked at the fat stack of bills on Mason's desk.

"Um, Ms. Bedford is here to see you," said Linda

"Right. Gimme two minutes," said Mason. "Can you park her in the conference room, please?"

Linda nodded, snuck one last look at the cash, and left.

"Ok, Jalen. I've got another meeting. You and I are good for now. If you need anything, you know how to reach me, day or night."

"Bet," said Jalen. He rose from his chair and fist-bumped Mason. "Love."

Carrie Bedford was seated at the conference room table as Mason entered. He extended his hand and greeted her, "Hi, Mason Mitchell."

"Carrie Bedford. Nice to meet you." Polite and neatly dressed, she rose to shake his hand before sitting back down. With her slight frame, she looked small in the chair. She had angular features and a face weathered from time spent outdoors. Mason guessed she was in her mid-fifties. Her eyes were puffy, and she clutched tissues in her hand. Mason offered coffee or refreshments, which she declined. He set his laptop on the table along with a printout which contained information about Lori's case.

"How are you feeling?" asked Mason. People didn't meet with him unless they were having a bad time, but simple small talk helped to get the ball rolling.

"I'm fine, considering," she replied.

"That's good," said Mason, then slid the printout across the table. "This has the basic facts so far."

Carrie took a moment to look it over. "Attempted homicide," she whispered, while dabbing her already red eyes with a tissue.

"I wasn't able to get much more information since we spoke, but I did learn that Lori's being moved to Waukesha County Jail and her initial appearance will be Thursday morning at the Waukesha Courthouse. I expect my current trial to be completed by then, so I should be there."

"Ok, what will happen then?"

"At that time, her bail will be set and a preliminary hearing will be scheduled. After that, you can bail her out and then we go from there."

"How much will bail cost?"

"I don't know exactly, but since she has no record, I'd say around fifteen to twenty thousand. But that means you must pay all the bail. Wisconsin doesn't have bail bonds, so that means fifteen thousand in cash."

"Oh, ok," said Carrie. She was putting up a brave face but Mason could see the fresh worry behind her eyes.

"Is that something you could post?"

"I'm not sure, but I think we could come close. I would need to talk to my husband, Tom. That's Lori's father."

"There is also the matter of my initial fee, which is ten thousand dollars, up front."

The difficulty of the situation was not lost on Mason. Frequently, clients and families of clients had to choose between paying bail or paying Mason. Another byproduct of a system with an unlevel playing field. Early in his career, Mason took a few cases on bail assignment, with his fee being paid from the bail money at the end of the case, relieving clients of the choice between posting bail or paying him. After getting burned by a series of fickle clients, he stopped offering.

"Well, we need a lawyer now and we can figure out the bail in the meantime," said Carrie. "Where do I sign?"

"Right here." Mason handed her a pen.

"How do you want me to pay?" asked Carrie.

"Take your pick; cash, check, credit, debit, PayPal, Venmo, Cash App. We take it all." It sounded too rehearsed, but it was true. Mason even accepted in-kind payments occasionally. Carrie handed over her debit card and Mason produced a wireless terminal to process her payment. He scanned a copy of the retainer and gave her the original.

"I'm in trial this week, so I will not be meeting with Lori before court." Mason always told clients he was in trial or court, even when he wasn't. This lie gave him some measure of flexibility with his time. "But I will be at her initial appearance to set bail and her next court date. If you talk to her, tell her you hired a lawyer, and to keep her mouth shut and be patient. I know that is easier said than done."

"Ok, I will. Do you need anything else from me?"

"Not right now. Carrie, thank you for coming. You did the right thing. I'm going to do everything I can to help your daughter." Mason looked at his watch. "Now, if you'll excuse me, I'm due in court so I need to run."

Carrie stood and followed Mason to the reception area. "It was nice to meet you," she said.

"You too. And I'll see you on Thursday."

Mason returned to his office, packed his briefcase, and grabbed the 500 dollars off his desk. On his way out, he stopped at reception and handed the money to Linda.

"What's this?" she asked.

"Call it a bonus. Or an apology. Or a token of my appreciation. You deserve it."

Linda slipped the bills into her purse. "Thank you."

"And what about the proposal I left for you?" he asked, flashing a winning smile.

"It'll do for now," said Linda.

Mason clasped his hands together and pressed on. "Excellent. You know I can't do this without you."

Linda shook her head and sighed. "You've got that right."

Mason blew her a kiss as he headed out the door.

**12**

On a normal day, the courthouse was a beehive of activity, this morning it was more like a recently kicked hornet's nest.

An unexpected delay in the Dixon trial allowed Mason to duck out of Borowski's court, but he soon found himself squeezed into the crowd that filled the main corridor. He elbowed his way to the stairwell and went down one level, then turned right at the landing, where he found Mister Cee's Top Shine. This shoeshine stand and its eponymous proprietor, Harold Clinton, had been here as long as anyone could remember. Some attorneys joked that Mister Cee's came first and the courthouse had been built around it.

"Have a seat, Two-Tone!" said Harold, without looking up from his work. "Be with you as soon as I can see my face in Mr. Nantz's oxfords."

Mason nodded at this sole patron, a public defender named Kirk Nantz.

"Two-Tone?" said Nantz.

"Yeah. It's a term of endearment. And he just calls you Nantz, huh?" said Mason, as he settled in two seats down and placed his custom-made brogues on the footrests. "No hurry, Harold. I'll take a perch and wait."

Five years ago, Mason marched into Allen Edmonds, the go-to shoe boutique for Wisconsin's legal set, and ordered three pairs of custom-made Wingtip Spectators – black and white, brown and white, burgundy and white. Today, he wore burgundy. For him, the shoes, the well-tailored suits, and the French cuff shirts projected an image. It was the same with his splashy car, on-trend loft, and office that was bigger than he needed. He justified all the expense with a belief that it was important to appear polished, confident, and professional. He built his practice from nothing by presenting himself as an attorney who knew what was up, who was going places.

He caught Nantz staring at the shoes and shaking his head. "Something wrong, counselor?" asked Mason

"I don't know what you're going for," said Nantz, taking in Mason's outfit, "but you're a pinky ring away from looking like a mob lawyer."

Mason rolled his eyes. Nantz had the holier-than-thou attitude found in some public defenders. But Mason guessed this dismissiveness masked a lack of self-belief. Nantz worked hard, and while he was a sharp enough lawyer, there was no real cutting edge. Some attorneys ended up as PDs because they were true believers, while others simply didn't have the talent to justify proper hourly rates. With Nantz, it was a mix of both. Upper middle class, Northwestern grad, literate parents, suburban socialist, he'd been dealt a good hand and was almost breaking even. Still, he was a big step up from the truly useless no-hopers that Mason called 'public pretenders'.

"Juries like a sharp-dressed man, Nantz. Helps them focus. And judges don't like to admit it, but they'll defer to someone who looks the part. Trust me, if you traded in that burlap sack for a real suit to go with your cheap but shiny shoes, you'd get a few more breaks around here."

Nantz looked down and adjusted his baggy blazer. Harold let out a low whistle and said, "Go easy now, Two-Tone. Every man has his own style. And look at this stitching." He pointed to the seam that joined the sole to the upper on Nantz's shoes. "That is top quality."

"Thank you, Mister Cee," said Nantz.

Harold gave the oxfords a final snap with the buffing rag. "And now they *look* top quality."

"Thank you again," said Nantz, and handed over a couple of rumpled bills that amounted to a decent tip for a public defender.

Harold pocketed the cash and began laying out the tools of his trade at Mason's feet. Nantz rose to leave then sat back down. "What are you doing down here, Mitchell? Shouldn't you be in trial?"

"Already was. But the DA's witness is in the wind. They asked for a couple of hours to find him, Borowski gave them one. So, I have time to kill."

"Think they'll find their witness?"

"Not sure, but the break doesn't bother me. I just wanted a place to relax, but this morning it's nuttier than usual around here." Mason leaned back as Harold went to work on the leather uppers. "Do you have any idea what's going on?"

"You didn't hear?" said Nantz, incredulous.

"Hear what? I'm asking you."

Nantz shook his head. "Don't you ever check Twitter?"

"I'm a little busy for Twitter," said Mason.

"And I'm not? Alice Decatur is up from Chicago. She's taking the lead on that football coach who killed his wife."

"Decatur? What the fuck? Who roped her into that?"

At this point in her career, Alice Decatur was better known as a media personality than a trial attorney. She spent a lot of time on TV, preferring to try cases in the court of public opinion rather than in front of a judge and jury. In his less charitable moments, Mason figured that was because she was much better on screen than in court. Still, she brought the spotlight and the megaphone wherever she went. This football coach had a heavy hitter on his side.

Nantz looked over his shoulder like he was about to dispense valuable intel. "The case got assigned to Eliana Hysen, but before she knew it, someone convinced the coach to ditch her and go with Decatur. I heard it was the MJB."

"MJB?"

"Jesus, it wouldn't hurt you to watch the news every once in a while, Mitchell."

"Hey, if I'm not on it, I'm not watching. Some of us have to hustle for work."

Nantz snorted and turned away to study his phone. "Fine. Find out for yourself, big shot."

"Oh, don't be so sensitive. I'm just messin' around. Come on, what's the MJB? I would love for you to enlighten me."

"It's the Milwaukee Justice Bloc."

"And?"

"And they take on social justice cases, civil rights stuff. They organize and protest and all that, but more and more they're facilitating legal representation. They say that Michael Key is being railroaded because he's black. Or, more to the point, because his wife was white."

"And they got Alice freakin' Decatur up here." Mason looked up and imagined the venerable courthouse crumbling under the pressure. "This is going to be a circus."

"Call it what you want, but it's going to get a lot of attention. Decatur and the MJB are having a press conference on the courthouse steps in," Nantz looked down at his phone, "fifteen minutes."

"So that's what's got this place buzzing. The Decatur show taking over the county courthouse."

This time Nantz allowed himself a chuckle. "Well, she's never been shy about taking up space."

"And how's Hysen taking it?" Mason was aware of Nantz's young colleague. She was bright, tenacious, and well-prepared; a rare combo in the State Public Defender's Office. Her type usually took a few years to burn off their idealism before moving on to corporate law.

"That's the interesting thing," said Nantz. "She's pissed because she wanted a shot at something big like this. But part of her is glad someone of Decatur's stature is on it now."

"Oh yeah, why's that?"

"Hysen thinks he's innocent."

"Well, that's a rookie for you. Wife gets killed, it's usually the husband."

Nantz shook his head, "You don't get it. Hysen's nobody's fool. She really believes him."  He stepped from the stand. "I'm going to try and grab a live view of the circus, see you later, Mitchell."

———

Mason tucked himself in a quiet alcove on the second floor of the courthouse, far from the front steps, to watch the live feed of Alice Decatur's news conference on his phone.

*"...and so I have come here to ensure that this is not another case that gets swept under the rug. Another case of an African-American man being manipulated by a justice system that is historically and inescapably unjust. For too many years now we have marched, we have protested, we have organized, and we have vowed that things will be different. We have been steadfast in our belief that genuine change can happen. And still, to this day we see that so much remains the same. We see that change sometimes happens at the margins but that at the core of the matter, at the very*

*heart of this country, we encounter the rot and the stench of systemic racial injustice. Sadly, we've seen it at work so many times that, in a way, Michael Key's case is not special. And yet, his case is very special. Because it is an opportunity for us to put this police department, this city, and this nation on trial. The facts are plain as day. I wouldn't be standing here if I didn't believe that. And in presenting the facts we will also lay bare the soul of our system so that each and every one of us can take a good long look. Michael Key is innocent. It is America that is guilty. I'll be taking no questions at th is time."*

Mason pocketed his phone and hustled back to Judge Borowski's court just in time to learn that the prosecution's key witness had failed to materialize. Mr. Dixon's Sixth Amendment right to confront his accuser required the witness to show-up, which meant the prosecution had no case. With the jury already sworn in, double jeopardy came into play, and Borowski had no choice but to dismiss the case for good. Unlike his victim, Kevin Dixon had dodged a bullet.

After the gavel banged the case closed, Mason accepted an awkward hug from his client, packed his briefcase and shook hands with the red-faced prosecutor. "Tough luck, man."

---

Alice Decatur left the courthouse, crossed the plaza to Wells Street, and jumped into the back of a waiting Cadillac Escalade. Her assistant, Benny, was already there and handed her a fresh coffee.

"I watched the whole thing," said Benny. "You were great. The cameras loved it."

"That's just the appetizer. We are going to make a meal out of this case."

The driver pulled away from the curb and pointed the black SUV south for the drive back to Chicago. Alice decided years ago to employ a full-time driver, with the vehicle acting as a well-stocked and fully functional mobile office that allowed Alice to maximize her billable hours. Beyond the efficiency, she would admit to enjoying the prestige factor, though it wasn't a seamless fit with her carefully cultivated image as the people's champion.

"We just got this an hour ago," said Benny, handing her several stapled pages. "The autopsy protocol on Robin Key."

Alice set the document down on the seat and blew the steam off her coffee. "Anything interesting?"

"Not relating to the injuries. The cause and manner of death are as expected. But the blood screen results on page seven show the presence of HCG."

"Jesus!" said Alice. "She was pregnant?" She flipped through the pages and looked for herself. "Why the fuck didn't you give this to me an hour ago?"

Benny stayed silent. One hour ago, Alice instructed him that she was not to be disturbed until after the press conference. He knew that mentioning this would only fuel her frustration.

"Shit." She took a deep breath to compose herself. "Ok, this is not a disaster, it's just news. In any event, we should expect an amended indictment."

"What are you thinking?"

"They'll add another count of homicide, for the unborn baby."

"Can they do that?"

"Up here, yes. Wisconsin law recognizes the killing of a fetus, against the mother's wishes, as homicide. And the DA can charge it as such, assuming they can show Michael knew about the pregnancy."

"What do you need me to do?"

"Prepare a press release for when the additional murder charge is announced. We'll meet this head on."

**13**

Mason exited I-94 westbound and joined the morning rush hour traffic heading south, making the turn onto Redford Boulevard just as the light went red. His day would be a full one, beginning with Lori's appearance in Waukesha, followed by a sentencing hearing back in the city.

His navigation system estimated the drive from his downtown loft to Waukesha Courthouse would take twenty-five minutes, but he usually made it in twenty. His record was fifteen minutes, door to door, and today he was not far off that pace.

He parked in the ninety-minute lot in front of the courthouse. To him, the convenience was worth more than the cost of a ticket, and he always parked there regardless of how long he would be staying.

The court complex was a low jumble of structures centered on the original building, a drab product of 1970s civic architecture. Rising behind it was the secure courthouse, a newly built concrete box that was flanked by an admin building and the county jail.

Unlike in Milwaukee County, here Mason had to pass through security. He placed his phone and keys into a small plastic bin as instructed, put his briefcase on the x-ray machine, and walked through the metal detector.

*BEEP!* Every time. He never got through clean in Waukesha.

"Suspenders?" offered Mason.

"Sorry," said the guard. "Gotta wand you."

After a cursory inspection that confirmed Mason was free of forbidden items, he made his way to the intake courtroom at the back of the secure courthouse, closest to the jail.

The room was overtly functional, with no frills. On the bench sat a court commissioner who handled all pretrial procedures – arraignments, setting bail, preliminary hearings – deemed too mundane for elected judges.

Mason nodded at the bailiff. "Here on Lori Wells, in-custody."

"Got it. You're checked in."

He took a seat among the lawyers waiting for their cases to be called, each one glued to a phone, tablet, or computer, trying to look like they were working. Mason pulled out his laptop, connected to the court's wi-fi, and joined the group.

The job entailed a lot of sitting and waiting for cases to be called, idle windows he used to sift through backed up emails or quickly draft and file pleadings. For some unknown reason, Wisconsin's legal system was a leader for internet tools and e-filing, and the state's Circuit Court Access Program (CCAP) put all cases and filings online. This let Mason manage his practice on the go, a massive upgrade from his early years as an attorney.

The court clerk called out, "Wells is next." This was the bailiff's cue to retrieve Lori from the holding cell and for Mason to step-up to the podium.

Lori entered the courtroom wearing a green prison coverall and shackles that required her to shuffle more than walk. Her eyes were raw and tired, her hair disheveled. The brief stay in jail had not agreed with Mason's newest client.

"State of Wisconsin versus Lori Wells, case number 22CF0521. Appearances, please," said the commissioner.

"James Thurston for the State."

"Attorney Mason Mitchell on behalf of the defendant, who is in-custody and in-person."

Mason leaned over to Lori and whispered, "I'm your lawyer. Your mother hired me. Just keep quiet and do what I say. Only talk if I tell you. We're trying to set bail to get you out today, ok?"

Lori stared at Mason for a beat, not seeming to understand, then nodded in the affirmative.

"Ms. Wells, I am Commissioner Reitz. My job today is to inform you of your charges, some of your rights, and to set bail."

Lori turned her blank stare to the commissioner, who continued, "For example, you have the right to an attorney. It looks like you've hired Mr. Mitchell, who is here on your behalf. You also have the right to a preliminary hearing and one will be scheduled at the end of this hearing. You are charged with one count of attempted first degree intentional homicide. This is a Class B felony which carries with it a maximum possible penalty of sixty years in prison, do you understand the maximum penalties?"

"She does, and we waive formal reading of the charges," answered Mason.

"Ok, as for bail, State?"

"We ask that bail be set at fifty thousand dollars cash, given the serious nature of the crime and the potential exposure. Further we are seeking a no-contact with the victim, D.W., and his family."

"Defense?"

"Your honor, we are seeking a modest cash bail, around five thousand dollars. Ms. Wells has no record at all. She is a lifelong Wisconsin resident and is employed in the community. She has hired private counsel and cooperated fully with the police during her arrest. Further she has no objection to the no contact orders–"

Chains clanked as Lori grabbed the sleeve of Mason's jacket. "One second, please," she whispered.

"What?" said Mason.

"What do they mean? Why do they think I hurt David?  He's my husband, so why can't I talk to him? I don't understand!"

"Not now," replied Mason, before returning his attention to the commissioner. "As I was saying, she has no objection to the no-contact orders, and given that she was living with her husband, she will agree to reside with her parents."

"Wait, what is happening? I don't want to live with my parents!" Lori hissed. Mason ignored her and continued.

"Finally she will also agree to electronic monitoring if the court deems it necessary." Lori began sobbing almost silently and stared at the floor, refusing to acknowledge her attorney and the rest of the room.

"Ok, I am going to set bail at ten thousand dollars cash, with the no-contact orders as requested," said Reitz. "Ms. Wells is ordered to live with her parents. Counsel, after this hearing will you provide that address to my clerk?"

"Yes."

"She will also have no contact with the victim, D.W. You know who that is right?"

"She does. Her husband, David Wells," said Mason. The State's practice of using initials for the victim when issuing a Criminal Complaint never made sense to Mason, as everyone involved knew the identity of the victim.

"Ms. Wells, no contact means no contact by any means. Not through electronic means or a third-party. No phone calls, text messages, instant messages, no contact at all. If you can think of a way to have contact, do not do it. Do you understand?"

"She does."

"I want to hear it from her, counsel."

Mason looked over at Lori and nodded at her answer.

"Yes, I understand," she mumbled, not looking up.

"Now, we need to schedule this for a preliminary hearing," said Reitz.

Mason knew Lori's family could post the ten grand cash bail so pressing for a quick date was not necessary.

"How is October 28th in the afternoon?" offered the clerk.

"That works for the State."

Mason scanned the calendar on his phone. "I can make it that afternoon, with the usual caveat that I may be in trial that week. If that happens, my office will let you know ASAP. Otherwise, I'll be here."

Reitz nodded. "The next court date will be October 28th at 1:30 p.m. before the Honorable William Hulse. Case adjourned."

The bailiffs escorted Lorir out of the courtroom and back to the jail, where she would wait until bail was posted. Before disappearing through the doorway, she looked back at Mason, fresh tears welling in her eyes.

Mason exited the courtroom and found Carrie Bedford leaning against a wall in the main corridor.

"So what does all that mean?" she asked.

"In short, she must live with you and Tom once you post her bail. Also, she *cannot* speak to David or his family. I mean it. If she attempts any contact, they will raise her bail and arrest her. They also could charge her with bail jumping, another felony crime."

"What if I contact David or his family?"

"Absolutely not. Third-party contact is not allowed. Even if you think you're being nice or it's for a good reason, it will only hurt Lori's case. No contact, period."

"Ok. How do I get her clothes and stuff from their apartment?"

"Let my office handle that. We will contact David, and my private investigator will go over there to retrieve Lori's belongings. Just call Linda and give her a list of the things you need."

"Does she really need to live with us? She'll hate that."

"Look, the idea of setting the initial bail is to get her out, then we can chip away at the conditions and limitations, assuming no mistakes on her part. So, yes, for now she needs to live with you."

Carrie looked worried but didn't speak.

"She should count herself lucky," said Mason. "Ten thousand cash is low for a charge of attempted homicide." An alarm buzzed from his phone and he silenced it. "I'm sorry, but I've got to get back downtown. Let me know once you've posted bail and Lori's back home, then we'll schedule a meeting at my office." Mason shook Carrie's hand and turned toward the front doors, calling over his shoulder, "And don't forget to give Linda that list."

---

Lori shuffled to keep pace with the bailiff who led her back to jail, her head spinning from the appearance in front of the commissioner. The madness of the last few days left her confused and so tired. She still had so many questions and no one was answering them. *Was David ok? How badly was he hurt? What did this all mean?* And most importantly – *When can I get out of here?*

"Wells, returning from court," said the bailiff.

"Ok. Wells, report back to your cell, 13B," the guard said as she unshackled Lori's leg and waist restraints. Lori was happy to be free of the restraints again and walked quickly toward her cell. As she crossed the floor, an inmate yelled out, "What's your bail at?"

Lori recognized her, the girl who told her to call Mason Mitchell. "Ten thousand, I think."

"Oooohh. Mommy and daddy gonna post that rich girl."

Lori knew it might not be best to advertise that her family could afford the bail. "I'm not so sure. They still need to pay the lawyer. But thanks for recommending him."

"Shit, I called him and he didn't call back. Maybe if I tell him I sent you and he'll talk to me."

"Yeah, maybe," said Lori before ducking into her cell. She flopped down on the paper thin mattress and tried to sleep, praying for her bail to get posted before she had to spend another night.

**14**

A sentencing hearing could be the best and worst part of Mason's job. It meant the end of a case and a fully earned fee, but often signaled a sour turn in the attorney-client relationship. Even after a skillful defense and minimized sentence, clients and their supporters would loudly assert that Mason should have done more.

Today's client had exchanged fire with a police officer after a short chase, and there would be no mystery to the proceedings. After several rounds of negotiation, Mason hammered out a deal with the district attorney to reduce the sentence from a potential sixty years down to just six years in prison and six years extended supervision. They agreed to submit a joint sentencing recommendation to the judge, which made the hearing a formality. Mason had taken great pains to convince his client the deal was a big win.

As he settled in at the defense table, Mason felt a buzzing in his breast pocket. He pulled his phone out to set it on silent mode and saw the text message from Linda:

*Just received an email from Alice Decatur's office. Said they want to talk to you and it was urgent. Didn't say what it was regarding, but I replied with your phone number. Hope that's ok.*

"State of Wisconsin versus Donte Givens, case number 20CF0418," announced the clerk.

Before Mason could process the implications of Linda's message, Donte emerged from the bullpen, his entrance accompanied by the metallic rustle of belly and leg irons. The orange overalls issued by the county hung loose on his lanky frame, making Donte appear even younger than his twenty-two years. He reached the defense table and took the remaining seat and Mason placed the phone in his half-open briefcase on the table.

He laid a reassuring hand on Donte's arm but Mason's mind was still on the enigmatic message. A few years earlier, Mason attended a luncheon with Alice Decatur where he met her just long enough to exchange pleasantries. Otherwise, he only knew Alice by her stellar, and no doubt well-crafted, reputation.

From the bench, Judge Grambling cleared his throat and barked, "Someone remind me what was negotiated here!" With his gruff tone and sagging jowls, he reminded Mason of a cranky old mastiff.

"Plead to the amended charge, one count of first degree recklessly endangering safety. Joint recommendation of six in and six out, Judge," offered the prosecutor.

"Ok. State, proceed."

"As you know, the three sentencing factors the court must consider are the need to protect the community, the seriousness of the crime, and the character of the defendant."

"We get it," growled the judge. "Let's keep this moving, counsel."

"Of course. Mr. Givens was pulled over for expired tags, but as the officer approached the vehicle, the defendant drove off at a high rate of speed. The officer gave pursuit for five miles, at which point Mr. Givens struck a parked car, then left his vehicle and fled on foot. While running, he fired two shots over his shoulder. Fortunately, no one was hit. Officer Keller returned fire and wounded Mr. Givens, who spent two weeks in the hospital before being transported to the County Jail."

Mason's phone lit up with an incoming call. Unknown number from the 312 area code, Chicago. *She's calling me NOW? What the hell does she want?*

The DA moved on to describe Donte's criminal history for the court. Recounting the full record of violence and mayhem perpetrated by Mason's client took several minutes, but Mason barely heard a word. He couldn't be sure what Decatur wanted from him, and as the prosecutor droned on, Mason ran through possibilities in his head.

"Your honor, we believe probation would unduly depreciate the seriousness of this offense," said the DA, "and join with defense counsel in submitting a recommendation for a sentence of six years initial confinement followed by six years of extended supervision."

"Thank you for that, counsel," said Grambling. "Officer Keller, I will now hear your victim statement, with the polite request that you keep it as brief as possible."

Keller rose to deliver a concise and dispassionate account of the incident. The details of the chase and firefight barely roused the interest of the judge, who buried his chin in his chest until Keller finished and sat down next to the prosecutor.

"Very good, Officer. The court thanks you," said Grambling, then pointed at Mason. "Counsel, your sentencing argument please."

"Thank you, your honor. Since this is a joint recommendation, I won't take much of the court's time." He ran through the contributing factors of the sentencing recommendation, highlighting Donte's childhood hardships and letters of support from family members. The result of the hearing was a foregone conclusion, but Mason tried to paint Donte as a remorseful young man who simply wanted another shot at becoming a productive member of society. Mason almost felt guilty for speeding through his argument, but he'd already done the real work on Donte's behalf and wanted to wrap up the hearing and return the mysterious call from Chicago.

Grambling, who remained unmoved, interrupted Mason just before the end of his prepared remarks. "Counsel, I'm inclined to follow the sentencing recommendation, and I'd like to move things along. So, do you want to keep talking?"

"No, that'll do it, your honor," said Mason. He glanced into the briefcase as he sat down and saw a new alert on the display of his phone.

"Young Mr. Givens," said the judge, "you may address the court before I pass your sentence. Anything you want to tell me?"

Donte stood slowly, shifting to find a comfortable stance for his injured leg. "I just want to apologize to the court for wasting your time, and I also wanted to apologize to my family for putting them through this."

Mason casually leaned forward until he could see the display showing that he now had one new voicemail. He slowly transferred the phone to his lap and checked the call details; the same Chicago number.

"Mr. Mitchell! Are we boring you?"

Mason looked up to see the judge staring daggers at him.

"We all wish we were somewhere else," said Grambling, "but I won't have you checking TikTok in my court. Understood?"

"My apologies, your honor," said Mason, and made a show of placing the phone in the briefcase and closing it shut.

The judge sighed heavily and turned his attention back to the defendant. "Mr. Givens, as you were."

"Um, I just wanna tell you that my kids need me, your honor. Unlike my dad, I want to be involved in their life. Locking me up won't help them. So, I still want to ask for probation, and I promise you won't see me again. I want to make something out of my life. That's all I have to say, Judge."

"Very good," said Grambling, sounding pleased for the first time during the proceedings. "Mr. Givens, the law requires me to first consider probation, and I did. For about a second. This is clearly a prison case. What message would it send the community if I sentenced a guy like you to probation? We've tried that and, as we can see, it did not deter you from committing more crimes."

Donte looked straight ahead, stone-faced, as Grambling continued, "Your record is appalling. In your short but action-packed career, you have racked up seven convictions, five of them felonies, three with a firearm. At some point, we need to put you in prison and the only question is for how long. As to your alleged desire to be there for your children, I am unconvinced."

Mason winced. He had warned Donte that the 'I want to be a father to my kids' argument would only rile the judge.

Grambling leaned back and shook his head. "You know, it's hard for me to buy your story when it's clear you weren't thinking about your children. Not when you led police on a high-speed chase, and not when you shot at Officer Keller. From what I've heard, you only thought about yourself."

Mason heard Donte's grandmother sniffling as she wept softly in the gallery. She was there with Donte's girlfriend, who was the mother of his two youngest kids. Their support was admirable but would not move the needle today. If Donte was lucky, they would still be there for him after his release.

"Mr. Givens," the judge continued, "I'm going along with the joint recommendation for six in and six out. For that, you can thank your attorney, who apparently sees more in you than I do." Grambling held Donte in his sights for an extra beat, then looked down at his notes. "The defendant will receive 184 days credit. This sentence is consecutive to any other sentence. Mr. Mitchell, will you advise your client of his appellate rights?"

"Already on it, your honor."

"Very good. Court is adjourned."

———

Mason walked into the hall outside the courtroom and retrieved the phone from his briefcase. He swiped the voicemail alert, punched in his passcode, and listened:

*"Mr. Mitchell, this is Alice Decatur. I'm going to be in town representing Michael Key-"*

"Hey! I need to talk to you." Donte's girlfriend had followed Mason out and approached him, an adorable toddler on her hip. Mason covered his free ear and tried to digest the rest of the message before the girlfriend laid into him.

*"...and I'd like someone from here in Milwaukee to round out my team. Jim Preston gave me your info and said you'd be the right person to talk to. We should meet so I can pick your brain about a few things, see if you're interested. Call me back at this number. Sooner rather than later, please."*

It took Mason a moment to recover from the shock of the phone message and realize that Donte's girlfriend was speaking to him. "I just wanted to say thank you," she said. "I know you did the best you could."

"Oh. I, um, that's nice of you to say. Sorry, your name again?"

"It's Sierra."

"Right, of course." Mason was relieved that Sierra wasn't there to yell at him, but his pulse was quickening at the thought of Decatur's proposal.

"That judge was an asshole," said Sierra. "I know it was all figured out already, but he didn't have to be that way. Donte can appeal, right?"

"I already filed notice with the clerk, but it could be months before they appoint his new lawyer and an appeal can take years. "

"Years? Oh my god." Donte's little son started squirming, and Sierra shifted him to her other hip. She smoothed her hair down on one side, and Mason could see her hand was shaking.

"Hey, do you have people to support you, to help with the kids and all that?" asked Mason. He wasn't about to tell her that things were going to be ok, but she clearly needed someone to care.

Sierra drew a deep breath to settle herself before she answered. "My mom, a little, but she works a lot."

"You know, there are services that can help, with the kids, with education even."

"Yeah, whatever."

"I'm serious. I know some people with community services. Here's my card. You call that number and talk to Linda. Tell her I said to put you in touch with them."

She accepted the card without looking at it. "Alright. Just wanted to say thanks." Sierra wiped a tear from her eye, then returned to where Donte's grandmother stood, holding the hand of another small child.

Mason would be surprised if Sierra called, and wasn't sure how much his contacts could help if she did. *You did the job. Now shake it off and move on.* Mason watched the two women in Donte's life console each other for a moment, then turned and walked away.

Rounding the corner, he ducked into an empty meeting room and shut the door. After swallowing a mouthful of Tito's, he drew the phone from his jacket and tapped the Chicago number.

"Hi, Alice Decatur? It's Mason Mitchell."

**15**

"Wells! Lori Wells, get up here!"

Lori sat up and looked across to the central pod desk and saw the guard with the handlebar mustache waving her over. Waukesha County Jail had been built at the height of the criminal justice reform movement in the '70s, and the rectangular layout of each pod was designed to promote rehabilitation, with modular seating in an open central area bordered on one side by a guard desk and phone banks. The other three walls were lined with cells, each fitted with a sliding metal door and two-inch thick glass sidelights. In theory, this floor plan gave a sense of community, but the reality was an almost total lack of privacy. Everyone knew everyone else's business.

Lori's cell was directly across from the guard station. As she walked the length of the common area to comply with her summons, fellow inmates added commentary, "Look at Miss Thing." "You getting out?" "Must be nice to be you." One inmate stared dully at Lori as she walked past, causing her to step a little faster.

"You Wells?" barked the guard.

"Yes."

"Lemme see your wristband."

Lori held out her arm and he ran his finger along the ID number. "Yep. Lori Wells, inmate number 519003. Bail has been posted. Grab your stuff and go to that door." The guard pointed at the only exit, to the left of the desk.

"Got everything I need," said Lori, and walked to the heavy door, fighting the urge to shout, cry, something. Only a few seconds passed before it began to open but it felt like an eternity. She stepped into the vestibule beyond and waited for the next door to slide open, one step closer to freedom. She had learned that in jail, only one door opens at a time, but in her eagerness to be out of this place Lori wanted to bang on the door and run like hell. She navigated the series of checkpoints, stopping to sign her bond, no-contact order, and other paperwork, none of which she read. The closer she got to the outside, the more afraid she was to look back, afraid it was all a joke. In the processing area, she was handed a plastic bag containing her clothing. She changed quickly, trying to ignore the musty smell and dark blood stains but thankful to feel real fabric against her skin. One minute later, after a terrifying four days and three nights, Lori stepped out of the Waukesha County Jail.

She saw her mother standing at the edge of the parking lot and ran to her. They embraced, sobbing, neither wanting to let go.

"I am so sorry. I am so sorry," said Lori through her tears. "I really need a smoke and some real food."

"Oh, angel, you don't smoke."

"Mom, please."

"Of course," said Carrie and opened her pack and passed a cigarette to Lori, who lit up and inhaled deeply. Carrie put an arm around her daughter. "Now, let's get you out of here."

They walked to the car, not really speaking. Lori's father sat waiting behind the wheel, with the engine running. He greeted Lori with a smile while fighting back his own tears.

"You wanna go get something to eat?" asked Tom, as he drove out of the lot.

"Yeah, dad. Thanks."

They drove in silence, Carrie clutching Lori's hand for dear life, and stopped for McDonalds. Lori ate as if it was the best thing she had ever tasted, which it was that week. As they drove toward home, Tom kept looking at her in the rearview mirror, his face etched with worry. Carrie tried to make small talk, with no mention of her daughter's ordeal or the night of the crime. Lori knew they must have a thousand questions, but was thankful they didn't ask them. That would come at another time.

"You can sleep in your old room," Carrie offered brightly as they pulled into the driveway. Lori nodded, but did not respond.

"We can schedule a meeting with the lawyer in the next few weeks. I'll let you know." Again, Lori responded with only a polite nod. "I know you must be exhausted. Get some rest, angel. We can talk about all that in the morning."

Lori walked into her childhood home, the surroundings at once familiar and disorienting. She hugged her parents, then went upstairs, locked herself in the bathroom and took a scalding hot, twenty-minute shower. Lori padded across the hall to her old bedroom and changed into the pajamas her mother had laid out. She walked around the room, looking into dresser drawers and inspecting the menagerie of porcelain animal figurines on the small shelf unit below the window. As a girl, she had been so proud of her collection. Now, they seemed like relics from a different life. As dusk gave way to night, she lay down on her bed and fell into a dreamless sleep.

**16**

Mason left Courtroom 520 and stood against the wall in the main hallway of the Safety Building. The hearing that concluded minutes earlier had been a limited success. His client was in court after opening fire at a family party and seriously wounding a friend of her cousin. With little leverage to call on, Mason had still managed to talk the DA down from attempted murder to injury by negligent use of a weapon. All in all, a decent day's work.

"The fuck you think you were doing in there?"

Mason looked up from checking emails on his phone and saw the client's boyfriend making a beeline toward him.

"Probation for eighteen fuckin' months! She's gonna have an ankle monitor!" The man stopped just within arm's reach. "How do you think she's gonna work now, huh?"

"Look, that's not my problem," said Mason. The client and her belligerent boyfriend had been a massive headache to manage. If he was spoiling for a fight, Mason was in the mood to give him one. "She shot the guy, ok? Then she confessed to the police that she shot the guy. You should thank me she's not going away for five-to-ten! Now it's time for you to support her for once."

The man glowered at Mason, unsure of how to proceed in the face of resistance.

Mason looked over the boyfriend's shoulder at an approaching court officer. "Now, get out of my face before one of the nice police officers cuffs you and frog-marches you over to the jail."

The boyfriend got right in Mason's face and snarled, "Fuck you, punk." He put a forearm across Mason's throat and drove him back against the polished marble wall.

Mason landed a jab to the ribs and tried to wriggle free. The client's mother hurried over, screaming at them to break it up and swatting the boyfriend with her handbag. The court officer shoved his way through the crowd, yelling at the man to let Mason go. A Sheriff's deputy appeared at the other end of the hall, spotted the commotion, and broke into a run.

The corridor emptied in a ten-foot radius around Mason, the boyfriend, and the client's mother. The court officer broke through the circle, one hand resting on the gun at his hip. "Get your hands off him, now!" he shouted.

The boyfriend's eyes remained locked on Mason, but he released his grip and took a step back, raising both hands above his head.

The deputy burst through the wall of onlookers and fired his Taser at the boyfriend, sending him to the floor in a twitching heap. The crowd let out a collective "Ooohhhh." They kept watching at a safe distance, a few onlookers with their phones were out, capturing the action on video.

The deputy flipped the boyfriend face down on the floor and placed a knee between the shoulder blades, forcing the air from his lungs. The court officer used his body weight to pin the man's legs to the floor. More phones were out now.

"Yo! Can't breathe, man!" The boyfriend's words came in clipped, hoarse bursts.

"Stop resisting, sir!" yelled the deputy, still kneeling on his back.

The court officer radioed for back-up then looked at Mason. "You ok, counselor?"

Mason could feel a sharp pain around his Adam's apple. "Yeah, I'm alright," he said, "but you need to get off this guy's neck."

"Don't tell us how to do the job," said the officer.

The boyfriend writhed against the carpeted floor, trying to raise his head. "Can't breathe," he croaked. The client's mother shouted, "You're gonna kill him!"

"She's right," said Mason.

The officer stepped into Mason's space. "You need to back away, counselor."

Mason pointed to the crowd with phones in hand. "Fine, but if you don't get this dude upright and out of here right now, you're going to end up on the national news."

The officer looked around and saw the people recording. He tapped the deputy's shoulder. "Hey, ease up, man. Let's get him on his feet."

---

Ten minutes later, Mason checked in at the Marquette Club. He needed a cold drink to soothe his nerves and the painful throbbing in his throat.

Situated two blocks from the courthouse, the Club was Mason's preferred after court watering hole. Some days, he would drop in before or even between court appearances. At its inception a century ago, membership was open only to alumni of Marquette University, but in the years since, the old boys' club had been infiltrated by all manner of non-Marquette men, and even women. A certain faction of the current membership took a dim view of this surrender to cultural trends.

For decades now, it served mainly as a downtown clubhouse for the lawyers and judges of Milwaukee County. With the ancient facilities overdue for a facelift, the Club got by on reputation and proximity to the courthouse, but one or two spaces in the building retained their upper class elegance. Nowhere was this more true than in the Gold Room, where Mason now stood, notable for the baby grand piano by the window and a requirement for men to wear jackets on weekdays.

Mason crossed the room and settled onto a weathered leather stool. His regular bartender was there to greet him with a smile. "Afternoon, Mr. Mitchell."

"Hey, Smitty. How was the lunch rush today?"

"Just fine, thanks. What can I get you?"

"I could use a tall Sprite."

"You got it. Coming right up."

Smitty knew the drill and was back in a flash with a tall glass of clear and bubbly Sprite that contained the requisite three shots of vodka. Mason took a sip and winced.

"Something wrong with the drink?" asked Smitty.

"Not at all," said Mason, massaging his swollen throat. "I just had someone try to crush my windpipe."

The bartender conjured a look that communicated an appropriate amount of concern, but didn't pursue it.

Mason took another sip and grinned. "Nothing a good drink can't fix." He looked around at the almost empty room and realized his heart was pounding. The scuffle and ensuing civil rights violation had gotten to him. "Smitty, do me a favor."

"What's that, Mr. Mitchell?"

"Make that two favors. Number one, and I keep telling you this, call me Mason. Number two, don't ever get arrested."

Smitty chuckled but didn't skip a beat. "You got it, Mason."

"No, I'm serious, my friend. Don't let them get their hands on you. But if they do, pray it's in a public place."

Smitty noted Mason's earnest tone and stayed quiet to let him keep talking.

"Even with people watching and cameras...you never know." Mason looked up from his stealth vodka to see Smitty nodding, his features inscrutable. "Sorry, I'm just rambling."

"Don't worry about it. You're fine."

Mason slurped an ice cube into his mouth, crushed it between his molars, then let the slushy mix slide down his throat, momentarily dulling the pain. "Can I tell you something?"

"You bet," said Smitty without looking up from his glass polishing.

"Most of the lawyers you see in here don't give a rat's ass about anyone they represent. Guilty, innocent, they could care less. They aren't in the law business, they're in the processing business." Mason was rolling downhill, and didn't notice his bartender glance around for a plausible excuse to walk away. But the other bar stools sat empty, so Smitty focused on his tray of glasses as Mason kept talking.

"Judges, too. Just processing. Most of 'em, anyway. And the cops? I'm no bleeding heart, but they will fuck you over without even knowing it. Believe that. They don't have to be dirty or racist or inhuman, it can be the ones that just try to do the job. But that job involves processing people who are unlucky enough to run into cops." Mason exhaled loudly and then downed his drink. "One more Sprite, please."

Smitty paused for a moment to take stock of Mason's state before he went about pouring another.

"All these people end up standing next to me in court," said Mason, "and I try to give them the best defense possible. I try to keep them from just getting processed, you know?"

The bartender had heard many rambling drunks before, but this wasn't Mason's style. Something was up. Smitty was becoming concerned, even a little intrigued.

"Anyway, if you ever get picked up," Mason placed one hand on his chest, "you call me, ok? I won't let them railroad you." He fished a business card out of his coat and planted it on the bar. "I mean it."

Smitty picked up the card and tucked it in his vest pocket. "Thanks, Mason. You'll be the first person I call."

"And don't say a word to the cops or there's only so much I can do." Mason watched the bubbles ascending in graceful lines to the surface of his drink.

Smitty made it his business not to get too involved with his customers, but this outpouring left him feeling a little sorry for Mason. "Tough day at work?"

Mason didn't respond for a few seconds, then looked up at Smitty as if returning from somewhere far away. "Yeah, you could say that. Got into it with a client's boyfriend after keeping her out of prison. Fucking ingrates."

"So that was the thing with your, uh–" Smitty pointed at his neck.

"Yup. You know, I've done eight trials in four months. In five of the cases, my client confessed, but I managed to win two of those. In the other cases, there were no confessions and I had a decent amount of evidence, but lost two out of three. That means my record is better than most, but still...fucking juries, man."

"I guess you never know what you're gonna get," said Smitty.

"You know it. And after a while, it starts blending together. You've got to keep your distance with cases, keep it mechanical, you know?"

"I get it. Best not to get too close."

"Exactly. You get in trouble when you start caring too much. I have one like that now. A woman, in way over her head and I feel like I need to look after her. She stabbed her husband. The guy's a real prick and probably deserved it. Unfortunately, that is not a legal defense."

"She killed him?"

"No, no. The knife only went in this far," Mason held up his thumb and forefinger about an inch apart, "so he got off easy." His focus shifted to the TV mounted behind the bar, which showed a local news reporter standing outside the County Courthouse. "Hey, can you turn that up for a sec?"

Smitty picked up the remote and raised the volume just enough to be heard close to the bar.

*"Prominent Chicago civil rights attorney Alice Decatur has arrived in Milwaukee as she prepares to defend local high school football coach, Michael Key, who stands accused of double homicide in the October stabbing death of his wife, Robin Key, who was three months pregnant at the time. Last week, Decatur spoke to assembled media here at the county courthouse after filing briefs on behalf of her new client, saying she was determined to shine a light on systemic issues around policing and race in Milwaukee in order to exonerate her client. At this point, no court date has been set, but Decatur's presence figures to bring further national attention in the lead up to the trial. Paige Tyler, Fox 6 News."*

"Jeez. What am I getting myself into?" muttered Mason.

Smitty lowered the volume, his curiosity piqued. "Sorry, what was that?"

"Alice Decatur. She contacted me. Asked me to help out with the case."

"And?"

"And what do you think? I said yes. Meeting with her tomorrow."

"For real?" said Smitty, sounding impressed by Mason's step into the limelight.

"Yup. You don't pass up a case like this. But I have a feeling it's going to be a mess."

Smitty nodded knowingly. "I've been watching the news. It's kind of a soap opera, huh?"

"You've got that right. Black football coach kills his white wife. It's like our own mini OJ case. Now we find out she was pregnant? The cops say the guy confessed under questioning and they have video of the murder. I know enough not to believe everything that gets leaked out of police headquarters, but with all that, defending this guy is gonna be a tall order." Mason swallowed the last of his drink, the icy vodka soothing his bruised voice box. "I still think they could've found local counsel for the case, but it's no wonder someone like her came up here to take it on."

"Yeah, even I know who she is," said Smitty. "I think I saw her on The View one time. She was great."

"Well, for Michael Key's sake, I hope she's as good in court as she is on TV."

"Right. Another Sprite?"

Mason ran a hand across his tender throat. "One more sounds good, just for medicinal purposes. Then I really gotta go."

Smitty served up one last drink, then called for the club limo to take his customer home, charging the service to Mason's account, with a generous tip for himself.

## 17

Alice flashed her TV-ready smile and shook Mason's hand with a surprisingly firm grip. "So, you're young Mr. Mitchell? So nice to have you on the team." Mason's first thought was that Alice was short. In his memory, she was much taller, a testament to the outsized presence that naturally put her in command of any room.

"I appreciate the opportunity, Ms. Decatur and I – "

"Please, call me Alice. We'll be working closely, so first names will do."

"Works for me, Alice. As I was saying, I'm very happy to be joining the team and ready to get to work."

"That's good to hear, Mason. Please, have a seat. You'll have to excuse the last minute setting," Alice shot a pointed look at a young man sitting by her desk, "but we're still in the process of securing offices here in Milwaukee." The meet and greet was taking place in an upper corner of the County Courthouse, inside the chambers of Judge Chavez, who was off for the week and had given Decatur the green light. Alice and Mason were joined by three members of her staff who busied themselves with tablets and files while sizing Mason up.

She perched on the edge of the oak desk that dominated the room. "Now, you'll notice that I've brought my people in from Chicago, but you're here because I think it's important to have someone local on our side. Someone sharp, who knows the landscape and can keep up. It was slim pickings up here, but you have a good amount of trial experience and came highly recommended."

Mason forced a smile. "That's nice, thanks."

"Sorry, that came out wrong. My apologies. I only meant that I'm happy to have you on board. Jim Preston had only good things to say."

"That's alright. I get it, and I'll do my best to repay your faith in me. Since you spoke to Jim, I'm sure you know I've tried quite a few homicides, so I'm able to dive in wherever you need me. I can start by giving you some background on the judge and I'd be happy to assist with jury selection, you name it."

"That's exactly why we chose you," said Alice, "and I'll need everyone on the team pulling in the same direction, playing different roles as needed. Now, I want to tell you up front that I believe the details of this case, while compelling, are secondary to the larger factors at play. It seems clear that, with the police and racial issues, this is a touchstone case for the community. It illustrates societal failings that have been allowed to fester for too long. Michael Key is just the latest in a long line of defendants who have been mistreated by an unfair system overseen by an unfair society."

Mason nodded along, unsure of what to say, so he said nothing. It sounded like Alice was looking for a soapbox, not a courtroom.

She rounded the desk and continued, "It's my intention to bring even more light and heat to the media attention surrounding this case. This is bigger than Michael Key, bigger than Milwaukee. These are deeply rooted American issues, do you understand?"

"As you've laid it out, I suppose I do."

Alice smiled. "Great."

"My only question is what you would need from me as we prepare for trial?"

"Well, for starters you could tell me the best place to get decent coffee beans around here. I'm having an espresso maker brought in."

"Uh, yeah. Sure. I know a good spot by the lakeshore."

"Excellent," said Alice, and pointed to the young man by the desk. "Let Benny know and he'll take care of it."

"Sure. Anything case-related you want me to start on?"

"As a matter of fact, yes. We've been doing a bit of research on Judge Francis, but if you have any firsthand experience with him, I'd love to hear about it."

"Yeah, I've tried a few cases in front of Francis. I can write a memo on him for you."

"That'd be great, but I'd love to hear your impressions of him right now. Is there anything we need to be aware of? You know, tendencies, likes and dislikes, that kind of thing. Who are we dealing with here?"

"Ok. In my experience, he's a pretty straight shooter. He likes to keep things moving along, but will let you follow a line if it's got some meat to it. I'd say he's not fond of grandstanding. He doesn't necessarily want to be part of the show, but he'll step in and crack the whip if he feels like the lawyers are trying to turn his courtroom into a theater."

Alice nodded along, signaling for Benny to take notes on his laptop.

"That's a good start. What's his style when it comes to handling a jury?"

"No nonsense. He's direct and keeps them on course. He'll be paying attention to that in a case like this, if I had to guess."

Alice raised her hand. "Objection. Speculation."

Mason smiled at her joke. "I just think he's going to want to keep a tight lid on things. Jury selection could be a minefield. I've already heard he's not a fan of the news spectacle around the case."

"Yes, judges are like that, aren't they? But if I do my job right, the attention won't go away, so that's something he'll have to live with. Still, it's good to know that he's sensitive to it. What about his demeanor? Any quirks?"

"Not quirks, per se. He's just been on the bench a long time and knows everyone around here. In Milwaukee, he's the big dog. With you being from out of town, don't be surprised if he makes a point of establishing who's in charge."

"Oh, I'm used to that. These big dog types like to bark at someone like me, but I can handle that."

"I'm sure you can."

Alice moved back behind the desk and sat down. "I guess that will be all for now. It's been good getting to chat with you, Mason. We'll be reaching out tomorrow with next steps, but for now, just give some thought to jury selection. I'd be interested in your take on things."

"Will do."

Benny popped out of his seat to get the door and Mason rose to leave. Before he was out of the office, Alice called after him "And Mason? Don't forget about the coffee beans!"

**18**

Mason's loft and office formed two points of a triangle, with the Milwaukee County Courthouse as the third. The distance between each was walkable but Mason insisted on driving. He couldn't see the point of walking as a mode of transportation. It was too slow and exposed to the elements, and if it wasn't for Clyde he would never bother. Mason's meticulous sartorial flair would be wasted if he arrived at a destination sweaty and out of breath, and the climate-controlled style of his Mercedes (and the Jag before that, and the Audi he had his eye on for next year) completed the look, bolstering the reputation of Mitchell & Associates. The fact that Mason had no associates was beside the point.

But a more practical benefit of driving everywhere was that it allowed Mason to be nimble. He never knew if his day would include a court appearance in the suburbs or a spur of the moment client meeting at one of the local or state detention facilities.

Today being a Saturday, he was driving to a fourth point, outside his normal circuit. Communauto Coffee sat across from McKinley Park on the shore of Lake Michigan. His visits were reserved for occasional weekend mornings, like today. Mason was no coffee snob but he did appreciate the bump in quality compared to his weekday Starbucks.

He parked out front and walked in, happy to see no lineup and the co-owner, Denise, behind the counter. She looked up from her inventory list and smiled. "Hey, stranger."

Mason's order never changed, and Denise put down her clipboard to start working on a large latte. They had an app for ordering ahead but Mason didn't use it. A visit to Communato was all about taking his time.

He once overheard another customer refer to Denise as a 'business hippie', and he found that the term fit. She looked the part of a free spirit – formless batik smocks, earthy bangles, thick black hair piled high and held in place by a chopstick – but Denise carried herself with the no-nonsense authority of someone responsible for the bottom line. She was far removed from his world and in a committed 'emotional union' with Communato's co-owner, Colin, but Mason was undeniably attracted to her energy.

"Been a while," she said, "You good these days?" Her pale green eyes and steady, unselfconscious gaze made Mason feel exposed.

Denise began steaming a canister of milk for his latte and Mason had to raise his voice to compete with the noise. "Not too shabby, thanks."

Mason found out about Communato while representing Colin in a case a couple of years back. It was an OWI, Operating While Intoxicated, all too common in Wisconsin. Colin got picked up late one night after taking out a stop sign, ironically, right in front of a coffee shop. No one was hurt, but the whole thing was witnessed by a young cop grabbing a cup to go, who administered a breathalyzer test on the spot. Colin blew well over the limit, but the cop made a rookie mistake, taking Colin to the hospital to collect a blood sample *after* booking him at the station. By then, it had been over three hours since the observed incident. In Wisconsin, this rendered the sample inadmissible in court. The state's eccentric (and sometimes astonishingly lax) drunk driving laws meant the sample never came to light at trial, and as a result, Colin was found not guilty. His license wasn't even suspended. Mason enjoyed favored customer status at Communauto ever since.

"And how's your little dog?" asked Denise.

"Oh, Clyde is living the life. He parties all night and sleeps all day."

"Good for him." Denise turned off the machine and banged the canister against the hardwood bar top before pouring the milk slowly into the cup of steaming espresso. "Hey, you want a pound of the Ethiopian Blend? Roasted yesterday."

"Make it two half pound bags and you've got a deal."

Mason laid a twenty-dollar bill on the counter beside his latte. Denise had used the foamed milk to create an intricate leaf pattern on the surface. Beauty and talent.

"That's fourteen for the beans and the latte's on me this time."

"Have it your way," said Mason and deposited his change in the tip jar with *Good Karma* scrawled across the front. Denise shook her finger at him. "What?" he protested, "I need all the good karma I can get!"

Mason took a seat at the picture window and set his latte aside to let it cool. The muted buzz of Communato's weekend business and aroma of roasting coffee lulled him. He gazed absently at the scene outside and slowly let his mind unwind while waiting for his meeting to arrive.

On the weekend, downtown belonged to its residents. No commuters rushing in, clogging the streets and restaurants. In the warmer months, the majority of weekend traffic outside Communato's window consisted of cyclists and runners on the lakefront, today it was reserved for the few Milwaukeeans willing to brave the winter chill. Mason allowed his thoughts to wander, unfocused and uncluttered by court dates or client demands. *Maybe Denise and Colin have it all figured out. What would a different life look like for me?* Idle thoughts coalesced into a daydream of a cabin up north, just him and Clyde. Maybe even a woman.

Denise set two brown paper packages on the table, "Here you go. Coarse grind, just the way you like it." Mason looked at her dumbly, the warm glow from a fireplace fading in his mind's eye.

"Did I wake you?" she asked, flashing a carefree smile. He resisted the urge to read anything into it.

"No. Not at all. Thanks, just waiting on someone," he said.

"Right. Well, enjoy the coffee."

The door chimed and he looked over to see Benny in the doorway, ushered in by a chilled blast of wind off Lake Michigan. Mason waved him over. He guessed that Alice's devoted assistant wasn't more than five-foot-nine and 150 pounds, but he carried himself like a bigger man. He knew his role and took pride in anticipating the needs of his boss. To Mason, he had the air of a true believer who enjoyed working for someone who could 'fight the man' and win. It probably didn't hurt that he earned top money for a paralegal.

Benny took the stool next to Mason. "Nothing for me, thanks," he said, before Denise could offer.

"Ok then. I'll see you around, Mason," said Denise. "And you know, we're also open Monday to Friday, so don't be a stranger."

"Yeah, I'll keep that in mind," said Mason. "Maybe next time I'll bring Clyde."

Denise nodded her approval and walked back to the bar.

Mason turned to Benny and handed him a bag of coffee. "Here you go, half a pound of the good stuff, my treat."

Benny smiled. "Thanks, I'm sure Alice will enjoy it."

"You said you had something for me?" asked Mason.

Benny produced a small black disc on a key ring and handed it to Mason. "It's a rolling password fob, the code changes every twenty minutes. It will give you access to the dedicated portal for the entire Key case." Benny looked over his shoulder then back to Mason, like he was passing nuclear secrets in Moscow. "You can access anything but print nothing without approval. Alice would like you to submit your invoices through the portal as well. The MJB will send checks to our firm, and then we'll pay you."

"Ok, got it." Mason slipped the fob into his pocket, motioned Benny closer and whispered, "I have a client meeting so I've gotta run. Wait two minutes before you leave so they can't follow us both."

Benny took a beat before registering the sarcasm. "Ha-ha. Just don't lose the fob, please."

"I'll guard it with my life. And I hope Alice likes the coffee," said Mason. "It's the best in town." He waved goodbye to Denise and walked back out into the blustery afternoon.

**19**

Mason took a moment to look over the evidence in the Lori Wells case arranged on his desk. This material, known in legal parlance as 'discovery', had been sent over from the DA's office yesterday, and today, Mason would go over it with his client.

Defendants would pester Mason to file a 'motions of discovery' to gain access to all evidence the State had against them. This request was often made on the advice of so-called jailhouse lawyers who convinced their fellow inmates that the district attorney was always withholding some evidence and that if they could prove that – voilà! – their case would be dismissed, and they would go free. Mason had to explain to clients, usually more than once, that the State was required to turn over all evidence, even if he didn't ask for it. He would stress that no district attorney would knowingly hide evidence because it would end their career and even land them in jail. In the annals of jurisprudence some corrupt district attorney somewhere had withheld evidence, but Mason had never seen it, nor had anyone in Wisconsin in the last seventy years. So when a client asked Mason to file a motion of discovery, he replied with a lie ('I'm happy to do it...') and the truth ('...but it won't result in a dismissal.') Eventually, most clients accepted this explanation and moved on to other arguments.

For her part, Lori Wells was simply eager to learn the details of her case. Despite weeks of trying, she was still unable to locate any memory of the crime in her mind. This blank space and the sequence of events since then left her feeling detached from reality. She knew she stabbed David only because she'd been told she did it. Lori could recall being at the party and seeing David by the fire with another woman, but the next thing that came to mind was Officer Logan asking to see her hands. In between, her mind held no images, nothing concrete.

She arrived at the offices of Mitchell & Associates, accompanied by her mother. Lori walked into the reception area wearing jeans, a zip-up hoodie, and sneakers. With her long blonde hair in a ponytail she almost looked too young to buy alcohol.

Linda rounded the reception desk and welcomed them with a smile. "Ms. Wells, I presume? Pleasure to meet you."

"You too," said Lori, shaking Linda's hand. "And this is my mother, Carrie."

"Yes, we've met. So nice to see you again. Please, if you'll both follow me to the conference room. Attorney Mitchell will be in soon. Can I get you anything, a coffee or water? What about you, Carrie?"

Lori and her mother declined, then took seats next to each other on one side of the long glass-top table. The wall across from them was floor to ceiling glass, with the door set in the center. The other three walls were Cream City brick, the longest one adorned with framed copies of the Declaration of Independence, the Constitution, and the Bill of Rights. On the short wall to the left hung the logo of the firm made from stainless steel, on the right a large flat-screen monitor.

On her first visit, Carrie had been too preoccupied to notice the decor. "Hmm. Seems like he's doing well."

Lori chewed her thumbnail, lost in thought.

"Angel, please don't do that," pleaded Carrie. "It makes you look coarse."

Lori stopped just as Mason breezed into the room. He wore no blazer or tie, with the top button of his shirt undone and his sleeves rolled up to the elbow. It was a calculated weekend look he called 'Relaxed Office', meant to put his visitors at ease. For some clients, Mason might employ 'The Floor Show' – suit, suspenders, cuff-links, the whole nine – but there was no need for shock and awe this morning. Mason wanted Lori and her mother to see him as a real person who cared about the case.

"Hi, good to see you both again." Mason took a seat across from them. "Carrie, it's great that you came down to support Lori, but I need you to understand that if you are in the room during my conversation with Lori, everything we say would no longer be covered under attorney-client privilege."

Carrie and Lori exchanged a nervous glance but didn't speak.

"In other words, Lori," Mason continued, "the District Attorney would be able to subpoena your mother and force her to testify about our conversation.  So, to be on the safe side, I'd advise that she wait in the reception area, but it's entirely up to you."

"Oh, ok. But, I would really like her to be here," said Lori. "What do you think, mom?"

"Angel, it's fine. If the lawyer thinks it's better with me not here, then I'll go. But I'll be right out there if you need me."

"Yeah?" Lori looked skeptical. "Ok. I guess." Carrie patted Lori's hand and picked up her purse.

Mason gave Carrie a reassuring smile. "If you need anything at all, just ask Linda."

Carrie nodded and made her way out of the room. Mason wasn't lying about the privilege rules, but mainly he was happy to have her gone because it increased the odds of full disclosure from Lori. Not many people enjoyed airing dirty laundry in front of their mother.

After the heavy glass door swung shut, Mason turned his attention to Lori. "Ok, I'd like to review the evidence with you now. We have the police reports, witness statements, and the 911 call from your case."

Mason laid out copies of each on the table in front of Lori. Her brow furrowed as she scanned the documents.

"Hey, it's going to be ok," said Mason. "Let's dig in, shall we?"

The reports revealed that Lori and David arrived at the party around 9 or 10 p.m. Most in attendance were drinking heavily, some were smoking weed, others were rolling on ecstasy and oxycontin. By all accounts, everyone, with the notable exception of Mason's client, appeared to be having fun. That is, until a young woman named Destiny showed up. It became evident as the night progressed that Destiny and David were involved. Several witnesses claimed to know that the two had been engaged in an affair for months, but that night it became clear to Lori for the first time. Around 1:30 a.m., Lori confronted Destiny and they got into a physical fight on the front lawn of the property. Although the statements conflicted slightly, all agreed that David inserted himself into the fight and led Lori away around the back of the property, by the out building.

At this point, there were no witnesses who saw what transpired between Lori and David, as most partygoers had returned to their activities. Destiny briefly followed Lori and David, shouting at them, but was removed by another friend and they went back out front to have a smoke. The next part of the account was from David only.

In his statement, he described Lori as irrational, drunk and out of control. He claimed that several times she tried to hit him, but he was able to fend off her attacks. He further stated that any injuries Lori suffered must have been from the fight with Destiny. Over and over in his statement he insisted *'I never touched her'* and *'I would never hit a woman.'*

"Bullshit. What an asshole." Lori said, under her breath.

"What was that?"

"Nothing," said Lori. Her jaw was clenched as she spoke. "Let's keep reading."

"No, wait. If you have anything to add, this is exactly the time to do it. That's what this meeting is all about. If you want me to defend you, I need to know everything, ok?"

"It's nothing. Please, just keep going," Lori urged.

The statement continued, with David claiming that Lori was so out of control and irrational he felt it would be best to just leave. He said he tried to do so more than once, only to have her call him back. Then David stated that as he walked away for the last time, she grabbed a knife from her purse and stabbed him, right in the stomach. David claimed that Lori then pushed the knife deeper and twisted. He was asked by the officer how Lori was able to stab him in the stomach, if he had been walking away from her. He explained it away saying, *'I must have turned around at the last second.'*

Statements from witnesses at the front of the property picked up the story from there. One partygoer saw Lori emerge from around the side of the house, walk to the end of the driveway, and make a call on her phone. According to everyone who saw Lori then, there was blood clearly visible on her hands and clothes. It's assumed that the call was not picked up, because she put the phone away and just sat down on the curb, motionless in a trance-like state. A short time later, David stumbled out of the back yard. Partygoers saw him collapse at the side of the house, at which time they called 911.

Next, Mason played a recording of the 911 call. Lori was still in her head, replaying the events and struggling to put a hand to any clear memories of the back yard, the knife, anything at all about the incident. Nothing had changed. Her knowledge of the crime was not tethered to any sense memory. No sights, sounds, or sensations. It remained unreal to her.

Lori realized Mason was looking at her intently from across the table, and she tuned in to hear the 911 caller say, *"...the blonde one! The little blonde did it! She's all covered in blood, and she was fighting! Please hurry!"*

The playback stopped and Lori nodded her head. Reading and listening to accounts of that night was making her feel a little insane. "Mm-hmm. Ok," she said. "Anything else?"

The remaining reports discussed ancillary parts of the investigation and interviews with attendees that saw nothing of note. When they reached the end of the materials, Mason sat without speaking, waiting for Lori to fill the space. He wanted to gauge her state of mind.

"It doesn't look good, does it?" Lori asked.

"I wouldn't go that far. It is what it is. And I still need to talk to the district attorney, see what they are offering, see what else our investigation reveals."

"Ok, but it's clear that I did this. Sounds like I'm in a lot of trouble." She began sobbing.

Mason reached for the Kleenex box on the conference table and handed her a tissue. "Hey, I've seen worse." He tried to make his voice as soothing as possible. "Trust me. It will be ok."

He saw a lot of crying in his line of work, but it still made him uncomfortable. "I am not saying you are going to walk away clean, but rest assured I will do everything I can to keep you out of prison." He truly meant that. Mason felt bad for Lori. His practice revolved around 'bad guys'. Repeat customers, no-hopers, and some genuine sociopaths. It didn't mean they always deserved what they got, but most knew what they were getting into. In Lori, he saw a lost soul wandering into the labyrinth of the criminal justice system without a clue.

"I'm so scared. I have never been through something like this before," she said through the tears, her breathing coming fast and shallow.

"I understand," he said, and handed her another tissue. "I know this is hard for you, but now we need to talk about the abuse."

"What do you mean?"

"You know what I mean. This is why I encouraged your mother to leave. I know David was abusing you."

"Wait, how do you know about..." her voice trailed off.

"In a follow-up interview with David, he provided some documents to the police."  Mason opened a folder and slid it across to Lori. "I'm sure you recognize these."

Lori's face dropped. "Where did you get these?" she whispered.

"When David was in the hospital, he told the police where to find them at your place, and they were collected as evidence. David believed they were important and wanted to make sure the police got them before you could destroy them." Mason struggled to contain the note of triumph in his voice. "He seems to think they prove that *you* were abusive towards *him*!"

"Please, please don't show them to anyone. They are embarrassing. I don't want my mother to see them, I don't want anyone to see them."

"Lori, listen to me. These documents help our case. We can use them to build a solid defense."

"Please, don't," she pleaded.

Mason considered pushing back, then thought better of it. Lori was on edge. This had all been too much at once. He closed the folder and dropped it onto the chair beside him. "Fair enough. I will keep them to myself for now. But if we go to trial, I think we'll need them, to show the truth of what went on between you and David leading up to that night."

Lori crumpled her copies into a ball, tears welling in her eyes.  "I don't want that to happen. I can't have people knowing about all that."

"Ok, I won't use them." Mason knew he would have to break his promise at some point, but now was the time for reassurance. "I can figure out different ways to go about this."

Lori pulled a compact out of her purse and checked her makeup, wiping away muddy streaks on her cheeks. "Thank you. I'm sorry I'm like this."

"It's ok. Forget the documents. We have other things to discuss, and privilege won't be an issue," he said, "so, maybe it'd be good to have your mom back in here?"

Lori nodded and wiped her nose again.

Mason hit a button on the phone sitting in the middle of the table. "Linda, can you send Ms. Bedford back in? Thanks."

When Carrie re-entered the room and saw her daughter's red eyes, but before she could comment, Lori told her, "I'm fine, mom. It's ok."

"We were going over the details surrounding the stabbing," explained Mason. "Understandably, it was a little emotional for Lori. In any case, thanks for your patience, Carrie. Now that you're back, I want us to talk about the next step in the process."

Carrie took Lori's hand and nodded for Mason to proceed.

"Excellent. I have an investigator on staff, Ozzy. Best in the state, I trust him with my life. He will try to interview David and gauge his attitude regarding this case, although I suspect I can already predict his reaction."

"That boy is an asshole," said Carrie, slapping the tabletop to punctuate the operative word.

"Mom, stop!"

"That's ok," said Mason. "I'll be getting in touch with the district attorney's office to see what type of deal they are prepared to offer. If we don't like what we hear, we take your case to trial. Simple as that."

Lori's eyes widened. "I do not want a trial."

"We are nowhere near that point yet. First, let's see if Ozzy turns up new information, then we'll find out what the DA is offering and go from there. I'll call you once I hear something. Until then, try to relax and just be there for each other. I know this is an emotional time but we're a team now, so let's stick together and stay calm. Can you do that?"

Carrie took Lori's hand in hers and squeezed it. Mother and daughter shared a look, then nodded.

"Very good," said Mason. "That's going to make all the difference."

20

Mason and District Attorney James Thurston had gone back and forth negotiating a deal for Lori but failed to reach an agreement. The DA's last offer was to drop the charge from attempted first degree intentional homicide down to first degree reckless injury, reducing Lori's overall exposure from sixty to twenty-five years. Mason's recommendation had been to reject it and Lori agreed.

On the morning of Lori's trial, Mason walked briskly across the parking lot of the Waukesha County Courthouse, rushing to meet his client and her family. He entered the low-rise sandstone building and scanned the lobby directory, silently cursing Thurston and convincing himself he was ready for trial.

Mason stepped into the elevator and closed his eyes in time with the doors. During the shuddering ascent he tried to clear his head. The exhaustion from consecutive late nights working with Decatur's team and drinking until bar close weighed on his limbs and mind. Eye drops and a well-tailored suit were enough to keep him from looking as haggard as he felt, but on this morning, Mason was running on vodka fumes and denial.

Lori, her parents, and another middle-aged couple were gathered in a small conference room next to Courtroom SC217 when Mason arrived.

"You're late," said Lori's father.

Lori looked at him with annoyance, "Dad, relax. It's nine o'clock. He's on time."

"On time is late, if you ask me." Tom was retired military and the transition to civilian life as a mechanical engineer had not softened his manner.

Mason checked his watch. It read 8:59. "Sorry to keep you waiting, Tom. Hope you all had a good trip down this morning. I know the traffic is killer these days."

The other couple were introduced as Lori's Aunt Cindy and Uncle Ken.

The family had made the sixty-five mile drive down from Fond du Lac. The quiet town of nearly fifty thousand sat at the foot of Lake Winnebago, an outwardly unspectacular example of good clean Midwestern living. Lori lived her entire life there until a year ago. Mason could sense that her family blamed the 'big city' as much as anything else for the situation Lori found herself in.

"Saw you on TV last night," said Tom, his voice clipped. "Working with that Chicago lawyer. For the football coach who killed his wife."

"Right. Allegedly killed his wife. And I'm just helping with that case," replied Mason as he opened Lori's file and placed it on the table.

"Must be a pretty big deal for you, that one," said Tom.

Mason was too tired to even consider taking the bait. "I suppose. But I'd like us to go over Lori's case right now and–"

"With all the attention on that case," Tom's voice was rising now, "you still focused on keeping our Lori out of prison?"

Lori put a hand on his arm. "Dad, c'mon. Mason has been working hard for us the whole time."

Mason saw Tom's anger for what it really was, an outlet for the tension. He felt it weighing heavily on the whole group. Facing the criminal justice system was enough to rattle anyone's cage, even if you weren't the one whose freedom was on the line.

"Mr. Bedford, I know you're hoping for the best outcome for your daughter." Mason looked to the other family members, "You all are. That's what I'm focused on, too. I want the best for Lori. And the best thing we can do for Lori right now is stay calm, united, and supportive, ok?"

Lori smiled weakly and squeezed her father's hand. He turned his gaze down into his lap with a loud sigh but gripped her hand in return.

So many of his clients unraveled just before their day in court but Lori was holding up better than could be expected. Mason could see how shaky and on edge she was, but still made a show of being ready for the ordeal ahead. Maybe there was more steel to her than she let on.

There was a knock on the door and James Thurston poked his head in. "Mason, can I have a word? Won't take long."

"Sure thing," said Mason. "Lori, I'll be back in a minute. You sit tight." He nodded towards Tom and Carrie, then joined Thurston in the corridor.

"What's up, James?"

"I wanted to take one more chance at a deal."

"On the morning of the trial? What, did charming Mr. Wells fail to show? Your case must be falling apart."

"Actually, no. David's here. In fact, he arrived thirty minutes early and spent that time expressing to me how insistent he is about going forward."

Mason raised his eyebrows. "So, why are you talking to me?"

"I have some hesitation," said Thurston, then looked over his shoulder. "The kid's a real ass, and the documents he provided to the police are, um, concerning. I want to see if we can work something out."

Mason nodded soberly and rubbed his chin. Partly to indicate he was mulling things over, partly to make sure he wasn't drooling over this gift. "We can work something out, but not at first degree injury," he said. "It's too much time. She has no record. The stab wound was basically a scratch. And with David," Mason looked over Thurston's shoulder, "being such an ass, he won't present well to the jury. You want to talk about those concerning documents? The women on the jury, and I'll make sure there are plenty, will hate him!" Mason was bluffing. Lori had still not approved the use of those documents.

"Look, I agree with you," said Thurston, "I don't want a jury to meet David. I'm making this offer without his approval, ok?"

"Legally, you don't need his approval."

"I know, but our office likes to have it, so I'm out on a limb on this one."

"I appreciate your maverick spirit, but is there an offer to go along with this, or do we start a trial and let Mr. Warmth put on a show?"

"Very cute, Mason. I can do a plea to second degree reckless injury, both sides free to argue. This reduces her exposure to ten years max, five in and five out. And the judge won't give the max, you know that."

"Can't say yes to that. For my client, that's still too much time." Lori hadn't said any such thing, but with Thurston eager to keep his victim away from a jury, Mason was happy to paint outside the lines and press the advantage.

"Ok, what were you thinking?" Thurston raised his index finger to stop Mason before he could answer. "And be realistic."

"Realistic? Fine. The amendment to second degree makes sense, but you need to go along with the recommendation in the pre-sentence report, whatever it is, and we are free to argue."

"I think I can make that deal, but David won't like it. He'll still ask the judge for whatever he wants."

"I don't doubt it," said Mason. "And another thing, bail continues until sentencing."

Thurston considered it for a moment then nodded. "Agreed, she's not a flight risk."

"Thank you. Ok, let me run this by my client and I'll get back to you to confirm."

Thurston pointed to the clock mounted above the courtroom doors. "Tick-tock, Mitchell. Don't keep me waiting."

"Yeah, yeah." Mason turned toward the conference room where Lori and her family waited. "Tick-tock. Don't I know it."

A whispered conversation between Lori and her mother cut off abruptly as Mason entered the room and took a seat.

"As you know, I've continued to press the DA, and he has just now conveyed to me they are ready to offer a new plea deal."

All eyes were on him, but Mason focused on Lori as he slowly and clearly outlined the terms of the offer. She nodded along as he went over numbers and variables.

"If you ask me, they are wary of a trial," said Mason. "They don't want David on the stand as he is not a sympathetic victim. So, that's where this is coming from. Like I said, we went back and forth and this offer is in line with what I was hoping we could get."

Aunt Cindy spoke first, "You say this deal is for five years in and five years out, but that's still a long time. Way too much time for what happened with Lori."

"I agree," said Mason. "But with the way sentencing works with charges like this, the recommendation of the department in the pre-sentence report gets followed, and I believe that with Lori having a clean record and good family, that recommendation could very well be no prison time, all probation."

"You say that, but she can still get the max of five years inside a prison," said Tom. "Plus, she will have a felony conviction for life. She's not a criminal!"

Lori was still silent, processing what she heard. Mason squatted down beside her, "Hey, Lori. I know this is a lot to take in, but if you have questions, now's the time to ask them." He looked at his watch. "Trial starts soon and the judge will want any plea agreement to be in place before we begin."

Lori chewed her lip and kept her eyes lowered. "I don't know what to say yet."

"Look, the good news is the DA is offering to be bound by the rec-ommendation of the pre-sentence report. That could be probation, maybe six months conditional time, but I don't foresee a prison recommendation. Still, David will be able to ask for whatever he wants."

"That son of a bitch," said Tom.

Lori ignored him and looked at Mason. "I hear what you're saying. Like, maybe there are better odds if I take the deal? But I can't handle going to prison at all. I just want to go home." Lori dropped her head into her hands and let out a shuddering sigh. "I feel like I can't make sense of this anymore."

"Ok. That's ok," said Mason. "Let me help you out. We can still go to trial if you want. Like I mentioned, I don't think David will do well with a jury and your personal history is a plus for us."

"And if we win then it's all over and I go home," she said quietly.

"That's right. You'd go free, nothing on your record. But you never know with a jury. It's tough. Sometimes they just want to convict. They want someone to pay. And if we lose at trial, it would be bad."

"How bad?" asked Carrie.

"Then we get the full force of the sentence, fifteen or twenty years. We don't want that."

Lori looked at her mother, "What should I do?"

"I don't know, angel. You need to trust your lawyer, trust your instincts, trust your heart," Carrie offered in her most reassuring voice.

Tom thrust his finger toward Mason, "Well, you're the lawyer! Stop dancing around and tell us what to do, then!"

"Dad, please," said Lori.

Carrie lowered Tom's hand with hers. "We need to stay calm, Tom."

"That's ok," said Mason. "I understand this is a lot. Thing is, I'm not going to tell Lori she should or shouldn't take the deal. She needs to decide. I will give her the best advice that I can. Right now, knowing what I know, I'd say that we have a strong probability of getting five years probation, no prison time, if we take the deal. We can go to trial and have a chance of getting a not guilty verdict, but there's the risk of a long time in prison."

Carrie shook her head bitterly and Tom remained frozen in impotent rage. Cindy clung to Ken, looking at Lori with pity. The atmosphere in the room was heavy, and Mason could see Lori shutting down.

He handed her a tissue so she could dab her eyes and blow her nose. "Look, everyone, this is a very difficult and personal choice for Lori. There's obviously a lot of pressure. Maybe you can give us a minute or two so I can go over this with her one more time?"

Tom glared at Mason for a beat then went straight for the door, followed by Cindy and Ken.

Carrie took Lori's hands in hers and whispered, "Take your time, angel. We support you. We love you." She gave her daughter a kiss on the forehead and went out to the corridor, shutting the door behind her.

Mason and Lori sat without talking for a moment. The fluorescent lights above them buzzed softly. With her family gone, Lori had wilted.

"Sometimes it's harder with them around," she said. "I know that sounds bad, but it's too much. I feel like I have to keep it together for them. They love me and they're trying, but it just stresses me out more."

Mason nodded and tried not to check his watch again. "I get it. I do. But now it's just you and me in here. So we can take a big breath," he inhaled deeply, gesturing for her to join, which she did. They exhaled slowly and sat in silence for a few seconds. "And now," he said, "let's go over this one more time."

Lori straightened in her chair and said, "Ok. I can do this."

"I know you can. As I said before, if we go to trial, the jury could very well hate David and feel like the stabbing was justified, which is how I would frame it. But they might simply see it as a case of 'she stabbed him, end of story'. We have no witness and you can't testify since you can't remember what happened."

"I don't know. I mean, I stabbed him. At least it appears I did. Everyone said I did, so I don't know."

"Well, if we go to trial I will use David's documents against him. I think they show you were the one being abused. I would argue that he was exercising power and control over you, and when you stabbed him you had no other option. An act of self-defense."

"But I don't want anyone to know about that stuff."

"I know, Lori. But if we go to trial, all of that information is our best chance. "

"Will it work?"

"Not sure. Juries don't like letting defendants go free, but they also hate spousal abuse. If we go to trial, it's a tough call. I can't say for sure how it would go."

"Uh-huh. And the deal?"

Mason leaned forward and looked directly into Lori's eyes. "At worst, it's a couple years in prison but I'd say that's unlikely. There's a good chance you would never see the inside of a jail cell again. If we go to trial and lose, it would destroy your life. The plea deal would let you put all this behind you."

"What do you think I should do?"

"If I were in your shoes, I would take the deal. Probation is likely. It eliminates a long prison sentence, and you move on with your life."

"Yeah, I understand. I get it. But ..."

"But what?"

Lori opened her mouth to reply, then paused. "Nothing. Never mind. Let's take the deal."

"You sure?"

"Yes."

Mason pulled the forms from his briefcase and laid them on the table when there was a knock at the door. "Bailiff here, Mr. Mitchell."

"Come in," said Mason.

"Judge wants to know what's happening. He wants to get things moving."

"Tell him it will be a plea, but we need a new sentencing date. It'll just take a minute to complete the paperwork."

"Got it. I'll tell him but make it quick. He wants to move forward now-ish."

"Will do." Mason turned his attention back to the plea forms. They reviewed the amended charge, the elements of the crime, and all the constitutional rights Lori was now waiving. They reviewed the maximum penalties and, finally, the felony warnings stating that once she pleads, she could never possess a firearm for the rest of her life and could not vote in any election until her entire sentence was completed.

After the final signatures, Mason looked at Lori. "It'll be ok. This is the right decision. You get peace of mind, a chance for a real future, and closure."

"Right," said Lori, staring at the documents on the table. "Thanks, really. I think this is good."

———

An hour later it was done. Everything went as expected, like the thousand other pleas Mason had handled. The only exception was one outburst from David when he heard the charges were being reduced. He was so disruptive the bailiffs had to remove him from the courtroom.

After it was over, Mason stood with Lori and her family in the courthouse lobby.

"I'll call once the pre-sentence report is completed and filed." He put a hand on Lori's shoulder and smiled reassuringly. "I know this was hard, but you did well. You should feel good about it."

Lori nodded. Her posture was lighter, youthful again, like some of the weight had been lifted from her shoulders. Even her father appeared more at ease, or at least less likely to punch someone. Mason shook Lori's hand and congratulated her for holding up so well, then made for the parking lot. He was dying for a drink.

**21**

Michael Key was sitting at a small table, under harsh lights in a cramped interrogation room. He did not move. Detective Roland Chase was in the chair across from him, also frozen in time.

Alice Decatur leaned forward, her chin resting on steepled fingers, studying the scene. "Chase has him on the ropes."

"Yeah, I think this next part is very telling," said Mason, then hit the spacebar on his laptop. The two men projected on the conference room screen came back to life.

*"Mike, we can't keep going in circles like this. If you keep dodging the question and not owning up to what you did, we can't move forward."*

*"Ugh. I hear you say that, and I want to tell you. I do."* Michael shifted in his seat and buried his hands in the front pocket of his hoodie. His movements were halting, sluggish. *"I just can't see it in my head, man. It's not there."*

They were watching the third, and longest, interrogation Michael Key had endured in as many days. The first two yielded nothing but denials, despite several hours of questioning from a revolving team of detectives. Now that Key was alone in the room with Chase, the tone of the conversation became more familiar and more insistent. The detective spoke like he already knew the answer to each question he asked.

*"Ok. Ok. Just take a deep breath and let's go over it again. After the altercation at the barbeque you drove around for a bit, had a drink to*

*calm yourself down. You ended up back at the house and waited for Robin. When she got there you confronted her by the porch, right?"*

*"Yeah, I guess."*

*"She said some nasty things. It got overheated, maybe she hit you again, like at the park earlier. Then ..."*

*"I don't know, man. I don't know."*

*"Come on, Mike. We've been over this. Then you pulled out the knife and you stabbed her. You did."*

Key slumped down in his chair and threw his head back, as if seeking heavenly guidance. Despite the low-res quality of the video, they could see clearly his agonized features.

*"Hey, stay with me,"* Chase continued. *"It's ok. We need to get this out in the open and then we can move on. The first time you stabbed her was where?"*

*"Um, maybe it was, like, around here."* Key waved his hand over his neck.

*"No. Not there. That was later. Remember, Mike? You stabbed her in the abdomen, right?"*

Alice Decatur shook her head in disbelief, "You can pause it there. Jesus, it's a fucking kindergarten guessing game. I'm going to have a field day with this."

For the past hour, the two lawyers had been reviewing interrogation footage. This conference room was part of Alice's temporary Milwaukee homebase, composed of two unused offices at one of Milwaukee's white-shoe law firms. The space had been generously donated by a partner who Alice impressed as an intern years ago. The room they were sitting in was just a few blocks away from the room in which Michael Key was kept for three days, slowly eroding under waves of questioning.

Mason's eyes were blurry, and he looked almost as haggard as their client on the screen. He had gone from Lori's plea appearance straight into a marathon all-night session reviewing the entire Key interview from start to finish, a task he finished just one hour before meeting Alice. He was running on nervous energy, knowing that his presentation could bolster Key's defense and boost Mason's profile in the team. Alice had tasked Mason with identifying the detectives who conducted the questioning (there were six in all), noting their tactics and Michael Key's demeanor as the interrogation wore on. She also asked him to keep an eye out for illegalities, but that was a long shot. Cops were given a great amount of leeway when questioning a suspect and short of direct physical coercion, there wasn't much that was off the table.

"I think I've isolated the worst of the worst, but it wasn't easy. As you can tell, it's just hour after hour of this same kind of thing," said Mason.

"Skip to the end," said Alice. "I want to hear him say it."

Mason scrubbed through the video and the scene on the wall moved in fast motion; Michael fidgeting and Chase gesticulating, Michael pacing the windowless room, and one time escorted out to use the toilet. When video playback resumed, the two men sat on opposite sides of the small table with a pen and paper between them, and Chase was speaking.

*"It's ok. Don't worry about what the paper says right now. We can have you sign that later and it'll only say what you've told me here. Now, you've done a great job, Mike. I know this has been hard. I do. But I'll level with you, this is gonna help your case a lot. I'm the guy who talks to the prosecutor and I will make sure he knows how you cooperated with us. In this job, I deal with a lot of bad dudes, total psychos. That's not you. Not even close. You just lost control. It can happen to anyone. I'll make sure the prosecutor and the judge know what kind of guy you really are. And that is gonna make a big difference down the road."*

Key nodded, staring at the table.

*"We've gone over the whole story, and you've worked really hard at remembering. That's great. Now, let's just finish this off so we can get out of here."*

At this, Key looked up, a glimmer of hope flashing across his slack face.

Chase picked the paper up off the table. *"Great. I'm going to go through this step by step, and you just say yes ... or no."*

*"Yeah, ok. Let's do it."*

*"You stabbed Robin, first in the stomach, on the right side."*

*"Yes."*

*"Then on the other side of the abdomen, under the ribs."*

*"Yes."*

*"Then again, in the middle of her back, and the last time, in her neck."*

*"Yes."* Key's responses were lifeless.

*"So, you admit now that you killed Robin Key."*

Michael doubled over like he had been kicked in the gut. Chase came around the table and placed a hand on his back.

*"Hey, it's ok. Just do this last thing and we're done."*

A pained wail escaped from deep inside Key, his body shook as he sobbed. Chase kept at him.

*"Come clean, Mike. Then we can put this behind you and get out of here."*

*"Yes. I think I must've done it. I killed Robin."*

Mason paused the video. Without context, it appeared to show one man consoling another.

"Disgusting," said Alice. "This is the case. We need to destroy that statement. They had him in there for what, two days?"

"Just over seventy-two hours."

"Even better. And this Detective Chase, how much of the questioning does he handle?"

"Most of the back half," answered Mason. "He stays in the room with Key for twelve hours straight to finish it off."

"And from what we've seen, the tone of the interview takes a distinct turn when he takes over, yes?"

"I'd say so."

Alice stood and walked over to the window. "Ok, then he's our target. What we have on video is plenty, but I want to take Chase apart any way we can. Can you work on that?"

"You bet," said Mason, typing a note into his laptop.

Mason knew she planned to go hard at the false confession angle, systematically dismantling the foundation of the State's case against Michael Key. At this point, the prosecution had produced little physical evidence and without the confession they would have a difficult time meeting the burden of proof.

Alice turned back to the screen. "Classic. They took an inebriated suspect, isolated him, then psychologically tortured him, and after *three goddamn days* they finally prodded a bullshit confession out of a completely broken man. Every clip you showed me follows the Reid technique, but on steroids."

"Sorry, what was that?" said Mason. He'd been staring at his computer screen, thinking about Chase.

"You're kidding me, right?" said Alice. Before Mason could respond, she continued in a mock professorial tone, "The Reid technique, developed in the '50s by Tom Reid."

"Right," said Mason, "the psychologist."

Alice snorted and shook her head. "He's billed as a psychologist, but the thing to remember is that he was a former Chicago cop. CPD has always had issues, but those were the bad old days. After his years on the force, the playbook that Reid designed was solely aimed at extracting confessions. If you ask me, it's just a whole slew of methods to wear down suspects until they say what you want them to say."

"Got it. Accusatory versus information gathering, I just didn't hear you at first," said Mason. The flush of pride for a job well done was now tempered by mild embarrassment and the lack of sleep catching up to him.

"The Reid technique has nothing to do with information gathering or facts," said Alice. "It's just about the cops building a narrative. And police departments across the country have used it for decades, especially with black suspects."

Mason nodded, typing notes into his laptop. "They can get a suspect to confess, but if we can show that it results in a high rate of false confessions..."

"Exactly," said Alice. She snapped her fingers at Benny. "I want you to line up some options for expert testimony. Make sure Bowen and Stutts are on the list."

Alice turned back to Mason. "We should have them confirmed by tonight. You'll need to go to the jail and meet with Key, get him to sign off on the expense so we can get started. Make sure he realizes how important this is to his defense. We need these guys."

"You sure you don't want to do it then? He's going to want to hear it from his lawyer."

Alice waved off his suggestion, "My driver is waiting downstairs to take me back to Chicago in a half hour. Governor's Ball is tonight. Besides, you're his lawyer too. It'll be good for you to finally get some face time with him."

Mason still had an afternoon of hearings ahead of him and all he wanted was a drink and some solid sleep. A late night journey into the bowels of the County Jail was not an enticing prospect.

"Hey, if you just want to be the coffee guy, let me know," said Alice. "Or you can be a real part of the team and get this done for me, ok?"

She had him there. And he figured he could sneak a couple hours of sleep at the office. "You got it. I'll make sure he's on board."

**22**

I t was past 8 p.m. when Mason reached the after-hours entrance of the County Jail. The guard buzzed open the door before Mason had a chance to hit the call button.

"Hey Schmidt, another prime shift for you, I see," said Mason.

The guard smiled and shrugged in response. "Yeah, working a double. Only four more years before the pension kicks in and I'm done."

"On the home stretch. Good for you."

"How many guys today?" asked Schmidt.

"Four. Here's the list."

"Got it. I see Key on the list. You represent him? I thought that fancy Chicago lawyer had the case?"

"She does, but needed someone handsome on the team. So here I am."

"Ha-ha. That one's a big deal. Looks like you're moving up in the world."

"Not too far up. I'm more window dressing than anything."

"Got it. Well, here you go." Schmidt handed Mason the visiting documents for the four inmates, each one folded into quarters and signed by him. "And don't forget this," he said, handing over a PROFESSIONAL VISITOR badge. Mason clipped it to his shirt before placing his briefcase on the x-ray machine and walking through the metal detector.

*BEEP!*

It never failed. Mason stopped in his tracks, but Schmidt winked and waved him past. "Whatever you're smuggling, just give me some on the way out."

The process for an attorney to have a contact visit with clients at the Milwaukee County Jail involved passing through a series of secured doors. After being cleared by Schmidt, Mason pressed a small silver intercom button that alerted Central Command to his arrival. They could observe him via closed-circuit camera and buzz him into the elevator vestibule when they saw fit. After being granted access, he pressed the call button for the elevator, which Central Command then permitted to descend to the ground floor. While waiting for it to arrive, Mason checked the paperwork and noted that his clients were split between the fourth and fifth floor. He would start on the lower level.

Arriving on four, he encountered another door, another intercom button. A buzzer sounded to pop the door, which opened on a short, caged corridor ending at the control station for that floor. There, Mason slid his client's paperwork to the guard through a slot at the bottom of the pass-through window. The double-thick pane of security glass bore scars from years of violent outbursts.

"Looks like I've got three guys on this floor," offered Mason in a cheerful tone. He learned from numerous visits to the jail that kindness and patience produced better, if not necessarily faster, results.

"Lemme see who you got," said the guard, thumbing through Mason's documents. "Ok, come on through."

When the door buzzed open, Mason entered a hallway off of which there were three small rooms, each one containing two plastic chairs and a concrete table fixed to the wall. He entered the middle room and waited for his first client to be brought in.

———

The visits on the fourth floor passed in routine fashion. Mason informed each client of the state of their case, prospects at trial, and checked in on their well-being, offering the sympathetic ear that some of them needed. Jail was a scary place, overcrowded, violent, with strict codes of conduct enforced by guards and inmates. Any slip up could bring harsh punishment and not everyone could cope.

After saying goodbye to the third client, Mason was buzzed through yet another series of secure doors to reach the fifth floor, where he would visit Michael Key. He kept this one for last, not wanting to rush his first meeting with the most famous defendant in the jail.

When Michael entered the visiting room, he was breathing heavily as he tucked in his jail-issued gray t-shirt and pulled the orange tunic over it. Michael was bigger than he appeared in the interrogation videos, Mason guessed a few inches over six feet and a solid 220, looking more like one of his players than the coach. Mason knew this imposing size would be a disadvantage in front of a jury.

"I was playing hoops when they called me in. Who are you?"

"Mason Mitchell. I work with Ms. Decatur's team."

Key looked chagrined. "Justice In Society – you've got to be kidding me."

"Sorry, what's that?" asked Mason.

"You spoke at James Madison High School a few months ago. I was in the auditorium. I saw your talk."

"Ah, yes of course," said Mason. "It's a small world, Mr. Key."

"Never talk to the cops," said Key, laughing ruefully, "that's what you said."

"Well, let's keep our focus on the here and now, shall we?"

"Hmph. Right. So...what is this visit about?"

"They treating you ok in here?" asked Mason. "Anyone giving you trouble?"

"Look, no offense but, why are you here? Where's Alice?"

"She's stuck in Chicago and asked me to come see you."

Michael shook his head. "My lawyer, always stuck somewhere and never here talking to me."

"Um, I assure you it was unavoidable. In any event, Alice does send her regards."

"Right."

"And she wanted me to talk to you about your confession and potential defenses against it."

"Ok, fine," said Michael, folding his arms. "I'm all ears."

It didn't appear that Michael meant what he said, but Mason carried on as if he did. "As you know, when you confessed to killing your wife– "

"I know what I said! But it was bullshit. They made me thin –"

"Mr. Key, please don't get upset. I simply meant–"

"I was so fucking tired and out of it when they were talking to me! It was crazy. They messed with my head, you know that!" Michael's tone oscillated between anger and pleading.

"I get it," said Mason, "and that will be central to our argument. We plan to hire an expert who will argue your interrogation had all the hallmarks of a false confession and is therefore unreliable. He's published several studies on the topic."

"It was one hundred percent false. You know I didn't do this, right?"

"Not the point, Mr. Key, and I don't really care either way. My job here is not about what you did or what I think. It is about what the State can prove and nothing more." As soon as this stock disclaimer was out of his mouth, Mason regretted it.

"You don't care either way? Well, I do! So, what the fuck are you doing here? I did *not* kill Robin. If we're going to keep talking, I need you to believe me."

Mason put his hands up. "Ok. Mr. Key, I believe you."

"No, man. Fuck that. Fuck you. None of you guys believe me. Not Alice, not any of her little minions. Why should you be any different? All you guys care about is the press, but I'm tired of this shit. I'm telling you I didn't do this, but if you don't believe me, we're done here." Key stood up and headed for the door, muttering, "Interrupt my basketball game for this shit."

Mason saw Michael Key's patience evaporating, and with it, Mason's lucrative spot on Decatur's team. He was desperate to salvage the meeting. "Mr. Key, don't leave, that won't help you. Sit down and let's deal with this bullshit together. Please."

Key rested his head against the door. "I'm so done, man. Nobody is listening to me."

"Look, I know you're frustrated. I know you're afraid. Something terrible happened to Robin and now something terrible is happening to you. I'm here to put a stop to that. You got pulled into this and everything since then has shown you the system is not fair. That can shake anyone, so I get it."

"I thought I was doing the right thing. I know talking to the cops was stupid, but..." Michael trailed off.

"Hey, that's behind us. We can face it and fix it, Mr. Key, but you need to work with me."

Michael looked at him with sad, tired eyes. "I just need someone to believe me."

"I just spent a long time poring over the video of your interrogation. I watched every single second of you in that room, so I know exactly how they treated you. How they used every lie and trick at their disposal to get to you. I saw how they broke you down and made you say what they wanted to hear."

Mason looked at Michael, the slumped shoulders and look of resignation on his face. 'Innocent until proven guilty' was the code Mason claimed to live by, but now he was being challenged to buy into it.

"So if you're asking me if I believe you...after what I saw...yes, I do. I believe you, Mr. Key."

Michael walked back to the table, slowly lowered himself into the chair. He didn't speak, but looked straight into Mason, sizing him up. Mason remained silent, waiting for his client to react.

"Call me Mike."

Mason exhaled. "Will do, Mike. Now, I can't imagine how hard it is, being caged up for something you didn't do. But that just means we have a lot of work to do. So, shall we proceed?"

Michael nodded.

"Excellent. I need your approval to secure two expert witnesses." Mason slid a printout across the table that showed info about each one. "There's the false confession expert I mentioned earlier, and the other one can testify to the faulty police tactics. It'll cost you about ten grand, total. The MJB won't pay, they are only paying for Alice and her team."

"Yeah, MJB won't post my two hundred thousand dollar bail either. What do you think?" asked Michael as he scanned the page.

"Honestly, without these guys, a jury will find it hard to believe someone would confess to a crime they didn't commit. The default mindset is '*I would never confess if I were innocent*'. They just can't wrap their heads around it, especially with murder. These witnesses can neutralize that mindset."

"Ok, do it then," said Michael, rubbing his temples. "I'll need to take some money from my retirement account."

"Great. These guys will be worth the money. Beyond the confession, there doesn't appear to be a lot of strong evidence at this point. What we're working against is the assumption that when a woman is murdered, it's almost always the man closest to her."

"Yeah, but they can't convict me on an assumption, right?"

"Look, Mike, I meant what I said – I believe you. But forget about me, about Alice, whoever else. It's all about the twelve people who will sit in that jury box. Getting them to believe you is all that matters now. The truth is, their assumptions make a difference, but we can fight back, change the way they see things. That's how we're going to win this case."

"Got it," said Michael. He nodded his head and inhaled deeply, as if convincing himself it could be done.

"Good. I've got to run now, but I'll let Alice know you're good to go and the team will get to work. I'll be in touch soon, but in the meantime, just keep your head down, and stay out of trouble. If you think of anything that can help with your case, no matter how small, you tell the guards you want to see me and I'll be right back here."

**23**

After coming in off the street, Mason's eyes took a few seconds to adjust to the gloom inside Henley's Pub. Heavy canvas curtains kept the weak sunlight at bay and the overhead lights were dimmed to create an after-hours mood in the middle of the day. Mason scanned the dark wood booths but did not see the man he was looking for among the handful of dedicated day drinkers.

A whiskey-soaked voice called from the end of the bar, "Well, look who the cat dragged in!" Mason peered into the murk to see he had found his quarry, Jim Preston. When he reached the end of the bar, Jim greeted Mason with a firm handshake and hearty slap on the back.

Preston attended high school with Mason's father up north before going into law and serving as a prosecutor in the Milwaukee County DAs office. When the younger Mitchell graduated from law school, Jim tried to recruit him to the honorable side (as Mason's father called it), but Mason declined. He wanted the challenge of defense work, a fact his father never really understood or respected.

Mason and Jim were not exactly friends, but were always on friendly terms. Preston was avuncular, down-to-earth, one of the few lawyers Mason felt comfortable around. In his decades as a prosecutor, Jim had earned a reputation as a fine attorney before retiring about a year ago.

They faced each other just once in court, early in Mason's career, and his client was guilty as hell. The case was doomed from the start but Mason put up a good fight, mounting a spirited defense that pushed Preston on every point and drove the judge to distraction. Jim enjoyed the competition and took Mason out for drinks after the defendant was sentenced to twenty-five years. He became an unofficial mentor and regular drinking buddy, but before long, the two roles were indistinguishable.

Now, Jim was a widower and had yet to take up any hobbies in retirement, so Mason knew he'd be propping up the bar at Henley's on a Thursday afternoon.

"Imagine finding you here, Jim! How the hell are you?"

"Still tall and good looking. You?"

"Doing great. Busy as ever. And thanks again for referring me to Decatur. I wasn't aware you knew her."

"Yeah, I had a case a few years back prosecuting an overzealous cop and she handled the civil lawsuit. Sharp lady. Secured a pretty hefty amount from the city. Is she treating you ok so far?"

"Just fine, thanks. It's a learning curve, but I'm handling it."

Jim nodded and drained his glass. "What are you having? I'll get this round."

"Hold up," said Mason. "How 'bout we get some dice and make the house pay for a round?"

The bartender looked up at Mason, then to Jim, and shook his head. "I'm not doing it right now, Preston. Sorry."

Jim pulled a sarcastic frown and turned back to Mason. "You heard the man. What can I get you?"

"Come on, old timer," taunted Mason. "How about you and me shake for it then?"

"Are you turning down a free drink just for the fun of it?" asked Preston

"Exactly. Now get the dice. The drink will taste better when I win it from you."

"Have it your way, Mitchell." Jim caught the bartender's eye and said, "Danny, can you help us out?"

Danny produced a brown leather cup from under the till and placed it on the bar between the two lawyers. The leather was mottled from years of spills and thousands of sweaty, greasy hands. Two rearing stags were embossed on the outside of the cup, inside was well-worn rawhide. Next to the cup Danny placed five dice, translucent green with white pips.

"I don't want all the noise at the bar, fellas. Take it to that booth over there, ok?" said Danny.

Jim and Mason mockingly bowed, but did as they were told and settled into the corner booth.

Bar Dice and Shake of the Day are central to Wisconsin tavern culture. For as long as the state had been serving liquor, dice games were part of the bar experience. The games had too many local variations to count, but the basic idea was the same – you had to open the game by rolling a one, known as an 'ace', and get the most points in three shakes of the dice.

Mason pointed at his old friend, "Be my guest. Age before beauty."

Jim chuckled and placed the cup in his right palm. He shook it side to side as he raised it above his head. In one swift motion, he inverted the cup and brought it down, slamming the open mouth against the tabletop with a resounding smack.

He paused for effect, then slowly lifted the leather cup to reveal the dice. "An ace and two fives! I'll keep those." Jim set the three scoring dice aside, deposited the other two in the cup, then repeated the shake and smack. He was disappointed to see a pair of twos.

"Hmph." Jim popped them back in the cup. "Ok, third time's the charm!"

His final clattering roll produced a three and a four.

"Tough luck," said Mason, counting up the dice, "but thirty-five isn't bad."

"Don't patronize me, Mitchell. Just roll the dice."

Mason took his turn with a good deal less gusto than his opponent but the third and final roll put him over the top. "Well, well! Forty-four! We have a winner."

Jim headed to the bar to pay off his dice bet and returned with two blood red cocktails that Mason could not identify.

"Gee, thanks. Looks...unusual."

"My rule is the loser buys *and* picks any goddamn drink he wants," said Jim.

Mason took a cautious sip and felt it burn down his throat. Whatever it was, the recipe packed a punch.

"So, you got your free drink," said Jim, "are you going to tell me why you're here now?"

Mason smiled. "I need some advice. On the Key case."

"Not easy working with Decatur, is it?"

"Yeah, I suppose, but that's not it. It's something else I can't get out of my mind."

"Shoot, kid."

"Last night I met with Michael Key, and it was...odd."

"How so?"

"He just, um, professed his innocence to me."

Jim was nonplussed. "What, is this new for you? They all say they're innocent."

"No. Not like that. He really meant it. We're talking Shawshank, Andy Dufresne innocent," said Mason, drawing a laugh from Preston. "Seriously, it wasn't the typical denial. He didn't try to snow me and over-explain, or nitpick at the corners of the evidence. This was a direct plea for me to believe in his innocence. Actually, it was more of a demand."

"And what did you say?"

"I told him the truth, that I believed him."

"Dear god! Mason, I had assumed you were past the true believer stage."

"Jim, give me a break. I know bullshit, and this felt different."

"*Felt* different, you say? I think maybe you're a bit burned out, looking for redemption with that one righteous client. I've seen it before. Thing is, your job is not about redemption and you don't do salvation. You want those, go to church or volunteer in Haiti. Your job is to defend the client to the best of your ability, and at the end of the trial, you forget the result and saddle up for the next one."

"I know the fucking job, Jim. I'm not burned out, but I am kinda freaked out. That's why I came to you in the first place. The thing with Key last night felt different, and I'm trying to figure out if I can trust it."

Jim pushed his drink aside, laid both hands flat on the table, and studied Mason much like Key had the night before. "Hmph. Ok then. If you want to be sure your gut isn't messing with you, pay attention to the little things. The truth always comes out in the details."

"Right."

"I always found that during a trial, a hearing, or in your case, a jail visit with a client, when one little piece of truth showed up it would stand out, plain as day. In this line of work, we spend every day wading through a swamp of falsehood and misdirection, so when you encounter something undeniably genuine, it's almost impossible to miss. I'm sure it's happened to you before."

Mason snorted. "It has, but only to confirm that my client was guilty or that a witness was full of shit. Until now, I've never had that one little piece of truth show up and make me think *innocent*."

Preston smiled proudly. "That's because you, my son, are a true defense lawyer."

"But that's what it was like," Mason continued, "and that's why I noticed it. There was something about the way Key acted, the way he spoke, it just hit me in a different way."

"Sounds like you have your answer then," said Jim. He pushed the dice cup toward Mason. "Now stop stalling and roll the dice. I'm thirsty for another drink, so hurry up and lose."

**24**

Lori's old alarm clock went off just after seven on the morning of her sentencing. She hadn't slept a wink. In the years since she moved out, the bedroom, right across the hall from her parents, had been kept just as she'd left it, only cleaner. Staying in her old room added to the feeling of limbo that surrounded Lori since the night of her arrest, and her nights were plagued by sleeplessness. It had been two months since her plea and today, on the morning of her sentencing, Lori's body was leaden with fatigue while her mind raced.

She shuffled downstairs to the kitchen, hopeful that a coffee would chase away her stupor. Lori slipped a plastic pod into the machine and hit the button bearing a pictogram of three droplets. She closed her eyes and listened to the comforting whirr and gurgle of the brewing process.

Lori brought her cup to the table and watched the steam rise. Last week Mason had driven up from Milwaukee to sit with her at this same table and review the pre-sentence report. When they came to the sentencing recommendation – two years in prison followed by three years' probation – it knocked the wind out of her. Mason had tried to calm her down, explaining this was only because of David's statements to the department but the judge still had leeway and that a convincing argument could be made for no prison time. But as much as Mason minimized the recommendation, Lori could see he was angry about it.

For her part, she was scared to death. After the four days spent in jail, for Lori, prison was a nightmare scenario. Ever since her arrest, the fear lurked in the wings of her mind, but in the days since reading the report, it was center stage, producing vivid scenes of isolation and brutality.

For Mason, the sentencing recommendation allowed him to push for using the documents David put so much stake in. With the loss of her freedom now looming, Lori had quickly relented.

When Lori's family was brought up to speed, they reacted poorly. There were loudly voiced recriminations about the choice to accept the plea deal. Lori didn't blame anyone for being mad, but she was left feeling stupid and guilty.

"I thought I heard you get up." Lori looked up and saw her mother at the top of the stairs. Carrie squinted into the half-light, clutching her pale pink terry-cloth robe tight against her body. "You ok, angel?"

"Not sure."

Carrie gingerly made her way down the stairs and crossed to the kitchen. She sat down and stroked her daughter's head. "Tell me about it."

"I don't know. Nervous, scared, anxious, all of it. Couldn't sleep."

"Me too. I'm a wreck. Can't stop worrying about you."

"I'm sorry, mom."

"Don't apologize to me for anything, angel. I know your case, your so-called crime, and it's not fair. David was a monster to you. I just wish you had told me, maybe I could have helped. But he deserved what you did to him, and worse!" Carrie stopped, surprised by her own anger. She softened her voice and continued, "If you went to trial, no jury would convict you."

"We've been over this, mom." This rehashing made Lori's head hurt. "The plea was my best option."

Carrie shook her head.

"What if I went to trial and lost?" said Lori, and shrugged away from her mother's hand. "You want to be visiting me in Taycheedah till I'm forty-five? This way, at worst, I only get a couple years." Saying it out loud sapped her anger in an instant.

"David caused all this, not you!" said Carrie. "He should be the one going to prison!"

"Mom, you need to stop." Lori paused and took a sip. She wondered what coffee tasted like in prison. "Look, remember what Mason said? Maybe I'll just get probation. I'm not the kind of person they want to put in prison."

"I hope so, angel," said Carrie. "I have been praying so hard!"

"Thanks, mom." Lori got up and put her cup next to the sink. "I gotta go get ready. You should, too. We leave in an hour."

---

Mason steered his Mercedes into one of the ninety-minute parking spots by the front doors of the Waukesha County Courthouse. He turned the car off and sat there, a hum emanating from his gut. Mason was nervous, and he was almost never nervous for court.

Mason's typical client, by the time he met them, had been chewed up by life. Born into a bad home or no home at all, surrounded by substance issues, all kinds of abuse, in and out of custody. The sociological studies called these Adverse Childhood Experiences. Nine times out of ten, these ACE's led directly to a date in court standing next to someone like Mason.

For his typical client, the criminal justice system was just the latest in a series of societal structures to fail them. And while some committed grim and horrifying crimes, others were only trying to survive in an unfortunate zip code. Mason would defend each one to the best of his ability and a jury of their peers would inevitably find them guilty.

His typical clients had 'people' in prison and survival skills ingrained during a hard knock life. They at least had a shot, however faint, at coping on the inside.

Lori was not his typical client. She would be ignorant and alone. She would be prey. He took a deep breath, straightened his tie in the rearview mirror and stepped from the car.

Walking in he dropped his briefcase, wallet, and phone in a tub by the scanner and walked through the security portal. *Beeeeep!*

"Suspenders?" offered Mason. The guard swung a metal detector wand in a vague arc from Mason's shoes to his neckline, then waved him through. Mason grabbed his belongings from the plastic tray and started for the conference room.

He arrived to see Lori and her family seated in a cluster on one side of the room. The chair closest to the door was left vacant.

"Morning, everyone," said Mason. "Good to see you all here." He sat down directly across from his client. "How are you feeling?"

"Fine," said Lori, her voice shaking. "Do you think I'm going to prison?"

"She cannot handle prison," insisted Carrie. "She'll...I don't know. She just can't!"

Mason held up his hands. "Whoa. Let's all take a minute. Nothing is set in stone and there's a good chance that prison is off the menu, ok? It's up to the judge, and I don't think he likes David too much after his ranting and raving last time." The family looked at him, waiting for more. "Remember, Lori has a clean record, strong family support, decent employment history," Mason counted on his fingers as he spoke, "and she's white."

"What the hell does that matter?" said Tom.

"White defendants are sent to prison far less frequently than black defendants. It's not right, and I'm not going to get into the reasons why, but that's the way it is."

Tom looked unsure if he should be angry, but couldn't think of what to say.

"You said you saw me on TV, right?" said Mason. "Well, that lawyer I'm assisting has tons of statistics about sentencing disparities by race and gender, and they all favor Lori."

"So she might get probation?" asked Carrie.

"From this judge, yes," answered Mason.

Lori's eyes were already wet with tears but she nodded and straightened in her chair. "I hope so."

"Now, as we discussed," continued Mason, "David is going to speak today and you probably won't like what you hear. No matter what he says or how he says it, just stay calm and don't say a word. Not just Lori. All of you. We'll have our chance to talk, too. I'm going to bring up those documents from David. That means they become public record, ok?"

"Yes," she replied.

A knock on the door was followed by a bailiff poking his head in. "Judge is ready."

"Ok, thanks. There in a minute," said Mason. He turned to Lori, "You ready?"

"I guess."

———

Twenty minutes later, the prosecutor concluded his sentencing remarks, staying true to the deal made with Mason. "The State has agreed to abide by the pre-sentence report. Two years initial confinement with three years extended supervision strikes the right balance of the Gallion factors, and I ask you to follow that recommendation, your honor."

"Thank you, Mr. Thurston. Does the victim wish to say anything before we turn to the defense?

"Yes, he would like to speak, your honor."

"Very well. But I caution you, Mr. Wells, any outbursts and you will be removed from this courtroom. Do you understand me?"

David looked to the prosecutor, then back to the judge, and nodded.

Judge Hulse leaned forward and stared David down. "I need you to say out loud that you understand."

David stood up and replied, "I understand, your honor."

"Ok. You can step up to the microphone. Speak clearly for the court reporter."

Mason turned and made eye contact with the members of Lori's family, his silent reminder to stay strong and remain calm.

David placed a sheaf of handwritten pages on the narrow lectern, adjusted the microphone, and began to read. "Your honor, Lori's brutal attack on me that night changed my life forever. Sometimes I wished I died that night, so I wouldn't have to suffer so much. Just seeing her here in this courtroom fills me with…"

The sound of his voice hit Lori like a punch to the gut. A wave of revulsion washed over her as David warmed to his subject matter. He described a night of overwhelming terror that he would "never, ever forget". It was a tale of violent fury and gory details, coming back again and again to how he feared for his life.

Even though Lori had no memory of the stabbing, she could clearly hear the lies in his account. David was unchanged, and the crass manipulations were now plain for her to see. *How did I let it come to this?* she thought. A mix of anger and shame rose inside her as David spoke, and she felt diminished by both. Mason looked up from his note taking and sensed her difficulty. He laid his hand on Lori's forearm and leaned over to whisper, "It's just words. Let him dig the hole."

David went on, outlining the hardships he faced in the immediate wake of the attack and in the months that followed. He read from page after page, occasionally pausing for a sip of water before droning on with his hit list of grievances.

*"When I remove my shirt at the beach or the pool, children are frightened by my scar."*

*"I'm afraid that the emotional damage she did will prevent me from ever having a relationship again."*

*"How can I ever again trust in the people closest to me, your honor?"*

*"I live in fear that if Lori remains free, she will find me and finish the job she started that night."*

The entire exhausting performance seemed nothing more than an attempt to make one person pay for every slight or setback in David's life.

After thirty minutes, an exasperated Judge Hulse asked David to wrap up his remarks. Mason had long since stopped taking notes and sat calmly, biding his time. David closed by asking that the amended charge be thrown out and for Lori to serve the original forty year maximum in prison.

Hulse waved him to a stop. "Mr. Wells, even if I wanted to do that, and I do not, we are here because both parties have agreed to the reduced sentence outlined earlier. Now, if you have nothing further to add–"

David thrust his finger toward Lori. "She tried to kill me and she deserves to rot in jail! Thank you, your honor." He snatched up the papers and walked back to his seat in the gallery, across the aisle from Lori's family, his head held high.

Mason had never seen a less sympathetic stabbing victim. He was confident the marathon statement had not moved the judge. It was almost enough to make Mason think a trial would have been the better option.

"Thank you, Mr. Wells," said Hulse. "Attorney Mitchell, let's hear your sentencing argument."

Mason rose and cleared his throat. "Thank you, your honor. As you know, I filed letters in support of Ms. Wells prior to this hearing. Many are from family members, some of whom are sitting in the galley today. In addition, I filed letters of support from her employer and her pastor." Mason always tried to get a letter from clergy, and judges lapped it up.

"As you can see in the pre-sentence report, Ms. Wells has no criminal record, no prior arrests, and just one single speeding ticket. Let's see, it was," Mason looked down to consult his notes, "fifty-seven in a forty zone."

Mason paused, letting Lori's squeaky clean record linger in the air.

"But I would note that Ms. Wells has three prior law enforcement contacts as a purported victim, all at the hands of Mr. Wells. Although, in each case, she ultimately declined to press charges against her husband. This should not surprise the court, as abused women frequently recant or back down from their abuser."

David jumped up and shouted, "Abuser? She stabbed me! I'm the victim here, not her!"

"Mr. Wells!" said Hulse. "One more outburst like that and I will find you in contempt. You had your chance to speak, so now you sit down and be quiet. Do I make myself clear!"

David shot a spiteful look at Lori, then sank back into his chair and folded his arms.

"Continue, Attorney Mitchell," said the judge.

"Thank you, your honor. I think it is evident that Ms. Wells was abused in this relationship. And while she was not in imminent danger at the time of the stabbing, she legitimately feared for her safety. So, while the incident does not meet the standard for self-defense – and that is why she plead – the abuse she endured at the hands of Mr. Wells mitigates her actions."

Mason paused, took a sip of water. He was getting into a groove, but the anxiety persisted.

"I am filing with the court two documents that I believe are relevant." Mason rose and handed the pages over to the clerk, who file-stamped them and passed them to the judge. "Both clearly demonstrate the type of power and control Mr. Wells exerted over my client." Mason paused to let Hulse digest the submissions.

"The first is a letter written by Ms. Wells at the behest of her husband, dated seven months before the incident. The letter was dictated to my client by Mr. Wells. The central message of the rambling two and a half pages states, preemptively, that she would be lying if she ever claimed Mr. Wells hit her."

He moved to the second document.

"The other document is a contract of sorts, drafted by David Wells almost a year ago, just after they were married. According to the terms he lays out, she must never ask to move farther than fifty miles from his parents' hometown. She must agree that if they had an unplanned pregnancy, she would forfeit her parental rights. Furthermore, the contract forbids her from working any job he does not pre-approve, and stipulates that he has final approval of her daily wardrobe."

Mason paused allowing the judge to absorb the submission.

"Mr. Wells put my client under extreme pressure to sign both documents! Finally, she relented."

Lori and her family had reviewed these materials last week, but hearing them discussed in open court made the facts more painful.

Mason continued, "What is most telling is how we came into possession of these documents. After he was stabbed, David asked police officers to retrieve them from the apartment he shared with my client. He felt this nonsensical letter and warped marital contract supported his claim that Lori was abusive toward him! I'll be honest, your honor. After reading them, I'm inclined to believe he deserved to get stabbed, and amazed it was only once."

"Counselor!" yelled the judge.

"I'm sorry, I... my apologies to the court." Mason paused and took a deep breath, but the hum in his gut refused to go away. "My point, your honor, is that Ms. Wells is not a danger to the community at large.  She is not part of society's criminal element. Rather, she was a trapped woman who, when pushed to the breaking point by an abusive partner, lashed out, albeit inappropriately. But, with her family support and up to now clean record, my client is ready to resume her life as a productive member of this community. Given the totality of the circumstances, I hope you'll agree that probation is the appropriate course of action–"

"Probation?!" David was on his feet again. "Probation is nothing!" The bailiffs were on him before Hulse had a chance to speak. David continued to denounce Lori, Judge Hulse, and the justice system as the court officers dragged him from the room.

"I want to be clear. There will be no more outbursts," said Hulse, then pointed at Mason, "or inappropriate arguments today. Everyone in this room will display proper court decorum. Have I made myself clear?"

"Yes, your honor," answered Mason.

"Let's hope so. Now, you may continue."

"As I was saying, Wisconsin law requires the court to first consider probation and to impose the least restrictive terms that fulfill the objectives of the sentence. Given Ms. Wells' history and the circumstances surrounding this case, probation meets all sentencing criteria. Thank you, your honor."

"Ms. Wells, if you wish, this is your chance to address the court."

Lori looked to her mother for support, then stood and spoke clearly. "Thank you, Judge Hulse. I don't know where to start. I think my lawyer," she swallowed hard but the tears were already streaming down her cheeks, "said it best but I want to tell you I am truly sorry. I did not ever want to hurt David. I know what I did was wrong. I so badly want to remember the details of the incident, but I can't. It keeps me up at night." She paused to blow her nose and compose herself. "Please don't send me to prison. Please. I want to stay with my family. I want to go back to my job. I promise you will never see me again. I promise that–" Wracking sobs overwhelmed her, and she sank back into her chair.

"Ok, thank you, Ms. Wells," said Judge Hulse, his features inscrutable. Most judges rarely emoted, but it still put Mason on edge. "It is the duty of this court to take into account the gravity of the offense, the character of the defendant, and the need to protect the community. With that in mind, Ms. Wells," Hulse fixed his gaze on Lori and continued, "I note that you have good character, no criminal record, a solid work history, and strong family support. All of those things are excellent. On the other side of that coin, I can't look past the fact that, unlike many who come before this court, you had strong role models to teach you right from wrong." Hulse waved a hand toward the Bedford family in the gallery.

"Blessed with this support network and equipped with the tools to deal with adversity, I would expect you to make better choices." Many judges liked to play the firm but fair parent. Mason was used to Hulse's act, and patted Lori's arm to reassure her all was well.

"I don't believe you set out that night on a mission to hurt David Wells," said Hulse. "I have full confidence you have no interest in 'finishing the job' and that you will abide by the no-contact order I am entering. In my view, you are not a threat to the community at large and will not likely be back before this or any court in the future."

In the gallery, Carrie inhaled sharply and clutched Tom's hand in an iron grip.

Hulse removed his glasses and continued, "Yet, when set against the seriousness of the crime, I struggle to see how this is not a prison case. Therefore, I am sentencing you to two years initial confinement and three years of extended supervision, sentence to start forthwith." Without pausing, Hulse banged his gavel and walked off the bench to his chambers.

"Wait. What did he say?" asked Lori. She sat rooted to her seat, dumbstruck. Nothing made sense. A dull ringing rose in her ears.

"Nooo!" cried Carrie. "You can't do this!"

Lori tried to focus on Mason's face. "Am I...what did he say?"

"Two years in and three years out," said Mason. He was stunned. "Um, they're going to take you to prison today. Right now. I am so sorry."

Lori blinked rapidly and shook her head. "No. What about probation? You said probation!"

"I know. I know. I'll start the appeal paperwork immediately," said Mason. The hum in his stomach turned into a steady buzz. "I am so sorry." He could feel Tom Bedford's eyes boring into him.

A bailiff was walking over to their table. Mason asked Lori, "Do you have anything you want to give me to give to your family?" She looked puzzled. "Cell phone, jewelry, any valuables. They might go missing at the prison," said Mason. "Give them to me now!"

The bailiff asked her to put both hands behind her back. Lori's eyes went wide in panic. She quickly pulled the rings from her fingers and passed her purse to Mason before her wrists were pulled back and clasped in handcuffs.

"I'll give these to your mother," said Mason. "I'm sorry." The bailiff led her toward a doorway to the right of the judge's bench.

"Mom!" Lori shouted.

"Angel!" Carrie screamed at the bailiff, "Just let me hug her one time, please!"

"Can't do it," said the other deputy. "Safety reasons." Lori disappeared through the doorway. Carrie collapsed into her husband's arms and let out a long, pained wail.

Mason tapped Lori's aunt on the shoulder. "Hey, you can all go to the conference room. I'll be there in a minute." He grabbed his briefcase and walked past the gallery, trying not to rush. Outside the courtroom he turned right, ducked into the men's room, and locked himself in a stall. He sat down and sobbed silently. *What the fuck is wrong with me?* he thought. *It's just a case. It's just a fucking case, get a grip, Mitchell.* He retrieved the flask from his briefcase and took a long swig. Maybe it wasn't just a case. It was all the cases, catching up to him at once. He stared at the door, focusing on a cartoonish drawing of a woman's face in red marker. Mason tried to process what happened. The sentence, the hum in his gut, his angry freelancing in the courtroom. *She did not deserve that. It helps nobody.* One more long swig and two peppermint breath strips were followed by three deep breaths. "Fuck it," he muttered to himself. "Time to face the firing squad."

Mason entered the conference room, saw now two empty chairs, and elected to stand. Tom and Cindy were trying to console Carrie. Her sobbing had softened but she kept her face buried in her hands.

"What the hell happened?" yelled Ken. "You promised – no prison!"

"I didn't promise anything!" said Mason. "Look, I'm sorry. But I didn't think it would happen. We made a strong case for probation."

"Well, what now? I mean, where will she go?" Cindy had joined in and the questions came in a flurry. "When can we see her? Does she need anything from us? Can we appeal? What do we do next?"

"First off, let me explain her sentence. She got two years in, meaning Lori will be released from prison two years from today, minus the four days she served before."

"Can she get out earlier? Like, with good behavior or something?" asked Cindy.

"Sadly, no. Wisconsin has something called Truth in Sentencing, meaning you do not get any good time credit. So, if she keeps her head down and stays out of trouble she will be out in two years. Then she'll be on parole for another three years."

"Where will she go?" asked Aunt Cindy.

"Later today, they're going to take her to Taycheedah Correctional Institution for Women. It's a couple hours north of–"

"We know it," said Ken. The prison was a ten minute drive due west from Lori's childhood home.

"She will probably stay there for a year, maybe eighteen months," said Mason. "Then, if all goes well, she'll be transferred to a minimum security prison."

Lori's father, who had been glaring at Mason, addressed the room in a growl, "How can we listen to anything this guy says now?"

"Tom, you're not helping," said Cindy.

Carrie had calmed down enough to ask her own question. "When can I see her?"

"Maybe four weeks. Could be–"

"Four weeks!? Oh my god, that's forever!" shrieked Carrie.

"Could be more, could be less," said Mason. He wanted out of this room. "She has to go through A&E, that's assessment and evaluation, before she can receive visitors. Then you can see her."

"What about you? Can you see her sooner? Can you see her and tell her we love her? That we're going to appeal and get her out of there? Can you do that? Mason, you need to tell her." Carrie was becoming hysterical, tripping over her words.

"I can write her a letter and make sure she gets it once she arrives," said Mason. "And I will tell her anything you want." He took Carrie's hand and looked in her eyes. "But I'll be honest, we can't pin our hopes on the appeal."

Mason knew that almost no criminal appeals were successful. Of cases that went to trial and were appealed, less than five percent were successful. And when the defendant pled guilty, the percentage dropped to less than one percent. Clients and their families never understood that appeal could only deal with errors of law. It was no longer about the facts of the case. With her guilty plea, Lori waived almost all legal challenges. She had no real grounds for appeal. Her conviction and sentence would stand.

"I'll find out when she can receive visits and be in touch in a day or two, ok? Until you hear from me, just, uh, stay strong. She's going to get through this. I'm on it." The anxiety spread up into Mason's chest, strangling his pep talk. "Again, I am so sorry." None of the Bedford's responded. Mason picked up his briefcase and left, closing the door quietly behind him.

———

Four minutes later, Mason pulled over at a boarded-up plaza a few blocks from the courthouse. His breathing was finally slowing down. He pulled out his phone and linked it to the car stereo.

"Call Jalen."

The operating system obeyed with a stilted reply, 'Calling Jalen Demps.' Mason put the phone down and dug the flask out of his briefcase. It was empty.

After five rings a familiar, steady voice filled the car. "Mason. What's good?"

"Hey, I have a question. Your girl Marge, is she still up at Taycheedah?"

"Yup. She's got another three years."

Mason pumped his fist in triumph. "Shit. Sorry to hear that. Wish I'd handled her case. Anyway, maybe I can help her out a bit, but I need a favor. Where can you and I meet?"

The line went quiet for several seconds. Just as Mason was about to repeat the question, Jalen replied, "Not the usual. The other spot."

"Great. See you there in twenty minutes. Appreciate you." Before the words were out of Mason's mouth, Jalen ended the call.

———

Two days later, Mason sat at the desk in his home office, staring at the blinking cursor on his computer screen, which read 11:37 p.m. Minutes ago, he had typed the greeting, *Dear Lori,* and then froze, unsure of what to write next. Normally, clients had no further contact with Mason after they were sent to prison. Some held a grudge against him for their sentence, others shifted focus to the appeal process with their new lawyer. Most just wanted to serve their time and be left alone. For Mason's part, his job was usually done after sentencing. But Lori's parents had retained Mason to represent her in other matters and he had promised them he would write.

"Professional, but friendly," whispered Mason. "Try to be normal."

*Dear Lori,*

*I hope this letter finds you well, or at least hanging in there. I assume that since your parents live close by, you will be getting frequent visitors once you are out of A&E. I'm sure that will be nice.*

*As you know, David has begun divorce proceedings, and he is not going away quietly. His lawyer informed me that David will press for everything he can get his hands on. Once I have a settlement demand I will come to Taycheedah to go over all of that with you. My best advice for the time being is to just forget about him and focus on yourself. I will do what I can to have the divorce processed quickly and cleanly so that you can move on.*

*Other than that, I know the case is over and I can't be of too much help in your current situation, but I am always here if you have any questions or concerns.*

*I'll close this letter with a quote I came across recently. Perhaps you'll take some small inspiration from it:*

*'One who gains strength from overcoming obstacles possesses the only strength which can overcome adversity.' – Albert Schweitzer*

*Best,*

*Mason Mitchell*

"It'll do," said Mason. Clyde waddled into the room and sat down between Mason's feet, staring up at him expectantly. Mason smiled. "Ok, we'll go for a walk, you little goof."

*PS - I'm enclosing a photo of my dog, Clyde. He's always there for me, always cheers me up. I thought maybe he'd be good for you to have around, too.*

**25**

S ammi Mueller had traveled the eleven miles from James Madison High down to the Third Ward, located the converted old Cream City Brick warehouse, and was now six feet from the glass double doors of the office he was looking for. Sammi stood rooted in place, his foot wouldn't stop tapping and he couldn't keep himself from gnawing on his black painted thumbnail. He watched the woman at the desk on the other side of the glass talking on the phone. The nameplate on her desk identified her as Linda Green. Sammi looked again at the simple geometric logo that adorned the left door and the silver lettering below that read:

*MITCHELL & ASSOCIATES, LLC*

Sammi's pulse raced. Why had he come here? This was stupid. None of this was his problem, but if he went through with this it could become a big problem. He was about to turn away when the woman at the desk hung up the phone, looked up and waved at him to come in. *Fuck it. I'm already here*, thought Sammi, and went in.

He scanned the empty waiting area, then approached Linda's desk. "Hi. I'm uh..." he paused, unsure of how to even begin.

"How can I help you, dear?" asked Linda. She was unsure of how to take this new visitor, dressed in baggy jeans and a black shirt. The look wasn't her taste but she had to admit the kid's blue-streaked hair and eye makeup were very well done.

"My name is Sammi. Um…" he looked around again, taking in the plaques and degrees on the wall, feeling very out of his depth.

"Yes, Sammi?"

"I want to, uh…I want to speak to Mason Mitchell."

Linda's tone became more skeptical, "And what is this about?"

"He's one of the lawyers for Michael Key, right?"

This question seemed to put Linda on alert. "Yes, that's right. Do you have an appointment?"

"No, but, I just need to tell him something."

Linda's dubious expression deepened. "Tell him something about what, exactly?"

"It's about Ms. Key."

Linda raised her eyebrows in a silent question.

"Um, Ms. Key is, I mean, was my teacher. I know something about her and maybe it could be important. But it's private, ok? So is he in or not?"

"He might be, dear. Let me just check. You can have a seat over there." Linda pointed to the small waiting area, three aluminum and black cloth chairs surrounding a low maple table bearing a small pile of somewhat recent magazines and an outdated Wisconsin Legal Directory.

Sammi took a seat furthest from the front desk and kept his gaze on the table. He wondered if anyone ever actually looked through the directory.

Linda picked up the phone, "There's a young man named Sammi here. A student from James Madison. He has something to tell you about Ms. Key. Apparently it's important." She paused and nodded, never taking her eyes off Sammi. "Uh-huh. Ok. I will."

She replaced the receiver and waved Sammi over. "Mr. Mitchell has a very busy schedule today, but he can give you a few minutes right now. He'll see you in the conference room."

To Sammi, Linda took the same tone as the admin staff at school, like she assumed he was wasting her time.

"It's just around the corner to the right," said Linda. "Go ahead and have a seat there. Do you want water or coffee, dear?"

"No, I'm ok. Thanks."

Sammi followed the directions to the glass-walled conference room and sat down facing the door. His foot still wouldn't stop tapping as he went over the details in his head again.

One minute later, Mason strode into the room, set his coffee cup on the glass tabletop, and extended his hand. "Hi, Sammi. Mason Mitchell. Linda tells me you have some information?" He sat down across the table from Sammi and set a notepad and pen in front of him.

"Yeah. I dunno. I think it could be useful but I'm not sure."

"Ok, well I can be the judge of that. Did Linda offer you water or coffee?"

"Yeah. I'm fine. Maybe later."

"Ok then. Please, what would you like to tell me about Ms. Key?"

Sammi glanced at the notepad and looked around the room. Now that it was time to talk, he felt like a fool for coming all the way down there.

"It's ok," said Mason. "There's no recording or anything. I might take a few notes as we're talking. But nothing has to go beyond this room. Not right now. That'll depend on what you tell me."

"Right. Um, I don't really know where to start."

"How old are you, Sammi...?"

"Mueller. It's Sammi Mueller. And I'm seventeen."

"Alright. So, you were one of Robin Key's students?"

"Not this year, no. But last year I had her for Social Studies."

"Ok, that's a start. And what's this information you think might be useful?"

"Is anyone going to know I talked to you?"

"Sammi, this is just a conversation between you and me. We're not in court so you're not under oath. But I'm not your lawyer so there's no attorney-client privilege. Still, nothing has to go beyond this room right now."

"But maybe eventually?"

"Like I said, that depends on what you're about to tell me. But I want to hear it first, and if it's important, we can figure out what to do with it."

Sammi sat sullenly, fidgeting as he mulled it over. Mason could see the kid was likely a misfit at school. Sammi was probably used to keeping his head down. Probably unsuccessfully. Right now, Mason just needed Sammi to talk.

"Look, I know you might be a little nervous, but you came all the way here today for a reason."

Sammi nodded but didn't look up.

Mason sighed. "Sammi, I have a packed day, but I do want to hear you out, so we need to get this moving."

Sammi inhaled deeply. "Alright, fine. Ms. Key was having an affair," he said, then let the air out, "with Mr. Warnock."

Mason picked up his pen. "And who's Mr. Warnock?"

"He's the chemistry teacher."

"And you're sure about this?"

"Oh yeah, I'm sure."

"How's that?"

"I saw them doing it. In the library at school. I saw them."

"You saw them doing what, exactly?"

"I saw them like, you know. They were going at it."

Mason jotted down a note and paused. "Ok, Sammi. Let's take a step back. You were in the library at school. When was this? What date?"

"I'm not exactly sure, but I think it was the beginning of October. It was only a week or two before they told us that she had been killed."

"So, this was during the school day?"

"Not really, no. It was after hours. Maybe around five-thirty."

"And what were you doing in the library so late?"

"It's no big deal, really. I was just there."

"Humor me and tell me why you were there."

"I just go there sometimes after classes are out. For various reasons, I don't always like to go home, so I go into the library and hide out until the librarian leaves, then I hang out and read or do stuff on my phone for a couple hours. It's just a quiet space and nobody comes around. Until the janitor, his name's Eliot, until he gets there, around six-thirty, and tells me I have to go. But at least he's nice about it."

"And so you were in the library one day after classes, by yourself?"

"Yes."

"And you saw Robin Key with this chemistry teacher, Mr. Warnock?"

"Yeah, they came after I was there for a while already."

"Could you see them clearly?"

"Sure. I was in my normal spot on the upper level, on the side where the windows are. I like the light it gets at that part of the day. Best Wi-Fi signal, too. From there, it's easy for me to stay hidden but I can see the main doors, and most of the main floor, and the study rooms on the other side."

Mason was scribbling quickly and continued his questioning without looking up, "Ok. And what were they doing?"

"When I saw them come in it wasn't like they were sneaking, but they were quiet. And they were saying 'Hello? Anybody there?' but I didn't answer. I got under the table I was at. I didn't want to be bothered and...I dunno, I just figured they'd go away."

"But they didn't?"

"No. They walked around a bit down on the main level and kind of looked the place over. I guess they thought they were alone because they looked at each other and smiled. Then they came up the stairs and they were giggling, kind of like he was chasing her, then they started holding hands. I started to freak out that they would find me, but they went to where the study rooms are, across from where I was. Those rooms are always locked, but Robin," Sammi caught himself and looked at Mason, "sorry, Ms. Key took out some keys, and Mr. Warnock kind of moved in behind her, being all like, you know. He had his hands on her."

"He was touching her in more than just a friendly way?"

"He had his hands all over her hips and her butt and he was sticking his face into her neck. It was most definitely more than friendly."

"Ok, just checking. What happened then?"

"They went in and locked the room but the door and front wall of each study room is all glass except for the section across the middle that's like blurred, you know?"

"Frosted glass. Like this?" Mason pointed at the wall of the conference room.

Sammi nodded. "Yeah, exactly. If that's what you call it. Frosted glass."

"So, could you still sort of see what Ms. Key and Mr. Warnock were doing in the study room?"

Sammi took another deep breath and nodded slowly. "Yes. I mean...I couldn't see them from head to toe the entire time, thank god, but I could see enough to know what they were doing."

Mason paused. "And?"

Sammi sighed loudly. "You need me to spell it out?"

"That's kind of how this works. They were in the study room together. You could see them. They were, what? Engaged in...?"

"They were engaged in, ugh...all sorts of...sex. It was a lot of just whatever. They were definitely having sex." Sammi threw his head back, as if exhausted. "So there you have it, ok?"

"Almost. How long did this go on for?"

"Uh, I really don't know. I checked my phone to see how late it was and if Eliot was gonna be there soon and I think it was maybe five or ten minutes. I can't say for sure but I don't think it was super long."

"That's fine. And then after they were finished with the–"

Sammi closed his eyes, a pained expression on his face. "Please don't say it."

"After they were finished, they just left?"

"Well, first they, oh god, this is gross."

"What?"

"I couldn't totally see it but I think they used, like, I dunno, wet wipes or something to clean the table, and then I could hear them talking. Couldn't make out the words or anything but he got louder like he was angry or something. Then she kind of yelled at him, something like 'It's not your decision' or 'It's my decision', I can't totally remember. Then he left. By himself. He went down the stairs and out of the library, fast. I saw her sitting there alone in the study room. She looked sad. Or kind of mad. Maybe both? She just sat there staring at the wall and I kept watching her. I couldn't help it. The whole thing was so weird but I felt bad for her. It was like I just saw a breakup. After a minute, she sat up straight and nodded her head and said 'Fine'. Then she locked up the room and left."

"And neither one of them saw you?"

"No, they never looked my way. Not gonna lie, I'm pretty sure I was holding my breath the whole time. I didn't make a sound. After they were both gone I waited a few minutes. I wanted to get out of there, but I really didn't want to run into them in the halls so I only left when Eliot showed up. He said hi but I think I kind of walked right past him. I was freaked out. The whole thing just felt gross. And sad."

Mason leaned back and looked over his notes. "Thank you very much, Sammi. You were right."

"What do you mean?"

"I think what you just told me will be useful."

"Ok, great. So, is that it then?"

"Almost. Do you have classes with Mr. Warnock? Do you deal with him personally?"

"I don't deal with him personally, but yeah I'm in his AP Chem class. After what I saw them doing, it's fucking weird I have to be in a room with him for an hour, three times a week."

"And after you heard that Ms. Key was dead, did you notice anything different about Mr. Warnock?"

Sammi's brow furrowed. "Actually, yeah. Like, after we got the news, he was out of school for a few days. They said he had the flu."

"And what was he like when he returned to classes?"

"I guess he was sort of the same. Maybe more quiet than normal. But I think a lot of people were acting differently right after Ms. Key died. I mean, after she was killed. It's not like she just died. Someone killed her."

"Have you told anyone else about what you saw? Teachers or parents? Friends? Anyone at all?"

"No. I tried to forget about it at first, but then she got murdered. I mean, it's so fucked up. So I still think about it. Like, what did I even see, you know?" Sammi drew a fluttering breath. "She was pretty much the only teacher who was cool with me. Well, her and Eliot. But then, he's not a teacher. Whatever. I liked her a lot. She helped me, like with more than just class." Sammi's eyes teared up but he twisted his face to try and hold them back. He had learned not to show emotion in front of other people. "Look, I know everyone says Coach, I mean, her husband did it, but what if it was someone else, you know?" Sammi's big eyes bored into Mason, making the accusation without saying it out loud, "It's none of my business, but it just seemed like what I know could matter. For like, legal purposes or whatever. I'm sorry I didn't say something before, but I didn't know who to talk to." He looked into his lap, his face burning now. "Oh god, this was stupid."

"No, Sammi. Coming here was brave. I mean that. It was the right thing to do and I appreciate how hard this was. Do you want a tissue?"

"No. I'm fine." Sammi stood up. "I think I'm gonna go now."

He rounded the table and Mason rose to intercept him at the conference room door. "If it came to it, would you be willing to tell your story in court?"

Sammi threw up his hands. "I would very much *not* be willing to do that. To be honest, I didn't really want to come here."

"But you did, and it will help us figure out who is responsible for Ms. Key's death. However, I might need you to tell the court what you know to make sure an innocent man doesn't go to prison. Do you understand?"

"Yeah, sure. I get it. I do, Mr. Mitchell. But I just wanted to tell you so you could figure out if it helps. You're the lawyer, you can figure out how to use what I told you without me going to court. I just want to stay out of this, ok?"

"I understand, and I'll do what I can to keep you away from court." The lie rolled off his tongue easily. He couldn't afford to have Sammi getting skittish. Mason pushed open the glass door. "Linda can show you out."

"Thanks, Mr. Mitchell."

"Call me Mason." He waved Linda over and pointed to Sammi. She took the cue, leaving her desk to escort Sammi to the elevators.

Mason plucked the cell phone from his suit pocket and dialed Ozzy. "Yeah, we need to meet. When I'm done at court, let's say five o'clock at the after hours office."

"I'll be there, boss."

Mason ended the call then dialed another contact. "Hey Alice, when are you going to be back in Wisconsin?"

She sighed, "I'm back up there tomorrow afternoon. Why? What's so important?"

"I think we have a solid *Denny* issue."

"You're kidding! You have another suspect? Tell me all about it!"

"Let's talk it over when you're here. I need to sort a couple details so I know exactly where we stand."

"Hmm. Ok then. I'm doing some press here in the morning, then I'll drive-up. Should be at your office by three."

"Looks like I'll be done in court, so I'll see you then."

"Excellent. And Mason? Nice work."

# 26

Mason pushed open the heavy oak door and was buffeted by a warm gust that smelled of fryer grease and stale beer. He passed under the red lights in the entrance to the main room. An inch thick layer of posters – mainly Packers legends and decade old drink specials – had long ago buried all the windows and blocked all daylight. Morning, noon, and night, the interior of Walter's On Water never changed.

It was a prime example of a Wisconsin dive bar, with wood paneling on the walls and threadbare carpet on the floor. Fifteen stools lined the bar, all but three currently occupied by patrons scarfing wings, downing pints, and bellowing at one of the TVs above the bar showing a football game. This was the holy trinity of Walter's – fried food, televised sports, and massive amounts of cheap, cold beer. No craft beer, not at Walter's. Behind the plethora of taps at the bar, Mason saw John, the overworked and overfed bartender, squeeze into the small food prep area and drop another basket of wings into the rolling boil of the deep fryer. This 'kitchen' allowed the 'restaurant' to be open from seven in the morning until well after midnight. The menu contained breakfast and lunch options, but nobody who knew Walter's ordered anything other than wings, fries, and cheese curds. Still, ninety percent of their sales came from booze, and the majority of that came from a core group of regulars.

John glanced up from the fizzing oil and saw Mason. Just six feet away, he had to yell to be heard over the din. "What's up, counselor?"

"Not much! Is he here?"

"In the back, regular booth!" John dumped a batch of cheese curds into a wax paper lined basket, snatched the bottle of Tito's from the back rail and began to pour a double vodka and Sprite. "I'll bring this back in a sec."

Mason weaved through the full tables and slid into a booth against the back wall.

Ozzy greeted him, "Hey, boss."

"Jesus. Why do you insist on calling me that?" asked Mason.

"You sign the checks. What am I supposed to call you?"

"I don't know. Call me Mason, Mase, Mitchy, fuckin' anything, just not that."

"No thanks. So what have you got for me, boss?"

Oswald "Ozzy" Smith began working for Mason three years ago, right after he left the Milwaukee PD. At that time, he held the rank of detective and worked in the homicide unit. With his glowing service record, he would've had a chance to make Sergeant or even Lieutenant one day, but Ozzy's innate problem with authority set a cap on his upward mobility. It made him a kindred spirit to Mason, but displeased his superiors on the force. Ozzy's time as a cop ended with an internal affairs issue that resulted in department honchos strongly encouraging his retirement.

So, after more than two decades on the job, he walked away with a fully vested pension, just forty-five years old. Ozzy being at home every day was quickly followed by a second divorce that saddled him with healthy alimony payments. Add to that a daughter accepted at Michigan State, and Ozzy soon saw fit to launch a second career as a private investigator. It wasn't long before he hooked up with Mitchell & Associates. The two men had developed a mutual respect over the years, crossing paths several times in the courtroom. He liked working for Mason. It kept him 'in the game'.

"I need you to dig into someone," said Mason. "A kid named Sammi Mueller, attends James Madison High." John made his drink delivery and Mason took a big gulp as Ozzy began scribbling notes.

"Ok, what am I looking for?"

"One, see if he's full of shit. Two, if he's not, I need you to get him to sign an affidavit. He will probably resist."

"Full of shit about what?" Ozzy asked, keeping his eyes on the notepad. Mason took another swig, then recounted his earlier conversation with Sammi. When he was done, Ozzy put down his pen and gave his head a shake.

"Jesus Christ. That changes the landscape. Because if this Warnock really was sneaking around with Robin, you're thinking about a *Denny* motion, right?"

"Only if you can confirm the story."

"Sure. The big if."

"I'd like to get this moving as soon as possible. Linda can have the affidavit ready to go by Monday. And with your inimitable charm, I'm sure you can persuade him to sign it."

"Understood."

"And Oz, don't spook him too much. If we win the motion, we might need Sammi in the flesh at trial, but don't tell him that." Mason raised his glass in the air and rattled the ice, signaling to John his readiness for another.

"Not my first rodeo, boss," said Ozzy.

John was about to walk out from behind the bar and deliver Mason's next round when MJ, another regular, grabbed the drink off his tray. "Let me play delivery boy to our famous resident lawyer," he said, clearly amused with himself.

"Fine, have it your way," said John, and went back to frying wings.

MJ walked over to the booth and set the glass down in front of Mason. "Here you go."

"Can we help you?" inquired Ozzy in his stern cop voice.

"No, I just wanted to come see the big celebrity attorney."

"Don't go starting any problems, pal." Ozzy swiped his jacket aside to reveal the holstered .45 strapped to his belt.

"People call me MJ, not pal. And there's no problem. I just want to talk." He plopped down next to Ozzy, a crooked, buzzed grin on his face.

Mason gestured to Ozzy to back down. He had seen MJ enough times to know he wasn't dangerous, just a blowhard full of liquid courage.

"MJ, I'm just the guy who works for a real celebrity lawyer. So, why do you want to talk to me?" asked Mason.

"I saw you on TV, with that football coach who killed his wife."

"The football coach who *allegedly* killed his wife. What's your point?"

"My point is, this guy doesn't deserve a lawyer, he deserves a gas chamber."

Mason rolled his eyes and sighed. Ozzy took his chance to head to the toilet. He'd heard Mason debate drunks before and this barfly was no threat.

"Let me ask you this, MJ. Do you know anyone who has been charged with a crime?'

"Yeah, me! I had two OWI's, but nothing violent, not murder."

"And after you were arrested, did you get a lawyer?"

"Of course I did. Hired Duane Madigan, best in the biz."

"Yeah, he's ok for drunk drivers, I guess. And Duane fought for you, right?"

"You know it."

"He filed motions, negotiated with the DA, and argued for the lowest possible sentence, right?"

"Damn straight, paid him five grand for it." MJ was already empty again and waved toward the bar. "Another?" he asked Mason.

"If you're buying," said Mason with a smile. "Why did you hire Duane? Why not just roll over and take your punishment. I mean, you were guilty, so why even put up a fight?"

"The fuck you talking about? I know my rights. I get to defend myself."

"Same as Michael Key. I rest my case."

"Oh bullshit. You're just covering your ass. You know Key did it!"

"I do?"

"Course you do, and you don't give a rat's ass. Your whole job is getting paid to keep thugs like him out of prison."

"My whole job is to make sure that everybody gets their Sixth Amendment right to counsel and...and you know what, MJ? I'm so fucking tired of having this conversation."

"What's that supposed to mean?"

"It means that I'm tired of trying to convince you people that the law means something."

"You people? You don't know me, pal."

"Sure I do. And you people are everywhere, in the voting booth, on juries, and now you're here at my table while I'm trying to enjoy a drink. So please, let's talk about something else or you can just fuck off."

"Wait a second, you smug prick. You don't get to play the victim card here. There's a real victim. Her name was Robin Key and that baboon you're defending murdered her!"

"Baboon?"

"Ah, c'mon. Like an animal, whatever. You know what I meant."

"Yeah, I think maybe I do know what you meant, MJ."

"Right, now I'm the bad guy. Your client is a subhuman scumbag who killed his wife. We ought to string him up by his fingernails!"

"So, a lynching."

"Don't get all woke on me. They think they can kill our beautiful women and get away with it? Not anymore."

"Wow. You're doing all the Klan talking points here. Are you for real, dude?"

"Oh, I'm for real, big shot. And I'm not alone. You and Decatur can do your little dance in court, but one way or another, that bastard will get what he deserves!" MJ slapped the table to punctuate his tirade, overturning Mason's glass in the process.

Ozzy appeared beside MJ's seat and clamped a hand on the back of his neck. "Right, that's enough." He grabbed MJ by the arm, twisted it behind his back and yanked him out of the booth. "Time to go." Ozzy hustled him through the crowd and out the door, barely letting his feet touch the ground.

When Ozzy returned to the table he looked less than impressed. "I leave you alone for two minutes and you're about to scrap with some drunk hothead?"

"Hey, he started it," said Mason.

"Yeah, maybe don't take the bait next time. And don't get cute, there are some real nuts out there and this case is getting them all stirred up."

"What do you want me to do? Hide out at home? Tell Alice I quit?"

"Relax. It's just the mood in this city is taking a turn, boss. So just stay cool and keep your head on a swivel, ok?"

**27**

The small interview room at the county jail was stifling. Too many people in too small a space with no air circulation. Michael sat at the small table, smoke from his Newport filling the space between him and Alice. Decatur's star associate, Robert Lang, stood over her shoulder. Mason leaned against the back wall.

"It's called what?" asked Michael.

"A *Denny* motion, Mr. Key," said Robert. "From *State v Denny*. Under Wisconsin law, the defense must file this type of motion in order to argue that a specific individual perpetrated–"

Alice waved him to silence and took over. "Mr. Key, this is a huge development for us. We are bringing another suspect to this case, and will argue that he murdered Robin, not you."

Michael leaned forward. "Wait, you have proof someone else did this?"

"No, Mr. Key, we don't need proof," said Alice. "We just need to show there was another plausible suspect and the police ignored him. It's a big deal for your defense."

"Ok, so who is it?"

"It's, Trevor Warnock," said Robert. "Your colleague from James Madison."

"Trevor? What are you talking about?" Michael looked at Mason. "What the fuck did he do?

"Look, Mike, this isn't going to be easy–" said Mason, but a look from Alice cut him off before he could finish.

"Mr. Key, I can appreciate that this news might make you feel anxious." She detested cigarette smoke and this meeting had already taken more time than she wanted. Exasperation was creeping into her voice. "But I want you to stay calm and remember that we know what is best for your case."

"Will someone please just tell me what the fuck is going on?" Michael pleaded, tears welling in his eyes. "What did Trevor do?"

"Our investigation revealed that Robin was having an affair with Trevor Warnock," said Alice. Her voice was flat, expressionless.

Michael cocked his head as if her words were in a language he couldn't understand. "What did you say?"

"It went on for about a year before–"

Michael slammed his fist down on the table. "I knew it! Fuck! You've got to be fucking kidding me. A guy I work with. In the SAME BUILDING!"

The door opened and a guard entered the room, one hand on his baton. "What's going on?"

"We're good," said Mason.

The guard looked around the room, then pointed at Michael. "No more bullshit, Key." he said, and left.

"Really. Just some bad news. He's ok," said Mason.

When the guard left, Mason closed the door and Michael spoke again in a measured tone. "So, Robin and Trevor. And you think that he..." Michael couldn't finish the thought out loud.

"The law only requires us to show three things to make this argument," said Robert. "Motive, opportunity, and ties to the crime scene."

"I saw him just before she got killed," whispered Michael. "He was at the barbeque. I talked to him."

Robert continued, "We are arguing that Warnock had a motive to kill Robin since she broke off the affair shortly before the murder. He is also married, so being exposed might be a reason to kill. Or maybe he thought the baby was his? We do not know his exact motive, we only need to offer one. We can also show that he was not at home during the crime and has no alibi for the time of the murder. And the police fingerprint analyst found his prints on a beer bottle from the porch of your house. We did our homework, Mr. Key. Warnock is a very credible suspect."

"Oh my god. It all makes sense now." Michael buried his head in his hands.

"Mr. Key, please try to see the good side of this," said Alice. "What matters is we have another suspect to offer. A jury won't let you go unless they have someone else to blame, and we can give them Trevor Warnock." Alice continued, her tone sharpened by frustration, "We don't need to prove he killed Robin, but we can use him to create reasonable doubt. We'll argue that the police targeted you based on race. We can show they ignored a perfectly good white suspect in favor of the black man who married a white woman. It's our best defense."

Michael kept his head down and sobbed quietly. Alice looked at Robert and threw up her hands in exasperation.

"I can't believe they did this to me," whispered Michael. A long ash quivered at the end of his smoldering cigarette and fell to the floor.

"But they did, and that's what I can sell to the jury." Alice leaned across the table. "Mr. Key, for years, the justice system has blamed black men like you for everything, but we're going to turn the tables. We'll take your case to the media and the public. Everyone in this country will know your face and your name. We won't let this stand."

Michael lifted his head and looked at her, his eyes blank.

"Trust me, Mr. Key," said Alice. "The affair is a gift!"

Fresh tears spilled down Michael's face. "Not to me."

———

As they exited the County Jail, Alice flapped the sides of her blazer to air it out. "Goddamn Newports. Robert, do I have another suit at the office?"

"I think so. Maybe the blue?"

Mason stopped in his tracks. "Alice, are you sure the full court press with the media is a good idea? Judge Francis is going to get his back up and make things harder for us."

"He'll have to deal with it. I'm thinking beyond Francis and beyond Milwaukee right now. This is how we are handling the case. Do you have a problem with that?"

"No, but you wanted me for local knowledge, so I'm letting you know. Francis is not going to like all the attention and we need to be ready for that."

"Noted," said Alice and tried to move around Mason but he stepped in front of her again. "For Christ's sake, what is it, Mitchell?"

"You just told our client that his wife cheated on him for a year, with a man he knew, a man who may have murdered her. Maybe you could've softened the blow, or at least given him a minute to process it."

"Oh my lord. Just listen to yourself." She looked skyward and laughed. "Mason, you need to remember that what we offer isn't therapy, it's high level legal representation. So whatever misgivings you have about my interpersonal style, I need you to swallow them and get on-board with what we're doing here."

"I'm just pointing out that our client is a human being who needs some empathy."

"What Michael Key *needs* is a *Denny* motion filed on his behalf to create reasonable doubt in the minds of twelve jurors so that they find him not guilty and he goes free. So that's exactly what we're doing."

Mason was about to respond, but thought better of it. He had pushed his luck enough for one night.

Alice took a step toward the parking lot, then turned back to Mason. "I've seen so many guys like you in my career, and I know how you see me. My methods, my courtroom style, the media persona, the whole thing gets under your skin. You think you're some hot shot trial lawyer who could do it better. I'm sorry if you think I underestimate you, but the way I do things *wins cases*. And it will win this case. So if I rub you the wrong way, I need you to be a professional and put it to one side. Or, if you can't do that, step aside. You can man up and share in the glory when we're done, or you can get the fuck out of the way and go back to your little office and your little superiority complex because I will not let you mess up my case. Got it?"

Mason swallowed hard and nodded.

"Excellent. I'm glad we're clear." The smile returned to Alice's face. "Now, go get some rest and I'll see you in my office at eight o'clock. We have a lot of work ahead of us."

**28**

Decatur's defense team decided to leak the *Denny* motion to the press. Alice didn't have any local reporters in her pocket, so they would use Mason's contact, Paige Tyler, who covered the courthouse scene for Fox 6 News. Five years earlier, she and Mason shared a brief but intense romance that ended on mostly friendly terms. Since then, they formed a mutually beneficial relationship, trading information and access.

He found her number, still in the *Favorites* on his phone, under 'Fox Paige'. As he waited for her to pick up, he thought back to her smell and how his hand fit in the small of her back. For a split second he imagined asking her out for a drink, an idea that was quickly discarded. She married not long after their split and was now mother to two kids.

His reminiscing was cut short when her voice came down the line, "Hello, Mitchell."

"Hey, how's my favorite news reporter?"

"I'm about to go on the air. What do you need?"

"Got a tip, an exclusive. It's the Michael Key case."

"Did Decatur let you off her leash? Do you have her blessing?"

"Hey, I'm sitting second chair. Well, maybe third or fourth chair, but I'm on the case, and I can talk for the team," said Mason, sounding more defensive than he wanted.

He heard her cover the phone and whisper to someone else, "I can't. Tell them two more minutes" followed by a few seconds of muffled voices on her end. Then, "Ok, Mitchell. I'm listening."

"We're filing a Denny motion in the morning."

Paige knew the lingo from her years of covering the courthouse, so no explanation was needed. "And who is this red herring you're offering up?"

"One of the teachers at James Madison. He was having an affair with Robin."

"Oh shit, really? But if you expose the affair, can't the DA turn it around to show motive for Key? Michael finds out, gets mad, kills Robin."

"Yeah, it could cut both ways, but we need something, and this is our best chance."

"What can you tell me about the teacher?"

"Off the record, his name is Trevor Warnock. Teaches chemistry at the high school. And he's married, so I expect this motion will cause him some problems, not to mention the media storm that will land in his lap, but that's not my problem."

"And people say criminal defense lawyers have no soul."

"Doing my job, you know that. I don't love it, but then I wasn't the one cheating on my wife."

"Fair enough. Anything else I need to know about this guy?"

"Warnock is white, Michael is black. It's a layup for Alice. She'll argue the police focused on the black man and ignored the white suspect."

"Right. This will blow up the case, maybe even make national news. Will you go on camera?  We can have an interview team out to you in ten minutes."

"No can do. Alice is holding a press conference at the courthouse to-morrow at noon,  after we argue the motion.  You can run with this on tonight's broadcast, just keep my name out of it. Also, you can't disclose the teacher's name yet, that was strictly off the record."

"Got it, thanks! I'm going live in a minute so I gotta run. I owe you a drink!"

"Probably two. Press conference will be at the Wells Street steps. I'll save you a front row spot." Mason ended the call, turned to Robert and Alice and gave a thumbs up.

That night, the story broke, with Fox 6 reporting that a teacher (no name given) was being accused by the defense and that he had been having an affair with the victim. With the teacher being white, the defense believed that race, not evidence, had motivated the MPD. The story was picked up in no time and ran on the ten o'clock news broadcast for CNN, MSNBC, FOX News and all the national networks. Even Nancy Grace reached out to Alice's office. Clearly, the Decatur media machine was fully functioning. Across town, editors at the Milwaukee Journal Sentinel were already crafting the next morning's headline:

*MPD TARGETED BLACK COACH OVER WHITE TEACHER – ROBIN KEY NOT SO INNOCENT!*

At midnight, Mason sat in with Decatur and her team at their borrowed office, going over media reaction and planning strategy. He was mainly a passenger on this train, but Robert and the others were buzzing. Alice leaned back in her chair and looked out at the nighttime skyline, visibly pleased. "We'll have a good turnout for the press conference."

She turned to Benny. "Make sure all of our people know where and when."

"We have people?" asked Mason.

"Don't worry about that," said Alice. "Just pick out a nice suit, nothing too loud. You'll be on every channel tomorrow."

---

He walked into the loft, placed his briefcase and keys on the hall table and started for the patio door. Clyde followed and made a bee-line for the planter box. After doing his business, he jumped up on the sofa in the office, while Mason sat at his desk, opening the day's mail. He shuffled through the offerings and found an envelope that interested him. He opened it and read the handwritten letter inside.

*Dear Mason,*

*Clyde is so cute! I love his little black snout and those EYES! Oh my god! Thank you so much for the photo. I put it up beside my bunk. He's the first face I see in the morning and the last one at night. It's not like I have friends here, so it really does help.*

*But I guess I'm settling in. There's not much to do most of the time so I read and just try to stay out of everyone's way, the guards and the inmates. The whole thing is still so strange and intimidating. Being in here is very real and a weird dream all at the same time. I'm sharing a cell with a girl named Cherise. She's bigger than me and kind of pushy. She's not terrible but I'm pretty sure she's stealing from me. She doesn't say anything about it and neither do I.*

*To be honest, the visits with my folks and everyone in the family sometimes just stress me out. I love them and I know it's better than no one coming to see me. It seems like most people here don't get a lot of visitors. But when I see the angry look on dad's face or my mom starts crying (she does it every time she's here) I feel bad. It reminds me of how stupid I was and that I totally messed up and that's why I'm here. After they leave I go back to my cell and*

*I'm so mad and sad. Sorry if that all sounds weird and ungrateful. I just wanted to vent to somebody.*

*Thanks for the update about David and the divorce. Excuse my language but he's such a fucking pig. I think you were right that he deserved to be stabbed more than once. Anyways, I just want that to be done as soon as possible. I want him out of my life for good. We can talk about all that when you come here for the visit. Is that still supposed to be this month?*

*And really, thanks again for the Clyde photo. It was exactly what I needed.*

*See you soon?*

*Lori*

## 29

The press conference was scheduled for noon, but by quarter past, no one had appeared from Team Alice. It was unseasonably warm for early June in Milwaukee, with the temperature already pushing ninety and the lake effect adding a steamy haze of that hung over the city. Heat baked off the steps and paved plaza in front of the courthouse, sending the temperature closer to a hundred degrees.

A podium adorned with the Circle M logo of Milwaukee County and bristling with the microphones of two dozen media outlets had been placed at the top of the steps, overlooking several hundred people gathered on the sweltering plaza. Large contingents from the Aryan Brotherhood and MJB were easily identifiable, but smaller groups of all stripes were there to support Michael Key, Robin's family, or some other tenuously-related pet cause. Orders had been given to keep the situation from escalating, and fifty deputies formed a thin line down the middle of the plaza, separating the two major factions. Twenty more officers were posted along the metal fencing that ran the length of the steps, meant to keep the crowd from approaching the courthouse. On the other side of the barrier at the base of the steps, members of the media were packed shoulder to shoulder in a hastily erected pen. As Mason promised, Paige Taylor was up front with an unobstructed view of the podium.

With the oppressive heat and no focal point for their attention, tempers in the crowd began to fray, spurred on by agitators scattered among them. For weeks, public rhetoric around the Key case had drawn protests and counter-protest to the city center, and law enforcement officials were dismayed by the mob of white supremacists who arrived on buses from all corners of the state and beyond. They had become a regular fixture outside the courthouse, engaging in increasingly heated confrontations with members of the Milwaukee Justice Bloc. Some in the police department took a dim view of the MJB's ballooning membership coming up from Illinois, some said at the behest of Alice Decatur. Today, the scene on the plaza reached a peak in energy and numbers. As the delay stretched to twenty-five minutes, the sweating crowd was on a ragged edge, jeering and pushing. Megaphones blared competing slogans across the plaza, racial slurs were hurled, sometimes followed by plastic water bottles. Deputies eyed the crowd and each other with mounting anxiety, knowing the spark could come from anywhere at any time.

When Alice and the members of her entourage emerged from the courthouse doors at 12:28 p.m., they were met by a mixed chorus of support and derision.

Mason had followed her recommendation and dressed in conservative navy suit with a blood red tie. When he stepped out into the sunshine, the weight of the heat and the tension radiating from the assembled crowd caused a sweat to break out on his brow.

He had been involved in cases that garnered media attention, but nothing like this. It was now the top story on the news every night, and not just in Milwaukee. The firestorm of issues and opinions around the Key trial was growing, fed by deep-seated anger and wild allegations.

Alice walked to the podium and Mason took his place behind her shoulder. He looked past the forest of camera tripods to the restless mass of people beyond the barrier. In their faces he saw resentment, disaffection, and rage.

After waiting to ensure all eyes were on her, Alice began, "Good afternoon. I want to thank you all for attending. Today we struck the first blow in defense of yet another innocent black man victimized by the system." She wiped her hair from her face and continued. "Unlike the MPD, my team conducted a real investigation of this case. And we found the real killer." Alice let her words wash over the crowd. "This morning, we argued a motion that would allow us to reveal this person to the jury."

She looked down at her notes, then back to the cameras. "The court ruled in our favor, and we will present an argument based on *cold hard facts*, that Robin Key was not murdered by Michael Key, but by her secret lover." She paused again, a ringmaster drawing out the moment. "The real murderer's name is Trevor Warnock!"

A collective gasp rippled through the crowd. The reporters began to furiously scribble on notepads and type into their phones. The *Denny* motion and that morning's hearing had deliberately omitted Warnock's name, and this was the first time it was being made public.

"Warnock is a teacher at James Madison High School, where he and Robin Key carried on a torrid affair for several months. We have evidence that just days before the murder, Robin broke off the affair and, based on the State's own fingerprint evidence, we know Mr. Warnock was at Robin's house on the day of the murder." This was not entirely true, it couldn't be said with certainty when Warnock's fingerprint appeared on the beer bottle, but Alice was not the first lawyer to achieve success by making facts fit her narrative.

"Why did the affair end?" yelled one reporter.

Alice ignored the question and continued with her statement, "It is significant that this suspect was discovered in the course of *our* investigation. The police didn't find him because they never looked! For Trevor Warnock, there was no arrest in the middle of the night, no seventy-two hour interrogation, no leaping to conclusions. The detectives never even glanced in Trevor Warnock's direction! Because the MPD had found their black man to pin it on. This police department failed Michael Key and they have failed this community!" Cheers and whistles erupted from the MJB, quickly morphing into a chant.

*"Free Michael Key, Free Michael Key, Free Michael Key …."*

Alice raised her hands to settle the crowd. "They see a black man married to a white woman and say he must be guilty! I say the Milwaukee Police Department and the District Attorney are trying to get away with a lynching!"

Another roar from the crowd, louder now, cheers of defiance mingled with a cascade of boos and catcalls.

"But we can't let them," said Alice, her voice rising to the moment. "We are all created equal, and so justice must also be equal!"

*POP-POP-POP!*

The crack of three shots rang across the plaza, followed by a long moment of eerie silence, then chaos. Screams erupted from every side, the crowd running in all directions, dissipating and regathering like a cloud of starlings. Deputies spun round with weapons drawn, searching wildly for the threat. Mason had ducked on instinct and now lay against the foot of the podium. Below him he saw Paige, wild-eyed, crouched down in the media pen. His heart hammered against his ribcage. He put a hand to his chest and touched something wet. His fingertips came back stained red. Blood. He could feel more of it, on his face. There was no pain. *Am I hit?* He ran both hands over his body, frantically searching for a bullet wound.

Mason rolled on his side to check again and saw Alice slumped against the other side of the podium. Her eyes were fixed, vacant.

In a rush, he became aware of the blood, so much blood. The left side of her neck had exploded, the skin and tissue turned inside out, and there was a gaping hole in her skull just above the forehead. Her hair blew in the hot breeze, but otherwise her body was still. He could not look away, could not move.

An hour later, Mason was a few blocks from the courthouse, wandering the halls of Mount Sinai Hospital. A flurry of activity on the ward swirled around him, with doctors, nurses, and cops clogging the halls. At one point, he saw Benny wheeled past on a gurney, moaning in pain. Mason felt untethered, alone, and lost.

A heavy hand came to rest on his shoulder. "Hey, boss. There you are," said Ozzy.

Mason realized he had been hyperventilating and took a moment to slow himself down. "Ozzy, what the fuck happened?"

"Decatur is dead. One member of her team was also hit, Benny something. He's in surgery, it's touch and go."

"Oh, shit. Who..."

"Maybe you should sit down, boss." Ozzy guided him into a chair next to the nurses station.

"What have you heard? Do we know anything?"

"Right now it's looking like the Aryan Brotherhood got off some shots but nothing's been confirmed," said Ozzy. "Heard some young deputy chased the shooter and put him down. Quick thinking for a rookie. We're lucky it wasn't worse." Mason sat there shaking his head, not seeming to hear, and his ragged mental state worried Ozzy. "Did they take your statement already?"

"Did they do what? Oh, yeah. I didn't have much to tell them." Mason's eyes were wide, the shock was yet to subside. "Now what? I mean...what's next?"

"For you? I'd say a drink or two, then we can collect our thoughts tomorrow."

"Right, ok. Walter's?"

Ozzy put an arm around Mason and led him away from the nurse's station. "I'll drive."

# 30

*"At first I was afraid, I was petrified..."*

Lori looked up with annoyance to the screen on the wall of the TV lounge. On the garishly lit studio stage, a former congressman was dressed in a zombie costume and singing his heart out.

*"...and I grew strong, and I learned how to get along..."*

His tuneless wailing and crude dance steps were lapped up by the live audience, who whooped with delight, egging him on.

*"...you think I'd crumble, you think I'd lay down and die. Oh no, not I, I will survive..."*

*What an asshole,* thought Lori. She remembered the news of his scandal, apparently far enough in the past that he was once again fit for public consumption. During two terms in office, he lined his pockets with millions in taxpayer dollars while forcing himself on a series of young interns. After the story broke, he escaped with a slap on the wrist – a measly fine and a tearful press conference during which he declared his intention to 'Do the work, and reflect on my actions' before slinking off to accept lucrative corporate board positions.

After the final note of his shameless, sweaty exhibition the audience erupted in a rapturous ovation. The panel of judges stood and applauded, gazing at him with perfectly practiced admiration.

*"That was so brave!"*

*"I mean, WOW! Mr. Congressman, I am floored!"*

*"That was banger, my man!"*

Lori almost gagged. *My man? Jesus Christ.* She looked around the lounge at the other women, most of them plucked out of society for poor choices or worse luck. For them, there would be no triumphant reentry into public life like this celebrity talent show ratings bonanza. But a different kind of criminal enjoyed a victory tour in which he played a lovable dad who can't hit the high notes but tries real hard.

*And we're all watching it,* thought Lori. *Fuck him. Fuck this place. Fuck the double standards. That shithead got off scot-free, on TV acting like America's sweetheart. I'm in here, paying 200% markup on toiletries from the canteen, spending my time avoiding Officer Hal pushing his gross little dick at me.*

Lori had seen enough and stood to leave. The zombie congressman was in the middle of a cringeworthy monologue about redemption when the broadcast mercifully cut to a screaming red *BREAKING NEWS ALERT* graphic. Seconds later, the screen showed a live shot of Paige Tyler at the Milwaukee County Courthouse. She stood just outside an area cordoned off with yellow crime scene tape, the scene behind her was wall to wall with police and other first responders:

*"A gunman opened fire at the Milwaukee County Courthouse today during a press conference involving the Michael Key murder case. Early reports indicate that Attorney Alice Decatur died at the scene, and several people were injured."*

The feed cut to a video loop of the shooting as it happened. Lori almost fell down when she saw Mason standing next to the podium then hitting the ground when shots started flying. As the loop played again and again, she began to feel sick.

*"It is believed the gunman was killed during the exchange of gunfire with police. While details surrounding the attack have not been confirmed, it is presumed to be racially motivated. As we gather more information, we will pass it along to our viewers. This is Paige Tyler reporting for Fox 6 News. Back to you in the studio."*

Lori was approached by her old cellmate, Cherise. "Ain't that your hotshot lawyer on TV? Awww, you think he was shot too?"

"I don't know, Cherise. Back the fuck off!"

Shortly after Lori left A&E and entered the general population, she had ended up on the losing end of Cherise's fury. For some perceived sin of disrespect, she taught Lori a lesson resulting in a black eye, bloody nose, and two cracked ribs. The guards had been slow to react and it would have been worse if not for a girl known as Large Marge pulling Cherise off and pinning her against the wall. Lori did not know Marge and imagined she intervened due to some unrelated beef with Cherise, maybe something territorial. In any case, Lori was grateful. Since then, inmates tended to leave Lori to herself. Officer Hal was another issue.

Now, face to face with Cherise, Lori felt a rage rise in her. She planted both hands in Cherise's chest and shoved her back, hard.

Cherise's hip cracked against the edge of a metal table and she almost spilled onto the floor before regaining her balance. She stepped towards Lori with her fists balled up. "You know you fucked up!"

The brewing altercation brought an officer out from the guard station, shouting, "That's enough! Back away from each other NOW!" as he scampered across the floor. Lori felt the urge to sucker punch Cherise. A straight shot to the bridge of her nose. The broken knuckles would be worth it. Lori wanted to leap on her, pummel her stupid face, break all her fucking precious nails off and feed them to her.

"I SAID NOW!" The guard was only steps away.

Lori knew her violent fantasy was just that and nothing more. She could be scrappy, but Cherise was a fighter who had five inches and forty pounds on her. And Lori wasn't about to fuck up her release date for fleeting revenge with a no-hoper like Cherise.

The guard had reached them and stood between the two women. Lori raised her hands and took a few steps back.

"Fuck it," said Cherise. She sat down, stretched her legs out and leaned back, like she was sunning herself by the pool. "Trick ass bitch don't bother me."

Lori saw in Cherise's eyes the promise of trouble down the line. Nothing she could do about that now. Lori turned on her heel and retreated toward her pod, remembering her box breathing – *four seconds inhale, hold for four, four seconds exhale, hold for four, and repeat* – just like that motivational speaker last year had shown them.

Lori remembered him well. A former Navy SEAL. Any special visitor was an event, and this guy had been very fit, very cute, and way too motivated. He straight up told a room full of locked-up women surrounded by armed guards that they could take control and make something out of their lives, as if it wasn't some kind of sick joke. Still, Lori had taken it to heart. In prison, you would cling to anything that helped you get through the days. And the box breathing really helped. Ten of those usually brought her back to a good place. Back to the calm flat plain of serenity, or whatever passed for it in prison.

**31**

M ason flipped on the TV and saw Fox 6 News anchor Hal Booker sitting behind a massive plexiglass desk that bore the slogan, 'Local News You Can Trust'. The words BREAKING NEWS glowed white against a red banner at the bottom of the screen. A picture of the County Courthouse was projected over Booker's left shoulder as he delivered his script down the barrel of the camera:

*"In the wake of what many are referring to as the 'assassination' of prominent criminal defense lawyer Alice Decatur, Milwaukee PD has set up a 'hard perimeter' in a two block radius around the County Courthouse Complex. The Chief Judge has ordered the Complex closed for one week, adjourning all official business. The order indicated this time was needed for law enforcement to conduct an investigation without interruption. The order went on to say 'the men and women who work in the Milwaukee County Court System need time to process, heal, and grieve before returning to normal operations next Monday."*

*"Decatur, perhaps the nation's most high profile female African-American attorney, had come to Milwaukee to defend Michael Key, the local high school football coach accused of murdering his pregnant wife on the steps of their home last October. Yesterday afternoon, Decatur was speaking before protestors and assembled media on the courthouse steps when she was hit by three bullets fired from an assault-rifle. She was rushed to Mount Sinai moments after, and pronounced dead. The gunman has been identified as James Kilpatrick, a forty-four-year-old former Marine from the Chicagoland area. Kilpatrick posted a two thousand word manifesto to social media just hours before the shooting occurred. In it, he professed*

*his quote 'dedication to protecting white culture and our beautiful white women', and went on to decry what he called 'an ongoing invasion of lower order races' in the community. Kilpatrick was killed near the scene after exchanging fire with MPD officers."*

*"We are now going live to the press conference being held by Milwaukee County District Attorney, E. Michael Christenson."*

The broadcast cut away from the studio, and Mason saw the familiar figure of the DA on screen. Christenson was a wily veteran of Milwaukee's justice system, having occupied the office for twenty-six years. This made him the longest tenured district attorney of any major city in the country, although it was up for debate whether the rest of America saw Milwaukee as major. As a rule, Christenson was not controversial, and kept out of the spotlight. He liked the victories of his office to be shared by his soldiers on the front lines, and the failures to fall on others, usually law enforcement or local politicians. He knew where to step and where not to step, an instinct that was key to his longevity.

Christenson gripped the sides of the lectern and looked out to the media horde and their TV cameras crowding the Safety Building's ad hoc media room. His features were set in what he hoped read as grave determination, but his soft chin and sweaty brow made him appear more like a disgraced televangelist.

He bowed his head for a moment, as if in prayer, then began. "I am here to address yesterday's tragic events, pay tribute to my colleague Ms. Decatur, and call for calm. I represent the people of Milwaukee County, and I feel like I know the people of this county. And I know we are better than this. But as we've seen, the overheated rhetoric and lack of regard for our fellow citizens has real world consequences." He paused again and looked out over the room in a vain attempt to generate gravitas.

"The sober pursuit of justice demands that we all speak and act with consideration for one another, no matter the outcome of this or any other trial. This pursuit is a sacred process that underpins our society and embodies our highest ideals. We cannot let anger, divisiveness, and violence pervert the course of justice and in the process drive a wedge between us. There is much to be sorted out in the coming days regarding Alice Decatur's killer and the trial of Michael Key. I want all of us to be aware of the role we can play to ensure that justice is properly served in both cases. The District Attorney's office stands ready to defend our community in every way possible and I ask that you join us in calling for peace and togetherness as we move forward. That's the American way. That's the Milwaukee way. I have no further comment at this time, but Robin Key's family has asked to deliver a statement."

Robin's brother, Luke, broke away from the other family members gathered along one wall and joined Christenson at the front of the room. They shook hands, then Luke unfolded a sheet of paper onto the stand and loudly cleared his throat into the clustered microphones. "We too are saddened by the death of Ms. Decatur. We are even more saddened because we know this is another tragic, violent act that was spawned from the tragic, violent death of Robin Key. Robin was a wonderful daughter and sister. She was full of life and love and brought that to every situation. She gave her time and energy to many charity causes and volunteer organizations. Her work as a teacher was so important to her and she loved her students dearly. My sister believed that her love and light could be a force for good in the world. Robin showed that love and light to a man she thought would return it and paid for that mistake with her life. Now, because Alice Decatur chose to defend Michael Key, she is dead, too."

Luke's droning delivery was almost enough to dilute the crassness of his assertion, but he speedily continued over the commotion from the press corral.

"Michael Key is a beast and a murderer who thinks only of himself. He blamed Robin for all the mistakes that he made in his life. He abused my sister physically and emotionally, but saw himself as a victim in their relationship. Now, in this trial, he wants people to see him again as a victim. The truth is, Michael confessed to murdering our sweet Robin," here Luke choked up, his face contorting briefly as he pressed on, "and now, like the coward he always has been, Michael is unwilling to face the consequences of this heinous and brutal killing. We demand that he face the harshest punishment possible for his crime. Our family will no longer be commenting publicly and ask for everyone to respect our privacy as we grieve and attempt to process our loss. But we ask that any online tributes to Robin and support for our family use #justice4robin and would like to announce that we have opened a GoFundMe page to help us cover the costs associated with her death and trial. Thank you."

The feed shifted back to the Fox 6 News desk. The BREAKING NEWS banner was gone and Booker assured viewers that regularly scheduled programming would now resume.

**32**

The harsh sound of the buzzer cut through the late morning quiet, startling Clyde in his bed. Mason shuffled to his front door, the monitor on his intercom panel showed Ozzy standing in the lobby. Mason closed his eyes and leaned his head against the wall. "Fuck off," he whispered. The buzzer sounded twice more and Clyde began to bark. "Fine! Jesus Christ." Mason pressed the keypad to let him in.

Mason had spent the last three days holed up in his loft with Clyde and Tito's as his only company. Ozzy called again and again, leaving voicemails insisting he should swing by, which Mason ignored.

A minute later, Ozzy was standing in Mason's front hall. Clyde gave him a thorough sniff and accepted a brief head scratch. After realizing no treats were forthcoming, he returned to his bed and burrowed under the blanket.

"Hey, boss. How are you feeling?" asked Ozzy, scanning the scene with trepidation.

"I'm fine." Mason stood at the kitchen island in track pants and a rumpled old hoodie, pouring a healthy dose of vodka into his glass of orange juice. "What do you want?"

Seeing Mason in joggers and a sweatshirt had Ozzy worried. Casual attire was never a good sign. "Want? I want nothing. However, I do *need* you to get off your ass and get back to work. You have trials set, an inbox full of emails, a backlog of voicemails, and even a small pile of snail mail. Here." Ozzy slapped the stack of envelopes on the kitchen counter.

"I'll get to it later," said Mason, as he slid a pop tart in the toaster.

"When? When are you going to pull yourself out of this...self-indulgent spiral, and get back in action?"

"I'm in no rush."

"Yeah, well I am. So is Linda. Stop this shit and let's get back to work. People are counting on you."

"I could have been killed, Oz! Maybe I want a break. Do you get that?" said Mason.

"You know what? I do get it. I've been there, remember?" Ozzy shot back.

"Yeah yeah, the O'Haver case. You've mentioned it more than once. It was dark, there was a standoff, you took two in the chest–"

"Three, you little prick! Wanna see the scars?" Ozzy put himself directly in front of Mason.

"No, man. I know, I know." Mason took a step back and looked down at the counter, his face reddening with shame. Ozzy's chest rose and fell slowly as he tried to calm himself.

Mason kept his gaze lowered. "Sorry. I know it's not the same thing, but every time I try to leave the house...I can't. I keep thinking there'll be someone around the corner ready to take me out." He gulped down his spiked OJ and began mixing another. "I'm scared, ok?"

Ozzy briefly considered trying to take away Mason's booze and decided it wasn't the time. "Look, I get that. Shots fired, it can freak anyone out, believe me. But quitting? That's not you. And Mason Mitchell, I fucking *know* you. The world is full of crackpots and psychos, but so what? You already knew that."

Mason turned to the window and half emptied his glass in one go.

"Seriously? You're going to let them take you out of the game so easily?"

Mason took his time finishing the other half of his drink before speaking. "You make a good point. Fuck 'em."

"Exactly," said Ozzy, smiling. "Fuck 'em. And now I'm all out of pep talks, so can we talk business?"

Mason walked to the sofa and sat down heavily. "Fine. What have I missed?"

"Did you catch the news about the shooter?"

"Yeah, Kilpatrick."

"Right. Well, MPD is staying tight-lipped about the investigation, but I talked to a couple of my guys." Ozzy maintained strong ties with several former colleagues, most believed he got shafted by the department and were only too happy to help out when called on. "He was killed at the scene, and when they searched him he had no ID, no phone, no distinctive tattoos, nothing. But within a few minutes someone had given the detectives a name, home address, and other details. With that kind of speed, it looks like Kilpatrick had only one or two degrees of separation from somebody on the force."

"Jesus. So what else do we know about him?"

"A few minor arrests, disorderly conduct at skinhead protests, one time they got him carrying a .38. But there was nothing that would indicate he was going to do something like this." Ozzy pulled a small steno pad from his jacket pocket and looked at his notes. "He grew up two blocks from Wrigley Field. Twelve years in the Marine Corps, honorable discharge in '09. He worked at Walgreens in Evansville for the last ten years. No wife, no kids. His social media revealed a couple half-hearted tiki torch posts, but nothing that'd get him flagged by the feds or local law enforcement.

Then a few days ago he posted a manifesto before going downtown to shoot Decatur."

"It's weird, yeah, but every guy like this detonates in his own unique way," said Mason. "Anything else?"

"No, but there's obviously more to it, so I'm keeping my ear to the ground."

"Good. So, now that you got me motivated again," Mason ran both hands over his stubbled face, "guess I better clean myself up and get to work."

"Maybe open a window and let some air in while you're at it." said Ozzy. "What are you going to do about the Key case?"

"Not sure yet. Give me the afternoon to think about it and let's meet for dinner. Say, six o'clock?"

"Sure. Where?"

"Butch's. My treat."

"After making me drag my ass down here, it's the least you could do. See you at six, boss." Ozzy gave Clyde a pat on the belly and headed for the door, already planning what to order.

———

Mason sifted through the pile of mail on the kitchen island. One envelope caught his eye, stamped 'Inmate Mail - Taycheedah Correctional'. Letters from Lori arrived every two weeks, like clockwork. She didn't seem to have any social life inside and the regular visits from her family sometimes left her feeling guilty and ashamed. He guessed that writing to him was Lori's opportunity to talk to someone who wouldn't judge her, who didn't need anything from her. He would write back on occasion, when there were legal issues to discuss or sometimes when his stress levels had peaked and he wanted a break from normal life. With Lori literally separated from his world, he didn't feel the social anxiety that prompted him to keep others at arm's length.

Lori's divorce was still pending, and David had filed a civil suit against her for his injuries. Mason agreed to handle both lawsuits at a steep discount since they would take little effort and it gave him an excuse to keep up with the correspondence. He even made sure Lori had 'money on the books' at the prison store so that she would have the resources to write back.

He opened the envelope and unfolded the lined notebook paper filled with her tidy handwriting.

*Dear Mason,*

*I hope this letter finds you well. I saw the shooting on the TV and had to write because I was worried about your safety. I'm sure you were shaken-up by being so close to the violence and death. I know my trauma still affects me on a daily basis, so if you need to talk, you know where to find me, LOL. Seriously, please write back to let me know you're ok.*

*Things here seem to be improving slowly. Over the last few months I have grown accustomed to the routine. That is what prison is – routine. Seems like as long as you follow the routine, you can get by. It is mundane and makes me feel a little bit like a zombie, but it's also something to cling to each day.*

*I am learning which guards to avoid and which ones I can trust. The inmates are leaving me alone for the most part. After that first altercation, no one seems to bother me. I met a girl named Marge who isn't necessarily a friend, but kind of acts like my guardian angel.*

*I get along ok with my new cellmate and we both have long shitty stories to swap late at night. She might need a lawyer when she gets out, to get her kids back. I'm not sure if you do those types of cases.*

*As far as the divorce goes, can you please just get it done. I don't really care what he gets. We really don't have anything. He can burn all my shit for all I care. I just want to be rid of him and shed his last name. And is anything new happening with the personal injury case? Last time you said he wanted $50,000! Doesn't that shithead know I don't have fifty grand? He's such a fucking idiot!*

*Are you still going to represent that football coach? If not, who will? It seemed like Decatur was very good but you should take over if you can. And if you want my two cents, I would look at the chemistry teacher or anyone else Robin Key may have been with. I read in the paper that they found DNA under her fingernails that was not from her husband. Do you know whose DNA that was? I would look at that guy! Look at me telling you how to do your job! But seriously, you can feel free to bounce any ideas off me. Lord knows I have the time!*

*Anyway, I wanted you to know that I think you should still help him. This'll sound weird, but I think he just seems like a nice guy and for some reason I don't think he killed his wife. I don't know, call it women's intuition. I know they say he confessed, but we both know the cops can get anyone to say whatever they want. Maybe since I've been in here, I think everyone is getting railroaded. It sure does change your perspective.*

*I know you're busy, so I won't take up much more of your time. Please write back, maybe this time it will include a divorce settlement, fingers crossed.*

*Talk soon,*

*Lori*

Mason folded the pages and laid them on the hallway table, a visual reminder to write her back. "Ok, you little goof, it's go time!" He grabbed the leash off its hook, Clyde sprang from his bed and trotted to the front door, ready for action. Mason paused with a hand on the doorknob, went back to the closet, retrieved his Ruger Max 9 from the safe and tucked in his waistband. *Just in case,* he thought. *Just in case.*

———

Every time Mason walked through the front doors of Butch's Old Casino and Steakhouse he felt as though he was entering a different world. The decor – red velvet booths, coffered ceiling, embossed gold leaf wallpaper – suggested the middle-class glamor of Eisenhower's America, and he half-expected to see Teamster bosses conspiring in a corner, or Louis Prima serenading the diners. But rickety tables, mottled carpeting, and smoke-stained light fixtures were reminders that Butch's golden era had long since passed.

It was Milwaukee's only remaining example of an authentic supper club, and fittingly, the building sat alone on an otherwise demolished block next to I-94. With Butch now in his late seventies, and neither of his children showing an interest in the place, it was rumored he was ready to sell and move to Florida. Marquette University, his neighbor to the west, was looking to expand the campus and recently made Butch an offer too good to pass up. For Mason, it would be a sad day when Butch finally accepted. In a city dotted with ultramodern, minimalist steakhouses, the singular atmosphere and unfussy presentation of Butch's still couldn't be beat, and Mason would keep coming back until the doors were chained shut.

He found Ozzy waiting at their usual table, a high-top on the far side of the bar, next to the bank of ancient slot machines. The older man sipped a Brandy Old-Fashioned, a Wisconsin classic that fit the setting to a tee. As Mason took his customary seat facing the bar, a relish tray was delivered, joined moments later by his favorite martini – Tito's up, extra dirty, three blue-cheese stuffed olives.

Mason raised his glass, "Thanks, Jim."

Jim 'The Gent' Hallam presided over the bar, as he did on most nights. A flattened nose and thick forearms gave him the appearance of a backstreet brawler, which helped keep the clientele in line even though his hair now showed more salt than pepper. He started as a busboy in the '70s, one of Butch's first hires after buying the casino that had sat abandoned for twenty years. Together, they built the place into a Milwaukee institution.

Mason clinked Ozzy's glass, slurped the briny perfection, and began browsing the menu.

"Really?" asked Ozzy.

"I like to look, you know that." Mason's order never changed but he treated every visit to Butch's like a sacred tea ceremony in which no steps could be skipped.

Ozzy rolled his eyes and turned his attention back to his drink. Mason peeked above the menu and watched him gingerly slide a Maraschino cherry off the bamboo skewer and pop it in his mouth. Ozzy was a tee-totaler most of the time and a hard-ass all the time, and Mason couldn't stifle a chuckle.

"Look at you and your fancy cocktail," he said.

"Yeah, we can't all be macho men like you," said Ozzy. He scowled at Mason and bit down on another cherry.

"Ok, ok. Pardon me, detective."

A woman appeared at the table and laid a hand on Ozzy's shoulder. "Hello, handsome. What are we thinking, escargot to start?" Natalie Richter was another fixture at Butch's. Raven-haired, quick to smile, and a natural flirt, Natalie made you feel like her personal guest. Now in her early fifties, she'd been running the dining room since before Mason's time.

Ozzy gave her a sly wink. "As usual, my dear."

Butch's take on the French delicacy was mostly a garlic butter delivery system. Seven snails baked in pools of it, and the crostini on the side like-wise drenched. When the dish arrived, the two men savored it without speaking, until the coin flip that awarded the seventh and final dripping snail to Ozzy.

Natalie returned as Ozzy dabbed melted butter from his mustache. "Gentlemen, are you ready to surprise me?"

"Not a chance," said Mason.

Natalie pointed to Mason, "Lemme guess, bone-in ribeye, rare, with a side of hollandaise," then to Ozzy, "and ten ounce steer tenderloin, medium rare with the six ounce lobster tail, for you."

"You got it," said Ozzy. "And another round if you please, Nat."

"Already on the way, hon."

Ozzy watched her walk away with a boozy grin on his face. "That's some woman."

"You need me to give you a moment?" asked Mason.

Ozzy broke from his reverie, "What? No, I just....never mind. So, what's your verdict on the Key case? What happens now?"

"Not really sure. The reality is, Michael needs to decide what he wants. I was told the MJB is no longer footing the bill, so whatever is left of team Alice is gone, back to Chicago."

"What about you?"

"Don't know. Pretty much every part of me wants this case – high profile, false confession, all that. But things got so out of control. I mean, Decatur got fucking killed over this. Is it worth it?"

"You have to answer that for yourself, boss. But if you don't at least try, you know you'll regret it."

Mason rested his chin on his chest. In his head, images of carnage on the courthouse steps mingled with scenes from Michael's interrogation.

"I know you're right. Mike's been put through the wringer in so many ways and needs someone on his side. I know him and his case better than anyone right now."

"That's what I'm talking about. You can be the one to step up and really defend him."

Mason nodded. "I'll have a talk with Mike and see what he wants to do. Going down there to meet with him tomorrow."

"Good. Assuming he keeps you as counsel, how are you, a white guy in his thirties, going to deal with the race angle in this case?"

"I'm not sure I need to. That was Alice's approach, not mine. Between Warnock and the confession, I think there's plenty of compelling evidence on our side. I need to keep this simple and handle it my way. No playing to the press, no agenda other than Mike's innocence. With all the insanity around this case, I'd bet he feels more alone than ever, so I'm just going to focus on him."

"Sounds like a good place to start," said Ozzy as he stirred his drink. "But be careful how you handle things, boss. When you try to save a drowning man, he can drag you under."

**33**

Mason parked in the underground lot by the Courthouse, at MacArthur Square. He had driven a circuitous route to get there, constantly checking his rearview mirror for suspicious vehicles in his wake. Now, he craned his neck to double check the space between his Mercedes and the exit doors that led to the security station. Still nothing. He took one last swig of Tito's and set the bottle back in the glove box. He could feel the weight and bulk of the 9mm in its custom holster, clipped to his belt and hidden under his shirt. Mason earned his carry concealed permit ten years earlier, but he never felt the need to use it, until now. After one last check in the side mirrors, he took a deep breath and stepped from the vehicle. Mason's footsteps echoed off the concrete as he crossed quickly to doors, then across the street to the safety of the security checkpoint.

Due to security measures in the wake of Alice's death, the Courthouse Complex was kept sparsely populated, and Mason's journey from the garage to the County Jail was a breeze, passing without incident. He reached the entrance with little delay and was greeted by a familiar face.

"Top of the morning, counselor."

"Hey, Schmidt. How are we doing today?"

"Just fine, Mason. You holding up ok?" he asked with genuine concern.

"Yeah, not too bad. A little shaken up, but you know, the show must go on and all that shit."

"You've got that right. Speaking of which, how many today?"

"Just one," said Mason, then raised the corner of his shirt. "But I'm carrying, so I need a key for the lockers as well."

"Ok, here you go." Schmidt held the key aloft. "But FYI, those lockers are supposed to be for law enforcement only. I get why you're carrying, so I'll make an exception. Today only, ok?"

"I appreciate that. Next time, it stays in the car."

Schmidt placed the key in Mason's hand. "All good. So, name of the inmate?"

"Michael Key."

"Of course. Give me a second."

Schmidt printed off the paperwork, clearing Mason to begin his ascent through the sequence of security checkpoints to reach his client on the fifth floor. After fifteen minutes of waiting in the interview room, Michael was led in. The guard uncuffed him and left, closing the door behind him.

Mason laid a pack of Marlboro Lights and a book of matches on the table next to the small ashtray. "A small gift. Newports are disgusting, so I got you these."

Michael sat down, looking almost bemused. "Wasn't sure who was coming."

"What do you mean?"

"You're the first person from Alice's office to get in touch since it happened. But yesterday I got a letter from the MJB saying they would no longer pay for my legal fees. So really, I didn't know what to expect."

Robert Lang sent Mason an email the day after the shooting, informing him that Alice's team had decamped to Chicago and would terminate their work on the case. The message finished with instructions for invoicing Alice's firm and thanked Mason for his work, wishing him the best 'during this difficult time'.

"Well, just to be clear, I'm no longer working with Alice's office and I think we've both kind of been hung out to dry. But I'm here because I want to help you. And I can get Judge Francis to appoint me, so the County will pay my bill." In that scenario, Mason would represent Michael at a deep discount, but he wasn't worried about the money. "I know you, Mike. I know the case, and I know what you're up against. Now, I'm sure you're going to have other offers, but if you go with me...I can win this case."

Michael reached for the cigarettes and lit one up. Mason could see the exhaustion in his face. The months since the arrest had aged him. "It's almost funny. You stood on that high school stage and gave me the best piece of legal advice I've heard so far – never talk to the cops." Michael shook his head. "If I had listened, I probably wouldn't be here right now."

"Hey, you talked to the police because you trusted them. You knew you were innocent and figured it was best to tell them your story. I know that. And we can use that to our advantage. We can show the jury that your only crime was believing in the system."

Michael took a long drag, held it for beat, then slowly released the smoke from his lungs. "Ok."

"Ok what?"

"Ok, you're my lawyer. Talk to the judge. Do what you have to do."

Mason smacked the table. "Great! Good. Just one thing before we make this official. I want to be straight up with you, ok? I'm not going to play this the same as Alice. Even if I wanted to, I couldn't. I don't have a big team and all the resources to make this some larger than life cause. I mean, it's headline news every day, so that's already done. But you're the one on trial, so I'm focusing on you and you alone. Do you get what I'm saying?"

"Mason, I'm innocent, but I'm not stupid. I'm a black man in America, so I know what happened to me. Alice and I didn't see eye to eye, but she was right about a lot." Michael took another long drag. "Still, I'm not looking to be some kind of poster child. I just don't want to get convicted of something I did not do. I want to be a free man again, period."

"Ok, good. We understand each other. So, if you're not busy," Mason dug his pen and yellow legal pad out of his briefcase and placed them on the table, "we can dig in right now."

"My schedule is pretty open today," said Michael, drawing a low chuckle from Mason. "Where do you want to start?"

"I've reviewed the State's evidence, such as it is, and I've gone over the tapes and transcripts of your interview."

"So crazy to call it an interview. It was more like they fuckin' brainwashed me."

"I know, Mike. I know. But I need to hear the real story now. The whole thing straight from your mouth, ok? And only tell me what you can remember, what you can visualize. That's important. Try to leave out anything the police fed you during the interrogation and just tell me exactly what you remember happening on the night Robin was killed. I'm not here to judge any of your actions. We can get to context and all of that later. Right now, I want to learn about the sequence of events as you recall them. So take your time and start with your arrival at the barbeque in the park."

Michael repositioned himself in his chair, nodded as if securing the memory in his mind, and began. "We were both coming from the school."

"What time?"

"I'd say around 5 p.m. I had to clean up after practice, so I arrived later than Robin."

"You two drove separately?"

"Yeah. We were taking some time apart, so I was crashing with Flip–"

"Flip's real name is William Barris, right?"

"That's right." answered Mike.

Ozzy had already interviewed Mr. Barris and learned he could not offer Michael an alibi. On the night of the murder, Flip left work at 8 p.m. and when he arrived home he found Michael already there, 'kinda drunk and real sad'.

"And Flip is an old friend of yours? That's why you were staying with him when the police picked you up?"

"I've known him for years. He lived close by and he was one of *my* friends, separate from Robin. Fact is, Flip never really liked her, so I didn't get to hang out with him that much. But when things got rough with Robin, he was happy to take me in, and we'd stay up drinking and bitching about the whole thing."

"That's good to know. So, you and Robin arrived at the barbeque separately because of your seperation."

"Yeah, but even when we lived together, Robin and I usually drove our own cars. We had very different schedules and the athletic department is kind of a separate beast."

"Got it. Go on."

"When I pulled up to the park, I saw her car was already there, so I parked in the spot right next to her. I can remember how tired I was that day. Hadn't slept so well the night before and the day at school was not great. Kids acting wild and just wearing me out. So, I wasn't in the most social mood, but I knew a few people who would be there. Not close friends or anything. I mean, me and Robin only moved into the area like a year before, but a few neighbors were there who seemed nice enough and it looked like a couple of colleagues from school were also there."

Mason kept jotting notes. "Great. And what did you do after you arrived?"

"I said hello to a few people. Someone passed me a beer, and there were two grills going. You know, brats, hot dogs and stuff, it was cool. Nice day, still warm out, and people were in a good mood. I made the rounds, finished my beer before I finally went over to where Robin was. She was talking to some work people, including Trevor Warnock. I knew they were friendly, but they seemed maybe too friendly, if you know what I mean?"

Mason nodded, "Sure."

"Like I said," Michael continued, "I wasn't in the best headspace that day, so I approached them kind of aggressively, you know? Just butted in and sort of sent Trevor on his way so I could talk to Robin. I didn't even have much to say, I just was tired of her always talking to dudes. It was just a thing with her."

"Got it," said Mason as he jotted down bulleted notes on his legal pad.

"It was almost like, Robin had no female friends, but she could get along with any man, like she encouraged it or something. I know that sounds like I'm crazy, but you didn't know her, ok? And it just wore on me, you know? And Robin knew it. After a few years...I mean, I still loved her so much, but I felt like she enjoyed seeing me get aggravated."

Michael stopped and stared at the tabletop for half a minute. Mason didn't move a muscle. If his client was getting ready to fully open up, Mason wasn't about to disrupt him.

"It made me insecure. I know that. I let it get to me, inside my head. I got too obsessive. I just wanted her to act right. And I know how that sounds, too, but do you get where I'm coming from?"

"I think I do."

"You married?" asked Michael.

"I was. Divorced a few years ago."

"You still get along?"

"We do now that we're not together."

"Right." Michael paused again, and a bitter smile spread across his face. "Me and Robin, we probably would have eventually split up. Better for both of us. Our highs were really high, but the lows were bad. Brought out the worst in each other sometimes."

"I hear you. Let's get back to the park. To the barbeque, ok?"

Michael shook his head for a long time, then with a sharp inhale he straightened up and launched back into his account.

"I think I just asked her how she was doing and why she was acting so familiar with Warnock. I wanted to know how long we were, I mean, how long she was staying. We'd agreed to take a bit of time away from each other but we never really told anyone about it. Didn't want people talking about us. Especially when you're a teacher, you want privacy and it was nobody's business anyways. We also didn't want to attract extra attention in the neighborhood. A couple of the people on our street had acted kind of fucked up when we moved in. Nothing overt, but you could tell they weren't into us. Then our garage door got spray-painted one night. Big red letters. *JUNGLE FEVER.*"

"Did you report it?" asked Mason.

"Yeah, Robin got super pissed. Cops came by and made a report but nothing came of it."

Mason snorted, "No shocking doorbell cam video from across the street that time, I guess. But I digress. So, you were asking her all these questions, how long she was staying etc. And?"

"And she was annoyed with me real quick. Like I had spoiled things by showing up. Or by showing up in the mood I was in. We were talking, not loud or anything, nothing really bad was said, but I could tell people noticed and left us alone."

"Ok, and this was par for the course?"

"During that time, yeah. We weren't in a good place."

"What happened next? How did the police get involved?"

"We broke off our chat and each went off to mingle around solo. I was just small-talking and stuff, getting to know a couple of the neighbors. It was polite but kind of awkward. I felt like they were sizing me up, judging me. Might've been in my head, I don't know. I had a few beers, but I wasn't drunk or anything."

Mason knew that 'a few beers' was a Wisconsin euphemism for that window between buzzed and drunk.

"Maybe an hour after I got there I saw Robin say goodbye to the little group she'd been talking with and start walking to the parking lot. Didn't say goodbye or even look my way. I knew she was annoyed, but this was like showing me up in front of these people and I was pissed."

Mason made a note – *drunk and angry*.

"So, I followed her and was calling her name, but she wouldn't turn around or respond. I caught up with her by the cars and grabbed her by the arm to slow her down, just to get her to talk to me. I wasn't going to hurt her, ok?"

"It's alright, Mike," said Mason. "I only want to hear what actually happened."

"I remember she moved my hand away and told me not to touch her. I backed off, but I leaned against her driver door so she couldn't get in the car. I just wanted her to talk to me, you know? Like, I didn't even know what to say or anything but I wanted us to say something nice for once, or have her ease up for a minute and look at me like her husband. And I know how all this sounds as I'm saying it. I should've let her go, but at the moment I wanted to try and make it better. It was stupid."

Mason kept writing as Michael talked, but his story was matching up with the interrogation transcript that Mason had read, just with a little more reflection and soul-searching this time around.

"Then Robin started to get loud. She was mad now, calling me names and shit. Tried to shove me out of the way, but I wouldn't budge. She would step back and we would just stand there for a sec, then she would shove me again, shout some stuff at me. It was not good. A few people from the barbeque had kind of walked over to watch, but didn't get too close. The whole situation was just so depressing. I felt mad and sad at the same time."

"But you didn't put your hands on her while this was going down? When you guys were over by the  cars?"

"No. I mean, not really. When she'd try to get me off her car I stood my ground and maybe grabbed her wrist to get her hand off me. She would dig her nails into my arm, you know? But I didn't push her or hit her. I don't care what anybody thinks they saw, I didn't do anything like that."

"Ok, good to know. Keep going."

"I don't know how long it was, but it seemed like the cops showed up real quick. Two squad cars, four officers. They rolled in with lights and sirens, hopped out the cars and came straight for me, no questions asked. Just yelling to get my hands up, get on the ground, don't move, get your hands behind your head, all sorts of stuff. It was confusing. I was scared, man, because I know they'll shoot someone who looks like me and ask questions later. Or step on my neck and say I'm resisting. So, I did what I thought was best and laid down on my stomach with my hands out. I'm trying to talk to them, like 'Hey, I'm not armed, that's my wife, we're just talking', but they pounced on me, got me cuffed, and stood me up against the cruiser."

"And where was Robin?"

"She was standing by my car, and I could see she was freaked out. She was yelling at the cops, too. Telling them to stop hurting me, you know 'You leave him alone! That's my husband!' type stuff. I think she was afraid this was going to go too far. She must've finally gotten through to them because once they had me against the police car they seemed to relax and turned me around so I was facing them. They told me to shut the fuck up and asked Robin what was going on. She was explaining to them we were just a married couple having a disagreement and this was all a big misunderstanding. The cops weren't as amped up as when they arrived, but were still looking at me like I must've done something. She kept asking who called them to come there and they wouldn't answer."

"Ok, so Robin helped de-escalate the situation. She didn't say you'd done anything wrong or anything?"

"No. I know she was still mad at me, but she didn't want to see me dragged away."

"Right."

"After they got the story from us, they took my cuffs off and told me that I needed to go cool down somewhere, and they were going to wait with Robin until they felt everything was ok. The way they talked to me, it was like I was being disciplined or something. It was ridiculous. And by that time, everyone from the barbeque and the people who lived across from the park were all watching. I felt insulted and embarrassed, but I knew I couldn't do anything about it so I just wanted out of there. I got in my car and I drove away."

"Ok, so Robin was still there with the cops when you left?"

"Yeah."

"And you went straight to Flip's house?"

"Pretty much. I mean, yeah, I thought about waiting at the house to clear things up when Robin got there, but I was freaked out by what happened with the cops. I thought maybe it had scared Robin straight, to see how far we'd let things go, you know? So I cruised around the neighborhood a bit, hit the liquor store and went back to Flip's. He helped calm me down. I sent her a couple texts but she never responded."

"Right. I have your cell phone records and that all checks out. The State plans to use the location data to imply you were at your house that night but the signal radius is several miles wide, and Flip's house lands inside of that."

"Right, Alice's guy outlined all that stuff for me. That's good for us, right?"

"Sort of. If the data produced pinpoint accuracy we could show that you were never at the scene. Ok, you've sent texts to Robin, you're at Flip's place."

"Right. We kept drinking for a few hours. I kept him up kind of late. He can tell you exactly where I was the whole night. Right on his couch, getting wasted and talking about how I was going to save my marriage." Michael lit another Marlboro.

"And you were both still awake when the deputies knocked on the door?"

"No, Flip went to bed around midnight. He said he loved me and all, but he had to work early. Told me I needed to get some sleep, too. I stayed up for a bit, checking my phone to see if Robin wrote back. Think I passed out for maybe an hour. Got up to use the toilet and when I came back in the front room, I saw the flashing lights on the street. I figured I knew what was up, so I went and opened the door before they knocked or smashed it in. I didn't want them to wake Flip."

"And what did the officers tell you?"

"Said they wanted me to go with them to the station to talk about what happened with Robin."

"That's the way they said it? Nothing more specific?"

"No, not that I can remember. I was still kinda drunk but I don't think they said anything about Robin getting killed or even hurt. But I know they were on edge, man. I sensed it, 'cause it kind of sobered me up. Felt like they meant business. So, I just went."

Mason put his pen down. "Ok, this is a really good start, Mike. Really good. And between now and the trial, I want you to continue to think about that day. If you decide to testify, we will need your memory to be clear, so keep working on it."

"Yeah, I can do that. What's next?"

"I'll sort everything with the judge and come back here tomorrow to get your autograph on the paperwork. Otherwise, I have my investigator looking into Warnock to see what we can use and over the coming weeks I'll be prepping material for our witnesses. I'm going to be back here regularly to review this stuff because as far as I'm concerned, you're part of the defense team. We're in this together now."

**34**

Ozzy stood in the sally port of the Milwaukee Police Administration Building, waiting to meet someone. He checked his watch again and leaned against the wall next to a rusted, and very full, standing ashtray a few feet past the garage entrance.

At the far end of the port a heavy metal door swung open. A uniformed police officer emerged and nodded at Ozzy. He nodded back but didn't move, and the officer crossed to his spot by the ashtray.

"Thanks for meeting me, Matt," said Ozzy.

The officer pulled a folder from inside his jacket and put it in Ozzy's hand. "Here it is."

Their meeting took place in what many on the force called the Bermuda Triangle. This otherwise nondescript strip of concrete and cinder block, no more than six feet wide and fifteen feet long, lay in a blind spot for the security cameras. It was a handy location for unsanctioned meetings, 'vigorous' interrogations, any number of activities that didn't meet department rules and regulations.

"But you did *not* get this from me," said Matt. "We clear, Smith?"

Ozzy opened it halfway to confirm that it contained the personnel file for Detective Roland Chase.

"You bet. I know you're out on a limb here." He slipped the file under his coat and zipped it up tight.

"Yeah, well, it's easy to make an exception for a dude like Chase. That file makes for interesting reading." said Matt. He lit a cigarette and took a long draw.

"You're still smoking?"

"That's why I came out here, right?"

"Right." Ozzy scanned the sally port to confirm the coast was clear, then walked away, hugging the wall until he was around the corner to the street side of the building. After a couple of blocks, when he was sure he hadn't been noticed, Ozzy grabbed his cell phone and dialed.

"I've got it."

Mason's voice came down the line, "Meet me at Communato."

———

Although he visited less frequently, Denise knew Ozzy well enough to know he wanted a tall black coffee, no frills. Nothing that would, as he put it, 'taint nature's creation'. When he walked in, she began pouring.

"Here you go, detective." Denise wasn't sure if it was the correct designation for him, but she liked the way it sounded and he didn't seem to mind. Besides, she respected Ozzy. He was low maintenance and a gentleman, the polar opposite of the middle-aged clientele that hit on her in awkward and sometimes bizarre fashion.

Denise jerked her head toward the doorway behind the bar. "He's in the back office. You can come around the end of the bar."

"Thanks." He picked up his cup and followed her directions, pausing in the doorway.

"End of the hall, on the left," said Denise. "He's been back there for about an hour. Not sure why, but he seemed a little spooked."

"Got it." Ozzy walked through the beaded curtain to the back of the shop and knocked lightly before opening the door that read *Authorized Personnel Only.*

He saw Mason sitting across from Colin in the cramped office. Their conversation stopped as he entered. The sound in the small room was dampened by the sacks of coffee beans and wall shelves overstuffed with paperwork. Ozzy's eye immediately went to the 9mm on the small desk, which he recognized as Mason's.

"Hey Oz," said Mason, "Quick, close the door."

Ozzy complied and pointed at Colin. "Is he going to stay for this?"

"Don't worry about Colin. He's ok," said Mason. "Did you get it?"

Ozzy patted his chest. "Yep, right here."

"Let me see." Mason took the file from Ozzy and examined the contents.

He reviewed the basics – from when Roland Chase joined the force, his career path, moving up to detective and then to the homicide unit. Mason noted a couple of minor infractions early on, then his record was clean until three years ago. Since then, he had four reports of excessive force against black suspects and was reprimanded privately. Nothing formal.

"Oz, let me ask you this – what would've happened if there was a string of excessive force complaints against you only involving one specific demographic, but they want to keep it quiet?"

"It would pretty much end my career. I mean, I could stay on the force if it wasn't anything too heinous, but I'd never advance. It'd be a stalemate."

"Let me ask you another question," Mason flipped back and forth between two pages in the file. "How many detectives pass on taking overtime when offered?"

"None. I mean zero. That is the great loophole for cops. Base salary may be low, but you can make a lot of money padding it with overtime. One year, I almost doubled my take home that way. And it's easy to justify, especially in a homicide unit. Long investigations, endless records to sift through, nobody questions your hours."

"Right. But for the last three years, our boy Chase has declined overtime again and again." Mason laid the file in front of Ozzy. "I only know a few of these names in the log, but I'm sure you know more than I do. It looks to me that Chase declined overtime every time he might be partnered with a black cop."

Ozzy leaned over Mason's shoulder and ran his eyes down the shift request list. The pattern sure seemed to show Chase dodging assignments with black colleagues.

"You need to dig into this guy," said Mason.

"You bet." Ozzy tried to sound casual, but he knew sniffing around a homicide detective would be tricky. "Anything in particular you want me to look for?"

"I don't know exactly, but any extracurriculars. Did he start running a racket or fall in with some radical groups? Something changed three years ago and I want to know what it was."

Ozzy paused, then his eyes widened. "Don't need to. I was there. The O'Haver case."

Mason dropped the file on the desk. "That's right! Oh shit, how did I miss this? Chase was shot that night, too."

Ozzy took the folder in his hands and flipped to an incident report near the back. "Looks like he was convinced it was because a cop hung him out to dry. A black cop."

"Who?

"Me!" said Ozzy.

"Shit, are you for real?

Ozzy placed the file on the desk and pointed to the page in question. "This report shows he was the John Doe in my IA complaint."

"Why didn't you mention any of this?"

"I didn't know until just now! Fuck, I don't like this. If I go poking around and he gets wind, things could get uncomfortable. He may have enemies on the force, but he's still connected, a senior guy."

"You don't need to go anywhere near him," said Mason, "nothing in person. Just start with what you know, or even what you think you know, and go from there. Check his online presence, talk to your contacts on the street. Nobody's airtight, you know?"

"Gee, thanks, boss. I was hoping you could tell me how to investigate."

"Ha-ha. Just see what else you can dig up, ok? Something I can use in court."

"Sure, but can you do me a favor," said Ozzy, looking around the room, "and tell me why we're here and not at the office? You know I love the smell of coffee, but it's a bit cramped."

"I thought I was being followed. Coulda sworn I picked-up a tail when I was walking Clyde this morning, but I wanted to be sure, so I broke my routine and came here." Mason pointed to the cabinet next to the desk that housed a dozen small monitors showing different camera angles inside and outside the building. Colin hadn't taken his eyes off it since Ozzy arrived. "With Colin's top notch security set up, we can see who comes and goes."

"And?"

"And I was right. Look here." Mason jabbed his finger at a screen showing the customer parking lot. "That Chevy Impala. He arrived just after

I did and has stayed in his car since. Do you think it could be one of your former colleagues?"

"Not sure. I'll ask around," said Ozzy, then jotted down the vehicle description in his notepad. "But following a defense lawyer in the middle of a high profile homicide case, that's not the department's style."

"I agree. Maybe the Brotherhood, or even MJB for some reason? This case has brought all the overheated kooks out of the woodwork. Who knows what they think of me."

"I can't make out the plate, can you?"

"Don't worry," said Colin, a sheepish grin on his face, "I got it earlier, when I took some garbage out to the dumpster."

Mason shook his head. "I forwarded it to Linda to check, and it's registered with Enterprise Rent-A-Car at General Mitchell Airport. So that was a dead end."

"Can we subpoena the records to see who rented it?" Ozzy asked.

"No, I don't have some kind of carte blanche subpoena power. I'd need to show it was relevant to a case and convince some judge to sign off on it."

"Maybe I could try my contacts at the department, but–"

"But if it's MPD we don't want to tip them off," said Mason. "Need to find another way."

"Maybe I could ask around at the rental counter."

"I'll let you know. But let's stay focused on our top priority – Chase. See if there's anything there. And can you check-in on Sammi? He didn't return my call this week. In case we need him, I don't want that kid getting flaky on us. And last thing, take another shot at interviewing Warnock. With everything going on, a guy like him might be ready to crack."

**35**

The past few weeks saw Ozzy juggling his three witness assignments with varying degrees of success. With the start of Michael Key's trial fast approaching, it was time for another sit down with Mason to get him up to speed.

He arrived at the offices of Mitchell & Associates five minutes ahead of his meeting time, as usual. Ozzy walked through reception to the office and found Mason rummaging in a desk drawer.

"Hey boss. Hope I'm not too early."

Mason sat up and placed a bottle of Tito's on the desk. "What? No, it's fine. Have a seat."

Linda walked in and placed two copies of the prosecution's witness list on the desk. "Need anything else?"

"That's ok, we're good," said Mason as he poured three fingers of vodka into a heavy etched glass. "Thanks, Linda."

"Alright, I'm going to head home then." She eyed the bottle with disapproval, then turned to leave.

"You bet. Have a good night," said Mason. Ozzy gave her a friendly wave as she closed the office door behind her.

"Ok, so let's start with Warnock. What do we know?" asked Mason.

"I'd say his life is officially in the shitter. His wife has filed for divorce, he lost his job, and the media won't stop hounding him. I'm starting to worry he might come off as sympathetic to the jury."

"Find anything that ties him to the murder?"

"You mean other than an affair with the victim while they both worked in the same building as her husband? No. And I gave him a long look."

"Right. The State has him on their witness list, but I'm going to subpoena him anyway." Mason circled the next name on the list. "What about our friend, Detective Chase? The personnel file gave us some nice insight. You dig up anything else on him?"

Ozzy opened a folder containing his findings. "Sure did. As it turns out, Roland Chase likes to participate in a few sketchy communities online. My guy found him posting in fringe-y Blue Lives Matter stuff and Alt-Right forums. Nothing actionable, but his comment logs showcase some pretty distasteful views on a range of topics." He handed a printout to Mason. "And we didn't have to scratch too far beneath the surface to find this." Ozzy slid another piece of paper across the desk. Mason's eyes widened as he scanned it.

"Well how do you like that? An active member of the Aryan Brotherhood."

"For three years running," said Ozzy. "And I've got reliable sources who say Chase has made his way up the ranks. This is off the record, of course."

Mason let out a low whistle. "Three years ago. Really went off the deep end, huh?"

"I never got a good feeling off the guy, and by all accounts he's always had this in him. Nowadays, Chase is just like a lot of these people, doesn't feel like hiding it so much anymore."

"Yeah, that checks out."

"Anyways, he's written a string of posts on their social media accounts and in various chat rooms under the handle @whitebadge414. Most of it is pretty standard for the AB, but he makes his racial views pretty clear."

"Anything else?"

"There's a link to Kilpatrick, the guy who shot Decatur."

Mason put his glass down and leaned forward. "What kind of link?"

"The news says Kilpatrick worked at Walgreens in Illinois, but I found out he moonlighted tending bar at a place called O'Danny's near Wrigley Field. The owner of O'Danny's also has a place called McTavish Irish Pub."

"Why do I know that name?"

"Because it's close by, out in Brookfield. And that's where Chase had his side gig, picking up shifts as a bouncer. A few times a month, during baseball season, the owner would get Chase down to Chicago to bounce at O'Danny's during Cubs games."

"Is there anything that could show he got to Kilpatrick? Maybe Chase put it in his head to kill Decatur?"

"Nope. I can't even prove they spoke to each other, but it's all a little cozy and coincidental. I know the personnel file is out because of how we got it, but the AB membership, that's rock solid. Could we use it in court?" From his years on the job, Ozzy had more than a passing familiarity with the rules of evidence, but he wasn't sure what Mason could use on cross-examination.

"I'd have to be careful how I introduce it. If Francis gets the sense I'm reaching, trying to slip something between the cracks, he'll squash me. If I'm going to show up in his court and say that a decorated homicide detective is a racist and that's why he pushed so hard for Mike to confess, I better have something rock solid."

"Ok, what else would you need?"

"Dig into his whitebadge414 username," said Mason, referring to the printout, "and see if your guy can establish a concrete link to Chase. Login and account info, email address, anything. And see if those witnesses will go on the record."

"One's a cop, so he won't talk. The other one is intimately involved with Chase. I don't think she wants to go public."

"You never know. Just talk to them. Please. If you get something concrete, I can file a motion to allow it." Mason picked up the State's witness list again. "Ok, who's next?"

"Robin's gynecologist, Dr. Fehl. Why would they call him?" Ozzy looked puzzled.

"They need his testimony to prove she was pregnant, for the murder charge against the unborn child. They'll also use him for statements about Michael."

"What statements?"

"The medical records say that Robin told the doctor that Michael was not happy about the pregnancy. In fact, she claims he even questioned if it was his baby. They had tried before but were unable to get pregnant. According to the notes, Robin said that Michael thought he might be sterile and accused her of having an affair, which Robin denied."

"I don't understand. How can the doctor testify to what Robin said? That sounds like textbook hearsay."

"Normally it would be, but any statements Robin made to her doctor for the purpose of treatment are exempt from the hearsay rule. Judge Francis already ruled all of Robin's statements to Fehl can come in."

"You want me to have a look at him?"

"I don't think so. His testimony helps to prove there was an affair, which cuts both ways. And he can testify to Robin's denial of the affair, which was a lie. That might help us. I'll make him work on the stand but I'm not so sure it's a good idea to attack him."

"Got it."

"What about Sammi?" asked Mason.

"He is a little jumpy, no surprise there. But he'll be ready when we need him and I will make sure young Mr. Mueller gets to court, even if I need to drive him myself."

"Good. So, between now and the trial I'll be doing more prep and working with our two expert witnesses. Looks like we'll be in decent shape, or at least I hope we will."

"Sounds good to me, boss. And if that's all for now, I think I'm ready to get out of here." When Ozzy stood up and stretched, his spine cracked from top to bottom. "Or I could wait around? Follow you home?"

"That's a pretty slick pick-up line, Oz, but I think I'm good."

"Hey, I saw you've been carrying the Ruger. Figured you might be a little jumpy and could use the backup."

Mason got the sense that Ozzy was half concerned and half lonely, but Mason didn't want him hovering around like a bodyguard.

"No, really, it's ok. I'm going to be here for another hour going over this stuff. Why don't you get out there and try your lines on some poor unsuspecting divorcees?"

Ozzy nodded, gave Mason the finger, and left.

After finishing at the office, Mason went home to pick up Clyde and take him for a walk. Back in the loft after, Mason found his mind wouldn't stop racing. He kept thinking about the sordid private life of Detective Roland Chase, but it wasn't getting him anywhere and he suddenly didn't want to be alone. Mason knew it was too late to call Ozzy, so he made the short walk to Walter's for a nightcap.

When Mason emerged from the bar two hours later, sufficiently drunk, his attacker struck. The man wore a hoodie and a bandana covered his face. He had fast hands, delivering blows with brutal efficiency. Luckily, as Mason flailed in defense he smashed his elbow through the bar's front window.

A moment later, John the bartender burst out the door and pulled the hooded man off Mason. "Get the fuck off him before I call the cops!" The assailant whirled around and landed a clean right to the bartender's jaw before sprinting down the alley.

A moment later, a young bar-back joined them on the sidewalk, baseball bat in hand. "Which way?"

"Forget it," said John, "he's fucking gone. Call an ambulance."  He turned back to Mason "Hey! Can you hear me? You, ok?"

Mason spit a mouthful of blood onto the pavement. "I'm fine. Help me up."

John put his head under Mason's arm and hoisted him off the sidewalk. Mason's 9mm lay a few feet away, shining dully under the streetlight. He bent to retrieve it and stopped short as pain ripped across his midsection.

John picked the gun up gingerly and helped Mason replace it in the holster. "Who was that guy?"

"I don't know. He walked up out of nowhere, said something about me being a *'race traitor'* and cracked me in the ribs. I tried to grab my gun, but he knocked it away. I got a couple of shots in but he knew how to handle himself, like he'd had training. I was no match." Mason gasped for breath.

"Sounds like he did a number on you. You might have broken ribs or internal bleeding. Can you walk?"

Mason nodded slowly. John helped him inside, easing him onto a bar stool where he waited for the ambulance.

When the paramedics arrived, they strapped Mason to a stretcher and transported him to Mount Sinai Hospital, where he was fed some painkillers, then given x-rays and a CT scan. The police arrived to take a statement, but he knew it would amount to nothing. Unlike Communato, Walter's had no exterior security cameras, and both Mason and John had been unable to provide a detailed description of the attacker.

Mason lay in the hospital bed, waiting for his scan results. He drew shallow breaths so as not to awaken the pain in his ribcage. As the shock had worn off, fear settled in him. He didn't know what to do, where to go. Mason knew the assailant must have tailed him from his house. Now they knew where he liked to go at night. It seemed they knew everything, and everywhere he went. *Fuck, why did I keep this case?*

He grabbed his phone and dialed. "Meet me at Mount Sinai. I'm on the second floor."

Ten minutes later, two young men in baggy jeans and oversized t-shirts entered the room and stood guard on either side of the door. Jalen appeared in the doorway dressed in a similar style but accessorized with a fresh black Chicago White Sox Hat and what looked like fifty thousand dollars worth of jewelry. He walked to Mason's bedside without breaking stride.

"Hey, Jalen. Thanks for coming. Appreciate it," said Mason.

"Of course. You like family. So who was this, bro?"

"I really have no idea. Some nutjob. But I don't need any action, just someone to keep an eye out."

"Easy. Twenty-four seven?"

"I think I'm good at home or my office, and obviously in court. Just everywhere in between."

"Done. You strapped?"

"I am, but it didn't help much this time."

"Whatever. As long as you're gonna carry it, you gotta be ready to pull the trigger, right?"

"I know. I will be. But I just want an extra pair of eyes to watch my back for a while."

Jalen nodded. "Hit me up anytime you're gonna move and you'll have cover. How long?"

"I've got two weeks until the trial starts. After that, we'll see."

"Bet. Love." Jalen turned and walked out without looking back, taking one of the young men with him. The other stayed, standing guard as Mason slept through the night.

**36**

*"Downtown Milwaukee ground to a halt today as protesters and counter-protesters staged running street battles. The windows of several downtown businesses were smashed and three vehicles were set on fire, including one police cruiser. It all started after an initial demonstration here, in front of the County Courthouse steps early this morning. It's unclear exactly what set off the altercation, but tensions surrounding the Key murder trial have been running high for weeks. Recall only a few months ago, Michael Key's first lawyer, Alice Decatur, was assassinated on the steps of the Courthouse. And a couple of weeks ago, his current lawyer, Mason Mitchell, was attacked outside a downtown bar. The trial is scheduled to start today with jury selection, a process that will be made mor e difficult given publicity surrounding this case.*

*There were no fatalities as the demonstrations turned violent, but several injuries have been reported, and property damage estimates are unknown at this point. A massive police presence was deployed to make arrests and disperse both groups while enforcing a so-called 'no go zone' around the Courthouse Complex. As Mayor Douglas joined community leaders in calling for calm, his office has not ruled out a curfew for the downtown core. Reporting live from Clas Plaza, I'm Paige Tyler, Fox 6 News."*

---

"I brought two suits, the gray and the navy." Mason held them up for Michael. "Which one do you want?"

"I thought we already decided on gray today and navy tomorrow?"

"Right, the deputies will bring it back for you to change," said Mason as he looped a purple tie around Michael's neck and began on a half Windsor knot. "This'll go nice with the suit. Not too showy. Just friendly."

As a safeguard against suicide, inmates were not allowed ties, shoelaces or belts in their cell, so Mason always provided accessories for his high profile defendants. He would have liked to bring Michael a nice pair of shoes but they were also banned, and with the floor length table skirts in the courtroom the jury wouldn't see his feet anyway. There would be a full house for the start of the trial, not to mention an overflow room down the hall filled to capacity. All eyes and cameras would be on Michael Key – the black football coach accused of murdering his white wife. The Chief Judge approved a media request made under Wisconsin Supreme Court Rule 61, and would permit Court TV to film the trial. Consistent with the rules, both prospective and selected jurors could not be filmed and Judge Francis, already uncomfortable with the media presence, intended to ensure the rules would be followed. Otherwise, America would have full access from gavel to gavel.

"Thanks for the tie, and the suit. I'm nervous, Mason. Really nervous."

"I know. This is a big moment. But I'm here with you the whole way. The jurors will be watching you, so ignore everything else out there and just sit up straight and keep calm. I'll put a pad and pen on the table for you to take notes if that helps." Mason pulled a pair of tortoise-shell frame eyeglasses from his breast pocket. "I can't give these to you right now, but you can put them on once you get seated. They're not prescription or anything, and you'll have to surrender them before you leave each day, but I want you to wear them whenever you're in the courtroom."

"Are you serious?"

"Yes, I'm serious. The suit, the posture, the glasses, it all counts. When you get in there, the DA is going to paint an ugly picture of you for the jury. I want the real life Michael Key sitting in front of them to look as different from that as possible, like a guy they'd have over for dinner."

"Yeah, ok. I get it. I'll wear the glasses."

"Thank you," said Mason, straightening his own tie for the tenth time.

"Are you nervous?"

"Hell yes. I'm always nervous when I defend an innocent man." Mason stepped back and looked Michael up and down. "You're going to be great, just stay loose and let me do what I do. I'm going to head in now. Get dressed and I'll see you out there."

Mason left Michael in the bullpen, closed the door behind him, and gestured to the deputy sitting nearby indicating he was done. Mason walked past the desk and through the back door into the courtroom. This door served as the entrance for defendants, but to reach it they had to walk down a hallway that took them right past the jury room. This meant the deputies had to play a game of 'hide the defendant' each time they moved someone who was in-custody, trying (not always successfully) to shield them from the view of jurors who were about to determine their fate. This lack of separation is arguably a breach of the defendant's right to a fair trial, but with no budget to renovate the Safety Building, there were no other options.

Mason had conducted dozens of trials in the building, but this would be his first in Courtroom 620. As he walked through the door, he was struck by the energy of the packed house. He had never tried a case in front of a gallery this large, or felt an atmosphere so charged.

He had worked in front of courtroom cameras before, but the maze of wires leading to the soundboard manned by a producer sitting inches behind the glass partition took things to a new level. Court TV planned to air every second of the trial, while every major news outlet closely followed the case. A small conference space adjacent to the courtroom had been converted into a media war room, crammed with tables bearing banks of monitors for national and local media, along with the Court TV feed and other cable channels.

Mason walked to the well of the courtroom and stopped at the prosecutor's table, where Templis was arranging his supply of refreshments. "Morning, Grant. You ready for this circus?"

"Got my Diet Cokes all lined up. My witnesses, too."

"Funny," said Mason. He took his place at the defense table and began laying out his materials.

"Attorney Mitchell, Attorney Templis? Judge wants to see you guys in the back," said the clerk.

Mason and Grant walked to a door beside the judge's bench, opposite the door that led to the bullpen. Grant knocked.

"Enter," came the command from within.

They found Judge Francis seated in his austere chambers. The room contained nothing in the way of adornment, not even a family photo on the desk. The wall to the left was floor to ceiling shelving full of legal volumes, against the opposite wall was the only creature comfort in the room, a well-worn leather couch. Francis motioned for his guests to sit in the two hardwood chairs directly in front of his desk.

"How are you gentlemen this morning?" asked Francis. He did not particularly care about the answer, and neither attorney bothered to answer. "I know you both to be experienced trial counsel, so I'll keep it brief. This case may be fodder for the evening news, but I will run my courtroom in the same manner as always, holding you and everyone else in attendance to a high standard of conduct. I've heard the term 'media circus' being bandied about, but we will carry out this trial with professionalism and dignity. Is that understood?" Again, no response needed or expected.

"So, given the intensity of the media attention, we are going to bring up seventy-five jurors to start. I will ask my series of questions, and mine will be the only ones that address pretrial publicity. Based on their answers, I will strike the ones necessary on my own motion. I repeat – neither of you are to ask about pre-trial publicity."

Francis handed a copy of the jury list to each lawyer. "This is who we are starting with, and in the end we will keep fourteen. As I'm sure you both know, given the charges in this case, you will each have seven strikes. So, before the end of the day I'd like this list to be down to twenty-eight, and you can exercise your selections from there. If we can, I'd like to conclude jury selection today. Tomorrow, we can begin with openings and then start the testimony. Any questions?"

"No, your honor," said Templis.

"None from me," said Mason.

"Good. Let's get in there and get started."

Grant half-raised his hand. "Before we do, your honor, I need to inform the court about a development."

"What kind of development, Attorney Templis?"

"Yeah, what development, Grant?" Mason asked. A prosecutor with a 'new development' just before a trial started was never a good thing.

"Well, it seems that we have another witness. We were contacted three days ago and told that an inmate at the jail had information on this case."

"What kind of information?" The judge's tone betrayed his frustration.

"The inmate, Mr. Steven Baker, claims that the defendant confessed to him while they were housed together last week."

Mason exploded, "What a crock! Are you seriously telling me you have a last-minute jailhouse snitch? How fortunate for you!" He appealed to the judge, "I want this witness excluded, your honor."

"On what grounds?" Templis shot back.

"Take your pick!" said Mason. "How about unfair surprise, failure to disclose him on the witness list–"

"But we only learned of him three days ago. Then we had to interview him, which was done yesterday. I only received the police report summarizing the interview this morning." Templis handed Mason and the judge a copy of the report.

"So, what! We still did not know about the miraculous Mr. Baker and we have not had a chance to prepare for him. Also, how do we know–"

"Counsel, calm down," said the judge as he scanned the report. "As inconvenient as you may find this, the DA's account appears to check out. After learning about this witness, it looks like they were diligent in interviewing him and getting you the report."

"Yeah but–"

"Don't interrupt me."

"Sorry, your honor."

"I don't see that the State did anything wrong, and I am going to allow the witnesses. But Attorney Templis will make sure counsel has a copy of the recorded interview by lunchtime."

"I can do that, your honor," said the DA.

"You honor, please reconsider. This is a last-minute ambush. At least give me an adjournment."

"Attorney Mitchell, any adjournment will cause your client to waive his speedy trial rights."

"With all due respect, your honor, a speedy trial doesn't do my client any good if it's not a fair trial."

"Watch it, Mitchell. This is my courtroom you're talking about. You'll get the recording in a timely fashion," he paused to direct a look at the

DA who nodded like a dutiful schoolboy, "and we can proceed with your client's rights intact. That is, unless he wants to remain a guest of the county for even longer while we sort out your adjournment?"

"No, your honor. My client has made it clear he wants no delays. I guess if we get the recording by lunch, I can use the next few days to review and have my investigator look into it."

"Then it's settled. We need to place this discussion on the record before we bring in the jury.  If neither of you have anything else, let's get out there."

"Wait, your honor," said Mason. He was pissed about the snitch and wanted to claw back some leverage. "If you are going to allow this last minute witness, I would like you to reconsider the admission of the posts made by whitebadge414 when detective Chase testifies."

"Counsel. That issue has been litigated, and if you have nothing new to add I see no reason to revisit it."

"With all due respect, your honor, Mr. Baker is being called to bolster the confession given to Detective Chase. If Chase had a motive to push a false confession we should be able to explore that. The whitebadge414 posts clearly bring his motives into question."

"Your honor!" said Templis, his voice rising to a whine.

Francis raised his hand to cut off all discussion. "At most, Mr. Mitchell, you have posts that are tied to an IP address at a coffee shop *near* detective Chase's home, nothing more. My ruling stands. All whitebadge414 posts are out. Now let's get in there."

———

After a long day of jury selection, Mason walked into the office and plopped down in his chair. Ozzy and Linda filed in after him and settled into the two seats on the other side of the desk. One of Jalen's 'cousins' took up his post by reception. Ozzy still didn't like the choice of security, but he understood the need.

"How's Mike holding up, boss?"

"Fine, but he's as pissed as I am. Says Baker is full of shit and that they never spoke. But he remembers a time about a week ago when he got back to his cell and his discovery materials seemed out of order, like someone might have messed with them. Figured it was a random inspection."

"They scan all those materials into an inmate's property. That record could show us if anything is out of place."

"That's what I'm thinking. Can you look into it?"

"You bet," said Ozzy as he scribbled in his notepad. Mason had long ago stopped trying to get him to use a phone app for notes. "How did Baker get on the radar in the first place?"

"Officially? He asked to talk to the detectives. But I figure he's either an opportunist who saw Mike as his golden ticket, or somebody from homicide put Baker up to it. Whatever the real story is, there's no way this guy is on the level. I need to neutralize him on the stand."

"I'll see what I can dig up for you." Ozzy set his pen down and studied Mason. He looked tired, agitated. "What do you think of the jury?"

"Not in love with them," said Mason. He seemed distracted.

"Right, but I'm surprised we got Juror Eighteen," Ozzy paused to check his notes, "and Sixty-Three. Both had prior arrests for domestic cases, so I would've bet on Templis cutting them."

Mason loosened his tie. "Yeah, maybe. All I know is, the demographics on that panel were not ideal."

"In a pool of seventy-five, I counted just eight black candidates," said Linda. "That didn't help." Normally she didn't attend court, but Mason wanted her there for jury selection on the big cases. He believed that non-lawyers got a better read on prospective jurors and would consult with Linda and Ozzy during the breaks.

"There are never very many. Not in Milwaukee," said Ozzy, "Even though the county is, what, twenty-five percent black?"

"Closer to thirty," said Linda.

"Right. So, it's even more out of whack."

She nodded in agreement. "And for all the wrong reasons."

Mason reached into his lower desk drawer, producing a bottle of scotch and three glass tumblers. "Well, you need to be a registered voter to get a summons," said Mason, anger rising in his voice, "so that skews the numbers. And maybe you're scraping by on shift work or your boss is a dick who won't let you miss time."

He poured a generous measure into each glass and set two of them on the desk in front of Ozzy and Linda. Mason picked up the third and began pacing behind his desk.

"Even though employers are legally required to let workers take time off," said Linda, then felt Ozzy's hand on her arm, stopping her. He could see Mason needed to blow off steam and the less Ozzy and Linda said, the sooner it would be over.

"And you're not about to press your luck and get fired over fucking *jury duty*," said Mason, waving his hand dismissively. "So you don't show! That's why half of my goddamn panel today were the slack-jawed morons who can afford to take a few days off work!" Mason shook his head as he swirled the amber whiskey in his glass. "Some people don't show because they're convinced the system is rigged, and I can't say I blame them. The worst part is, this kind of bullshit isn't even malicious; it's *mindless*. Jury disparity isn't a problem with the summons system, it's a problem with the machine, with society. You add it all up, and that thirty percent ends up more like ten percent." Mason stopped pacing and downed his scotch in one gulp. He saw Ozzy and Linda looking on with concern. Both of their glasses were untouched.

"Shit. Guess I got into a bit of a sermon there," said Mason.

"Maybe a little," said Linda.

"C'mon, boss," grumbled Ozzy, "Let's stay on track. You can make this work."

"I don't know, can I? The confession was bad enough, but now we have Baker and this sketchy jury." The madness of the past few months seemed to weigh him down, and he slumped into his chair. "How's Mike supposed to get a fair trial with all this shit?"

"Hey, you've said it yourself, the State's case is thin and you're as well-prepared as you've ever been, so don't tighten up now. This is it. You get to walk in that courtroom tomorrow and put on a show."

Ozzy knew which buttons to push. For Mason, trial was the most comforting thought.

"I know. Just a little frustrated. Anyway, the rant is over and you're both free to go." Linda looked relieved. Mason reached across the desk and grabbed her glass.

"Anything you need before I take off, Mason?" she asked. "You're all set with the, um, young gentleman out front?"

"All good, Linda. And really, thanks again for today. It was good to have you there." Mason took a sip and leaned back in his chair.

"I'll walk you out," said Ozzy, falling in behind Linda. He stopped in the doorway and looked back at Mason. "Do yourself a favor and don't stick around too long, ok? You look like you could use some rest."

Mason saluted. "I'm heading home soon. Clyde awaits, plus I bought groceries. I'm going to cook dinner."

Ozzy's eyebrows shot up. "No shit?"

"No shit. Taking a night off to be a homebody and prepare for my opening tomorrow."

"Good call. Just try not to cut off any fingers, Chef Mitchell. At least not any important ones."

Mason raised his glass as the two left the office, then emptied it, closing his eyes as the familiar whiskey warmth spread through his chest.

He picked up Ozzy's abandoned whiskey glass, took a sip, and began scrolling through his emails, stopping when he saw one sent that afternoon from [WIDOC] with a subject line that read EMAIL FROM TAYCHEEDAH CORRECTIONAL INSTITUTION - CLICK LINK BELOW. The instructions directed him to a Wisconsin Department of Corrections portal, where he was required to answer a series of verification questions. This produced a code that he received in yet another email, along with a link to his registered WIDOC account. "They gotta do everything the hard way," muttered Mason. Only after entering that code was he finally able to view the correspondence.

*Mason,*

*I finally got an email account approved! So now you have no excuse for not responding, LOL.*

*Did you know you're famous in here? Everybody knows that you're my lawyer so it's like I know a celebrity! The Key trial is on Court TV and that's all anyone wants to watch in the lounge, especially since that poor lawyer got shot. That's so messed up! Do you have police protection or something?*

*Anyways, we've all been watching the lead up to the trial, so today was super exciting. No one in here likes Judge Francis, but most of us think you picked a good jury. Are you nervous?*

*I hope you don't mind that I write to you so often. I know you're busy so it's no big deal that you don't respond each time. The reality is I don't have many people I write to anymore. Actually, it's just you. All my friends from before have cut me off or just ghosted. And I see my family every week but you already know about the good and bad of that. When I write a letter to you it's almost like therapy in a way. I know that someone who works here probably reads my letters before they get sent but I treat it like my little tunnel out into the real world and I know you get what's happening with me and you don't judge or put pressure on me. I hope that makes sense.*

*I have some good news! You remember Cherise, my old cellmate who was bothering me and taking my stuff? She got beat up pretty bad by another inmate. I know I shouldn't be happy about someone getting hurt but I am. I don't know exactly why it happened, but that bitch had it coming, for sure. But the best part is that since it happened, Cherise keeps to herself. I can leave my cell and not have to feel like I need to watch my back all the time.*

*I want to tell you again how good it felt to sign off on the divorce. I don't care AT ALL that David is taking all the things we had. It's not like it was anything that great and besides, all of it reminds me of him and I want none of it. The only thing I want is him out of my life and that's what I'm going to get. No more David is the only good thing about being in prison. And I appreciate you making the process easy on me.*

*Write back soon.*

*(Especially now that all it takes is hitting REPLY!)*

*Lori*

## 37

The natural acoustics in Courtroom 620 were less than ideal. The thirty-foot ceilings and walls clad in oak paneling would swallow a normal speaking voice whole. After years of complaints from court reporters, microphones were installed to compensate. These were sensitive enough to amplify any statements or testimony, and sometimes even private consultation at the counsel table.

Currently, only the clear, sober voice of the Honorable Jeffery Francis could be heard as he read his opening instructions to the jurors. The full capacity gallery of family, media, and select spectators sat in silence, hanging on every word. The atmosphere was like a school library on the day before spring break, hushed but ripe with anticipation.

The instructions included standard, dumbed-down legal explanations all judges were required to read to a jury in Wisconsin, along with the substantive instructions specific to each crime. The script Francis read from was the product of a Jury Instruction Committee composed of sitting judges, academics, and attorneys. These committee members would debate and eventually compromise on the language, which was then published statewide by the Board of Regents at the University of Wisconsin Law School. To Mason and many other members of the bar, this product of collective authorship resulted in jury instructions that made the law more difficult to understand. But then, no one asked him.

Courtroom 620 was the largest secure courtroom in the entire complex, and the only one on the 6th floor of the Safety Building. The size and isolated location made it the venue of choice for high-profile cases; it was in Courtroom 620 that Mason's old mentor, Gerry Boyle, had conducted the Jeffrey Dahmer trial back in the '90's.

After completing the jury instructions, Judge Francis turned to Grant Templis. "Does the State wish to make an opening statement?"

The answer was always 'yes' but either party could elect to not make an opening statement, so the question had to be asked. The defense also had the option to defer their opening to later in the case, but that was trial suicide.

Templis stood and answered, "Yes, thank you, your honor." Mason knew him as a capable trial attorney and a fixture in the DA's office for almost two decades. They had faced each other in trial once before, a loser of a case that Mason rescued by seizing on evidentiary errors by the police. Since that day, they had developed a mutual respect.

Grant's courtroom style was reminiscent of the Woody Hayes offense – three yards and a cloud of dust. He was a straight shooter, if a little unimaginative, and embraced the burden of proof with a keen eye for detail that allowed few openings for the defense. This relentless, no-frills approach had turned Templis into one of the state's top homicide prosecutors.

"Ladies and gentlemen of the jury, this is a simple case of anger and rage resulting in murder. The State will prove that Robin Key was brutally stabbed to death by her husband, Michael Key." Templis placed a large photo print on an easel next to the podium. Taken a few weeks before the murder, it showed a beaming Robin Key at her classroom desk, surrounded by devoted students presenting her with a giant birthday card.

"The defendant is charged with two counts of first degree intentional murder. One count relates to Robin Key, the other is for her unborn child." Templis paused to let the jury absorb the horror of the second count. "We will prove to you beyond a reasonable doubt that Michael Key committed these heinous crimes."

He turned to the next page in his folder and continued, "We intend to prove this through concrete evidence. You will hear from Robin's doctor about her pregnancy and how her husband was convinced this baby was a product of infidelity. You will also hear that the Keys' marriage was on the verge of collapse and that Michael and Robin were separated when the murder occurred. We will present DNA evidence found under Robin's fingernails that proves she had a physical altercation with Michael on the night of the murder. You will hear about their heated argument at a neighborhood barbeque earlier that day, where the police had to intervene and subdue Michael. We will prove that the defendant did not stop, even when the police told him to go home and stay away from Robin. Instead, Michael Key followed Robin back to their marital home where he attacked her on the front porch, brutally stabbing his pregnant wife and leaving her for dead. We will show proof he was there, with phone records that recorded his movements on the night of the murder. And crucially, you will hear a confession from Michael himself, describing to detectives in detail how he murdered Robin Key. A confession repeated just days ago as he boasted of his horrific crime to a fellow inmate in the jail."

Another pause for dramatic effect, another turn of the page. "At the end of this case, after you have heard all the evidence, I will come back before you. I will ask you to reach the only possible verdict based on the evidence – guilty. Guilty for the murder of his wife Robin and guilty for the murder of their unborn child. Thank you."

Templis returned to his table and sat down, his face a mask of quiet confidence.

"Attorney Mitchell, do you wish to make an opening statement?" asked the judge.

Mason nodded to the bench, rose, and buttoned his jacket. He stepped to the easel, took down the photo of Robin, and handed it to Templis. It was an old prosecutor tactic, to put up a picture of the victim during an opening statement or closing argument and conveniently forget to remove it after they were done. If left on display during defense remarks, the jury would be too focused on this sympathetic picture of the victim to pay any attention.

Mason stood behind the podium, opened his laptop, and began. "Prosecutors like Mr. Templis are trained to present theories as facts. In the opening statement you just heard, he used words like 'proof' and 'evidence' in an attempt to convince you that the facts are on his side. But, his presentation was based on nothing more than a collection of conjectures, assumptions, and downright falsehoods. Mr. Templis speaks with the voice of authority, and for you, that might give his words the veneer of truth. But I want you to be careful not to buy what he's selling before you know the whole story, the *real story*, about the death of Robin Key."

He took two steps toward the jury and continued. "Studies have shown that seventy-five percent of jurors make up their minds right after opening statements." Mason loved that statistic. He couldn't remember where he got it from, but it sounded scientific and always got the jury's attention. "Now, this is truly terrifying because, at this point in the trial, no evidence has been presented. And how do we know that?"

Mason picked up a spiral notebook and held it up for the jury to see. "Because you don't have one of these yet. The court will hand out notebooks to each of you at the beginning of the evidence phase in this trial, not before. Nothing said in an opening statement, by me or the State, is evidence. When evidence *is* presented in this courtroom, it will come from one place and one place only," Mason pointed to the raised box behind the court reporter, "the witness stand."

This was a stock opener for Mason. Contrary to the law, most juries presumed the defendant was guilty, and shaking them out of this would require a combination of charm, storytelling, and misdirection. At this stage, he focused on reminding the jury of their duty to listen critically, because the evidence presented at trial generally did not favor the defense.

If Mason's client was guilty, and most were, the evidence usually bore that out. But in the case of an innocent defendant, the system still heavily favored the party with the most investigative resources, and that was always the State. Materials gathered by law enforcement tended to support their theory of the crime and ignore everything else, but if Mason could prepare jurors to question this so-called evidence, he would have a chance.

"Those studies I mentioned also show that people are disposed to side with those in authority. In other words, people overwhelmingly tend to believe that the authorities get things right and we shouldn't question them. I'm sure if you think about it for more than two seconds you'll see how dangerous that kind of thinking can be, but let me tell you a story to illustrate the concept."

Like most trial attorneys, Mason was a fan of Hollywood courtroom dramas. And, like most trial attorneys, Mason was not above borrowing from their scripts. He couldn't get away with half of what his on-screen counterparts said in court, but sometimes the writing was too good to pass up. James Spader's character on *Boston Legal*, Alan Shore, was a particular favorite, and Mason routinely paraphrased him during opening statements.

"It's about a painting by Matisse, entitled *Le Bateau*. Now, I don't know a whole lot about art, but this painting is a favorite of mine for a few reasons. The colors, the simplicity, I guess I just like the way it looks hanging on my office wall. And that leads us to what I really love about this painting. You see, a curious thing happened when the Museum of Modern Art in New York City displayed *Le Bateau* in 1961. Over forty-seven days, this famous masterpiece was seen by over 116,000 people, without incident. These people admired the painting, much as I do, and thought nothing was amiss. And it was only after forty-seven days had passed and so many thousands had seen it that the authorities who ran the museum realized they had hung the painting upside down!"

As usual, this revelation produced snickers among the jurors. Mason smiled inwardly. He didn't have Spader's polished delivery, but this pet device had struck a chord.

"Why do I tell you that story? To illustrate the danger of assuming that authority gets things right. That painting was presented by a world-renowned gallery, the ultimate authority, but they got it wrong for forty-seven days. Even more telling is that the 116,000 witnesses did not challenge their authority, they simply assumed the museum got it right! That lesson applies in our case, but rather than an upside down painting, this is about a man's freedom, his very life. I'm asking each and every one of you to not assume the State got things right."

Mason stepped closer to the jury box. "During this trial, as you examine the evidence and listen to witness testimony, I want you to challenge the picture presented by the State. Do that, and you'll realize they've got it all upside down." Mason returned to the podium and pretended to consult his notes.

"For example, Mr. Templis said that you will hear Michael Key confess to the murder. But he failed to mention the coercive, outdated interrogation tactics used by police, and how they produce false and misleading confessions. We will present expert testimony to show you how it happened in this case."

Mason pointed directly at Templis. "He said you will hear about Michael's DNA being under Robin's fingernails, but he did not mention the fact that another unknown man's DNA was also found under her fingernails." Mason closed his laptop and leaned on the podium.

"These days, we're always hearing that our country is divided, that Americans can no longer agree on what's right and what's wrong. We see it on the news, on social media, and sometimes even around the family dinner table. We've even seen displays of division outside this very courthouse and, tragically, on the steps of this sacred institution just a few months ago. But I don't believe that's the end of the story."

Years ago, Mason's ex took him to the Oriental Theatre and made him sit through Jimmy Stewart's classic courtroom drama, *Anatomy of a Murder*. Mason loved it, and returned by himself the next day for another screening. He had watched it many times since, including last night. Now, Mason put a spin on his favorite speech from the movie.

"I believe that twelve people, with twelve different minds, twelve different hearts, from twelve different walks of life, with twelve sets of eyes and ears, can come together and sit in judgment of another human who is as different from them as they are from each other. And in their judgment they can become of one mind, unanimous. The ability for juries to do this is one of the miracles of man's disorganized soul. In most instances they do it well, and I know you will, too." Mason picked up his laptop and returned to his seat next to Michael.

"Thank you Attorney Mitchell," said Judge Francis. "Bailiff, please hand out the notebooks. Attorney Templis, call your first witness."

---

Mason sat on a barstool in Walter's, replaying the day's events over his third Tito's and Sprite. Next to him sat Tre, the newest face from Jalen's security service. Tre didn't smile or speak, just watched the room while ignoring his glass of water. Mason had grown used to the shadow by now and found that he enjoyed the undemanding company.

That afternoon, Templis had called his opening set of witnesses. First up was his crime scene detective, who gave a fairly straightforward account of what he found on the blood-spattered porch, while Templis introduced far more photographs of the scene than were necessary. It was an example of Grant's 'belt and suspenders' approach, but in general he played fair and kept the more gruesome photos to a minimum. Templis knew that these images could engender sympathy, but a jury might resent being exposed to gratuitous amounts of graphic brutality.

The State's second witness was the fingerprint expert Macy Jordan. She testified they found nothing other than prints from Warnock on the glass beer bottle from the porch. This was another Templis technique. Even when part of an investigation turned up nothing, he would parade the non-findings before the jury to show how thoroughly the police investigated the case. Templis never mentioned they were only looking for Michael Key's prints in the first place, and Mason was only too happy to highlight this detail with his cross-examination.

The last prosecution witness of the day was a neighbor, Anika Jenkins, who lived across the street from the Keys. She supplied the video doorbell footage showing the Keys' porch on the evening Robin was murdered. Jenkins lamely attested that Michael and Robin were quiet but seemed to be 'having troubles'. The video was entered into evidence and played for the jury, but even after being enhanced, it was dark and grainy. The footage showed two indistinct, shadowy figures moving back and forth for several seconds, after which one disappeared from the frame and the other remained, on the ground, motionless. It was evocative and drew low gasps from a few in the courtroom, but was still a far cry from the clear depiction of murder described by detectives in their interrogation of Michael Key.

A quick cross by Mason neutralized the neighbor's flimsy statements about the state of Michael and Robin's relationship, and made plain to the jury that due to lighting, distance, and myriad other factors, the doorbell camera was entirely unsuitable for identification purposes.

In Mason's estimation, it had been a strong opening session with a lot of jury buy-in and no major damage from prosecution witnesses. The first day of what the local news had dubbed 'Milwaukee's Trial of the Century' had gone well for the defense.

Mason tapped Tre on the shoulder. "Hey, you want a burger or something? On me."

The two of them ordered and ate, then propped up the bar for another two hours, all without exchanging a word. Eventually, the clock above the bar and the buzz in Mason's brain told him it was time to get some rest.

He pulled a roll of cash from his breast pocket, peeled off two fifty dollar bills, and laid them on the bar. Mason patted his bodyguard turned dinner companion on the back. "Thanks for the chat," he said, earning a side-eye from the bored young man. "You've been charming. Now you get to take me home."

They stepped out into the chill wind blowing down Water Street. Mason pulled his coat tight and turned toward the parking lot. He hadn't gone five paces when something solid, wooden, slammed into the back of his head. The contents of his skull rattled and pressure hammered into his ears and sinuses. Warmth soaked Mason's shirt collar as his equilibrium went haywire. His body hit the pavement and he received a kick just above the beltline that missed his spine by an inch. Then everything went dark.

When Mason came to, a friendly face framed by a crisp new White Sox cap filled his vision.

"Good thing you just fight for me in court and not on the street," said Jalen.

Mason's hearing was muffled, and his neck felt sticky. He was sitting on the sidewalk, propped against a wall. "Where'd you come from?"

"I'm always where I need to be."

Mason glanced left and right but saw no one else around. "Tre?"

"Don't worry about him. He went to finish doing his job."

"Wha' the fuck happened?" said Mason, his head still swimming.

"Nothing we couldn't handle. Sorry you got touched up."

Pain throbbed between Mason's ears and the scene began to slowly spin. He clamped his eyes shut. "Thanks, man."

"Love, bro. But from now on, you're at home, office, or in court, nowhere else. At least until the trial is over. Got it?"

"Understood."

**38**

"The State calls Trevor Warnock." Grant Templis opened a folder on his table as his witness made his way to the stand.

When preparing their materials, trial lawyers tended to fall into two camps – binder or folder. Templis was a leading proponent of the latter, employing a proprietary system, refined over years, of fastidiously organized folders for every case. In this system, he would devote a folder to each witness, regardless of their importance or the length of their testimony. He attached all relevant reports on the left side of the folder, and his always extensive hand-written notes on the right. With the pressure of a packed house and TV cameras in the room, a well-organized folder put Grant Templis at ease.

After Warnock entered the witness box, the clerk approached and asked, "Do you solemnly swear that the testimony you shall give in this matter shall be the truth, the whole truth and nothing but the truth so help you God?" to which Warnock replied, "I do."

"Can you please say and spell your name for the court?"

"Yes, it's Trevor Warnock. T-R-E-V-O-R, W-A-R-N-O-C-K."

It was just like the jurors had seen on TV, and seeing their favorite show come to life made some of them temporarily forget the tedium of jury duty. But in the next moment, the illusion was ruined as they saw that, in Wisconsin, lawyers did not prowl the floor when questioning a witness, but were required to do so from their table or the podium in the well of the courtroom.

"Thank you, Mr. Warnock," said Templis, choosing to remain seated at his table. "How are you employed?" Mason never understood why, but this was always the prosecution's first question, even when the witness wore a badge and uniform.

"I am, I mean, I was a high school chemistry teacher."

"And where were you teaching in October of last year, when Robin Key was murdered?"

"James Madison High."

"Did you know the victim?"

"I did. We taught together."

"Did you two also have a relationship outside of work?"

"Yes, we had a, um, personal relationship."

"What was the nature of your personal relationship?"

"We were friends."

"But more than friends, yes? Meaning you had a romantic relationship?"

"Um, yes."

Templis shifted in his chair and consulted the notes in his folder. "Let's get more specific. How long was the affair?"

"Oh, I don't know. Um, I would say...about a year, I guess." Warnock spoke like he wasn't one hundred percent aware of every detail by now. Mason almost found it amusing. "Yeah, I'd say a year, and then I broke it off."

"And when was that?" asked Templis.

"It must've been a week or two before she was killed."

"Why did you end things, Mr. Warnock?"

"Well, it was after she informed me she was pregnant. She seemed to think it was mine, but I had a vasectomy three years before, so I knew it couldn't have been. Anyway, Robin and I argued. It was getting too complicated. There were all sorts of reasons for it to end."

"Can you tell us about these other reasons?"

"Objection, relevance," Mason interrupted.

"Overruled," said Francis. "You may answer, Mr. Warnock."

"We were both married, so the whole thing was just wrong in the first place. I felt bad, you know. And then her husband, Michael, he was so volatile. She was worried he would do something–"

Mason sprang from his chair. "Objection! Move to strike."

"Overruled, the answer will stand."

"Sidebar, your honor?"

"Fine. Approach." Francis waved both attorneys to an area next to his place on the bench, away from the jury. He turned off his microphone and flipped a switch that played white noise over the courtroom sound system to obscure their conversation.

"Your honor, the witness is talking about prior bad acts," said Mason, "and that is not allowed. No motion was filed. It's clearly 'other acts' evidence."

Francis turned to the prosecutor. "Mr. Templis?"

"I'm not asking about other acts, judge. We are only talking about why the affair ended. He said the defendant's volatility was a reason. He did not get into specific acts."

"Ok. I will let the answer stand. But tread lightly, Mr. Templis." Francis switched off the white noise, and the lawyers returned to their tables.

Templis continued, "Did you and the victim interact after the affair was over?"

"Yes. After I broke it off, she said Michael had confronted her about—"

"Objection, hearsay," blurted Mason.

"Exception, your honor," replied Templis.

"Sustained," said the judge. "Next question."

Templis ran his finger down a page in the folder to find his place, then looked at Warnock. "What did the victim tell you about her husband's accusations?"

"Objection, hearsay!" Mason raised his arms in frustration.

The judge spoke in a voice cold as the grave. "Chambers, gentlemen." Francis then turned to the jurors. "Members of the jury, we need to discuss a legal matter in chambers. It should be brief, but please feel free to stand and stretch while we are gone." He stepped down from the bench and entered the door to his right, followed by Templis and Mason, who closed the door behind them.

Once inside, the judge unzipped his robe and hung it on the coat rack. He sat on the edge of his desk and directed the attorneys to two chairs in front of him.

"What are you doing, Grant? You know better," said Francis, his tone scolding.

"What Michael Key said is a statement by a party opponent, and therefore an exception to hearsay."

"True, but you're taking us into a second layer of hearsay because your witness heard it from Robin, not from Michael. So, no exception there.

And it is not a dying declaration or excited utterance, so I'm shutting it down. You already got him to say Michael was volatile and I let that stand. Now we're done, understood?"

"Yes, your honor," replied Templis.

"Anything you want to add to Attorney Mitchell?"

"No. I think you're doing an outstanding job," said Mason, stifling a chuckle.

As they returned to the courtroom, Francis took his seat on the bench and quickly jotted a reminder to place the sidebar and chambers discussion on the record later when the jury was out. "You may continue, Attorney Templis."

"Mr. Warnock, did you have interactions with the victim outside of school after you broke off the affair?"

"Yes."

"I want you to tell us about that. Not what was said, just what happened."

"I went to her house the day before the murder. We sat on the porch and talked for a few minutes, I drank a beer, nothing really happened, and then I left. That's it. That was the last time I saw her."

"Thank you. No further questions."

"Counsel, cross-examination?"

"Thank you, your honor." Mason strode to the podium and opened a thin binder.

"So, you were at the Key residence with Robin the night before she was killed, true?"

"Yes."

"Not the night of her murder, October 8th?"

"Correct," said Warnock.

"But you did see Robin at the neighborhood barbeque earlier that day, correct?"

"Yeah, I was there, but I did not see her that night."

"Ok then, where were you on the night of October 8th?"

"Um, at home, I think."

"You think? Was anyone with you?"

"No, my wife was out that night. She was staying with her sister in Chicago that whole week."

"How convenient."

"Objection," said Templis.

"Withdrawn." Mason plowed ahead. "You stated earlier that you and Robin were having an affair for about a year, right?"

"Yes."

"You were doing this behind your wife's back, correct?"

"Yes."

"And behind Michael's back, correct?"

"I guess."

"And you knew Michael, because he was a member of the faculty at James Madison with you and Robin, correct?"

"Yeah."

"So, you would see him around the school?"

"On occasion, yes."

"Of course, you would see Robin around the school *and* elsewhere, right?"

Warnock paused. "Yes."

"So, you lied to your wife and colleague for a *whole year*, isn't that right?"

"I wouldn't put it that way!"

"What other way could you put it?"

"I wasn't...it's just...I didn't tell my wife and I assume Robin didn't tell her husband."

"For a whole year. And you never did tell your wife or Michael Key, but they found out later, didn't they?"

"I guess, yes."

"Let's get into that. Did the police talk to you about the affair?"

"Yes."

"And isn't it true they only came to you about the affair after we did? That is, *after we* filed our motion? After it was already reported on the news, isn't that true?"

"Objection, compound question."

"Sustained," said Francis.

"Ok. I'll break it down and we can go through this together." Mason leaned against the podium and slowed his pace. "Mr. Warnock, the police talked to you after my private investigator tried to contact you, correct?"

"Yes."

"And that was after your affair was reported on the news, correct?"

"Yes."

"So, just to clarify, no one from law enforcement spoke with you at all, until after your affair with Robin was discovered by us, yes?" Mason could feel Templis itching to object. He was not enjoying this line of questioning but had no grounds to stop it.

"That's correct."

"Ok, let me shift gears." Mason paused to flip a few pages in his binder, but he already had a line of questioning lined up in his head, and this pantomime was used for pacing. Once he had a witness on the 'yes train', Mason would make occasional stops to let the jury absorb the testimony. "Mr. Warnock, you told the court earlier that you ended the affair, not Robin. Correct?"

"Yes, I ended it."

"The evening in the library. You said about two weeks before Robin was killed, right?"

"Yeah, that's right." Warnock looked puzzled, as if unsure of where to step.

"What if I told you a student witnessed the two of you together that evening in the library, and that student says it was Robin who broke up with you?"

"They must have it wrong. I'm the one who ended things that day."

"Oh. Ok," said Mason. "So, when you went to Robin's house the night before her murder, it was to what, break it off again?"

"No, we were friends, and I still loved, I mean...I cared for her." Warnock was flailing, desperate to stay afloat. "I don't know, I just wanted to see her, I guess."

"Got it. And while you were there, you drank a beer, right?"

"Yes."

"And that is how your fingerprint got on that bottle found on the porch, right?"

"I guess."

"Isn't it true that you waited until law enforcement confronted you with the fingerprint on that bottle before you *confessed* that you went to see Robin at the house the night before her murder?"

"I don't know. I guess so."

"You guess so? I don't want you to guess, Mr. Warnock, so let's break this down too, ok?"

"Mm-hmm."

"In your first statement to the police, you confessed to the affair, correct?"

"Yes."

"And you told them the last time you saw Robin for, let's say 'personal reasons', was the night you broke it off in the library, correct?"

"Yes. I had forgot–"

Mason plowed on, "And the second time you spoke to the cops was three weeks later. Only then did you mention meeting Robin on the porch the night before her murder, correct?"

"Yes."

"And that was when the cops mentioned the fingerprint, right?"

"Yeah, I think so."

"Good, because I think we had it right the first time – it was only *after* the police confronted you with the fingerprint that you came clean about meeting Robin on the porch of the Key residence the night before the murder, correct?"

"Yeah. I forgot, I was–"

"Did you also forget about seeing her on October 8th?"

"No."

"You never told the police, during any interview, that you were at the barbeque, correct?"

"No, but, I forgot."

"You forgot that, too?"

"Objection, argumentative," said Templis. He needed to protect Warnock before his earlier testimony was rendered obsolete.

"Sustained," said Francis.

Mason continued without skipping a beat. "Isn't it true you went to the Key residence on October 8th and you and Robin got into a fight?"

"No!"

"Isn't it true you knew Robin and Michael had fought at the barbeque, so you took that chance to confront her yourself?"

"No way, that didn't happen."

"And during that confrontation, you grabbed a knife and stabbed her over and over?"

"No. I didn't!" Warnock wailed.

"You have no alibi for that night, correct?"

"No, but–"

"So, we should just take your word for it, right?"

"Yes!" Warnock shouted, his hands shaking.

Mason turned to the jury and continued his questioning, "Mr. Warnock, you want us to take the word of a self-confessed liar? Someone who deceived his trusting wife and coworker for a year? Someone who changed his statements to the police over and over?"

"Objection, argumentative," snapped Templis.

"Withdrawn, nothing further," said Mason. He closed his binder and returned to the table. Francis was clearly unhappy, but Mason had scored all the points he needed. Templis declined to re-direct, wanting Warnock off the stand and gone.

———

The next State witness called to the stand was their DNA expert, Dr. Melanie Gayle, whose testimony held no surprises for Mason. She discussed her qualifications, then, under Templis' methodical direction, launched into a long and boring explanation of the testing process, explaining how samples are magnified to determine if enough DNA is present to render an opinion. The prosecutor then prompted her to deliver a rambling lecture to the jury about what she called 'touch DNA' and how it can be left behind at a crime scene. In the end she offered her findings – the DNA found under Robin's fingernails came from two people, both male. One profile was a match with Michael Key, the other was unknown.

This was far from a shocking revelation, and Gayle's prosaic delivery had rendered the jurors nearly catatonic. When the opportunity came, Mason decided on a fast-paced cross examination to refocus their attention.

"Dr. Gayle, you testified that under Robin's fingernails there was a mixture of DNA from two men, correct?"

"Yes."

"And one of those men is Michael Key?"

"Yes. He is the source of one of the profiles to a reasonable degree of scientific certainty."

"It's not strange for one spouse to have the other spouse's DNA under their fingernails, is it?"

Gayle looked at him blankly. "I wouldn't say, uh..."

"Never mind. Let's talk about the other DNA sample. It came back unknown, correct?"

"It did not match any of the profiles submitted for comparison."

"And which profiles were submitted for comparison? Which samples did you test?"

"The one's given to us by law enforcement."

"I see. Did the police give you a profile for Trevor Warnock to test?"

"No."

"Did they give you any profiles to test other than the one for Michael Key?"

"No."

"Thank you, nothing further."

After a short recess, Templis resumed with a shift to nailing down basic facts, calling two 'chain of custody' witnesses – the cop who took the buccal swab of Michael's DNA pursuant to a search warrant, and the officer who transported the sample to the crime lab. Mason used his cross of both men to establish that the police could easily get a warrant to collect DNA if they wanted, but had chosen not to seek any other warrants.

For the State's final witness of the day, Templis called Robin's OB-GYN, Dr. Lawrence Fehl.

When he entered the courtroom, Dr. Fehl appeared nervous, overly aware of the cameras. In Mason's experience, most doctors were self-assured on the stand, using their intellect and command of the subject matter to take control of the proceedings. They would wow jurors with a flurry of medical terminology and belittle any lawyer who tried to question their expertise. The interrogative format of witness examination favored the lawyer, particularly during cross-examination when they could lead the witness. Not so with doctors. But if this was Fehl's first time on the stand, the packed courtroom and media scrutiny would be enough to make him anxious. Mason saw it as a rare break from the norm that worked in his favor.

Templis used his time with Fehl to establish one fact – Robin was pregnant at the time of her death. This proved the existence of a second victim, the unborn child. The doctor also testified that Robin shared with him her concerns over the pregnancy, implying that Michael was not overjoyed at the news. According to Fehl, during Robin's last visit to his office, she related that Michael accused her of having an affair. Templis elicited a final opinion that Robin felt unsafe in her marriage and was, according to Fehl, "deeply troubled."

Despite the hearsay and pre-trial objections, these comments were ruled to be exempt under the medical provider exception, and Mason did not object in front of the jury. He hoped that Fehl's skittish demeanor and lack of command had lessened the impact of his testimony. But on cross, the doctor held his own, leaving few openings. Mason managed to score one point before Fehl left the stand, establishing that Robin had denied her affair, even to her doctor.

After Judge Francis brought the day to a close, Mason squeezed Michael's shoulder. "This was a good day for us. No big hits from Templis, and we worked Warnock over pretty good."

"Yeah, I'm with you on that." said Michael. He had enjoyed watching his former co-worker crumble on the witness stand and Mason couldn't blame him.

"Anyways, you rest up tonight. I'll see you back here in the morning." The two men shook hands before the bailiff arrived to escort Michael back to jail.

———

Lori sat at the edge of a semicircle of chairs arrayed below the single 32-inch TV. It was mounted high on the wall of the lounge, too high to reach or damage, at least not without great effort. Today, and for the last several days, it was tuned to Court TV, with almost every inmate captivated by the Michael Key trial. The chairs in the lounge were spoken for early in the day and argued over often, with standing room spectators filling in behind them. Raucous play-by-play came from all points in the room. Many inmates fancied themselves as jailhouse lawyers and most presumed to know more than their real attorney, so the running commentary was non-stop. As Lori watched Dr. Fehl give his testimony, someone called out "Wouldn't let that weird little man put his hands on my shit!" The consensus in the room was that he looked creepy, and Lori had to agree.

A woman two seats over shouted, "Can we change the fucking channel?"

"NO!" came the chorus from all across the room.

Lori recognized the woman from her rounds delivering inmate mail to their cells. Deena Oliver. She would get one or two letters a month that looked like they were from her kid.

"Fine, fuck this shit," said Deena. "Fucking pig!" She stood up and hurled her shoe at the TV, an act that caused no damage, but got her hauled off to segregation.

⸻

Mason and Clyde stepped off the elevator after a successful evening walk and ran into their neighbor outside her door. "Hey Donna."

"How are you?" she asked.

"Good thanks. Just took my boy out on the town."

"I've been watching you on TV."

"Are there cameras in the courtroom? I hadn't noticed."

Donna smiled. "Must be weird in there. Outside too. A lot of people making a lot of noise."

"Yeah, I try to tune them out," said Mason, unlocking the door to his unit.

She bent to give Clyde a scratch behind the ears. "Well, if either of you ever need anything, you know where to find me."

"I sure do. Thanks, Donna." Mason nodded goodbye and followed the little dog into his loft. He let Clyde off the leash and retired to his office. Mason woke his desktop and opened a blank doc. As he began typing, Clyde joined him and laid at his feet.

*Lori,*

*Thanks for your letters. Sorry it's been so long and that I haven't been able to write more. You mentioned you've been watching the trial, so you'll know it's getting pretty involved. That being the case, I am working longer hours than usual. A pretty unoriginal excuse, I know.*

*So you say I'm a celebrity now? I like the sound of that. And say hi to my fans, LOL.*

*Witness testimony started today. Maybe you caught parts of it. I think it went ok. We scored some good points and didn't take much damage. I got the jury thinking about the chemistry teacher, Warnock. I don't know how he looked on TV, but in the room he seemed kind of unhinged. Then Robin's doctor was unpredictable and had me on the wrong foot. It's like the whole feeling in that courtroom is off. Or maybe it's just me, a jaded lawyer who thinks everyone seems shifty now.*

*I just want to do right by Michael. He's been lied to and pushed around and manipulated through this whole thing, so I can't let myself get freaked out by the noise surrounding this case. Gotta stay focused.*

*Wow, that was a bit much. My apologies. I've been wrapped up in the bubble of this case and don't get much time to decompress or talk to anyone who isn't involved in the trial. Not comparing my situation to yours, but it starts to feel very isolating. So, I'm glad to have the opportunity to communicate with someone just for the sake of it.*

*Anyway, from what I can tell, you've been coping really well so far and I think you should be proud of yourself. I know that Taycheedah has a couple pretty good professionals you can talk to, but I also know you hate formal therapy. So, I'm totally fine with being your outlet if you need to get things off your chest or just rant and let off some steam. I'm far from a qualified therapist but happy to listen, as long as you don't mind me being late to respond.*

*That's probably why I'm writing this right now. I guess we're both in a position of wanting to have someone to talk to. In any case, I'll continue checking in and working on filings for your civil suit. As you know, that's nearly wrapped up. I'm sure the process continues to be painful, but legal closure is not far off now.*

*Which brings me to your inspirational quote:*

*'If you're going through hell, keep going.' – Winston Churchill*

*I believe in you, Lori. I'll see you on the other side of this, and I'll try to write more often once the trial is over.*

*Best,*

*Mason*

**39**

"*M*an, *I know you keep saying this stuff to me...but I'm telling you...it's just not there. Like, it's not in my head, not at all."*

The overhead lights in Courtroom 620 were dimmed as a video played on the projection screen opposite the jury box. It showed Michael Key slumped in a plastic chair in the corner of Interview Room B at Milwaukee PD District 4. The other figure in the video was seated across a small table with his back to the camera.

*"I hear you, but it's gotta be up there somewhere,"* insisted the seated figure. *"Sometimes people block things out and I get that. It's not always easy to face things that happen, especially when it's like, you know, something that isn't what you're really like. Do you get what I'm saying, Mike?"*

*"I'm trying this whole time to do right by you guys and by Robin...and...oh man, oh my god....I can't even–"*

*"Look, Mike, I know this is hard, but we have to face up to things we do, right? I know it's hard, but we have to."*

The Michael Key in the video began to sob, his hands covering his face. In the courtroom, Michael Key sat completely still and watched, his face expressionless.

*"Noooo. No, man. It's not there. It didn't happen. You got to stop because I can't do this."*

The seated figure slid his chair closer to Michael and leaned in.

*"Yes, you can, Mike. Yes, you can."*

On screen, Michael was doubled over, his body spasming as he wept.

*"Mike, you gotta start telling me how it all happened, ok? I already know about it but I need to hear it from you. We have the video from across the street and it shows everything clear as day. So, this isn't like, something where we have to guess. We know what went down but it has to come from you, here in this room, so we can move forward. Do you understand that?"*

Mason paused the video playback. A timestamp in the corner of the screen showed 04:32:51. The colors in the flickering freeze-frame washed out as the courtroom lights were brought back up. He turned to the man on the witness stand.

"Detective Chase, that's you in the interview room with my client, correct?"

"Correct."

"At this point of the interrogation, how long had you been at it?"

"I would say a few hours. Maybe three or four."

"And this was after he had already been in that room for over twenty-four hours?"

"I think that's probably in the right ballpark."

"And, as we just heard, it was at this point that you told Michael Key you had video of him killing Robin?"

"Yes."

"But what you really had was a grainy porch-cam video from across the street. And as the court heard in earlier testimony, that video only showed blurry, indistinct figures by the front of the Key's house for a few seconds, and that those figures could not be identified in any real way, correct?"

"Yes, that's correct," said Chase. He was calm, sitting tall in the witness box as he delivered his responses in a practiced, matter-of-fact tone.

"Now, I know you're allowed to do this. It's not illegal to lie to a suspect and say you have DNA evidence or a damning eyewitness statement or even video of them committing the crime. You're allowed to lie like that, right?"

"Yes, we're allowed. In our department training, we're taught the effective use of, um, I think the word is subterfuge."

Mason stepped from behind the podium with hands clasped behind his back, and looked Chase in the eye. "Yes, subterfuge. That is another word for lying."

"Well, it's–"

"It's ok, detective. Let's keep moving. So, why did you lie to him?"

"I was attempting to use this technique to...spark a reaction. I wanted to see how he reacted to me disclosing that we had video of the crime."

"Disclosing is the wrong term to use since, as we just established, you made it up. But you wanted a reaction. Ok. When you told Michael Key that you had this video, how did he react?"

"He denied it."

"Denied what?"

Chase took a beat and folded his arms. "Denied that he was there. That it was him in the video." Mason loved the detective's textbook defensive body language and snuck a glance at the jurors. A few had picked up on it.

"Ok, so when you told him this false story that you had a video of him killing his wife, he denied that it was possible."

"Yes."

"In other words, he didn't go along with your false story and expressed once again that he was innocent. And there was no clear video of him, so the defendant was telling the truth, was he not?"

"As you said, he expressed that it couldn't be him."

"Now, I want to recap the interrogation up to this point. You and your fellow detectives, five in total so far, have questioned a still intoxicated man without letting him know exactly why you brought him in. Then you inform him that his wife has been murdered. Then, as he struggles with the shock of this news, you lie to him, saying that you have video of him murdering her. Does that all check out for you?"

"Uh, we have methods that we use to get perpetrators to reveal what they know, and we use these methods when we, according to our training and years of experience, believe we have the right guy for the crime."

"That was an awfully long answer when just a yes or no would have sufficed, but I'm interested in a word you just used there. *Believe.* When you believe you have the right guy for the crime, you want to do everything you can to nail him. Lie, harass, intimidate, break him down, yes?"

"We work very hard to get bad guys off the streets."

"Based on a belief. More like a hunch, a feeling, a gut instinct. A belief that the very first person you get your hands on must be the guy?"

"Objection!" said Templis. "Argumentative, your honor."

"Sustained. Attorney Mitchell, behave yourself."

Mason ignored the reprimand and kept his eyes locked on Chase. "You told Michael Key you had video, and you told him his DNA would be present because of the struggle on the porch, correct?"

"Yes."

"In fact, you told him that given the nature of struggle on the porch, the attacker's DNA would be under Robin's fingernails, right?"

"I don't remember. But it turned out his DNA was under her fingernails, counselor." Chase's tone indicated that he thought he won the point.

Mason walked back to his laptop and played another video clip of the interrogation, with Chase once again speaking to Michael.

*"You do realize it's not just the video. There are going to be a lot of factors that come into this. It won't just be the tape. We'll have all the evidence leading up to the event and a lot of evidence at the scene. We know there was a violent struggle on the porch, ok? And what happens with something like that is DNA gets left behind. We find it in all sorts of places, Mike. We're going to swab her hands and get under her fingernails. If someone else's DNA is there, it'll show."* Here, Chase slid his chair close to Michael. *"But you and I know that it's not going to be anybody else's DNA, don't we?"*

Mason paused the video and read from the transcript in his hand, "'But you and I know that it's not going to be *anybody else's* DNA, don't we?' That is what you just said, correct?" Mason could see that his emphasis was not lost on the jury.

"Yeah, but–"

"But, after the examination was conducted, you did find someone else's DNA, isn't that right?"

"I don't know. I don't work in the lab. You'd have to ask them!" The tempo of the examination was rattling Chase, and Mason pressed the advantage.

"We did, detective. They told us you never gave them anyone else's DNA to test, despite Robin having two different DNA profiles under her fingernails."

Templis jumped up. "Objection, this is an argument, not a question."

"Sustained," growled Francis.

Mason ignored them both stayed trained on Chase. "You never collected a DNA sample from Trevor Warnock, did you?"

"No."

"And after you learned that two different DNA profiles were found under Robin's fingernails, did you go back and investigate further?"

"No."

"Why not?"

"We already had our guy. We had extracted the confession. In order to close cases successfully, we need to manage our resources, so looking elsewhere was a waste of time."

"I see," said Mason. He walked slowly back to his table, giving the jury a moment to absorb Chase's admission. "Let's shift gears Detective. You are trained to, as you said, 'extract the confession'. You are allowed to use a variety of methods to do so, including psychological pressure and manipulation. Would you agree with that?"

"Yeah, that's one way to say it."

"Right, and another way to say it would be that you keep a suspect in isolation and present a false narrative that preys on their fear. Would you agree with that?"

"I'm not sure what you mean."

Mason signaled again for the lights to be dimmed, selected another clip, then hit PLAY.

*"Mike, you need to tell us what happened. If I can get it down on paper here, your side of the story, then I can go to the DA and tell him what kind of guy you are because look, you're not some kind of monster. You told us about how she cheated, how she lied, and wasn't exactly treating you so good as a husband. There's context here, and that's what we need from you. That's what this is about, ok Mike?"*

*"Ok."*

*"Let me put it to you this way, man – when it comes to trial day, it's going to make a big difference to that jury if you came clean when you had the chance. But if you keep fighting this, and it's only after you see the video that you admit what happened? I can't lie, Mike, it's gonna look bad."*

*"It's gonna look bad if I want to see the video, right?"*

*"Right. And I'll show it to you if I have to, but you know it looks better for you if you man up and come clean now."*

*"But if I…"*

*"How much credit is your family and her family going to give you if you don't admit it until finally, after the last straw, you're forced to admit it? You know what I mean? How much credit do you think a jury or judge is going to give you when they find out that you had these opportunities to tell the truth, to say what happened, but you waited until you watched it with your own two eyes. And by the way, I don't think you want to see that video, Mik e."*

*"When it…when it comes down to that, about credibility, about how every-body's going to look at me…"*

*"I mean, maybe you don't even care. Mike, do you care how people are going to see you? I mean, some people don't."*

*"Yes I do, 'cause I don't want people to look at me as a monster, like I killed my wife and don't care or something."*

*"Okay."*

Mason paused the video, "For the record, I paused the recording at 4:51:18."

"You weren't sure what I meant, detective, so I just showed you. Something like that" said Mason, pointing to the projector screen, "that's what I mean. You bait him, saying that unless he confesses, everyone will think he's a monster. You tell him that at trial, the jury will think he is a monster. You tell him that a confession is the only way not to *be a monster*. That's what I mean."

"Objection," said Templis, his tone aggrieved. "Compound and argumentative."

"Sustained."

Mason waved it away and didn't break stride. "Clearly you assumed my client's guilt at this point, correct?"

"Assumed? No. We don't assume in my business."

"So sorry, you *believed* he was guilty."

"Yeah, he was," said Chase. His professional calm was starting to fade. "And we got him to say so."

"Yes, Detective, you definitely got what you wanted."

Francis looked up from his notes, impatience written across his face. Mason could feel the thin ice start to crack and moved quickly to his next argument. "Now, at this point in the interrogation, you hadn't gathered all the evidence or made an exhaustive search for suspects, correct?"

"This was hours after the crime, and we were urgently–"

"Detective Chase, this is simple. Please answer with a yes or no."

"No."

"So, what formed the basis of this...*belief* that Michael Key was the right guy?"

"There was a history of violence in their marriage and–"

"No, wait. I'm going to have to stop you there. My question was, at this point in the interrogation, what formed the basis of your belief that

Michael Key had murdered Robin Key? Did you know anything about Michael Key's whereabouts that night? Or something about the crime scene? I'm asking you to leave belief aside and tell the court, what *facts* you had in hand that made you think my client was the right guy?"

"We had information regarding the altercation between the Keys earlier that day at the park."

"Just to clarify, were there any injuries stemming from this so-called altercation?"

"No."

"Did either party seek to press charges?"

"No."

"Did the incident report from that day indicate that Michael struck or attacked Robin in any fashion?"

"No, but he had blocked her from–"

"The 'no' was good enough, detective."

Chase looked to Templis and then to Francis, hoping for assistance that didn't come.

Mason pressed on, "Did the report indicate that, in fact, it was Robin who had lightly struck Michael on the arm?"

"I don't recall details from the incident at the park."

"I'd like to refer to exhibit number forty-one, the Milwaukee PD incident report filed by the officers at the park, on the afternoon of October 8th." Mason held aloft the report and brought it to the witness stand. "Detective, can you read where the report indicates Michael Key attacked Robin Key?"

Chase donned reading glasses and scanned the two pages.

"No, it's not there."

"But you do see where it says, in Robin Key's own words, that she struck Michael Key during their argument?"

"Yes."

"If you had evidence of anything, it was that tempers flared, they argued briefly, and Robin hit Michael, but no one was hurt, correct?"

"I guess so."

"Sounds to me like a married couple having a bad day. Have you ever argued with your wife, Detective Chase?"

"What?"

"Does it get heated? Anyone ever call the cops on you?"

Templis rose from his chair, "Objection, your honor! The witness's marriage has zero bearing on the matter."

"Sustained" said Judge Francis. "Attorney Mitchell, keep it professional and on point."

Mason nodded gravely in a show of contrition, and continued, "Ok, while the Keys argued, someone called the police to the scene. And Robin Key was shocked and dismayed by what ensued, correct?"

"I don't know what her thoughts were at the moment."

"Luckily, we have some indication about what she was thinking, don't we?"

"I don't know."

Mason returned to his laptop and opened up a screen shot from a smartphone that now showed on the projection screen "This is a text message exchange between Robin and her sister just minutes after the incident. Detective, are you able to make out the highlighted passage?"

Chase turned to the screen. "Yes."

"Good. I'm just going to read it out loud for the record, you tell me if I miss anything."

*Robin: the police went nuts on mike! so messed up.*

*Tina: police? Why? U ok?*

*Robin: I'm fine. mike was being a jerk and i guess i lost it a little but they made a bad situation worse. i don't know what asshole called the cops but mike could have been really hurt. i don't want all this. Im so close to running away from everything and everyone. fml.*

"Detective Chase, when you read that, do you take it as evidence that Robin Key felt threatened by her husband?"

"Not directly, not in that exchange, no."

"Great. So, without any evidence that Michael Key was physically threatening towards his wife, and armed only with conjecture and guesswork, you questioned him like he was the killer?"

"We had reason to believe he had information and was involved. We questioned him with the aim of finding out everything we could."

"But you and the other detectives also asked him," Mason made a show of picking up a page from his table and pointing out the pertinent passage, "ninety-eight times over a three-day period, why he killed his wife. Sounds like more than information gathering. That sounds accusatory. That is central to the Reid technique that you were trained in, correct?"

"I'm not sure what you mean by that."

"Sorry, I'll be more clear. Did your training lead you to accuse Michael Key of murder at a rate of more than once an hour even though you had no solid evidence to back up that accusation?"

Detective Chase's sour look deepened and he leaned in to the microphone, "Our training and my extensive experience as a police officer who arrests criminals and solves crimes leads me to use every legal method available, and that includes putting pressure on a suspect when I have reason to believe he was involved in a murder, yes."

"Great. There's that word again. *Believe.* Belief is a powerful thing for you."

"Objection!" said Templis. "If Attorney Mitchell doesn't have questions for the witness, we should move on."

"Sustained." Francis was scowling now. Mason had tiptoed up to the edge to make his point in the mind of each juror and the reprimand was expected. "Attorney Mitchell, I have given you leeway with the witness and you are making me regret it. Are we done here or do you think you can finish without further incident?"

"Of course, your honor. I don't have much more to go over with Detective Chase."

Francis held Mason's gaze for a couple more seconds to make sure his point was well taken. "Good. Let's finish this questioning and we'll break for lunch. Proceed."

"Detective Chase, let's go back to the interrogation we were watching earlier." Mason toggled the laptop screen back to the interrogation room scene frozen at 4:32:51. "Up to this point, Michael Key was adamant in his denial."

"Correct. But that's par for the course in cases–"

"Let me stop you there, thanks. In fact, more than anything, Michael Key seemed concerned and then grief-stricken as the full gravity of the situation became clear, correct?"

"He did seem to be in distress, but that happens with many–"

"That's fine, Detective. He did seem to be in distress."

Templis interjected with another objection "Is Attorney Mitchell going to let the witness finish his answers?"

Mason held out his hands in an appeal to Judge Francis, "I'm only asking for basic yes-or-no answers, your honor. I'm trying to keep things moving and not waste the court's time."

Judge Francis' face registered annoyance as he looked from Mason to Templis, "Overruled, Mr. Templis. He's allowed to move the witness along once a question has been answered sufficiently."

"Thank you, your honor." Mason returned his focus to Detective Chase, "But once you entered the idea into his head that you had video evidence of him committing a murder, things began to change, didn't they?"

"I suppose. Well, what do you mean exactly?"

"I mean, he was no longer as sure of himself."

"That's correct. We had broken down part of his wall. I felt that when Mr. Key realized we knew he did it, he would come clean."

"There's that magic phrase. 'Come clean'. You kept Michael Key isolated in that tiny room, awake for most of seventy-two hours, and fabricated a story about having video evidence. And even lied to him about Robin's last words, right?"

"I guess."

"Don't you think it's possible that, faced with such extreme duress and repeated lies, he began to also believe that something might have happened?"

"Yes. What I mean is, due to our questioning he dropped his guard and finally wanted to tell us the real story."

"Even if it didn't happen?"

"I don't believe that was the case."

"Oh, that much is clear, detective. No further questions."

"Thank you," said Judge Francis. "We will break until one-thirty for lunch."

**40**

G rant Templis rose and announced, "The State calls Steven Baker to the stand."

A low murmur of anticipation rose in the gallery, the spectators keen to hear explosive testimony from the so-called snitch.

Templis walked his witness through the story like it had been re-hearsed for months. Baker described the layout of the jail and affirmed he and Michael Key were housed in the same unit. He testified that the two men shared the same gym schedule, and it was there that Key's confession occurred. Templis knew Baker's credibility would be an issue, and he meticulously presented documents from the jail to corroborate his witness testimony.

Under the direction of Templis, Baker outlined the encounter in the gym during which he claimed Michael confessed to murdering Robin Key. According to Baker, Michael described the attack in detail, admitting he 'stabbed her so many times he must have blacked-out from guilt,' and went on to boast that he was 'going to get away with it because the police lied to him about the evidence and it would be tossed out of court'. After fifteen efficient minutes of direct examination, Templis thanked Steven Baker and returned to his seat.

"Your witness, Attorney Mitchell," said Judge Francis.

294

"Thank you, your honor." Mason stood, moved to the podium, opened his laptop. "Mr. Baker, isn't it true that you wanted consideration for your testimony?"

"Consideration? What do you mean?"

"Consideration means favorable treatment. You are hoping that testifying in this case will help you with your own case, correct?"

"Nope. I'm doin' it because it is the right thing to do."

"Really?"

"Yep, to help that poor family get peace."

"Didn't you tell the police that you would only talk to them if it would help your case?" asked Mason. He spoke with intent, hoping to push the pace with Baker.

"Nope, check the tape."

"The tape? You mean the tape of your interview with the police the other day?"

"Yeah. I never ask for nothin' on that tape. Check it if you want."

"I did. And you are right. It's not on the tape."

"Told ya."

"How many times did you talk to the police in the last week or so?"

Baker shifted in his seat. "What are you talking about?"

Mason noticed a quick glance to Templis and suspected that Baker might not be as sure-footed as he seemed.

"Well, isn't it true that you talked to Detective Chase twice last week? Once with your lawyer and once without?"

"I dunno know his name, but yeah. Once with the cop, and once with my lawyer and the cop."

"But we only have a recording from one interview, the one with your lawyer. Did you know that?"

"Yeah, I told them I would not agree to being taped until my lawyer was there."

"Ok. What did you talk about in the first, unrecorded interview?"

"Same stuff as the other one."

"During that unrecorded interview you didn't tell the police you wanted something for your testimony?"

"Nope. Ask them."

"And before you talked to the police, did you tell anyone you wanted something in exchange for your testimony?"

"Objection, relevance," snapped Templis. He wasn't sure what Mason had, but he wanted to put a stop to it.

"Overruled. You may answer," said Francis.

"Nope," said Baker. "I already told you, I'm doing this because it's the right thing to do. Don't you listen?"

"I heard you, Mr. Baker," said Mason. "That is why I'm so confused."

"About what?"

"Well, I'm trying to figure out why you are lying to this jury."

Baker sat up straight for the first time. "I'm not ly–"

"Objection, argumentative," snapped Templis.

"Sustained," agreed Francis. "Mr. Baker does not need to answer. Strike any portion of the answer made by the witness."

"Sorry, your honor. Let me try a different angle." Mason paused, then studied the jury as he posed his next question.

"How did the police know you had information about this crime?"

"I wrote to Detective Chase," answered Baker.

"Not to your lawyer?"

"No, that takes too long. We can send notes to the guards saying we want to talk to MPD. Just fill out a form and tell them a little about what you got, and then police come to meet with you if they want. So, that's what I did."

"Did you know that all written material you send from jail, except for legal correspondence, is scanned and saved to your file with the jail?"

"Objection, lack of foundation," said Templis. "This witness would have no knowledge of the jail procedures."

"Sustained."

"Fair enough," said Mason. "Let me see if I can lay a foundation." He was a little surprised that Templis had taken the bait. Setting up the objection was an old DA's trick used against the defense, and Grant didn't see it coming from the other direction. "Mr. Baker, how many times have you been in custody in the County Jail, in total?"

Templis, only now sensing the trap, rose from his seat. "Objection. Sidebar, your honor?"

Francis looked none too pleased. "Chambers."

All three convened in the judge's office, and as soon as the door closed, Templis jumped in. "He knows he can't get into that. It's misconduct. I could ask for a mistrial or sanctions–"

"Relax, Grant. Take a beat," said Francis. "Mason, what are you doing asking about prior incarcerations?"

"Judge, I asked the witness about jail procedures with correspondence. The DA objected on foundation grounds, so I am simply laying that foundation." Mason grinned as he saw realization dawning on the prosecutor's face. "With that objection, Baker's knowledge of the jail and its procedures became relevant, which would include the amount of time he has spent at the jail. That's why I'm asking."

Judge Francis realized Templis had stepped right into the trap Mason set and was annoyed because now he would have to allow ordinarily inadmissible evidence. "He's got you there, Mr. Templis. Questions about Mr. Baker's prior knowledge of the jail, including how much time he has spent there, are in bounds."

"But Judge, that's never admissible. Prior bad act. It's not fair."

The judge held out his hands. "Don't look at me. I'm not the one who fell for it, Grant. That was all you." He opened the door and a chastened Templis returned to his table while Mason strode confidently to the podium.

Francis mounted the bench and took his seat. "Continue, counsel."

"I'll ask you again, Mr. Baker," said Mason, "how many times have you been in custody in the Milwaukee County Jail?"

Baker looked to Templis for help, but the prosecutor remained silent. "Uh, I don't know. Three, maybe four times. I'm not sure. Maybe more."

Mason knew it was six, but didn't really care about the precise number. His point was made. "Did you know that all written material you send from jail, except for legal correspondence, is scanned and saved to your file with the jail?"

This time, Templis didn't dare object.

"No," answered Baker.

"Did you know that this includes any notes you write requesting to speak with law enforcement?"

"No."

"If you saw your note, the one you wrote telling police you wanted to talk to them about Michael Key's case, do you think you would recognize it?"

"Yeah, and I would know if you changed anything, too!"

"Sir, I am handing you what has been marked as Exhibit Two-Eighteen, do you recognize that document?"

Baker took a moment to inspect the sheet of paper. "Yeah, I do."

"That is the request you made to speak to the police, correct?"

"Yes."

Mason handed a copy of the note to Templis, and another to the clerk, who passed it to the judge. "The document reads as follows: *I have information on a murder. I will tell you what I've got if I can get my case dismissed, or something good.*" Mason allowed a moment for the jury to fully absorb the new information. "Mr. Baker, did I read that correctly?"

Baker slouched in his chair again, looking deflated. "Yes, that's what it says."

"And it continues: *The murder is the one on TV. With the football coach who killed his wife. That's got to be worth a lot.* Did I also read that correctly?"

"Yes, but it's not like–"

"Those are your exact words when asking to speak to the police, correct?"

"Well, I mean–"

"That is a yes or no question, sir. I read what you wrote, correct?"

"Yes."

"Thank you. The defense moves for the admission of Exhibit Two-Eighteen."

"Hearing no objection, it is admitted," replied Francis.

"Mr. Baker, do you know what discovery is?" asked Mason. He could sense Templis, eager to object but wary of another misstep.

"Yes."

"Great. Discovery is the police reports, crime scene photographs, videos, and other evidence against a defendant in a case, right?"

"Uh-huh," said Baker.

"And lawyers are required to give their client a copy of discovery, correct?"

"They should. My lawyers always gave me mine."

"Where do you keep your discovery when you're in jail? Do you have a locker or someplace secure?"

"Nothing like that. No privacy in jail," scoffed Baker, drawing snickers from the gallery.

"So then, discovery is kept in your cell, unsecured?"

"Yeah, but you don't touch another guy's discovery. You catch a beating for that."

"I bet. And I'm sure an experienced guy like yourself would know that, right?"

Baker stared at Templis for a long moment, then answered, "I guess."

"So, it's common for discovery, which includes police reports and other evidence in a case, to be unattended in your cell, correct?"

"Yes."

"When you leave for a visit, or a court date, or go to the gym, it stays in your cell?"

"I said yes."

"Ok, I just want to make sure we're clear. And your cells are unlocked during the day, right?"

"That's right," said Baker. He sat slumped in the witness box now, as if half the air had been taken out of him.

"In fact, during the day, cells are only locked during count or if a lockdown is ordered. Otherwise, they stay open, correct?"

"Yep."

"I suppose that means someone could walk into a guy's cell while he's not there, and go through his discovery, read the police report, and learn all the details of his case."

"I dunno. I mean, yeah, whatever's in there."

"And then you could simply present those details to the cops as something that guy told you. Right?"

"Objection, argumentative," said Templis, but his tone had changed. He knew the damage from the cross-examination was already done.

"I'll withdraw the question," said Mason. "Mr. Baker, your story here in court is that you learned the specific details of Robin Key's murder when Michael Key confessed to you in the gym one day."

Baker paused, wary of any line of questioning. "That's right."

"Had you met Michael Key before that day?"

"I seen him around once or twice."

"Right, but had you ever spoken to him before that day in the gym?"

"No, that was the first time."

"So, for the jury to believe you, they must believe that Michael Key simply volunteered that he killed his wife, and gave specific details, to a total stranger, correct?"

"Uh-huh."

"Out of the blue, he divulged his deepest, darkest secret to someone he had never met before."

"I guess, yeah."

"And I assume you confessed your crime to him, right?"

"No way. I'm innocent. I'm a victim of the system," said Baker, his chin jutting forward.

For all Mason knew, that was true, but Baker had picked the wrong way to try and get out of his predicament. "I see. So what would make Michael divulge this information to you? Your winning personality?"

"Objection, argumentative." said Templis. "How much more of this can we allow?"

"Counsel," said Francis, "do you have any more?" By now, the judge was exasperated with the entire Baker episode.

"No. I think the jury has heard enough from Mr. Baker," said Mason.

"Attorney Templis, do you have any redirect?"

"No, your honor." Templis didn't want Baker on the stand for another second. "With that witness, the State rests."

"Ok, we will take fifteen minutes, and when we come back the defense will present their case." Judge Francis banged his gavel. "We stand adjourned."

**41**

M ason rose and flashed his best smile in an attempt to spark some warmth in his witness. "Doctor Bowen, I want to establish your credentials up front. Is that ok?"

The man on the stand was in his early sixties and wore a burgundy turtle-neck under a navy corduroy blazer. Were his face not set in a permanent grimace, he could be a Carl Sagan impersonator, thought Mason. He had asked the man not to wear a tie and keep his appearance 'neat but casual.' Clearly he should have been more specific with his sartorial directions. Between the wardrobe and the resting elite face, Bowen was not the friendliest character.

"Of course. I'm currently a professor and chair of psychology at the University of Wisconsin-Green Bay. I earned a Ph.D. in social psychology from Northwestern in 1987. As a professor I teach courses on legal, criminal, and social psychology. I am the author or co-author of thirteen published studies on law enforcement interrogation and interview tech-niques with a focus on the phenomenon of false confessions. I conduct-ed field research with law enforcement agencies across the country and have presented my findings to professional and academic organizations here in Wisconsin, across the country, and internationally."

Mason could frame Bowen as the unassailable expert, but it would be a real challenge to make him appear human in the process.

"Very impressive. Now, knowing what you know, what do you think would happen if a group of police detectives kept you, or anyone here,"

Mason extended his arms towards the jury, inviting them to imagine the scenario, "isolated in a small room for three straight days and asked them ninety-eight times if they murdered someone when they didn't do it?"

Templis reacted in an instant, "Objection. Speculation and lack of foundation."

"Sustained. Attorney Mitchell, would you care to lay the proper foundation?"

"Absolutely. Dr. Bowen, do faulty interrogation techniques lead to false confessions?"

"Yes, they can and do. I can point to several studies in recent years that confirm the phenomenon of improper interrogations resulting in false confessions."

"Ok. So, that's a fact. But it's still tough for many of us to wrap our heads around. Anyone can understand a person saying they *didn't* do something when they actually did. People do that all the time. But the opposite is harder for us to grasp. I mean, why would anyone say they did something when they didn't do it, right?" Again, Mason held his hands out and looked to the jury, as if inviting them to ask the question they all had in mind.

Bowen fixed Mason with a look of scholarly seriousness. "Although it may seem counterintuitive on the surface, there are many simple ways in which an innocent person can be coerced into confessing to a crime."

"And the police who produce these false confessions, are they doing this deliberately? With malice?"

"I would say in most cases, no. What I mean is, even law enforcement officers with the best intentions will end up producing false confessions if they are using faulty interrogation techniques."

"Can you explain that to us a bit?"

"Of course. There are two major strains of police interview techniques - information gathering and accusatory."

"Those sound fairly self-explanatory, but if you could just give a quick overview so we're all clear on the difference between the two."

Bowen straightened up and cleared his throat. It was clear that he enjoyed being asked to showcase his expertise for the lay people. "The information gathering technique focuses on teasing out facts from the interview subject through methodical, targeted questioning. The idea is to take the information the subject gives and use it to understand the scope and details of the crime, and hopefully, if you've done the job well, use that information to eliminate them as a suspect or determine with relative certainty that they can be charged and tried."

"That sounds effective. And the accusatory technique?"

"As you said, it is what it sounds like. The police take a confrontational approach, questioning the subject as if they are guilty, not presumed innocent. The police may lie or intimidate, and rather than gathering information, they will often supply information. In this technique, a number of methods are employed to build a narrative of guilt."

"Can you outline some of these methods? What goes into producing a false confession?"

"We can start with sobriety. Questioning someone who is under the influence of alcohol or drugs, or one who recently is coming off a high, is a red flag. The interview subject is not in the right state of mind to be accurate and truthful in their statements; not mention they are highly suggestible."

"That seems fairly straightforward and I'd imagine we've all been there – a little tipsy, a little high, a little hung over. It's probably not a time when we're going to do well under questioning."

"That's right. And sleep-deprivation is another significant factor. It has the same effect as intoxication on accuracy and coherence, along with severely damaging the suspect's ability to reason."

"Ok, that's two factors. Keep going, Doctor Bowen."

"Isolation plays a large part as well. When an innocent party is kept for a long time in a situation where they have no contact with the outside world, in other words their real life, it can affect their relationship with narrative, chronology, and reality. They can be influenced to entertain or accept alternative viewpoints to what they initially believed was real."

"You can tell them up is down and left is right."

"So to speak, yes."

"What else have we failed to mention?"

"Minimization is another interrogation tactic that can lead to false confession. It's explained to the suspect that the crime in question is really not that bad and that if they can just help the officers out and explain what happened it can all be cleared up with no great consequences. A version of what we do with children, saying it's ok, just tell me what you did and you won't get in trouble."

"Ah, I see." Mason angled his head and nodded along, showing the jury how much he appreciated the good doctor's generous explanation of such complex and compelling ideas. "And what else can contribute to a false confession?"

"Fabrication. The police are allowed to lie to the suspect, to claim that they have things like DNA evidence, eyewitness accounts, or like in this case, a video of the subject committing the crime."

"You've listed five factors now. Anything we've missed?"

"Yes, and I think this is a very important factor – indifference to claims of innocence. When police are convinced they have a guilty party, they are not going to care if that person says 'It wasn't me!' The police will ignore it or accuse them of lying. But when this tactic is applied to an innocent person, this outright rejection of their pleas of innocence has a damaging cumulative effect when combined with the other factors I've already mentioned. If you believe that the only way out of the interrogation room is to give the police what they want so you can go back to your life, then you are far more likely to do just that, to tell them what they want to hear. By that point, you might even believe it when you tell them."

"And according to research done by you and other top experts, the presence of any of these factors during an interrogation can increase the likelihood of a false confession?"

"That's correct."

"How do researchers know these are false confessions?"

"Well, one study focused on defendants that have been exonerated by the Innocence Project, based on DNA evidence. Believe it or not, thirty percent of those exonerated initially confessed to their crimes. So, we know they were false."

"I suppose you could say it's shocking but true." Mason paused to let the jury process Bowen's case study before asking his next question. "If all these factors you've outlined were at play during an interrogation that led to a confession, would you find that to be a problem?"

"Very much so. I would have grave doubts about the confession due to the circumstances under which it was obtained."

"Were all these factors at play during the interrogation of Michael Key?"

"Yes, they were."

"I think it would be helpful to show some footage of the interview, and you can help us understand what we're seeing, ok?"

"Certainly."

At the push of a button, the courtroom's big screen showed the now familiar confines of Interrogation Room B, with Michael Key seated at the small concrete table, under questioning by Detective Chase.

*"I can understand if you're up on that porch and you don't remember what happened, but I have to believe that leading up to that point, you can at least remember walking up there."*

*"I kind of–"*

*"You may not remember the struggle, you may not remember what happened to her, you may not even remember leaving, but everything leading up to that? I'm pretty sure you'd still remember those details."*

*"I don't remember, I don't remember hurting her at all. And it hurts that I don't remember if I did this. My next...my next memory is going to Flip's house and crashing. Maybe if you can show me the video, show me what you have seen and maybe I can explain."*

*"Come on, Mike. You've got to stop with the video. I mean, it shows the struggle, and you can see everything. Plus, we're going to find your DNA. We will. So, let's stop messing around here. Time for you to dig deep and tell us more. Tell us what you remember."*

*"I know. I know. I want to remember. I want to get past this with you. I'm not a monster, man."*

Mason paused the video. "Right there doctor, what did you see?"

"Michael's body language has changed. He is clutching himself tighter, his head is down, buried in his chest, and there is intermittent sobbing."

"Anything else?"

"Most telling, Detective Chase is trying to convince Mr. Key that not having any memory of the killing could be due to the trauma of the event itself."

"Why does that matter?"

"It shows a concerted effort to shape narrative, no matter the facts. Chase is compressing Michael's worldview, like an altered reality, and nothing is allowed in that doesn't fit the narrative. Everything that Chase introduces to the conversation creates a sort of funnel that leads to a predetermined conclusion, extinguishing the possibility of innocence. In other words, Chase explains away the inconsistency in Michael's head – that he cannot remember a single detail about the murder. The possibility that this is because Michael was not there and did not commit the murder is completely dismissed and discarded."

"Understood." Mason clicked play again.

*"That's right, Mike. You're not a monster. We know that. You can just explain how it happened, because we're not here to judge you. We want to help you get free of this, but you need to come clean, for your own sake. So, you approached her on the porch. Did she see you approach?"*

*"I don't really know, man. I don't think so."*

*"C'mon Mike. Think about it."*

*"No, I mean. She didn't scream or anything. I think I must've just...I must've just got her with the knife before she saw me."*

*"Uh-huh."*

*"I was so wound up. I was hurt, man."*

*"I know, Mike. Just like we talked about. But there's more. Keep going. You stabbed her before she turned, right? The first couple times you got her in the abdomen, right?"*

*"Yeah...yeah. It would have been in the abdomen, I guess."*

*"We need you to be sure, Mike."*

*"It was the ribs. And then I got her again when she turned, like in the chest."*

*"It was a little higher than that, wasn't it?"*

*"In her neck? Like the throat or that area. She's short so it would be the right height for where my arm is at."*

*"Yeah, ok. In the neck. That's good. What happened next?"*

*"You got to tell them, man. You got to. I'm not a monster, like you said. This wasn't supposed to happen."*

*"We know, Mike. But let's keep going here so we can get the story right."*

*"Shit. I don't know anymore. I'm trying to help you."*

*"You're helping yourself, Mike. Remember that, you have to come clean."*

*"I know, and I want to, but I can't see it, I just can't!"*

*"That's because you're blocking it out. I get it. This is a hard thing to face. But we've already talked about how she pushed you, she hurt you and so you were out on the edge, like you weren't still yourself. That makes sense and we get that. So, I know it's hard to think of yourself doing this but in a way it wasn't you doing this, do you understand?"*

*"Yeah."*

"Paused at 6:15:40," said Mason, providing the timestamp for the record. "Dr. Bowen, what did you see there?"

"Again, the detective has told Michael it makes sense he does not remember, but tells him he still committed the murder."

"And what does that do to Michael Key's mental state?"

"This creates dissonance in the mind of someone who has been made vulnerable, under great stress from the barrage of questions, from grief, from sleep deprivation. Under these circumstances, someone in Michael's position will start to second-guess their perceptions. In short, they can lose touch with reality. At that point, Chase is free to tailor the story to fit his own conclusion, in essence providing a new reality for Michael Key."

"What do you look for to indicate that this is happening?"

"Well, one way to determine if a confession is reliable is to see if the details of the confession match the crime."

Mason turned to the jury, nodding his head. "Makes sense."

Bowen continued, "The police have been trained to get suspects to provide details of the crime. In theory, this makes sense, with a series of questions and answers painting a full picture of the event. But in practice, if the suspect is unable to provide details, the police redirect them, leading them to the desired answers by introducing details into the conversation. This is done in such a way that the suspect might believe they know things that were never in their head before then, before the police put them there."

"So, rather than accept that they may have the wrong suspect, the police manipulate the interview to make it appear that they do."

"Yes."

"And you saw that in this clip?"

"Most definitely. When Detective Chase asks about the location of the injuries, he has to correct Michael several times, trying again and again until Michael gives the right answer, the one that agrees with the evidence. With a pliable subject like Mr. Key was at that point, it's more akin to a guessing game than a confession. The result is that now these facts are introduced into Michael's mind, and treated as if he volunteered the information rather than coming to it by what amounts to a multiple choice quiz."

"Would the detective have even known the location of the injuries? The autopsy protocol is dated four days after the homicide." Mason said while needlessly referencing his notes.

"Yes. In my review of the photos of the crime scene and the victim, the location of Robin's injuries were easy to identify. And remember, I am not a medical doctor."

The attempt at humor fell flat and Mason ran right past it, "In other words, anyone looking at photos of the victim's body could tell where she had been stabbed?"

"Yes."

"Doctor, based on your decades of education, training, and research, and all the available literature on the subject on which you are an eminent authority, is it your opinion that the statements made by Michael Key are unreliable and probably false?"

"Oh yes. This interrogation was like an instructional video for producing false confessions. The presence of intoxicants, the sleep deprivation, the extended length of the interrogations, the shaming and repeated rejections of claims of innocence, all of this left Michael Key in a state where his world had closed in on him. And the only possible exit, the only way Michael Key believed he could survive, was to say whatever the police wanted, despite having no independent memory of being involved in this crime."

"Thank you, Dr. Bowen," said Mason, returning to his seat.

Templis rose for his cross-examination. "How many times have you testified in court as a defense witness, Mr. Bowen?"

"It's been fifty or sixty by now, I would say."

"I looked it up, and this is your sixty-fourth trial appearance. Does that sound right to you?"

"Yes, that sounds about right."

"Earlier, you told the court about your role as a professor, chair of the department in Green Bay, your study and publishing, presenting at conferences, and heading up organizations. You have a very busy professional schedule, yes?"

"Yes, I am fortunate to have a lot to do in my roles."

"But you manage to find time for a side job, parachuting into cases and delivering testimony on demand, yes?"

Bowen paused, his lips pursed in annoyance, then replied, "I offer my analysis based on years of research and study, if that's what you mean. And far from 'parachuting' in, I spend a good deal of time with each case, going over all the evidence and relevant materials until I am satisfied that a proper evaluation can be delivered."

"When did Attorney Mitchell contact you with a request to look at the Michael Key interview and submit your findings?"

"It was, uh, about six months ago."

"To be exact, it was May 7th."

"Ok."

"And when did you return your finding to Attorney Mitchell?"

"I'm not sure what the date was."

"It was May 21st," said Templis.

"Objection. Your honor, perhaps Attorney Templis can save the court some time and give us the answers to his questions to start with?"

"Sustained," said Francis. "Keep it moving, counsel."

"So, Mr. Bowen, just two weeks after hearing of this case for the first time, you were able to supply Attorney Mitchell with what you feel is a comprehensive and accurate report of what transpired during the interview of Mr. Key?"

"Yes."

"In two weeks, despite all the time you had to devote to your many professional commitments, not to mention sleeping and eating, you managed to process so many hours of interview tapes and transcripts and render a solid professional judgment?"

"Since my student days I've been used to managing my time and working quickly and accurately. So, yes, I managed."

"That's impressive. I know I wouldn't have been able to prepare for this trial so fast. Not very well, at least."

"Is that a question?" asked Bowen, exasperation seeping into his tone.

If this kept up, Mason was worried the jury would turn on his expert witness. His credentials only worked well when paired with a relatable persona. His demeanor on the stand right now made it too easy to cast him as a smug, ivory tower academic. Mason guessed that more than a few jury members had been spoken down to by a man like Bowen in their time.

"No, I suppose it isn't," replied Templis. "But here's one - are you really comfortable putting your two weeks up against detectives who have interviewed countless suspects during decades serving on the force?"

"Very comfortable. As I mentioned, I have also conducted extensive field research, much of it in the room with police officers like Detective Chase, evaluating their methods in real life situations and studying how these interrogations contribute to outcomes in the justice system, positive and negative."

"And it's your belief that the officers involved in Mr. Key's interrogation had somehow forced him to say he committed a murder?"

"I wouldn't say forced. It's more subtle than that. I have watched every minute of his questioning. I've seen the duress and coercion applied by the officers. I've observed Mr. Key's body language and emotional state. When I compare and contrast these things with the hundreds of other interrogations I've studied and factor in the relative lack of physical evidence in this case, I can only reach one conclusion, which is that Michael Key gave an unreliable statement."

"You mean confession?"

"No, that would mean you could conclude what he said was reliable and true, and under these circumstances, you cannot."

"Mr. Bowen, I–"

"It's *Doctor* Bowen," interrupted the professor. There was that tone again. Mason wanted him the fuck off the stand, now.

"My apologies, Dr. Bowen." Templis knew how this was playing with the jury and was more than happy to let Bowen have his way. "You're saying the officers involved deliberately set out to make Michael Key say he murdered his wife?"

"I make no assumptions about their intent with Mr. Key other than to follow the methodology of their training, meaning the Reid technique."

"And these officers didn't care if Mr. Key was innocent or guilty? They just followed the book and took leave of their own thoughts and impressions?"

Bowen shook his head and replied to Templis as if he were a challenging student, "Once again, I don't know what was going on in their minds during the three days of interviewing Mr. Key, but I do know that the tactics and practices proscribed by the Reid technique create a perfect storm of factors that can lead to false confessions."

"Would you agree that, with the vast amount of historical evidence of spousal violence and homicide, these experienced and dedicated law enforcement officers that interviewed Michael Key had good reason to speak with him in the first place?"

"Yes, but I would–"

"No further questions."

Mason was loath to have the jury see more of Bowen but needed to get a last word in. He rose from his table. "Re-direct, your honor."

Francis nodded his assent. "Proceed, Attorney Mitchell."

"I think Attorney Templis cut you off there, Dr. Bowen. Can you finish your last answer?"

"Yes. Thank you. I would say that the police had reason to question anyone that was close to Robin Key and anyone that saw her on the day of her death."

"And yet they only questioned one person, Michael Key."

"Correct."

"In your expert opinion, did they have good reason to accuse Michael Key of murdering Robin Key almost a hundred times as they questioned him over seventy-two hours?"

"No, none whatsoever."

"And yet here my client sits," said Mason. He raised his eyebrows and turned to the jury. "Why do you think that is, Dr. Bowen?"

Templis wasted no time, "Objection. Argumentative."

"Withdrawn. I have nothing else."

---

After Bowen stepped down and was released back into the gallery, Mason returned to his table. "You good?" he whispered to Michael, who replied with a thumbs up. Mason nodded and took a drink of water before quickly checking his notes for the next witness. "Your honor, the defense calls Vernon Stutts."

The bailiff popped open the secure door in the safety glass partition, allowing a slim fifty-something man to enter from the gallery and walk purposefully towards the witness stand. His face was well-scrubbed and freshly shaved, his light green eyes were hyper-alert, like a bird of prey. From his jawline to his gait to the cut of his plain black suit, Vernon Stutts was all hard angles. Mason was happy to be the one asking questions rather than vice versa.

"Mr. Stutts, thank you for being here. I want you to quickly tell us about your expertise in the field of interrogation."

"I was a police officer in Chicago for twenty-three years, made detective, and conducted hundreds of interviews with suspects in that time. Fifteen years ago, I co-founded Laufen & Stutts,"

"That's just a couple hours down the road in Naperville, right?"

"That's right."

"And what does your firm do?"

"We conduct training courses for law enforcement agencies across the country, specializing in interview and interrogation techniques. We draw on our training staff's decades of experience, and our constant research and review process, in order to remain current on best practices. Our intensive instruction and top notch curriculum lead to real world results, making sure law enforcement officers get the right guy and get him off the streets."

"Excellent. And your firm is recognized as an industry leader?"

"That's right. We have been awarded over a dozen citations for Exemplary Service to Law Enforcement from the National Association of Police Organizations."

"And you?"

"I have been fortunate to have my work recognized for several years running as a top instructor in the country."

"Given your experience, you must be familiar with the Reid technique of suspect interrogation?"

"Yes, I am."

"We heard Dr. Bowen talk about information gathering versus accusatory interview methods. Would the Reid technique fall into the accusatory category?"

"Yes, definitely."

"And the Milwaukee Police Department training for suspect interviews is based on the Reid technique?"

"That's correct."

"And does Laufen & Stutts teach the Reid technique?"

"No, we do not."

"Why is that?"

"The strategies and the methodology it employs are problematic. The Reid technique has been found to produce too much variance in the veracity of interview outcomes."

"Can you dumb that down for me a little bit?"

"It can lead to incriminating statements by innocent parties and even false confessions."

"Even in the hands of officers who are genuinely trying to get to the truth?"

"Yes."

"So, the technique itself is faulty no matter who uses it?"

"That's right."

"Thank you, no further questions."

"Mr. Templis," said Francis, "any questions?"

"Yes, thank you, your honor," said Templis, rising from his seat. "Mr. Stutts, your firm no longer includes the Reid technique in your course materials, correct?"

"That's right."

"You no longer believe that it produces the best results?"

"Correct."

"And that was due to a policy review and change that your company conducted and put into effect just under two years ago, yes?"

"Yes."

"So, if we had you on this stand two years ago you would've testified to the effectiveness of the Reid technique, yes?"

"Well, at the time, perhaps. We always like to follow the most up to date and proven methodologies."

"I see. So if we get you on this stand two years from now, there's a decent chance you'll have a completely different answer regarding the most effective interrogation techniques, is that not so?"

"Objection," said Mason, "speculation...and argumentative, your honor."

"Sustained. Point made, Mr. Templis. Move on."

"Of course. So, Mr. Stutts, is it fair to say that in the field of interrogation, an *expert*," Templis made exaggerated air quotes, "like yourself, can change their ways and start to espouse new and even contrary techniques to what had been used before?"

"I think it's fair to say that we like to follow the most up to date and proven methodologies."

"Whatever they may be from year to year, month to month, day to day."

"We like to adhere to the most current science and research."

"As it stands for now," said Templis.

Stutts paused, clearly unhappy with the prosecutor's characterization. "That's the best we can do."

"No further questions."

**42**

Mason returned to the jail at seven that evening and went through the security charade with Officer Schmidt, who informed him that Michael Key was waiting in Room 5, the one with the mildew odor. Mason stopped at the coffee station just beyond the security area and filled two cups; black for him, two sugars for Michael. The coffee smelled stale and his first taste confirmed it. He grabbed one extra cup to use as an ashtray for the soft pack of Marlboro Lights in his blazer pocket. Depending on how the conversation went, Mason might want one, too.

He entered the room and set his gifts down on the table. Michael blew away the steam rising from his coffee and took a sip. "Thanks, man," he said, then leaned back in the chair, his face creased with worry.

"Listen, today was good for us," said Mason. "Bowen was good, Stutts was strong and credible. I don't think Templis put much of a dent in either one of them. That leaves just one thing on the table."

"Mason, I know you don't think I should testify."

"I never said that, Mike. Just figured that, if I did my job right, we wouldn't need you to take the stand."

"Sure, but now that we're here," Michael let out a weary sigh, "I don't want to leave any stone unturned."

"And I don't blame you for feeling that way."

"I'm just...I'm really scared, man." Michael's eyes were glassy now. Tension radiated off him.

Mason nudged the Marlboros and lighter across the table, but Michael took no notice of them, so he reached out and put a hand on his client's shoulder. The muscles were taut. "Hey, Mike, I've got your back no matter what you decide. But we're in good shape so far and I can close this. I'm getting through to this jury. Believe me."

Michael nodded, trying to compose himself. "No, I know. I watch you every day in that courtroom and I see it. But like, in the end, if I go down for this and I didn't even speak for myself, it wouldn't sit right. That'd be enough to drive me crazy, you know?"

"Honestly, I can't say I do know, Mike. I feel for you. You know I do, but it's my duty to tell you that it might not be in your best interest."

"Yeah, and you told me before. But I want them to hear from me that I didn't kill Robin, that I'm an innocent man."

"Of course, you do. But listen to me, we don't need to prove your innocence. Templis needs to prove your guilt, ok? He has the burden of proof and that's our biggest advantage."

"Don't you think the jury needs to hear certain things from me? Hear why I confessed, or said what I said?"

"Stutts and Bowen already told them why you confessed. They gave the jury the cold, hard truth and the science to back it up. From you, it could come off as self-serving. Like, of course, the guy who confessed to a murder now wants to say he didn't do it. I'm just not sure how much your testimony can help."

Michael shook his head. "This is so fucked up, man."

"You're preaching to the choir, my friend. I know it's frustrating and you just want to help your case."

"So, I have to just sit there and do nothing?"

Mason was tempted to paraphrase Abraham Lincoln - 'Better to remain silent and be thought possibly guilty than to speak and remove all reasonable doubt.' - but thought better of it.

"Mike, your job in that courtroom is to appear sympathetic. My job is to show the jury how many holes there are in the prosecution's story, and there are plenty. Both our jobs are not necessarily made easier by having you up there answering questions."

Michael traced a figure eight pattern over and over again on the surface of the table. Mason could see he was struggling to accept the idea.

"Hey, let's say you decide to testify. Fine. I can set you up with some easy questions and get you rolling, telling your story to the jury. The police screwed you, it was a false confession, there's not enough evidence. It is a good story. And it'll be told well because you present well. Good looking, well-spoken, professional, you'll look like who you really are – a solid member of the community who was simply in a bad place in life and got worked over by the system. If it could happen to you it could happen to anyone."

Michael looked at him expectantly, waiting for the other shoe to drop.

"But then Templis will have his shot at you, and he's very good at what he does. That's when we lose control of the narrative. He will drill down into every little detail about you, about the day Robin was killed, and he'll have a field day. Troubled marriage. You were drinking way too much. Jealous and insecure. The altercation at the park. You confessed to the murder. He will fire a ton of questions at you and whip from topic to topic. He'll try to get a rise out of you, catch you in any tiny inconsistency. And I know you think you can handle it, but trust me when I say that you'll be walking a tightrope. There's a very narrow window of behavior that will play well when you're under questioning. If you're too cool and calm, the jury will see you as a cold fish, an emotionless sociopath. That's a guilty verdict. You stand up for yourself, spar with

Templis, and show too much emotion? Well, now it's easy for them to see you as a hothead, a guy who lashes out when he's pushed. Again, guilty verdict. There's maybe one way it goes right, and a hundred ways it goes wrong. Once Templis is done with his cross, those twelve peers of yours will have forgotten all about the nice, solid guy I had in the witness box."

Michael closed his eyes, his face twisting into a grimace at the prospect of being grilled in open court.

"I know you're scared," said Mason, "and more than anything you just want to take the stand to show those jurors that you're a real person, a good guy. If they could just see the Michael Key that I know, that most people know, they'd understand. But what I'm scared of is that you will be helpless up there, and in the end, the jury won't see you as that Michael Key. To them, you'll be nothing but a murderer."

Michael slid a cigarette out of the pack and lit up. His hands moved slowly and methodically. He inhaled deep and chuckled derisively as the smoke left his lungs. "But it's still up to me, right?"

"It is, yes," said Mason. He wasn't sure if Michael would see the light. Anxiety flared in his gut and he almost reached out for a cigarette. "Hey, if you do decide to testify, I will do everything I can to make you look like the nicest guy in Milwaukee. Pillar of the community, couldn't hurt a fly – an innocent man."

Michael nodded and buried his chin in his chest. "Do I have to decide right this second?"

"Nope. But tomorrow, before we get to court, I will have to let Templis and the judge know what's up."

"Jesus. I don't know what to do, Mason."

They sat quietly for a minute, both men loath to say much more even though there was so much more that could be said.

"Ok, maybe just sleep on it, then," said Mason.

Michael took another long drag and exhaled slowly, filling the space between them with smoke. "Don't think I'll be able to sleep."

"I hear you," said Mason. "Either way, I'll be back here first thing in the morning. You can tell me what you want to do, and I'll inform the court. Then we can go over our notes if necessary. Cool?"

"Cool."

"I can't say I know how hard this decision is for you, not truly. But I've given you my best counsel and I just hope it helps."

Michael nodded and stubbed out his cigarette.

"Whatever you decide," said Mason, "I know it'll be the right thing. And I'll support you one hundred percent. Testify, don't testify; I will make it work to get the outcome we want."

A sardonic smile spread across Michael's stubbled face. "Justice In Society, right?"

"Right," said Mason. He had hated being in that high school. "Well, fuck society. Let's start with justice for you."

———

Mason left the County Jail and headed straight for home. His security detail this evening was a tall and no doubt well-armed young man named Tracy, and the pair drove in silence, the younger man impassive and alert, Mason lost in his own thoughts. He made it a rule not to put himself in a defendant's shoes, but now Mason couldn't help but imagine the torture of Michael's dilemma.

By the time they arrived in the parking garage of his building, Mason's uneasy feeling was spiking. The meeting with Michael had left him anxious about what tomorrow would bring, and with each passing second, Mason became more convinced that testifying would sink his client.

When the elevator opened on the fourth floor, Mason's bodyguard stepped out first to confirm the hallway was clear of threats. "Ok, you're good."

"Thanks, Trace," said Mason, holding the DOOR OPEN button, "but I think I can make it from here."

Tracy nodded and stepped back into the elevator. "Bet. Back here in the morning. What time?"

"Make it eight," said Mason. He watched Tracy disappear behind the closing doors, then turned down the hallway, jingling his keys as he walked. As Mason approached his home, the door next to his opened and Donna emerged, standing between him and a quiet evening alone. "Hey there, neighbor!" She said with a smile.

Mason's shoulders dropped as he realized Tracy had been dismissed too soon. "Hello, Donna."

She didn't move out of Mason's path, and when he came to a halt, she studied his face with concern. "Looks like you've got a lot on your mind."

"Just trying to get home." He was tired and wanted nothing more than the company of Clyde and a Tito's martini.

"I guess I can't blame you, with your client hitting the stand tomorrow."

"What?" Mason snapped. "Who told you that?"

"Been watching the case, like everybody else. On Court TV they were saying Key could testify in the morning."

"Oh, is that what they said? We'll see."

"I get it. Keeping things secret."

"Not really." Mason kept his tone polite, but anxiety rose in his chest. "Like you and the guys on Court TV, I won't find out til tomorrow morning."

"Are you serious? You don't know yet? "

"Yes, Donna, I'm serious. I've given him my advice, but the decision is his to make." Mason sighed loudly. "After everything that happened to him that was out of his control, at the last moment, he gets the responsibility of determining his own fate. So, right now, Michael Key is alone in a cell, grappling with a choice that could determine his freedom, and I'm still standing here talking to you." Mason stopped when he saw the look of alarm on Donna's face. "I'm so sorry. That really was not meant for you. I'm just–"

"That's ok, really," said Donna, moving to one side. "You must be under so much stress and here I am, just getting into your business. I should be apologizing to you."

Mason stepped past his neighbor, embarrassment adding to his agitation. "Really, Donna, it's just been a long day," he said, turning his key in the lock. "Actually, it's been a long few months." When he cracked the door open, Clyde nosed through the gap and waddled into the hall.

"Of course. I can only imagine," said Donna, crouching down to scratch Clyde's head. "If you want to talk about it sometime, I'm around."

"You have a good night, Donna," said Mason. "C'mon, Clyde. Let's go, you little goof." The dog trotted back inside, followed by his master.

"Good luck tomorrow," said Donna, but the door was closed before the last word left her mouth.

———

The next morning, when Mason arrived at the jail, his client wasted no time in delivering his decision.

"I really want to tell my story," said Michael.

Mason's heart sank, but he set his features with a look of grave understanding that he hoped would mask the disappointment. Testifying was the wrong choice.

"But, I can do that after this is over," continued Michael. "Maybe write a book or something. So, I'm not going to take the stand."

A shuddering breath escaped Mason's chest. "Oh, ok. Ok then. If that's what you want, that's great."

"I trust you, Mason, and I think you've done the job. Other than my confession, they don't have much against me. And you showed how messed up my interrogation was." Key spoke as if he was making the case to himself one last time, just to be sure. "The jury is going to see that. They know the police didn't do their job. We just need a reasonable doubt, right?"

"Exactly."

"Besides, the whole reason I'm in this situation now is because I thought it was a good idea to sit down and tell my side of the story. Don't want to make the same mistake twice, right?"

"Yeah, I mean, you could say that," said Mason.

Michael put his hands on Mason's shoulders and looked him in the eye. "You said you can close this case. So, go do it."

**43**

"**A**ttorney Mitchell," said Judge Francis, "you may proceed with your closing argument."

"Thank you, your honor." Mason rose, buttoned his suit jacket, and faced the jury. "Ladies and gentlemen, the judge just read an instruction to you about reasonable doubt. It states that," Mason read from his notes, his voice slow and clear in the stillness of Courtroom 620, "if you can reconcile the evidence upon any reasonable hypothesis consistent with the defendant's innocence, you *must* do so and find the defendant not guilty."

He looked up at the jury and continued, "I remember hearing that on the first day of law school. My criminal law professor read it to the class, then asked us to try and explain what the instruction meant. Our answers were all over the place."

Mason had no recollection of what really happened that day, mainly because the parties leading up to it had been so memorable. But the jury's understanding of reasonable doubt was of crucial importance, and he frequently used this small fiction to introduce the concept in his closing arguments.

"My professor shared with the class an analogy for reasonable doubt that I think will help you in your deliberations. It's a simple thought experiment called Mouse in the Box."

Mason paused to scan the jury. When he was satisfied he had their full attention, he continued, "It goes like this. You place a mouse inside a cardboard box, and put that box in a room with a cat. You close the door to the room and leave it overnight. You come back the next morning and check the box. If the mouse isn't in there, you know the cat ate the mouse. And you know it beyond a reasonable doubt."

He took a beat to ensure the jurors were following along. "Now, you could come up with some ridiculous explanations for the missing mouse – it had super strength like Mighty Mouse and leapt out of the box, or aliens appeared in the room and beamed the mouse onto their ship. But those explanations aren't reasonable." Mason took a swig from his bottle of water, adjusted his tie, and pressed on.

"Now, let's replay that same scenario, but this time," Mason formed a circle with his thumb and index finger, "the box has a hole in it. When you come back the next morning, check the box and find the mouse is gone, you can no longer conclude, beyond a reasonable doubt, that the cat ate the mouse. Because there's clearly another possibility. The mouse in the box escaped through that hole! Ladies and gentlemen, that hole in the box is reasonable doubt! And the State's case is *full of holes!*"

Mason now referred to his notes. "There is almost a complete lack of physical evidence tying Michael Key to the crime. Police did not find a murder weapon or any bloody clothing in the house where Michael was staying, despite him being arrested only hours after the murder. Another man's DNA was found under Robin's fingernails. The State has no eye witnesses to the murder. They have no clear video, and no fingerprints, at least not Michael's. Cell phone data shows that Michael was within a three mile radius of the crime scene, but that radius *includes* the friend's house where he had been staying and where he told officers he spent the night. The testimony we heard from Mr. Baker is suspect to say the least, and leaves much to be desired regarding his motivation and truthfulness. You add it all up and there's simply not enough to convict. Not beyond a reasonable doubt."

While he delivered this meticulously rehearsed argument, Mason watched the scene as if outside himself. There he stood at the podium, trotting out his reliable stories, rhetorical tricks, and appeals to logic. He saw spectators in the packed gallery, with their desire for revenge, closure, or entertainment; Judge Francis, sternly watching over the spectacle from his perch; and finally, the jurors, listening but not hearing.

"From the start, the police operated solely on assumptions, not proof. They assumed the husband killed his wife, but failed to investigate other credible suspects. They assumed the physical evidence would show Michael Key was the killer, but ignored the DNA found by the lab. They assumed that Michael Key lied in his interrogation, but they were the ones lying to him. They fabricated a story to fit these assumptions, then they pushed and pushed and pushed using techniques they know produce false confessions."

The faces Mason saw in the jury box were preoccupied with the prosecution's story of saintly Robin, the argument at the barbeque, the bad marriage, and Michael's confession. Mason could see that, to them, he was defending a murderer. The realization caused him to lose his bearings, until a cough from the gallery brought him back to the moment. Mason looked back at Michael seated behind the defense table, his heavy shackles hidden from view. He looked so alone. Mason needed to shift gears.

Mason stepped out from behind the podium and took two steps toward the jury box. He stood silent for long beat gathering himself, then looked directly at the jury and asked.

"Have you ever had a bad day?" Jury members looked at each other and back to him, unsure of what to do with the question. "Of course you have. Well, what about your worst day? Take a second and think back to that day." Mason paused to let everyone in the courtroom locate an unwelcome memory.

"Were you under a lot of stress? Trouble at work, or bills piling up? Was your relationship falling apart and you felt heartbroken? Did you lose a loved one? Did you feel like the world was against you and it was all too much to bear? Well, imagine if all those things happened on the same day."

He stopped and let each juror retrace the emotional scars now being called to mind. Several leaned forward as Mason continued in a clear, deliberate voice, "What if, on that day, the people who were sworn to help you did their utmost to hurt you instead? I think you'd call that your worst day. And in my line of work, we know it's a mistake to judge someone solely on the worst day of their life.

On October 8th last year, Michael Key was frustrated, angry, confused, and very sad. His marriage was falling apart, and the woman who once loved him now looked at him with disdain. It's true Michael Key was in a bad place that day, but he was looking for ways to make things right. That resulted in him having a loud and embarrassing confrontation with Robin at the barbeque. But that day was about to get so much worse!"

As he spoke, a surge of indignation rose in Mason's chest. He struggled to tamp it down and keep his voice level.

"Just a few hours later, police officers picked up Michael Key and told him his wife was dead. Murdered in front of their home. The home in which they tried to build a life, where they had dreamed of raising children. The same home that was subject to hateful vandalism because some of their neighbors could not accept a mixed-race couple. And the nightmare wasn't over yet."

He walked over to where Michael sat and placed a hand on his shoulder. "Police showed my client horrifying photos of the crime scene and placed him under arrest. When they should have been hunting for the animal who butchered Robin, detectives were psychologically torturing her grieving husband!"

Mason walked back to the podium. He took a sip of water, waited a few seconds before turning to the jury.

"The police took a broken man who was clearly in a vulnerable state, and they lied to him. Plain and simple. We all watched them make up a story about having a video of my client murdering his own wife! It was outlandish and offensive, but they did it anyway. Was it malice or just professional laziness? Neither option is acceptable, ladies and gentlemen. But they didn't stop there." The jury sat motionless, hanging on every word.

"Detectives kept him in a tiny room for seventy-two hours, pummeling him with a barrage of questions and suggestions, dangling a promise of salvation if he would just *come clean*. That's how they systematically and deliberately convinced an innocent man to say he murdered his wife!"

Mason was letting his anger take over. He was fed up with the rigged system, with sketchy police interrogations and rubber stamp judges. Fed up with everyone, including himself, assuming guilt. Mason truly believed in Michael Key's innocence, and now he needed the jury to believe it, too.

"The cops supplied all the details of my client's supposed crime, and filled in all the blanks. They worked as a team, taking advantage of Michael's tired mind, broken spirit, and essentially decent nature, until he was ready to tell them anything they wanted. Detectives backed him into a corner, leaving only one way out! Confess, they said, and this can all be over. My god, the police convinced Michael Key they were helping him! And he wanted to do the right thing. "

Mason slowly scanned the jury, holding eye contact with each one in turn.

"To these officers, it was ok to send a man to prison for the rest of his life simply because they couldn't be bothered to do their job." Mason's voice grew louder, filling the room. "Detectives didn't find Trevor Warnock, we did! What about the unknown DNA? Did it belong to Warnock? Someone else? We don't know, because the police never checked! They went straight for an easy target, and called it a day."

"I wish I could say this was unusual, that police are always objective, and don't assume guilt. But the truth is, once the police have you in their sights, the system is designed to convict. Remember, Detective Chase told us himself that lying to Michael Key about the video was allowed, that it was legal. And he's right, it was. And remember what our expert said – it's well known that these interrogation techniques lead to false confessions, yet the police still use them. I think that's sick, and a perversion of everything the criminal justice system stands for."

Mason could feel Francis glaring at him. With this off-the-cuff performance verging on accusations of police misconduct, Mason had walked right up to the red line of contempt, or even a mistrial. He needed to step back from the edge and wrap this up before the judge punished him for the impassioned display.

"Ladies and gentlemen, there was no investigation here, just a series of lazy assumptions. Now, the authorities want to make Michael Key, an *innocent man*, pay the price for their laziness. Don't let them get away with it. Don't let them turn the worst day of his life into the rest of his life!"

―――――――――

"Ladies and gentlemen," said Judge Francis, "since the State has the burden of proof, they get the last word. Mr. Templis, your rebuttal."

"Thank you, your honor." Templis rose from his seat and stepped to the podium with no folder full of notes, just a remote in his hand.

"Worst day for Michael Key." Templis shook his head as if puzzled. "Let me remind you that on October 8th of last year, Robin Key lived her *last* day." The DA's emphasis was not lost on the jury. "The judge told you to use your common sense, and common sense tells you that Michael Key is guilty. To believe otherwise, Michael Key would need to be the unluckiest man in the world. The defense would have you believe that, about an hour after Michael instigated a violent and public fight with his wife, some unknown person happened to find, attack, and kill Robin in front of the Key residence. All this while Michael Key's cell phone also happened to be in the area. What luck!"

Templis clicked a button on the remote and a photo was projected on the screen opposite the jury box. It showed a visibly happy Robin Key celebrating her last birthday. The jurors could not look away from the image of her smiling face.

"This trial is not a referendum on the Reid technique. This trial is not about the police not doing their job. This trial is about the savage murder of Robin Key. It is about a husband's uncontrollable rage after learning of his wife's infidelity." Templis turned and walked over to the defense table. "Ladies and gentlemen, you have probably never been in a room with a murderer before. But make no mistake, you are in the room with one today." Templis pointed to Michael. "And there he is."

Templis took his time returning to the podium, letting the accusation sink in. "We know he is a murderer based on the evidence. The evidence shows his phone was in the area at the time of the murder. The evidence shows that about an hour before, he was in a violent fight with Robin. So violent that police needed to intervene. So violent that his DNA ended up under Robin's fingernails. And that evidence has nothing to do with police tactics." Templis walked over to his table, glanced at his notes, then stepped toward the jury box.

He dropped his voice low, as if sharing a secret. "And you know what else? Michael Key confessed. He told the police he stabbed Robin. That he plunged the knife into her, over and over in a violent rage. Then he told his fellow inmate. And nothing in the record shows that Mr. Baker employed the nefarious Reid technique." He clicked the remote and a picture of the bloody porch filled the screen.

"Michael Key waited for Robin, his pregnant wife, in front of their marital home. And when she arrived, he stepped onto that porch, and brutally, *viciously* attacked her. He repeatedly plunged the knife into her to satisfy his all-consuming rage. It's that simple. Take him at his word, believe his own statement. Hold him accountable for the two lives he selfishly took from this world. Find Michael Key guilty and give Robin and her baby the peace they deserve."

The courtroom seemed to hold its breath as Templis quietly returned to his seat. Judge Francis broke the deathly silence to deliver his final jury instructions, after which he selected and excused the alternate jurors. Everyone in the room remained seated as the bailiffs, sworn to keep the jury sequestered from the outside world during their deliberations, funneled the jurors out of the courtroom and down the hall. When Michael Key's twelve peers reached the jury room, bailiffs collected their cell phones in exchange for notebooks, and closed the door.

**44**

Mason stopped just inside the threshold of the Gold Room and loosened his tie. He spotted Smitty behind the bar and gave him a wave. His 'Sprite' would be on the way shortly. Mason put his head down and made a bee-line for the bar, hoping to avoid any incidental socializing with the other members in the formal lounge of the Marquette Club.

"Thanks, Smitty," said Mason. He took a sip of his drink before sitting down and gave the bartender a thumb's up. "Perfect, as always." He mounted his usual bar stool and grabbed a handful of dry roasted peanuts from one of the heavy cut glass dishes that the bar always laid out for patrons. Smitty and salty peanuts; two reasons Mason always waited on his Milwaukee County verdicts at the club.

Mason downed the last of his drink, and without a word between them, Smitty began mixing one more.

Another club member appeared over Mason's shoulder, and exclaimed, "Would you look who it is!"

Mason recognized the voice, and kept facing the bar. "Yeah, it's me alright."

Geoff McLean Jr. had known Mason since the first year at law school. He worked in corporate litigation for a large downtown firm, a species of lawyer you'd find on Law Review, recruited directly from law school. Geoff's species monopolized the lucrative summer internships and six-figure starting salaries. He spent the first years of his career hustling, desperate to impress the tyrannical partners, no doubt including Geoffrey Sr. After several years, he made partner and gained his own minions whom he could flog in the same manner. He would likely end his days drinking whiskey and telling old war stories at the Marquette Club before dropping dead from boredom, completing the life cycle. Geoff, like all of his species, was secure in the belief he was a *real* lawyer doing important work.

"What are you doing here in the middle of the afternoon?" asked Geoff. "Don't you have clients to save or money to chase?" It wasn't that Geoff didn't like Mason, he didn't *approve of* him.

"Nope, waiting on a verdict. You know, like in a real case where lives are on the line, not just zeros at the end of a check." Mason just plain didn't like Geoff.

"Yes, I think I saw it on television. I never understood how you could represent those people, if you catch my drift."

"Of course. Why would *those people* deserve a defense, or any rights at all?" said Mason.  Smitty placed a fresh drink in front of him and retreated down the bar to slice some limes, just within earshot.

"I'm not saying that," said Geoff. "It's just that with your clientele, you get your hands so dirty. Aren't you worried they'll rub off on you?"

Mason raised his eyebrows in a question.

"Oh, come on. You know what I mean, Mace," he said, and gave Mason a mock punch on the shoulder. Geoff was the only person who called him that. The forced attempt at bonhomie was equal parts amusing and annoying.

"Yeah, I think I know exactly what you mean, Geoffrey," replied Mason, returning the punch, harder. He was warming to the argument just to make the waiting go by faster. "And while I do appreciate your heartfelt concern for my integrity, as you can see," Mason smoothed his hands over his pinstripe blazer, "I'm doing just fine."

"Yes, in a manner of speaking, I suppose you are," said Geoff. He looked Mason up and down and shook his head. "Yet you spend all that money just to look so...down-market."

Mason chuckled. "It's called panache, Geoffrey. You look like the Mormon that other Mormons find too boring. I mean, Jesus, your wardrobe doubles as a sedative. You may have sold your soul but it looks like you rented that suit."

He saw Ozzy arrive and start to cross the room toward the bar, but waved him off and pointed to a pair of unoccupied high back leather chairs by the window. Mason looked back at Geoff and realized he was talking, "...and this whole sanctimonious act of yours doesn't wash, Mace. Your whole practice runs on drug money and–"

"You don't have to stop talking, Geoff, but I gotta run," said Mason. He left the corporate litigator stammering for a comeback and joined Ozzy.

"Hey, boss. Who was that back there?"

"What? Oh, just some rich dickhead. Get you a drink?"

"No thanks," said Ozzy. Mason could tell his private investigator was anxious.

"Oz, it's not like you to hang out when I'm waiting on a verdict. What gives?"

"Not sure. This one feels different. Feels like I should be here. Besides, it might be a long one."

"You never can tell."

"I guess. Noticed your security isn't here. You call him off?"

"It's not exactly his type of crowd here, so he's out front. Anyway, now I have my great protector with me," said Mason.

Ozzy shook his head. "You're lucky I came over here to keep you company."

"Since you did, you want some food, Oz? I'm buying."

"Not hungry."

"Yeah, me neither," said Mason.

The two men sat for a while in silence, watching the traffic on Jefferson Street.

"Liked your closing," offered Ozzy. "I've never heard you straight up claim innocence. That's a new one."

"Hmm. Felt like it kind of got away from me. You think I was pushing too hard?"

"Honestly? I have no idea. Couldn't get a read on that jury. But as long as you did what you thought was best for Mike…"

"Innocent or not, I know for damn sure there's enough reasonable doubt. You saw the trial. The State didn't do enough to earn a guilty verdict against Michael Key."

Mason's phone buzzed with a text message from the court clerk.

*Jury question. Please come back.*

Mason typed his reply – *On my way.*

———

Half an hour later, Mason was back at the Gold Room bar, watching Smitty prepare his next round. "I hate jury questions," he muttered. "They never tell me anything."

The bartender looked up to see no one else around and figured a response was the polite thing. "What did they ask about?"

"They wanted to see the video again. The same video the police lied about and said was clear as fucking day. More like, clear as mud!"

Smitty leaned over the bar. Insight into jury deliberation for the 'trial of the century' had piqued his interest. "What do you think it means?"

"Who knows? I mean you can guess and wrack your brain, but you never know for sure.  Trying to figure out what jury questions mean will drive you crazy, so I stopped trying a long time ago."

"I see," said Smitty, more than a little let down by the answer.

Mason collected his drinks and returned to Ozzy and the leather high back chairs. They passed the afternoon in conversation, taking turns retrieving each new round from Smitty. Ozzy tried to keep his employer loose, but Mason would steer things back to the trial, rehashing it blow by blow – each witness, every piece of evidence.

"Shit, maybe he should have testified," said Mason.

"Ok, why do you–"

"Definitely should have had another expert."

"You had the two best guys you could find."

"Yeah, but I feel like the jury hated Bowen, or at least tuned him out." Mason sighed and rubbed his temples. "And maybe I didn't go hard enough with Warnock, took my foot off the pedal."

"Hey, if you're gonna keep this up, I can leave," said Ozzy. "It's too early to be a Monday morning quarterback if the game is still on. What's with you?"

"This one is sitting with me differently. Fuck. Did I give Mike the right advice not to testify?"

"Don't start that, boss."

"A trial is about sympathy, Ozzy. You know that. Did I generate enough sympathy? If Mike testifies, maybe that seals the deal. But I got nervous."

"Stop. You did everything you could for him. No one else would have given him a better defense. Now, it's out of your hands."

Mason nodded, but didn't hear. He stared out the window, replaying a perceived missed opportunity from the cross examination of Detective Chase. The waiting was doing him no favors, leaving the field open to self-doubt and recrimination. Ozzy noted with concern the number of empty glasses on the table between them.

Mason's phone buzzed. The clerk again.

*Verdict.*

Mason jumped up and showed Ozzy the message. He gulped down the last of the Sprite, grabbed his jacket and began pulling it on as they made for the door. The fresh air and nervous anxiety sharpened him up, and he walked briskly with Ozzy and his young bodyguard in tow. Mason burned away the vodka aftertaste in his mouth with a spritz of breath spray as he went, inhaling the menthol deep into his lungs. He arrived at the Safety Building and entered from 9th Street, through the leftmost door. At security, Mason showed his pass and was ushered upstairs and through the overflow crowd outside Courtroom 620. A deputy escorted

Mason past the gallery, and opened the door that led to the well of the courtroom. Mason paused and studied the scene framed by the doorway – the cameras, family members, activists, police officers, and Michael Key.

Mason took a deep breath, then walked through the door and sat down at his client's side.

He saw that Michael was restrained with a belly chain and his ankle was shackled to the floor. "They're going to announce a verdict," whispered Mason, "and I want you to keep your hands down so the jury doesn't see the chains. You ready?"

"Yeah. I'm good," said Michael, his chest rising and falling faster than normal.

"And no matter what happens, please don't react. If we win, you will have plenty of time to celebrate. If we lose, this is your sentencing judge and we don't want to do anything to piss him off. Got it?"

"Lose? I thought you said that–"

"I say the same thing to all my clients and I'm saying it to you now. That's all." Mason could see Michael's mind was racing. "Hey, just try to stay calm. You've come this far. We're good."

Michael straightened up and faced the bench, making an effort to ignore the cameras, the spectators, and the chains. Twenty minutes had passed since Mason was notified that a verdict was reached. He knew the longer they waited, the worse it must be for Michael. Quiet blanketed the packed courtroom, every cough and creaking chair cut through the pregnant silence.

The door to the left of the bench opened, then a bailiff emerged and announced the jury. They shuffled in, single file, and Mason scanned their now familiar faces, looking for any sign that hinted at the verdict. Some defense attorneys believed that eye contact from a returning jury meant not guilty, and no eye contact signaled a guilty verdict. Mason didn't buy it, but he couldn't blame others for believing it. Made as much sense as any other trick for reading a jury.

Mason tried to make eye contact with jurors as they settled into the box, but none would meet his gaze.

Judge Francis returned to his seat on the bench. "Has the jury reached a verdict?"

Juror 12 rose, revealing herself as the foreperson. "Yes," she replied, the single word filling the hushed courtroom.

"Please give it to the bailiff," said Francis, and a binder containing a copy of the jury instructions and the verdicts was handed over and dutifully brought to him. He methodically donned reading glasses, opened the binder, and read the verdict to himself. The judge's features remained inscrutable as he made his way down the page.

"I have reviewed the verdicts. They appear to be in order and signed on this day by Juror Twelve, Ms. Sneed."

Mason searched for clues in the judge's tone and posture but found nothing. He heard Michael's breathing becoming ragged, and Mason could see the quickening pulse in his client's neck.

The judge continued, now addressing the gallery. "Ladies and gentlemen, a verdict in this case has been rendered and will be read aloud in open court. Regardless of the outcome or whatever personal feelings you have about the verdict, I will not tolerate any outbursts. If you cannot behave accordingly, you will be removed from this court and potentially face arrest. Do I make myself clear?" His question was met with church-like quiet.

Satisfied, Francis began to read out loud, "We the jury, in the matter of the State of Wisconsin versus Michael Key," Mason listened for one word, one sound, really – the *n* of 'not guilty' – nothing else mattered, "on Count One, first degree intentional murder as to Robin Key, we find the defendant guilty. On Count Two, first degree intentional murder as to John Doe, we find the defendant guilty."

As the words washed over the gallery, their silence was replaced by an eruption of wails and cheers. The judge's warning was ignored as cries of dismay, grief, triumph, and shock filled the room. Francis banged his gavel and called for order, but some spectators had already leaped from their seats. Finger pointing and taunting quickly led to shoving, sparking a chain reaction of increasing hostility. Four Sheriff's deputies left their post by the doors and waded into the gallery, the situation threatening to flare out of control.

Michael stared at the judge, seemingly uncomprehending. Mason couldn't move. A sickening, strength-sapping heat, like a gut full of hot iron, spread out into his limbs. Only the chair back kept him upright. *This is wrong. They got it fucking wrong!*

Judge Francis hit the panic button behind the bench, and the court officers sprang into action, escorting the jury out the side doors. Two bailiffs rushed past Mason, disconnected the chain from the floor, and hauled Michael from his seat. As they hustled him out a separate entrance, Michael looked back at Mason, his features contorted in anguish.

On the other side of the partition, a full-scale brawl was in progress, with bailiffs rushing in from other courts to reinforce the outnumbered deputies. Much of the crowd remained, forced to the edges of the courtroom but unable to flee the melee. Some stood on chairs, recording the scene with their phones.

Mason still hadn't moved from his seat. Templis was standing at the defense table, shouting at him, "Attorney Mitchell! Hey! Mason, come on!"

Judge Francis waved frantically to the two lawyers, beckoning them to follow into his chambers.

Templis grabbed Mason's arm. "You, ok? We've got to go. Now!"

Mason stood and let himself be pulled along until the judge closed his office door behind them and locked it with a deadbolt. He went to his desk and picked up the phone, "Yes, it's me. No, we're locked in back here. But listen to me, you keep this line open and buzz me the second that SWAT arrives."

Francis opened a desk drawer and pulled out a revolver. He spun the chambers to make sure it was loaded and set it on the desk. The three men sat stunned, not speaking, the floor rumbling under their feet. They listened to the muffled sounds outside the door – police officers shouting commands intercut with high-pitched screaming, the crack of heavy impacts against the security-glass partition, but no gunshots, yet.

Francis leaned back in his chair and exhaled heavily. "This is a goddamn mess."

## 45

"**H**ey."

Lori turned from the laundry press table and saw Deena, her jumpsuit unzipped to the waist and her hand held out expectantly.

"So, give it," said Deena.

Lori replaced the steaming iron in its wire cradle. She opened her coveralls and awkwardly removed a pack of ground coffee from inside her left pant leg, then a bottle of Dark & Lovely conditioner from the right, handing each one over.

Deena tucked the items into her jumpsuit, zipped up, and jammed her hands into the pockets to keep the cargo from moving around. The whole action took only a few seconds. "Meet me down in the yard in 5 minutes."

———

Lori found Deena strolling along the path that bordered the East Yard and tried to look casual as she fell in step beside her. They walked a few paces in the blinding white morning sunshine before Lori broke the silence.

"So, you know the doctor?"

"Dr. Fehl. Yeah, I recognized that piece of shit on Court TV. Dirty motherfucker."

"What do you know about him?"

"I know he's a dirty motherfucker."

Lori sighed but kept her cool. "Hey, I got your stuff. So, I need the whole story."

Deena kept her head down, studying the pathway for a few seconds, then began. "In those kinds of practices, nurses like me would move around every few years, and it's a small circle. People talk. We all heard rumors and stuff."

"What kind of stuff?"

"That he was friendly. Too friendly, like with his staff. He didn't care about the rules when it came to prescriptions and would offer 'perks' to the girls who played along."

"Played along? What do you mean?"

"What do you think I mean? He wanted you to wear tighter scrubs at work, he'd let his hands wander, and you just had to roll with it to get the perks, get it?"

"Hmm. Ok. And was he trying stuff with patients?"

"Like I said, we heard rumors. Then I got to see it up close."

"You mean you worked for him?"

Deena turned to Lori, squinting against the sunlight. "Yeah, Dr. Fehl. He was my last one before I ended up here. When I interviewed for the position he made a big deal out of saying the problems in my work history didn't matter to him, that he saw I was good at my job. Said he respected that I was a single mom. Kept talking about how he was sure we would make a great team. Kept repeating 'great team'." Deena shook her head, "He saw me coming a mile away. I should've known."

"So, you played along?"

There was a long pause, with only the rhythmic crunch of gravel underfoot. "Not at first, but yeah. He fed me the meds I wanted. Motherfucker would joke and call himself Doctor Fehl-good. So, I got all the pills I wanted as long as I kept my mouth shut about what went on in the exam room."

"And he was...what? Touching his patients?"

Deena stopped and looked Lori in the eye, her voice took on a sharper edge, "Look, he raped them, ok?" She exhaled, then resumed walking, her tone shifting back to neutral. "He made sure I was in his pocket, giving me the pills I needed. And he damn sure let me know he was going to take me down if I said a word or tried to quit. All he wanted me to do was leave the room for a couple minutes."

Lori kept walking, unsure of what to say in the face of such a horrible admission. She felt Deena's eyes on her, as if daring Lori to pass judgment.

"I had a kid, ok? I would lose the job *and* him if they found out I was using again." They walked a few more yards before Deena added quietly, "I lost him anyway."

Lori gave the last comment a chance to dissipate into the bracing air. There was unmistakable pain behind those words, but no invitation to console or relate. Everybody in here had a third rail that you didn't want to go near. Lori ignored Deena's heartache and continued, "You ended up here. Did you stop playing along or something?"

"He just kept pushing. That man was a pig! The last time, he 'accidentally' put a patient under, then told her after that she'd had a bad reaction to the local anesthetic, that it knocked her out."

"Oh my god."

"I walked in on it because I heard instruments hit the floor and I thought something had happened. Stupid piece of shit had just kicked the cart over while…getting between the stirrups."

"You mean he was–"

"Yeah." Tears rolled down Deena's cheek and she wiped them away with her sleeve. Her face flushed, the features twisted by the bitterness of the memory. "He just turned and looked at me, totally calm. His eyes were like a snake. He didn't say a word, but that look was all the threat he needed. So, I got the hell out of the room." A tormented groan escaped her throat before she carried on. "He came back out a minute later, like nothing happened. Asked me to come help revive the patient."

"And you didn't tell anyone?"

"Little fucker called the cops on me before I had the chance. Next day, they picked me up, searched the apartment and found my stash. He gave them the story that I'd been stealing from him and a whole bunch of other shit."

"Jesus. I'm sorry."

Deena glared at her. She didn't want her sorry, and Lori felt like a fool for offering empty words.

"I told the cops what Fehl was doing but they didn't even listen for a second. To them, I was just some junkie bitch trying to save my ass." Deena stopped dead in her tracks, fully under control again. "So, that's what you wanted to know, right?"

Lori nodded but couldn't bring herself to look Deena in the eye. "Yeah, thanks."

"Sure, whatever," she said, then turned and walked back to the dorm, alone under the late autumn sun. Lori watched Deena go until her outline was swallowed by the deep shadow cast by the prison block.

Lori looked around the yard, seeing no one who noticed or cared what she was doing. Her heart thudded against her ribs as she walked back inside, to the library, the draft of an email forming in her head.

**46**

"W here are you, boss? We need to meet." Mason was tempted to hang up. He knew where he was but didn't want anyone else to know.

"What is it, Oz? Not in the mood to talk."

"Too bad! This is important. It's about the Key case."

"That one's over, remember?" Mason slurred, "And we fucking loooost."

"Jesus Christ. I think I know where you are," said Ozzy, before ending the call.

Ten minutes later, he walked up to the bar at Walter's. "Where is he?" John pointed to the back, where Ozzy found Mason alone in a booth, a half-eaten basket of cheese curds and three empty rocks glasses scattered across the table. He took a seat and waved to John for a fresh round.

"What the fuck. Told you I didn't want to talk," said Mason.

"I bring you a bombshell and that's my greeting? You can be a drunk or an ingrate, but not both, ok?"

John arrived and set a beer down in front of Ozzy. Mason grabbed the highball glass from his other hand.

"Thank you oh so much for the drink, Ozzy. That better?"

"Just shut up and listen then. This could help Mike."

"Oh yeah? Guilty on both counts, sentenced to life. Unless you're about to tell me you invented a time machine, that's the end of the story." Mason finished his drink in one go and motioned to John for another, but Ozzy waved him off.

"Let's get you out of here. We'll go to Ma Fisher's, grab some food and chat. Ok?"

"Sure, what the hell," said Mason, pushing the curds away, "I could do with some real food." Mason stood, steadied himself, then followed Ozzy to the door, leaving a hundred dollar bill on the bar.

"Thanks Mason," said John. "And Oz? Take care of him, ok."

Ozzy struggled to keep Mason from weaving across the sidewalk as they slowly traveled the two blocks to the diner. Ma Fisher's was open twenty-fours a day, but the food always seemed to taste better in the middle of the night. Their slogan – 'Serving Milwaukee hangovers since 1968' – was an example of truth in advertising. The crumbling stucco exterior had been destroyed in a fire six years earlier and replaced with red brick, but inside, the classic diner decor remained, chrome and formica. Ozzy poured Mason into a booth by the front window and ordered two Denver Omelets with bottomless coffee.

"Alright. What's this bombshell?" asked Mason.

"It's the doctor. Fehl was arrested this morning."

Mason paused with the coffee cup at his lips. "What? You mean our tip from Lori...someone from the department actually followed up on it?"

"It would appear so. The way my contact tells it, a couple guys in the Sensitive Crimes Division gave our story a better look and found a patient willing to make a statement. What she said was a little vague, but she was sure something weird happened during a visit to the good doctor, enough to get a warrant."

The news was almost enough to sober Mason up. "Oh my god. So Lori's info was right on the money?"

"Yeah, and then some."

"What do you mean?"

"Fehl wasn't just assaulting his patients, he was recording it. Had a small camera set in the ceiling of the exam room. Police found a couple dozen videos on a hard drive. Like a trophy collection."

The food was delivered to the table, ignored by both men.

"And what about Robin? Was there anything involving her?"

"Yeah, she was one of them," said Ozzy. "Same M.O. Lori talked about. In the examining room, once she was under, he raped her."

Mason closed his eyes and kneaded his forehead. "Jesus."

"When investigators searched Fehl's storage room, they found the hard drive and some documents. One of them was Robin's chart with Fehl's handwritten notes. Not the same chart he provided to the DA for trial. This one showed she'd been asking questions about the pregnancy, denied the affair with Warnock, and told Fehl she was pretty sure Michael was infertile. Fehl knew Michael is black and I think he was afraid that if Robin carried that baby to term it wasn't going to come out looking like Michael. A paternity test could've brought it all crashing down for Fehl."

Mason stared out the window, almost in shock. "You think Robin's baby was his?"

"It would be a pretty big fuck up on his part, but my cop brain says the puzzle pieces are starting to fit."

"So he murders Robin to get rid of the evidence," whispered Mason.

Ozzy leaned in, "I'll bet you anything if they tested his DNA against the unknown sample from Robin's fingernails, we'd get a match."

Mason realized he'd been holding his breath and inhaled loudly. "Holy shit. This is insane. I fucking *knew* there was something with that guy!"

"We'll know for sure if we can test his sample. This has gotta be good for Mike. With the video, and especially if we get the DNA match, we can appeal!"

Mason shook his head. "It's not that simple. We'd need to get approval for the DNA test in the first place, and who knows if or when that'd happen. And the video probably isn't enough by itself. You know how messed up this process is, Oz. Judges and prosecutors hate reopening a conviction."

"But you *can* appeal, right?"

Mason slumped against the vinyl upholstery and closed his eyes. "Yes. I mean, sure, I'm allowed to file a motion. I think a post-conviction motion for a new trial with Francis would be our best shot."

He felt dizzy. Mason knew the statistics. Successful post-conviction motions or appeals were vanishingly rare. Even with new evidence, you had a better chance of being hit by lightning than to have the motion granted. On a double homicide, the chances would be slim to none.

Ozzy kicked Mason's seat under the table. "Hey! Look at me! You still believe in Mike, right?"

"Yes. You know I do, but–"

"Well, he's in a cell up at Boscobel looking at life! That's your client, and you're never shy about telling me you're a great lawyer. So you better pick your fucking head up off your shoulders and make shit happen. It's time to go to work, boss."

Mason knew he was right. A million to one shot was still a shot, and Michael deserved it. He nodded slowly. "Yup. I'll head up there and let him know it's on. Then we can get started on this."

"Good," said Ozzy. He pushed the plate of cold eggs under Mason's nose. "Now eat something. You look like shit."

**47**

The drive to Taycheedah was a comfortable hour which allowed Mason to go over the details of the post-conviction motion he just filed on behalf of Michael Key. The painstaking work that went into preparing it for submission had sparked fresh hope in Mason, leaving him convinced that Dr. Fehl's arrest would get Michael his new trial.

A wall of jack pines that bordered the road rushed past outside the passenger side window. As Mason drove on, the trees began to thin, an emptying of the landscape that signaled the prison was near. He saw the guard towers first, one on each corner of the perimeter, linked by a twenty foot high razor wire fence, with two more towers flanking the double layered entrance. He turned off the highway and slowly approached the security checkpoint, nosing his Mercedes past the first gate. It closed behind him, leaving his car stopped before the closed second gate, in a space that reminded Mason of purgatory, neither here nor there. A guard approached and asked for identification. Mason handed over his driver's license along with a card from the State Bar of Wisconsin that established his credentials. As he waited, Mason read the large sign posted outside his driver side window:

*ALL VEHICLES AND PERSONS WANTING TO ENTER THIS FACILITY ARE SUBJECT TO SEARCH WITHOUT EXCEPTION.*

*So much for the Fourth, Sixth and Eighth Amendments*, thought Mason. The guard handed back his ID and gave an 'OK' signal to the control booth. The second gate screeched to life, pulled along its track by a rusted chain.

358

Mason drove ahead to the parking lot, selecting a space far from the other cars. Prison parking lots were notorious for the mysterious appearance of a door ding or two. He walked the hundred yards to the prison entrance, an open distance that allowed visitors to be observed by guards and whomever else happened to be watching.

Once his clients reached prison, Mason's job was usually done, so his institutional visits were infrequent. But he knew enough that these occasions did not call for his usual polished look. Today he had taken it to another level, wearing jeans and a Marquette Law School hoodie that hadn't seen the light of day in over a decade.

The guard bellowed without looking up from his computer monitor, "Name of inmate?"

"Wells, Lori Wells." Despite the divorce and court order that restored her surname, the DOC system would not change Lori's name until she was released. For the remaining year of her sentence, Lori would remain tethered to David by this final thread.

"Pass through the metal detector," said the guard, eyeing Mason with suspicion. "Any unapproved electronics?" The prison did not allow laptops, cell phones, smart watches, or any device that could send or receive data.

"Nope, left it all in the car," said Mason cheerily. *And I know the drill, dipshit.*

After clearing the security check and affixing a VISITOR badge to his chest, Mason was led through a string of doors and hallways before being deposited in a small conference room containing two chairs and a small table.

"Wells will be in soon," said his escort, then left, leaving Mason locked in. Twenty minutes later Lori's face appeared in the door's small window. She pressed the button to request access and seconds later the door buzzed open.

Mason last visited several months prior, to have Lori sign her divorce papers. She had shuffled into the room, haggard and disheveled, refusing to give details about her black eye and bandaged ribs. Mason left the prison worried that she might not survive her two years inside. But the Lori he saw this morning appeared healthy and sure-footed, striding into the room with purpose.

"It's good to see you," said Mason. "You're looking well."

She pulled at her green DOC coverall, embarrassed. "Thanks."

For a moment, they sat not saying anything, each waiting for the other to begin.

"Hey, sorry about the Key case," said Lori. "Everybody in here thinks he got screwed."

"They're not wrong."

"But I saw on the news, the doctor got arrested. That fucking scumbag made videos?"

"Thanks to you, the police knew where to look."

She smiled shyly, but clearly pleased. "I just figured I could help."

"Well, it might have done more than that. After Fehl's arrest, I spent months putting together a post-conviction motion. Filed it a few weeks ago."

"You mean like an appeal?"

"Yeah basically. We are arguing for Mike to get a new trial. And this wouldn't have happened without you, so, you should feel good about that."

"Wow," said Lori, a blush spread across her cheeks. "That's nice of you to say."

"And you'll never believe what our DNA expert discovered."

"Let me guess – it was Warnock's DNA under Robin's fingernails?"

"Nope. The doctor."

Lori sat back, stunned. "Holy shit. So he killed her?" Her eyes went wide. "You think Robin got pregnant when he..." she couldn't finish the thought out loud.

"That's our guess. We'll have to work hard to make things stick, but our motion claims a gross miscarriage of justice. In essence, we're arguing Michael's innocence."

"So, what's going to happen?"

"We're saying that, that given this new evidence – the DNA, the altered medical records, Fehl's video of rape – the case should be presented to a jury in a new trial."

"You sound excited," said Lori.

"Yeah? Well, I am. I'll level with you, when I lost that case I was so despondent, even considered quitting the practice. But with a new trial, I can do right by Mike and we can get some real justice. I just want to see him walk free again."

"And I'm glad you didn't quit," said Lori, smiling, "because I still need you."

"Right! Sorry, to that point," Mason pulled a document from his briefcase and laid it on the table. "You just need to sign this and the personal injury case is also over. A fifteen thousand dollar lump sum and David is gone." He offered her his pen.

"You talked to my dad?"

"Yes, Tom has agreed to pay so we can put this all behind you."

Lori looked at the settlement agreement sadly, then signed. "What a fucking disappointment I must be to him, to everyone."

"Don't say that, Lori. You were trapped in an abusive marriage with a guy who made you believe you were worthless, but that's over now. You have value, ok? I see how much you've changed since we first met, and I know you have a lot to contribute to this world."

"Uh-huh." Lori looked down at the floor.

"Look at me," said Mason. She raised her eyes, now on the verge of tears. "You've survived over a year in this hellhole, and that took strength and guts. I've seen it with other clients of mine, this can be a chance to take control of your life. The experience will be a part of your story, but it doesn't have to define you. And when you get out, don't look back, not at David and not at this fucking place. Own it and become the best version of you, if for no other reason than to stick it to that asshole!"

Lori picked up the paper and studied her signature – *Lori Wells* – "Right."

Mason took the document from her hand and slid it back into his briefcase. "Signed, sealed, and after I deliver, David is gone."

"Good. That's all I want."

Mason stood and buzzed for the guard. "Now, I have to get back to the city. But you stay strong. I know you can do this."

"Does this mean we need to stop writing to each other?"

"Of course not. I said I'd see you through the two years, and I will."

Just as the guard arrived, Lori caught Mason in a hug. "Thank you."

"No contact with the inmate, counselor!" snapped the guard.

"Relax," said Mason, "it's just a little human emotion. You could try it sometime." He followed the guard into the hall, leaving Lori behind to wait for her escort.

"Hey, wait," said Lori. "What happens with the Key motion now?"

"Should be hearing back any day now. The waiting is the worst part."

Lori smirked, "Tell me about it."

# 48

"**M**otion denied?!?" screamed Mason. "Can you fucking believe this?"

Linda stood in the doorway of his office, not knowing what to say. She felt for him, for Michael Key, but there wasn't anything she could do to change the decision or calm Mason's rage.

"What is the process even for, if not for a case like this?" He slammed both palms down on his desk. "What the fuck am I supposed to tell Mike? He gets put through the whole nightmare again, except now he also gets to know that his dead wife was raped by her own fucking doctor!"

The phone at the front desk started to ring and Linda looked over her shoulder, then back to Mason.

"It's fine, you can go answer it. Just close the door. If anyone asks, I'm not here."

She ducked out, grateful for the excuse to leave Mason alone with his anger.

Mason had spent months crafting arguments, waiting for DNA results, and reigniting Michael Key's hope for justice, only for Judge Francis to summarily deny the motion. Although he could appeal to a higher court, Mason knew there would be no new trial now, Michael would live the rest of his life in prison.

Mason grabbed the balled up paper from the garbage can at his feet, smoothed the page against the desktop, and read the decision again:

*The argument presented to this court in support of the motion to vacate the verdict and grant a new trial for Michael Key is underpinned by three pieces of new evidence. One – the defense has presented evidence that Dr. Fehl sexually assaulted Robin Key and therefore may have been the father of the unborn child, giving him a motive to commit the homicide. Two – the unknown male DNA found under the fingernails of Robin Key identified Dr. Fehl as the source giving him the opportunity to commit the homicide. And three – the altered medical records discovered when Dr. Fehl was arrested on unrelated charges speaks to his credibility as a witness in the underlying trial. Considering these pieces, the defense argues that Dr. Fehl should have been presented as a 'Denny' suspect and this new evidence should be presented to a jury.*

*The first step in the legal process is to consider if this new evidence could have been discovered by the defense through diligent investigation, prior to the original trial. If not, it is proper for the court to consider this evidence in hindsight. This court finds the new evidence could not have reasonably been discovered prior to trial and therefore, counsel was not derelict in his duties.*

"Well at least I did something right," said Mason.

*The second step is to consider if the new evidence demonstrates 'actual innocence' as argued by the defense. Unlike a trial, which is designed to be a 'search for the truth', a post-conviction motion is not a fact-finding mission. Rather, the Court is limited to reviewing for legal error or for a gross miscarriage of justice. The latter requires a showing of 'actual innocence' – which is the rationale argued by the defense. Under that standard, the new evidence, taken in context, is insufficient to overturn a conviction. Simply put – this evidence does not support the innocence of the defendant. At most, this evidence presents an alternate viable suspect – another 'Denny' suspect. It does not, however, rise to the level of establishing innocence. Accordingly, the motion to vacate the judgment against Michael Key and to order a new trial is denied.*

———

An hour later, Mason pressed the intercom button on his desk phone, "Linda, can you come in here, and bring Ozzy."

When they entered the room, Mason stood at the sideboard behind his desk, pouring a scotch. The framed print of *Le Bateau* sat to one side, revealing the wall safe, which stood open.

"Either one of you want a drink?" asked Mason. "It might be that type of conversation." Both declined. Linda looked from the bottle to Mason, her brow furrowed with worry.

"First of all, I wanted to say a few things, and please do not interrupt. Just let me get it out."

Ozzy kept his arms folded across his barrel chest and said nothing. He was not a fan of mystery and being summoned by Mason with no explanation had set him on edge.

When Mason spoke, it came out flat and plain. "I'm out. I mean it. I cannot do this anymore."

Chagrin showed on Linda's face. "I knew it," she said under her breath. Ozzy said nothing.

"This has been on my mind since we lost the Key trial." Mason paused to sip the scotch, "and today's decision to deny Mike's motion seals it for me."

"Just like that?" asked Linda.

"Yep. For months now, I've been feeling lost. And now I don't know what I'm doing, like I don't have a purpose. I show up to court, fight hard, make my arguments, I do everything I can and nothing changes. The people I represent just get chewed up. In this system...there's no place for me anymore. So, that's the big speech." Mason turned and reached into the safe. "And now comes the good part."

He took out the Ruger and set it in his briefcase, then removed all the cash, arranging two neat piles on the desk in front of Linda and Ozzy, and placing the rest next to his gun.

"That's twenty grand for each of you. Call it severance pay."

Ozzy finally broke his silence, "Ok this is cute and all, but what exactly–"

Mason held up a hand to stop him. "Please, Oz. I'm almost finished." He turned to Linda, "I need you to file motions to withdraw on all my pending cases. Send the clients we like to Chad Resnick. You know him. He's young, he's good, he'll take care of them. The others will have to fend for themselves."

"What do I tell the courts?" Linda was put out by this development, but the pile of cash kept her from fully showing it. "If we're withdrawing, I'll need to give a reason."

"Tell them I'm retiring or taking a leave of absence. Hell, say I'm running away on a Great Lakes freighter if you want. Just as long as they know I'm out."

"Ok. Effective when?"

"Today. And email the landlord, tell them we're out of the offices as soon as possible. I'll arrange the movers."

Ozzy squinted at Mason, as if looking at an imposter. "Are you sure about this, boss? How much have you been drinking?"

Mason put the glass down and looked him in the eye. "I'm in my right mind, if that's what you're asking. Mitchell & Associates is done."

"It was just a bad loss. Everyone in this room felt it. But you bounce back and move on!"

"Not this time. The job just isn't me anymore. I don't fit. Police can coerce a confession, evidence gets ignored, and a jury signs off on whatever the DA puts in front of them. You've seen all the stats, Oz. With my clients, their race and gender can matter more than the facts. Decatur wasn't just talking to hear her own voice; it's not just the courts, it's the whole system, top to bottom."

Ozzy flicked at the pile of money in front of him. "So, I just take my parting gift and that's that?"

"Come on, Oz." He was tired, pleading with his old friend. "I appreciate how hard you had to work lately, keeping me on track and in the game, but I'm done." He forced a weak smile, "And who knows, maybe I'll be like you, get bored, come back and find a different way to do it. But not right now."

Ozzy shook his head but his features softened. "First Butch takes off, now you. Am I the only one who wants to work anymore?"

"Maybe I'll retire, too," said Linda, chuckling softly. She picked up a brick of cash and riffled through it. "I know Cliff wants to move to Arizona. Maybe this is our chance."

Ozzy raised a hand in warning, "Trust me, Linda. Retirement sucks."

"I'm not a glutton for punishment like you, Ozzy. And it's easy for you to talk when you have that police pension to catch your fall."

"I'm not touching one red cent of it until my girl is done at Michigan State. My boat can wait. For now, I'll deal with all the scumbags our fine city has to offer."

Linda rolled her eyes. The cash was now cradled in her lap like a beloved pet. "What are you going to do, Mason?"

"Take a few days to shut things down here, then...I don't know," he said with a shrug. "Maybe Clyde and I will hit the open road and just stop when we get tired."

Linda's phone buzzed and she looked down at the screen. "Speak of the devil. Cliff needs me at home. Are you ok here if I get going?" He nodded and she stood to shake his hand. "Thank you. And I'll start contacting the courts and clients as soon as I get home."

"On your way out, could you drop this in the mail?"

Linda looked at the address on the envelope, "You still write her?"

"Yeah. Kind of been like therapy the last few months. Please send that last one."

"I will."

**49**

M ason slid into a bench at the back of the courtroom, near the door. His attempt at remaining incognito – chinos and a windbreaker with a baseball cap pulled down low – was unsuccessful.

"Hey, what are you doing sitting all the way back here?" Assistant DA, Jean Lindeke crouched beside him on the aisle. "Hiding from someone?"

"No, no, just wanted to see how this goes."

"For a co-defendant or something?"

"Yeah, something like that."

Judge John Stevenson emerged from his chambers and Mason promptly removed his hat. Stevenson was scheduled to rule on the defense's motion to suppress evidence found during the execution of a search warrant.

Jean stood to go but Mason stopped her. "Do you think the motion has a chance?" he asked.

"To be honest? Not so sure. This one is sticky." Mason had learned the hard way that judge's almost never rule against police action so Jean's lack of confidence was startling.

"All rise," commanded the bailiff.

"Gotta go. And hey, tough luck on that football coach case. Let's grab a drink soon." Jean left Mason and walked to her table.

After hearing all the evidence and testimony, Stevenson ruled that the entry by police officers into Dr. Fehl's storage room was unlawful. The search warrant included the exam room and the doctor's office, but the hard drive that contained video recordings of the sexual assaults was recovered from a storage unit Fehl rented in the basement of the office complex. Stevenson concluded that the search warrant did not cover the storage unit, saying the incriminating evidence was obtained illegally. As a result, all videos and all other materials police took from the storage unit, along with all subsequently discovered evidence, including the doctor's confession, were ordered suppressed and declared *fruits of the poisonous tree.*

"Given my ruling, and exclusion of the evidence, how does the State wish to proceed Ms. Lindeke?"

"Based on the ruling of the court, the State has no choice but to dismiss the charges against Dr. Fehl."

"So ordered," said Stevenson. Mason was out the door before the judge's gavel came down.

———

"The fucking exclusionary rule, fruit of the poisonous tree. In this case, it's total bullshit." said Mason. "The search was good because the warrant was good. How is that storage room not part of Fehl's office? It's the same rental agreement! Stevenson is splitting hairs and that warped predator walks. Unbelievable."

Jim Preston eyed him wearily. "It's been the law for a long time, and it isn't changing anytime soon." Jim drained his drink and nodded to Mason, indicating it was his turn to get the next round. Mason waved to the bartender and held up two fingers. He had only come to Henley's because Preston refused to go anywhere else.

The back booth's red leather upholstery squeaked as Jim leaned forward. "But this gives you a glimpse of being a prosecutor. I know the defense has it hard, but you never had to tell a victim's family that the guy who killed or raped their loved one is going free, that justice is not being done. Now that's hard." Jim paused while fresh drinks were placed on the table. "Especially when everyone, including the judge who excluded the evidence, knows the son of a bitch is guilty! All because of the exclusionary rule that defense attorney's love so much."

"Yes, I've used it to my client's advantage. That's the job. But in this case, the judge is just wrong."

"It's always 'wrong' when evidence that proves someone guilty is excluded, but that's the law, Mason. And what's that saying of yours? 'Better that fifty guilty men go free than one innocent man be convicted' – well, that comes at a price!"

"Fuck it. I'm out anyway," said Mason, scratching at his beard. He stopped shaving a week ago. "Can't get justice in the justice system, but something needs to be done about this guy."

"Who, Fehl? What are you saying?"

Mason rolled his head from side to side, feeling a satisfying crunch in his spine. The drinks loosened his joints, but frustration from the ruling and the whole past year sat like a tight ball in his stomach. "I have a very broad client base, Jim. Some interesting characters who are willing to do all sorts of things. Some of them owe me."

"Don't talk shit, Mason. You think because you have a few hard-asses on speed dial that you're that kind of guy? If you do, you're a fool. When you do something like that, it can't be undone. Cause and effect, my young friend. Even if you just dip your toe in that swamp, you're still going to stink."

"Yeah, but Fehl, what he did to those women...and there's no way he didn't kill Robin. He could walk in here right now and have a drink if he wanted, while Mike will never see another day as a free man."

"With as many cases as you've handled, now you're getting idealistic? What's gotten into you? I know it's not just the booze."

"I just can't take any more, Jim. I've had my fill. Seeing it again and again, people processed and spit out, lives thrown away for nothing. I want it to mean something."

"I know, son. The ugliness gets to you. We wouldn't be human if it didn't. If you're in our business long enough, the ghosts start to pile up. You can't outrun them," Preston drained his glass and smiled. "but you can try to outdrink them. I've seen a lot of burnouts in my time and that's where you're at right now. You need to disengage, go somewhere else and do something else until you feel right again. I'm sure you've got some money stashed away. Go on hiatus. Live a little!"

Preston patted Mason's hand then heaved himself out of the booth and made the trek to the bathroom. Mason did have savings, but right now, his mind was on a different chunk of money. He had eight thousand dollars in an envelope inside his jacket and a recipient in mind.

He opened his phone, found the contact for Jalen and typed a message – *Need to meet tonight.* The reply came in just before Preston sat back down – *Bet. 20 mins. you know where.*

"You know, if it helps you, this doctor is fucked no matter what." said Jim, settling back into the booth's still warm, Preston-shaped divot. "He'll lose his medical license if he hasn't already, and with all those potential plaintiffs in a civil suit, he will get absolutely wiped out."

"You're right. I guess that's something."

"See? This guy is going to get his one way or another."

"I'm sure he will," said Mason.

"How long have you been at it, Attorney Mitchell?"

"Twelve long years."

"Over a decade in the trenches! That's long enough for anyone. Forget about Key, forget about this damn doctor, and ride off into the sunset for some well-earned rest and relaxation. But first, let's get ourselves one more round, shall we?"

"Wish I could, but I have to run." Mason downed his drink and slapped a pile of twenties on the table. He shook Jim's hand. "Thank you."

"For what?"

"Everything. For listening. Unlike my father, you never judged me. Thanks for that."

"Where are you headed?"

Mason stopped short, then realized Jim didn't mean tonight. "Not sure. North? I'll be in touch once I settle in somewhere."

Preston stood, pulling Mason in for a hug. The old man clapped him on the back then whispered, "Trust me, don't do it."

---

Mason parked his Benz at the curb and walked to the front door of 2720 West Melvina. His arrival garnered the attention of several neighbors, but nothing was said. He pressed the doorbell and looked into the surveillance camera above his head. After a few seconds a buzzer sounded and Mason opened the door. From the entry hall, he walked past a darkened room on his left and mounted the steep staircase that rose along the opposite wall. On the second floor landing he was greeted by a steel door with a button set at eye level. He gave it one long press followed by three short ones, then heard the telltale click of deadbolts turning over. When the door swung open, a thick cloud of marijuana smoke floated out, filling the landing. Jalen's hulking bodyguard appeared in the doorway. He nodded at Mason and offered a hit off his blunt.

Mason shook his head. "I'm good. Where's he at?"

"Out in a sec. Come on in."

A moment later, Jalen emerged from around a corner at the back of the room. "What's up?" He was shirtless and holding a two-foot-tall purple bong. On his head sat a fresh White Sox hat, white with black lettering. "You look like shit, bro."

"Thanks," said Mason. "Maybe some time away will help."

"Won't make you prettier," joked Jalen, but neither man laughed. "How long you gonna be gone?"

"Not sure yet. But I'm out, done practicing, done with the whole thing."

"And you said my guys, if they need something, they can go to this Chad–"

"Resnick, yeah. He's a good guy, good lawyer. I've already set it up and I'll text you his contact. Don't worry, he knows what he's doing."

"Hm. Ok. And the other thing?"

Mason removed the envelope from his jacket and handed it to Jalen. "Eight stacks."

Jalen set it on a table without a glance. "You know, once something like this starts moving, we can't go back. You get that, right?"

Mason exhaled heavily. "Yeah, I don't care. The other way, 'my way', didn't work. Hell, it never really did, if I'm being honest. I'd tell my clients I stand for justice and making things right, but it was bullshit."

"I know. Even the streets know that. Maybe the last to know was you." Jalen fired up the bowl of the bong, inhaled deeply, and held it. "This system is designed to keep us in place," he said quietly, before expelling a huge cloud of smoke.

Mason pointed at the envelope. "Right, so, I'm ok with this. At least I know how it's going to end and why."

"All due respect, you don't know shit, Mason." Jalen tapped the palm-sized platinum medallion in the shape of Wisconsin that hung over his bare chest. "*I know* how shit going to end, because I'm the motherfucker who deals with shit."

"Fine," said Mason. "The fucking judge made sure the evidence can never be used against this guy. He will never see the inside of a jail cell. He's untouchable. Or he thinks he is. So, if you're the motherfucker who deals with shit, do me a favor and deal with this fucking guy already!"

"Aaayyye, that's not the way we talk to each other, bro." Jalen's voice remained calm. "Now sit your fuckin' ass down."

It was all the warning Mason needed. "You're right. I'm sorry," he said, slowly lowering himself to the chair.

Jalen sat on the other side of the table and took a long look at Mason. "I know you are. But you're all fucked up right now. Not smart to make big decisions and spend big money when you're all fucked up. You know that. You've seen enough dumb motherfuckers with you in court. That path? It's not you." He slid the envelope across to Mason, who stopped it in the middle of the table.

"Jalen, I hear you, but this guy...this guy deserves it."

"Maybe. Not for you to decide," said Jalen. "And not for me either." He pointed at the envelope. "Now I think you better take this and go."

Mason stood up and walked to the door. "Keep the money. Do whatever you want with it."

"I'll hold it for you," said Jalen.

Mason almost laughed. "The last honorable man in Milwaukee," he said. "I'm gonna miss you."

# EPILOGUE

M ason grabbed the car keys and patted Clyde's round belly. "See you in a few hours, you little goof."

He had today circled on his calendar. The day he would revisit his old life, just for an hour or two.

It had been almost a year since Mitchell & Associates officially ceased operations. For the first couple of weeks Mason climbed into a bottle and didn't come out. One or two women were along for the ride, drunks like him. He had briefly paused his binge drinking to make the trip upstate to see Michael Key.

They had discussed details of the motion denial and Mason gave him the name of a good appellate lawyer, knowing nothing would come of it. Michael barely reacted, no histrionics or tears, but two days after Mason's visit, guards found Michael in his cell, his wrists slashed by a sharpened toothbrush. They got to him before he lost too much blood and Michael had recovered quickly before being transferred to a secure psych ward for two months of observation. After that, Mason continued to visit when he could. Michael spoke less and less, but was learning to paint and seemed to enjoy showing Mason his watercolors.

After Mason sold his Third Ward loft, for twice what he paid, he boxed up everything and put it in storage. Traded in his tailored suits, cufflinks, and suspenders for jeans and hoodies. The Benz was gone, replaced by a late model Jeep Cherokee that he drove out of Milwaukee, heading north until he stopped in Door County. He stayed in a motel for a week before pulling the trigger on a thirty-one foot Crossroads Sunset Trail RV that he parked at a permanent campsite on Clark Lake. Mason slowed down, depressurized, and barely thought about his law practice or the criminal justice system. He made weekly visits to Madison and had even convinced Kaylie to stay with him in the RV one weekend. Mason and Clyde passed most days relaxing in the shade or walking the lakeshore and spent their nights by the campfire, savoring their cigars and chew toys. On occasion, Mason would even join the other camp residents for cocktails and cards.

Mason steered the Cherokee past the camp gate and onto the road, breathing deeply to combat the anxiety rising in his chest. *They're just people. You don't have to stay long.* He had one stop to make on the way. When Mason left the RV park, Clyde was almost always along for the ride, safely ensconced in his custom-embroidered Snoozer Lookout dog seat. But not today. Mason pulled in at the small farm house a few miles down the road, went to the porch and picked up his parcel, then jumped back in the Jeep to continue the drive into Fond du Lac.

His emailed invitation said 'Anytime after 3:00 p.m.' Mason pulled up to the house closer to 4:30, hoping the crowd would have thinned by then. The driveway was filled with lawn chairs and party goers, so Mason parked two houses down and walked over. He spotted Tom and Carrie on the lawn with a small group of friends and family. As he hit the drive-way, Mason saw Lori walk out onto the porch. Her green prison scrubs were replaced by fashionably ripped jeans and a cropped sweatshirt, her curly hair fell down over her shoulders. He could see in her face that she was different now. The scared young woman that was hauled out of a courtroom two years before had been tested and came out the other side renewed, self-assured.

Lori saw Mason approach and waved. "Hey! You made it! Mom, Dad! Look who it is!"

She crossed the lawn to greet him and saw the small case in his hands. He unzipped the top and the fluffy head of a six-week-old Chihuahua popped up, excited to meet the world.

Lori's hands flew to her mouth, and she squealed. "Who's your friend? A new playmate for Clyde?"

"Nope. He's for you."

Lori's eyes went wide. "He is? Are you serious?"

"Absolutely." Mason put the puppy in her arms. "I thought you could use some unconditional love."

"Oh my god, I love him!" The dog yelped with excitement, licking Lori's neck as she beamed with delight.

"What are you going to name him?"

"I don't know, let me see...oh, I love all this reddish fur around his eyes, so maybe Rusty works? What do you think?"

"To me, he looks like a munchkin from the Wizard of Oz, *and* he scarfed down three treats on the drive over. I'd call him Munchie."

"What? That's no name for such a handsome boy!" Lori nuzzled the dog, who excitedly lapped at any part of her face he could reach. "No, I'm going with Rusty." She held him up in the air, then gave him a kiss. "You are so cute!"

"Rusty it is," said Mason. "I got you one more thing." He unfolded a Marquette Law School dog shirt and handed it to her.

"That is adorable!" She hugged him with one arm, cradling Rusty in the other. "Thank you so much. I love it, I mean him," said Lori, and gave Mason a peck on the cheek. "Thank you for coming, really."

"You're welcome. I know Clyde has kept me sane, so I thought maybe this guy," Mason gestured toward Rusty, "might do the same for you."

Lori smiled and knocked on the wooden picnic table. "Let's hope. Do you want a beer or something?" she asked.

"Uh, ok. Why not?"

They walked toward the house, stopping to chat with Lori's parents. Carrie thanked Mason for coming and Tom even shook his hand. Lori led Mason inside to the kitchen, passed him a cold Miller Lite from the fridge, then set to mixing herself a rum and coke on the counter.

He twisted off the cap and took a swig. It was his first drink in over a week. "I'm sure everyone is asking, so tell me to piss off if you want, but how does it feel being out?"

"Piss off," said Lori, and laughed at her own joke. "It's fine, but it's so new, I really don't know. Don't get me wrong, it's great and everything, but right now it feels confusing and kinda scary."

"I can only imagine."

They sat in silence for a moment. Mason felt out of place, unsure of where to take the conversation next. "Well, you look great!" he offered.

Lori blushed and smiled shyly. "Thanks."

Mason took a long pull off the Miller Lite. "So, what's next? I mean for you, what's on the horizon?"

"Not sure. It's kind of too much to even think about right now. I need to figure out all the normal life stuff, a place to live, a job. Not too many employers want a violent offender on staff..." Lori trailed off, then perked herself back up. "What about you? Are you really done practicing? Don't you miss it?"

Mason shrugged. "Yeah, certain things. Standing up in the courtroom, that used to be *my place*, like the best version of me. I miss the fight, but I can't go back. At least not to the way it was. But eventually I need to figure something out. I just want a new start, you know?"

"I do. Believe me, I do." Lori looked at Mason from across the kitchen. "Maybe I could help you with that."

# ACKNOWLEDGMENTS

It's impossible not to be humbled by the unfailing kindness and generosity shown by family, friends, and colleagues who helped bring this book to life.

We'd like to thank:

Laura, for her tireless support and patience during the creative process, and always.

Nina, for keeping the train on the rails and making all things seem possible.

Chris, for his invaluable insights and bedside manner.

Marshall, for his big heart and bigger talent.

Magda, for her good sense and human touch.

Reaching our destination was made more gratifying because the journey included so many wonderful people.

# ABOUT THE AUTHOR

Lewis Allan is a pen name used by the two authors behind Mason Mitchell — a veteran criminal defense attorney, and a well-traveled free-lance writer. These childhood friends reconnected after thirty plus years to create a story that is entirely fictional, except for Clyde, who is 100% real. Mouse In The Box is their debut novel.

www.ingramcontent.com/pod-product-compliance
Lightning Source LLC
Chambersburg PA
CBHW030106310726

48970CB00004B/1171